WINGED LION

WINGED LION

STEVEN ANDERSON

Published by Theropod Publishing
https://www.facebook.com/TheropodPublishing

RuComm352@gmail.com
https://www.facebook.com/RuComm352
https://RuComm352.wixsite.com/theropod

Cover by Fiona Jayde Media.
Interior Formatting & Design by The Deliberate Page.

Ebook ISBN: 978-0-9991788-6-7
Print ISBN: 978-0-9991788-7-4

CHAPTER 1

GATTINO ALATO

Captain Thomas Benson closed his eyes. The pulse of the engines gave a gentle, purposeful buzz to the deck under his feet, and he hoped the coffee he had swallowed would soon do the same for his brain. Ship's time was 06:00, and he was on the bridge of the *Gattino Alato*, where he was supposed to be. His first officer was late.

"Schiava, where is Ms. Vendramin?"

"Ms. Vendramin is at container eight. The aft lashings shifted this morning, and she is working with the younger Mr. Beauvais to correct it." The Artificial Intelligence system's reply sounded deferential, her voice soft, with a touch of sultriness in the Italian accent a programmer in the Meeker shipyard had added to her personality silo.

Tom liked his ship's voice. It reminded him of the summer he'd spent studying in Barcelona. The girl from Venice he'd met there had been his lab partner, and then more. Her voice had been soft and sultry too. The sound of it had seduced him into following her to *La Serenissima* and applying for work with the Trade Guild.

That was long ago.

"Please remind Ms. Vendramin of the time, and that I am waiting for her." Tom took another sip and the coffee burned his tongue. He closed his eyes a little tighter and thought of morning coffee at the Bambú Beach Bar just south of the Barcelona museum.

"Fiona," he whispered.

Schiava screamed his name. "*Capitano* Benson! Unknown craft in our path ahead. They have not replied to my challenge and they're spinning."

"Spin up. Tell Ms. Vendramin she damn well better have number eight lashed tight or we'll tear apart. Where the hell is our escort? You should be able to sense them by now."

"*Sì*, but I cannot feel them. Perhaps they have been delayed... or it could be because we transited the Chéng Nuò Deep Space Hole early."

"We're already through the DSH?" A shiver chased down his spine. "When?"

"04:06 this morning. I've already notified the docks at New Palisade of the change in our arrival time."

"Encrypted?" he asked, not that it mattered anymore.

"Of course. How else?" She sounded offended that he would think her that careless.

"Three hours early. Explain it to me. We've been underway three weeks and the nav charts don't reflect any deviance. Why haven't you told me until now?"

Schiava sighed. "A harmless secret. Mr. Beauvais, Simon, not his little brother, was first. He asked if I could nudge thrust up a percent on account of a girl he knows on New Palisade. It was important for him to meet with her as soon as possible. Then his brother, Mr. Tekanatoken Beauvais, asked the same thing, so I added another percent in the name of his friend, Delilah. Engineer Tulisan bumped me a percent and so did First Officer Vendramin."

She lowered her voice as though telling him a secret he didn't already know. "I think they have a date planned at the Bab al-Ahmar. Then *you* added two percent for–"

"I know what I did."

"–Elsie Campbell," Schiava finished anyway.

First Officer Gabriela Vendramin pushed past the door onto the bridge while it was still sliding open, her face flushed from the three hundred meter run from container eight. Her shoulder-length brown hair had come loose from where she'd tied it back, and she shoved it away from her face. "Sorry I'm late for watch changeover. We snapped two fiber lashings, but it's squared away now, sir." Her gaze drifted to the red flashes on the main display panels that covered one wall of the bridge. "What's happened? Is that...?"

"Fast Attack Craft," he confirmed. "They've cut us off."

Gabriela stepped in front of him and touched the image of the FAC. Her fingers sparkled in the coherent light of the display. "They've already spun up, ready to strike. How long?" Her voice had become soft, barely above a whisper, as she looked at her probable death.

Schiava answered. "Six hours, give or take. It depends on what our *Capitano* decides to do next."

Gabriela looked at Tom. The tightness around her eyes betrayed what she was feeling. She was afraid.

He shook his head. "Schiava, have everyone in the mess hall in ten minutes. Are we at full spin?"

"Almost. I can't spin very well with sixteen cargo containers lashed to my nose. They stretch out in front of me over five-hundred meters. It's ungainly, having a long snoot."

"You're a towboat, Schiava. It's what you were built to do."

"Still makes me ungainly."

"Is our armor in place?"

"I'm reconstituting the Holloman armor around my main hull and the shuttle while I get up to maximum rotation. The high-speed sintering printers will rebuild the honeycomb as it's ablated, so we should be able to endure their attack for an hour before they breach my hull."

"And we all die." Gabriela smiled sadly at Tom. "Well, at least my family will finally be proud of me."

"How's that?"

"Oh, the Vendramin name hasn't been worth much inside the Guild for years. We once were something, but that was a century or more ago. Lots of scandals in the pre-reunification days. We sold cargo to people whose payments never showed up on the books and spent a lot of money on things we couldn't afford. That sort of thing. I was trying my best to live up to the family reputation until Grandpa shipped me out on the *Agnello Participazio* when I was nineteen. 'Adapt or die', he told me. I adapted."

She twisted the lock of hair that had come undone around her finger. "I think I've done OK."

"You've done OK. I read your file to make sure the Trade Guild wasn't sticking me with another lazy Venice kid slumming for a year before they promoted her to a made-up job in the Guild hierarchy. You've earned your station."

She nodded and the confidence came back to her eyes. "The others should be in the mess hall by now, sir. They'll want to hear what you plan to do."

"Yeah," he answered. "Me too."

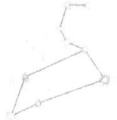

Engineer Owen Tulisan let go of Gabriela's hand, leaned back in his chair, and crossed his arms. "That's bullshit, Skipper. You expect us to defend sixteen containers full of ag products and clay with our *lives*? Let them have what they want. We can outrun them in the shuttle at max thrust. But we need to start now. Before they get in range. Now would be good."

Gabriela studied him with her eyes narrowed. "You signed a contract, Tuly. We all did."

He looked at her. "Right. The undersigned swear allegiance and fealty to the Trade Guild of Venice, they shall treat the Guild's property as their own and defend it unto death from all persons or forces that may attempt to seize it without formal contract or payment, blah, blah, blah. Out here, that means exactly jack shit. You don't think they actually expect us to *die* for what we have consigned in this tow, do you?"

Gabriela moved her chair away from him and didn't answer.

Tom answered. "That's exactly what they expect. It's what they demand. We will hold until our escort arrives or the privateers destroy us. There are consequences if we run. You know the stories."

Tuly's voice shook when he answered. "The oath was put in there to keep crews from selling cargo on the black market or making side deals trying to take a cut of the Guild's profits. That was before the war. That was before the Separatists started using letters of marque to send out attack craft to hunt ships loyal to the Union." He pointed at the main display. "God, Skipper. They'll kill us if we don't take the shuttle and leave in... Schiava, how long?"

"Five hours, twenty-six minutes, assuming the privateers intend to capture the *Gattino Alato* and the sixteen containers in our tow. If they plan to kill the crew even if you run, then you should leave soon."

"What are their demands?" Kahwihta Beauvais asked. She was the ship's bosun, responsible for managing the daily tasks needed to keep the *Gattino Alato* flying. Late-thirties, black hair pulled back from a high forehead, her hands rested in her lap, seemingly untroubled by the coming attack.

She had recruited her two younger brothers to come work with her almost two years ago, booming out with the Trade Guild and leaving their lives working the high steel of Bodens Gate's shipyards behind.

Simon and Tekanatoken watched their sister while they waited for Tom to answer. His words wouldn't matter to them, only her reaction.

"No demands yet," Tom answered. "They're jamming all RF comms to keep Schiava from screaming for help."

"I'm screaming anyway. You never know."

"Nothing's come through on the free-space optical. They might have something to say when they get closer." Tom tipped his head. "Were you expecting something special?"

"Not sure. Container one, out there on the port nose? Different locks and seals than the rest of the tow. A couple of Trade Guild suits were watching us close when we latched it down at the Chéng Nuò docks. Might mean something." Kahwihta shrugged. "Might not."

Tuly stumbled to his feet. "Open it."

"Sir," Gabriela reminded him. "You call him 'sir'." Her voice was steady. "And like hell are we going to crack seals on goods under our watch."

Tuly looked down at her, irritated. "*Sir*," he added. "If we're going to stay here and die, I want to know why. I want to know what we're sacrificing our lives to protect."

Gabriela stood, nose a few centimeters away from the Engineer's chin. "You think you can make a deal? Coward. You deserve what the Guild will do to you. We hold, like the Captain said. Maybe we live, maybe we don't, but I'd rather die here than be slaughtered by a Trade Guild *Vendicatore*. Shit, Tuly, why can't you–"

The Captain stopped her. "Enough. That's enough."

Gabriela turned to him, a hard look in her eyes, ready to argue that it wasn't enough. She had a lot more she wanted to say.

"Ms. Vendramin. Get the shuttle ready, sync the codes and logs, and make sure everything is hot."

"Sir..."

"I want the option. Make it ready."

"Yes, sir."

"Schiava, we were already pushing for the New Palisade DSH?"

"Five G push, plus a little."

"Turn us around and give me full thrust. We'll let that FAC look at our tail for a while and it should buy us a few hours before they're in range."

"One hour and nine minutes."

He shrugged. "Better than nothing. Kahwihta, you're with me. Let's go see what makes us so valuable."

"Sir, you can't," Gabriela protested. "The Guild is not forgiving."

He grinned at her. "Let me know as soon as the shuttle is ready if we're not back here by then."

"Yes, sir," she answered, but didn't move.

"Something else?"

She shook her head. "No, sir." She turned and gave orders to the Beauvais brothers to move gear and supplies.

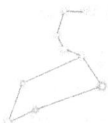

Tom and Kahwihta walked in silence down the narrow passageway linking the *Gattino Alato* to the containers making up the tow. The ringing of their boots was loud on the gray deck plates. He knew she would keep to her own thoughts if he didn't push her.

Tom stopped as they passed the aft airlock for container five. "Wait up a second. I need to know what you're thinking."

"Trying not to, Skipper." She had continued on a couple of meters after he stopped. She came back and stood close to him to whisper even though they were alone. "Opening the container is a bad idea. Running is a bad idea. Don't let Tuly push you. Don't make Gabriela try to stop you. She respects you, but she'll do it."

"You know what Tuly said has nothing to do with this."

She walked away from him.

"Kahwihta…"

She turned. "OK. You want my thoughts? I've killed my brothers. Let us die with our honor intact."

"No one will die today if I can help it."

She came close and put her hand on his chest above his heart. She'd never done it before, touching him like that. "Don't lie to me. Our escort missed the rendezvous. End of story. Don't make this…" She pulled away. "Sorry, sir."

He took her hand and placed it back on his chest. "Let's go see what cards we have left to play. Who knows? We could get lucky. We have a few hours left. Lots could happen." He kissed her hand gently and gave it back to her.

Kahwihta looked at her hand and nodded. "Not letting you into my bunk. We have work to do, and I expect a nice dinner first. Flowers too."

"I'll keep that in mind, but right now, you and I need to come up with a way to stay alive."

"OK." She walked away from him, keeping her thoughts to herself again, leaving him to wonder if they had just made a promise to each other.

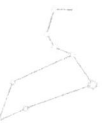

Tom placed his hand on the keypad. "Schiava, open the aft lock on container one, please."

"The locks on container one require you to acknowledge you understand the dire consequences of your actions."

"So acknowledged."

"The consignor will hold you personally and corporately responsible for any loss or damage to their property entrusted in good faith to the Trade Guild of the Most Serene Republic of Venice."

"Yes, I acknowledge that too. Open the lock."

"The lock is opened. May the Guild have mercy on you."

There was a soft sigh as the seal broke and the pressure equalized. The air coming out was hot, with a dry, dusty smell to it. Tom and Kahwihta stepped through the airlock into another world.

The interior of the cargo container was one-hundred meters long by fifty wide by twenty tall. Most shippers divided the space or packed it full of smaller containers. But not container one. The consignor had filled it with red sand shaped into ripples and dunes sloping up toward red rock cliffs. The lights were low, and stars shown in the evening sky. He could make out a few low red adobe buildings, and what looked like cave openings where the sand met the base of the nearest cliff.

Tom squatted and touched the sand. He picked up a handful and let it run through his fingers. "I thought this must all be a sim, but the sand at least is real." He stood and wiped his hand on his pants. "That sky though. So many moons. Schiava, who is the consignor for this container?"

"Captain Mala Dusa Holloman, Reunification Commission, on assignment to the Union Aerospace Force for the design of up-armored starships."

"And she's shipping sand from Chéng Nuò to New Palisade. A whole simulated sand world. Why?"

Kahwihta walked farther into the container and up the first low dune. "Not just sand." She put her hands on her hips, head tipped to the side. "What are they?"

Tom caught up to her. Several creatures looked back at them. Six legs supported a fat, rounded body the size of a large dog. And they weren't looking, he realized. The bump that must be a head didn't have eyes. Pairs of meter-long tentacles with flattened spade-shaped tips waved at them from below the front head bump while reds, browns, grays, and occasional flashes of blue pulsed through them. The closest one had its tentacles raised to full height with the tips slowly rotating back and forth as though scanning them.

"It's weird, Skipper. They just appeared. Five, then six, now what? Ten? I didn't see them come out of the buildings. There was nothing but sand, then... Oh! Did you see that? The light shimmered and there he is. He's a pretty one, purple tentacles waving at us." She put her hands by her head and wiggled her fingers at the creatures.

"They must be part of the sim." He walked down the dune toward them, expecting he'd be able to walk straight through the projected image. One creature scurried to meet him and pushed up against his legs, nearly knocking him over.

"Whoa, definitely not part of the sim." He laughed as it continued pushing against him, driving him farther away from the airlock toward where the other creatures were waiting with their tentacles held high, tips rotating. "They seem friendly enough."

"I want to touch him too."

Tom looked over his shoulder. Kahwihta's voice had gone soft and dreamy, and her eyes were unfocused as she walked down the dune toward him. She had one arm stretched out, and she was biting at her lower lip.

"Are you all right?"

"Let me touch him with you, Tom. We need to touch him together."

The reality of where he was came back to him and he pulled away from the creature, suddenly afraid. There was a Fast Attack Craft on its way to kill them. His crew was in danger. They had to run, and run now.

"No, we're leaving."

"We should stay with them." She took his hand. "We would be safe here."

He looked at her hand, at her fingers wrapped around his. He pulled her close and held her tight against him. They'd leave in a moment.

The creature nuzzled gently against their legs.

Tom closed his eyes. He could feel the beat of his heart in his wrists, in his chest, in his throat where the top of Kahwihta's head rested warmly against him. He counted his heartbeats. He'd hold her for ten beats. There was time enough for that. Ten more and then he'd let go. Ten more. There was a hum in his head and the sound of music playing from somewhere. He counted ten more beats, not afraid anymore.

"*Capitano*, First Officer Vendramin reports that my shuttle is ready for whatever the hell it is you plan to do with it. She is standing by for further orders." Schiava's voice reflected Gabriela's irritation.

Kahwihta stepped back from him, breaking the connection. "Let's go do it."

"Thank you, Schiava. Ms. Beauvais and I, um... we're on our way." Tom opened his eyes. They were alone. "Schiava, where did the creatures go that were here a moment ago?"

"You and Bosun Beauvais are the only living things I can detect inside container one."

Kahwihta planted her fists on her hips, fully alert. "Vendramin is good, but there's no way she and my brothers could have prepped the shuttle in the time we've been gone. How long have we *really* been in here?"

Schiava answered, "Twenty-seven minutes have elapsed since you opened the airlock."

"Damn good hug, Skipper. Were you singing to me?"

"I don't think so. I heard it too. We should leave." He glanced over his shoulder at the open airlock. "Do you suppose those creatures are in the *Gattino Alato* by now, or are they still in here hiding somewhere?"

They stared at each other for a half second and then ran. Kahwihta sealed the airlock behind them. "Schiava, is there anything else alive in the ship, or shuttle, or anywhere in the stacking frame other than crew?"

"Spiders," she answered. "Also, small mites and other insect-sized creatures native to sixteen planets. I was able to eliminate the last of the rats we picked up on Kudlow while we were docked at Chéng Nuò."

"I think we may have a problem, Skipper. That Union Aerospace Force Captain who consigned this container? You recognize her name, right? Holloman? She's going to be pissed if we've lost her pets."

"Yeah, I hear she's crazy. They talk about her on Bodens Gate. Weird stuff. And she's the creator of the armor system that I'm hoping will keep us alive until our escort arrives."

Kahwihta shrugged. "She patented the design for her armor while she was still a student at the Academy. Crazy and genius go together, I hear. I don't want her or anyone else in the Union military upset with me. Don't really want them to even know where I am."

"Is there something you want to tell me?"

"Not really."

CHAPTER 2

EMOTIONS

Kahwihta watched Tom as they made their way along the passageway linking the stacking frame to the ship. A sensation hummed in the back of her brain and she imagined she could feel what he was feeling. She could tell he was worried, but not scared. That made sense. He was working the problem, trying to find a way to keep them alive without angering the Guild. Maybe it was the slump of his shoulders or the way he watched his feet while they walked. No, she could feel something else in him too, something like longing or desire. More than desire, it felt like...

She pulled back, afraid to dig any deeper. "Skipper, you remember when we broke orbit from Bodens Gate with my brothers two years ago? On board the *Gattino Alato* was not exactly where they were supposed to be that morning."

"I know."

"You do?"

"You said they were good men. I believed you. I still do. It took you long enough, but I knew you'd get around to telling me." He looked back at her, a tight grin crinkling his eyes.

"Yes, sir."

Her brothers had followed the traditions of the Mohawk, erecting skyscrapers on Earth, and then working the ultimate heights building ships on orbit. They had gotten into trouble when they took work in the Bodens Gate shipyards. Their new friends weren't really friends, and what they did wasn't always legal. She had heard stories about them from her cousins, stories that worried her. She took it as her responsibility to lay them straight again before they got themselves killed.

Bringing them on with the *Gattino Alato* had cost her the price of a modest dinner, a couple of beers, and a slinky dress she'd only worn once. She hadn't been with Tom long and thought the favor might cost her something extra.

She smiled a little at the memory. That night at the café in the Bodens Gate docks, the planet hanging beautifully above them visible through the transparent panels, all it had taken was for her to tell him that her brothers were good men. He'd accepted it, and asked for nothing more than her word.

Sometimes she caught him watching her, though. She knew the look, that he wouldn't mind giving her a tumble if the situation was different. The longer she served under him, getting to know him, the more often she found herself watching him and thinking the same thing.

Tuly was waiting for them when they entered the shuttle. "What did you find? Something we can use, I hope. You were gone long enough."

"Sand," Tom told him. "Sand and rocks."

"Under a peaceful night sky," Kahwihta added. "There was a sim running in there for some reason. It was pretty."

"Did you look *everywhere*? Things can be hidden in a sim."

Tom pushed past him. "There was nothing. Ms. Vendramin, status please."

"The shuttle is ready. I synced the data and supplies are topped up. The Fast Attack Craft has altered velocity to maintain the original intercept time. We have about four and a half hours left before contact. What are your intentions, Captain?"

"To be ready for any eventuality. As ready as we can be anyway. Did you log that I opened container one?"

"Yes, sir." Her expression remained unchanged, but her cheeks flushed.

"Thank you, Ms. Vendramin. You did the right thing."

Gabriela nodded. "Thank you, sir. I'm not sure I did."

"Based on salvage records and survivor stories, the privateers will focus on stripping the armor away from the *Gattino Alato* when the attack comes. Then they'll force a boarding. They need the towboat intact, so damage should be minimal. Our shuttle is valuable on the secondary market, so they'll try not to damage it either."

"What about us, Skipper?" Simon asked. "I don't suppose they care much if we get damaged."

"The stories are mixed. If we resist, we die. That's for sure. We'll probably still die, even if we surrender. They might keep some of us alive if they can collect a ransom or if they think they can sell us."

Tom glanced at Gabriela. Kahwihta shook her head. He'd been glancing a lot at Gabriela since she'd joined them at Chéng Nuò. Kahwihta had little doubt what had made him accept her as first officer. The privateers would definitely keep Gabriela Vendramin alive if they could. She might bring more than the shuttle.

"Or you can try to volunteer," Tom continued. "The privateers are always looking for new recruits."

Simon looked at Tek and they both shrugged. "Tried that kind of thing once. We weren't good at it. I guess we'll take our chances and stay with the Union."

"So that's it, then." Tuly's voice quavered. "We sit here doing nothing. Waiting to die. Except for her." He pointed at Gabriela. "With her name, the Guild will pay a fine ransom. If the pirates don't use her up amongst themselves first."

Gabriela hit him, fist to face, with all the power of her body behind it. He staggered back. His hands came up to cover his nose, but they couldn't hide the blood pouring from it.

Tom stepped aside and let him fall. "Ms. Vendramin, what were you thinking?" He took her hand and examined it. "You could have broken your fingers."

She grinned at him and then winced as he moved her wrist. "Sorry, sir. It won't happen again."

"You best have Schiava look at this. We might need your fighting skills later. Simon, you and Tek please help our engineer get cleaned up."

"Yes, sir. Come on, Tek. Grab him under the right arm and we'll drag him."

"And confine him to quarters when you're done. Got that, Schiava? I can't believe what he did, assaulting a senior officer. He knows better."

After the others had gone, Tom sat in one of the seats in the shuttle's main cabin. "I'm too old for this, Kahwihta."

"Not too old to be flirting with your First Officer."

"Was I? I'm almost twice her age. I think of her as my daughter, that's all."

"Sure. A daughter you'd like to…"

"She reminds me of my ex-wife when we were that age. Fiona Grimani is from one of the old merchant houses too. She always wanted more for me than I wanted for myself. Something different, anyway. After I'd spent two years pushing cargo between Earth and the outer planets, she thought I was ready for a career at the center of Guild power working next to her.

The problem was I got hooked on this life. This is what I want. Small ship, tight crew. Even Tuly never gave me any trouble until today. We work well together and we've had a lot of fun on shore... well, you know. You've been there with us most of the time."

"I miss Mr. Caswell. He was a good First Officer and you didn't flirt with him. I was sorry to leave him behind on Chéng Nuò."

"Someday you may want to retire too."

"Someday." Kahwihta gave him a sad smile. "If we're not dead."

His gaze came back to hers and then to the display at the front of the cabin. Red flashes marked the FAC's position. The number next to it showed the time to conjunction, telling how long they had to live. "It might be easier to die. The Guild isn't going to be happy about that broken seal. And those creatures we let escape? I don't think that's going to end well either."

She shook her head. "Those tentacle things worry me. A little piece of them crawled up inside my brain and won't come back out. I keep imagining I can feel things. Like what's inside your head. There's music somewhere. I want to sing with it."

"Well, dying should fix that too."

"You're giving up. I feel it. Maybe you are too old."

"Maybe..." Tom sat up a little straighter and something bright came into his eyes. "Maybe. But we're not dead yet."

"You got a plan, Skipper?"

"More an idea than a plan. At least it's something no one's ever tried. I don't think. It might work. Or we might end up with all of them hunting us down, Trade Guild, Holloman, and the privateers."

"What do you need me to do?"

CHAPTER 3

INTERCEPT

Tom was irrationally confident despite being aware that his plan was probably just a complicated way to commit suicide. "Schiava, where are Tuly and the Beauvais brothers?"

"Still in the medical bay. Ms. Vendramin did indeed break Tuly's nose, but I should have him back whole again in a few minutes."

"What about his brain? Is that working again?"

"It would seem so. He's contrite now that the pain meds I pumped into him have taken effect."

"Good. I need him. Have him report to Engineering as soon as you're finished. Gabriela too. I'll meet them there."

"No longer confined to quarters? That didn't last long."

"And tell Simon and Tek to start arming all of the quick releases on the twist-locks and lashing bars."

Kahwihta squeezed past him. "I'll go help. With the *Gattino* spinning, they'll need to watch close. Cargo may have shifted. Bars under tension are twitchy."

"Wait."

She turned and tipped her head.

"Kahwihta..."

"Don't make me regret what we started."

"Be careful, that's all."

"Sure. I hope you know what you're doing."

"I don't, but it feels right. If this works, we'll be legends. And if it fails..."

"We'll still be legends," she finished for him.

"Not a bad way to die."

"Don't plan to die today, Skipper. I think I know what you're going to do. Might even work."

Tuly had a bandage across his nose and he kept glancing sideways at Gabriela, as though wondering if she was going to hit him again.

Gabriela had her arms crossed, ignoring him. "So Skipper, the Beauvais brothers are prepping the cargo for separation. That's your plan? Hand our tow over to the privateers?"

"Not exactly. They can't move any of it without the *Gattino*, and I'm still betting our escort is on the way. We just need to buy some time. We're running a little ahead of schedule for some reason."

Gabriela and Tuly finally looked at each other. "Sorry, sir."

"We've all done it. And other than Kahwihta, we all did it to ourselves this time. It bit us in the ass, but, with a bit of luck, it might not be a fatal mistake."

Gabriela put her hand to her mouth, eyes suddenly larger. "Oh, wow. I can't believe you'd do that."

"What?" Tuly was lost. "What are we doing?"

"We're going to break up the tow," Tom told him. "We'll scatter the containers as widely as possible, and run like hell. The privateers will have to capture the *Gattino Alato* before they can even begin to corral the containers. When our escort arrives, they'll have to thrust empty-handed for the DSH. A FAC is no match for a Union *Esprit*-class frigate. Then we come back and clean up the mess. No lost cargo, no stolen ship, no dead crew. We'll be a little behind schedule into New Palisade, but I think the Guild will forgive us."

"Wow." Tuly stared at nothing, his mouth slightly open. "There is so much that could go wrong with that plan. What if our escort never shows up?"

Gabriela jumped in before Tom could answer. "What if they chase *us* first? What if they start destroying the containers? Containers don't have armor. Every one they pop increases the chance we'll wake up some night to the sound of a Trade Guild *Vendicatore's* vibracore cutting through our foreheads."

"And you're going to have some pissed off privateers," Tuly added. "They know what ship this is. They'll hunt us down."

"You have a better idea? Either of you?"

Tuly and Gabriela looked at each other and shrugged.

"Tuly, work with Schiava to sequence the releases. She'll try to go unbalanced when we start shedding the tow, especially with this spin. And don't torque the stacking frame; we're going to need it."

"Sir, what about container one?" Gabriela asked.

"It's full of sand."

"Yes, but you and our Bosun were spooked when you came back; I saw it in your eyes. And hers. We could keep it attached to the *Gattino Alato*. I'll rig a grav generator on the starboard side to hold balance."

"No. Start with number one. I want it as far away as possible." Tom turned to his engineer. "Tuly, can you stagger the fore and aft releases to impart a tumble?"

"Sure. It would be almost impossible to keep that from happening anyway. It'll make it hard to put them back together into the tow, though."

"Let me worry about that part."

"Which means you'll ask me to do it for you later."

"Like always. Get to it. Start releasing as soon as Kahwihta is ready. Gabriela, you're with me. I want to see if we can't push the Beauvais brothers a little faster."

"I think I'd be of more use to Tuly, sir. We'll need to hurry to be ready before Kahwihta finishes. I don't want there to be much of a lag between her arming the releases and us kicking the containers free."

"Fine. Don't hit him again. If he does something else stupid, wait until we're out of this. I need him."

"Yes, sir. No hitting."

Kahwihta yelled at her brother. "Damn it, Tek. Look at this. That's twice you loosened the load binder and didn't release it. This is not a race."

"I know, sis. I'm not racing. It's just Simon's ahead of me." The hard work of removing lashing bars and kicking cones and clamps clear of the containers had made his face flushed. He bent to pull the binding free, moving it with his boot. "There. Have you checked his side? Maybe you could slow him down for me."

"Privateers coming to kill all of us and you're trying to beat your brother?"

"Sure. I might not have another chance, what with being dead and all."

"Start on the starboard side of container one, I'll work the port. Simon's working number four. We'll meet him in the middle. Last row."

"Thanks for the help. We'll beat him for sure now."

Kahwihta shook her head as she watched him working on the first lashing bar.

It was as though nothing had changed since the day she shipped out with the Trade Guild when they were teenagers. She'd left them behind, Tekanatoken happy and competitive and always looking for a shortcut to beat his brother. Simon was arrogant and condescending, but how often had she seen him pushing himself in school or sports, trying desperately to stay ahead of Tek, and then pretending his victory had been from his natural superiority? She'd thought they'd keep each other safe.

Simon led them astray. It was Simon that took work in the Bodens Gate shipyards. It was Simon that took them down to the surface one night with their friends. A pair of Union Marines died at a scruffy café on the edge of the massive slum called the Warrens while they were there. Simon told her he and Tek were innocent. That's not what the security AI had recorded. She chose to believe her brothers, and the Skipper had chosen to believe her.

Kahwihta had them check each other's work as they made their way back to the main body of the ship thirty minutes later. Tek bragged about his speed in getting the containers ready.

Simon was dismissive. "A half-assed job doesn't count. I fixed three of your mistakes. How many of mine did you find?"

"Stowing the bars to two lashing eyes instead of three? Not a mistake. I beat you. Get over it."

She let them argue and enjoyed the sound of it. The Skipper had given them more than a second chance when he took them on. It was a second birth. She followed her brothers, praying silently that their new life would be a long one.

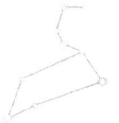

The door slid open granting Kahwihta access to the bridge. The main display panel was showing the view ahead, the *Gattino Alato's* hull visible under the layer of Holloman armor. She could see part of the Winged Lion of Saint Mark painted on the outer plates. The symbol of the Most Serene Republic of Venice had its sword raised in defiance, ready for war. She smiled to herself. It was a brave image for so tiny a ship.

Tom had his feet on the desk and his eyes closed while he listened to Schiava refusing his orders.

Schiava's voice was angry and her Italian accent more pronounced than usual. "*Capitano*, I will not allow my tow to be separated while we are in flight. I simply will not. No secret combination of words can override that function, no magical touch of your fingers on the keypad."

"Schiava, my one true love, it is temporary. Do you understand what 'temporary' means?"

No answer.

"I will do it manually if I have to. You know that I can do it without you."

No answer.

"We'll probably torque the stacking frame if you don't help us."

No answer.

"Fine." He leaned forward and his boots landed on the deck with a solid thump. "Kahwihta, we have work to do. You and your brothers suit up. We'll lose pressure in the gangways if the frame twists too far. Gabriela and I will join you while Tuly tries to hold neutral gravity."

"*Mio Capitano?*" Schiava spoke softly.

"What?"

"Am I *tuo unico vero amore*, your one true love?"

Kahwihta raised an eyebrow at Tom, head tipped.

"Yes, Schiava," he answered. "You are my life and my love."

"There are countermeasures. I could stop you. I will choose not to, but that is as far as I can go to permit this foolishness, this sin."

"Save your countermeasures for the privateers."

Schiava's voice brightened, as though she was looking forward to it. "*Sì, Signore*. If they make it on board, I'll have some fun with them."

Tom put his hand against the wall plate next to the door. He patted it a couple of times, caressing the gray painted composite. "Thank you, Schiava. We'll have everything put back together in a few days. You'll see."

Kahwihta stayed with Tom as they stripped down to shorts and t-shirts to slide into the pressure suits. "You have a problem, Skipper."

He grinned at her. "Just one?"

She glanced at the ceiling. "You know what I mean."

"Schiava will be OK."

Kahwihta shook her head. "She's not who worries me."

Gabriela came in as they were finishing and started shedding clothes to get suited up.

Kahwihta took a step closer to Tom, pretending to check the seal around his helmet. If she blocked his view of Gabriela in the process, well, that was just too bad.

Gabriela looked up at them from where she was lying on the floor, wiggling her body into the lower half of her suit. "Simon is already standing by at container four. I'll take number one. We'll need to kick five and eleven right after to keep balance. Tek's on his way to five."

"Kahwihta and I will take eleven," Tom told her.

Gabriela stood and rolled her shoulders, forcing the suit to conform to her body. "Thirteen and sixteen next. Need to work back out on the inside containers once the outer ones are clear. Tuly set a timer for each release, but with Schiava playing the good Guild Girl, we'll need to kick them manually when the timers hit zero. Schiava, what's the time?"

"Ship's time is 10:42. Estimated conjunction with the privateers is 13:10."

Gabriela nodded. "We need to run. One and four have to kick together. Six minutes. A little less."

They ran.

When they reached container eleven, Gabriela stopped and tapped the status panel. "Here. Countdown timer. Three minutes, eighteen seconds. Big green icon to release. It's live, no safeties. Touch it and the container is gone. OK?"

"Well done," Tom told her. "You and Tuly both. I thought you hated this plan."

She was already jogging away from them. "Still do, sir," she shouted over her shoulder. "We're all going to die, but…" She shrugged dramatically, arms raised above her head as she turned into the cross gangway, running toward the front of the tow.

Tom was smiling when he turned to Kahwihta. "I like her."

"Yes, sir."

Kahwihta watched the clock showing time slipping away from them.

Tuly's voice, steady, but tense, whispered in her ear from the helmet speaker. "Ten seconds, all. It's going to shake when one and four kick. Hold tight."

She wrapped one hand around the holdfast next to the display panel, sharing it with Tom. A ripple passed under their feet followed by the sound of groaning metal and composites trying to adjust to unexpected forces.

Tuly's voice in her ear was no longer whispering. "Shit! Shit, shit, shit. Gabriela, what are you doing? Kick it. Kick it now."

"I'm kicking. Nothing's moving. Big pop, little bangs, lots of groaning. It's stuck."

"OK, OK. Keep trying. Check the lashing bars. Everyone else, kick the rest of the containers as fast as you can, everything but... yeah, everything but seven. It'll sort of balance. Maybe. Punch the outer columns, then the inner. Order doesn't matter. Shed everything."

Tom touched the green icon. A moment later confirmation flashed on the screen. Container eleven was gone.

"Simon," Kahwihta shouted, as though shouting would help him hear her better through the suit's comm system. "Take number eight. We've got thirteen and nine. Tek, kick five. Then you and Simon move to the center containers."

"Copy."

"Number one is moving," Gabriela reported, her voice tight with fear. "It's got a shimmy."

"That ain't good," Tuly replied. "On my way to you. It's gotta be in the panel."

Tuly passed by Kahwihta and Tom a moment later at a dead run.

"Close that visor, Engineer," Tom shouted as he passed.

"No time. It's OK. I'll fix this."

"Idiot."

Kahwihta nodded. "Brave. Brave idiot."

Containers five, eight, thirteen, and nine separated cleanly. Tom skidded to a stop halfway to container ten, his head tipped as he listened. Kahwihta looked at him, not hearing the voice he was hearing.

He blinked at her. "Schiava, include Kahwihta in this."

"Yes, sir. I have received an answer to my hail. Captain Afweyne of the Independent Attack Ship *Mandirigma* wants to know what the hell you're playing at."

Tom chuckled. "Got their attention. Tell him to run before our escort arrives. I'm too busy scattering his prize to talk right now."

"Yes, sir. He's continuing to make demands and threats. He wants to talk to you."

"About five more minutes, then–"

Tuly's voice screamed in their ears. "Gabriela, what the hell? Why are you–"

The rest of his words were lost to a hiss of static. The gangway fluttered under them as gravity faded away and wind whipped past them to the sound of the decompression alarm.

"Tuly? Gabriela?" Tom listened to the silence. "Gabriela, report."

Schiava answered for them. "I lost internal sensors forward of container five at the first kick. External sensors show the stacking frame has collapsed in on itself, exposing the gangways to space. Container one is lodged perpendicular to container seven and appears stable for the moment. The other fourteen containers in my tow are gone and the stacking frame aft of container five is still intact and true. I have sealed the gangways and will have pressure restored in three minutes. Working on gravity."

"Can you see our First Officer and Engineer?"

"Ms. Vendramin is trapped on the port side between the containers and the remains of the gangway. I can see her through a gap where the wall plates have ripped away. She's not moving, but telemetry shows she's alive."

"Tuly?"

"Sir, he was ejected by the spin when the stacking frame collapsed. I am so very sorry."

"We can go after him."

"I'm still receiving his telemetry, but the images I captured showed his visor was still up. I am not receiving any signs of life in his telemetry feed. Engineer Tulisan was already dead when the spin threw him clear."

Tom looked into Kahwihta's eyes. "Schiava, where are the Beauvais brothers?"

"Near container seven."

"Unhurt?"

"Yes, sir."

Tom blinked hard, but there were no tears. Kahwihta had the hum in her brain again, as if she knew what it was costing him to hold back the pain. She could feel the piece of his heart that was screaming for Tuly, the guilt swelling as he blamed himself that Tuly was dead.

"Kahwihta, go to your brothers. Get Gabriela back inside. I need to talk to Captain Afweyne."

"What are you going to do?"

"Cut a deal if I still can. No one else..." Tom's voice broke. "No one else, OK?"

"I understand, sir." She nodded, feeling the emotional echo of her words in him, using it as a guide. She didn't understand where it was coming from or how it was possible, but she trusted it. "Tuly is dead. You gave us a chance to survive in a hopeless situation. You'd do it again the same way. Tuly would always run to help Gabriela. You play the cards you're dealt. Anything else is called cheating. When you draw the wrong card it's time to bluff, not fold." She felt his pain fading, leaving the grief behind.

The shadow of a smile touched his lips. "Where did that come from?"

"Don't know, sir. We'll think about it later, maybe over a bottle of wine at some quiet spot on New Palisade. Go talk to their Captain. I'll see to Gabriela and my boys."

The bridge display showed a view forward across the stacking frame. The far end of the structure was twisted and torn, what was left of it. Container one was wedged against number seven, held in place by the kinked remains of a long spar and parts of the gangways. "How could that have happened?" Tom asked aloud. Schiava didn't answer, having long ago adapted to the Captain talking to himself.

He could see figures working in the debris, the bright flare of a cutting torch. He wanted to watch. He wanted to go help. He shook himself.

"Schiava, tactical display." He studied it a moment. "Zoom out. Let me see the DSH behind them."

He traced a line between the *Gattino Alato* and their destination, the light from the display sparkling on his fingers as he touched the *Mandirigma*. "It looks like they're square between us and the Palisade DSH."

"Just over eleven degrees off the starboard bow."

"Hail the Union frigate *Esprit de la Légion* using the free space optical. Point it straight at the DSH."

"*Signore*, I am not showing a frigate having cleared the DSH. And our escort is—"

"Send it anyway. Make it broad enough so the *Mandirigma* sees part of it too. But only a little part. Do you understand?"

"I understand."

"Then pause a minute and act like you're responding to their questions. Give them our status, but make it sound better than it is. Let the *Mandirigma* catch about every other word."

"I like your new plan. I will be creative and subtle."

"Perfect. We'll feed them the lie for about five minutes. Then I'll be ready to talk to Captain Afweyne. Hold our current thrust and tell our imaginary escort we're slowing to reverse course and recover our containers. We need to do that anyway. I want to recover... We owe it to..."

"I am still tracking my Engineer. We'll get Mr. Tulisan home."

"Thank you. In your message to the *Esprit de la Légion*, ask them to wait with us after they've destroyed the *Mandirigma*. And thank their captain for his timely arrival."

He closed his eyes and listened to Schiava creating a reality better than the one he was living. She requested technical support in locating the containers and a share of the bounty for the destruction of the *Mandirigma*. He watched the transcript of Captain Afweyne's transmissions. His anger was growing the longer the *Gattino Alato* remained silent and he was making explicit promises about how he planned to kill all of them. Tom waited, trying to judge the exact moment to raise the stakes for the last time.

"Schiava, how long until he has to accelerate to escape the phantom we've created?"

"Twenty minutes, sir."

"Answer Captain Afweyne's hail, voice only. Can you modify my voice so he can't hear the way it's shaking?"

"Yes, sir. Stand by. His signal is also voice only."

"Mr. Afweyne, why are you seeking to intercept my ship?"

"Captain. I am Captain Afweyne."

"Really? Under whose commission? I am Captain Thomas Benson, by the authority of the Trade Guild of the Most Serene Republic of Venice. Perhaps you've heard of us. We have a maxim you should know. It says *Non stiamo perdonando*. We are not forgiving."

"How frightening you think you are. Perhaps *you* are afraid. You scatter your cargo to the deep and talk to imaginary ships. Perhaps you have gone mad from your fear."

"Ship? We've not talked to any other ship. Slow here next to us, Mr. Afweyne. We are quite alone and helpless. I'm certain your sensors would be able to detect a Union frigate, no matter how many layers of stealth armor the Hoog Schelde shipyard added to her. Tarry as long as you like gathering the scattered remains of your prize."

Tom waited for a response. Call or fold?

A telltale flashed on the bridge display next to the image of the *Mandirigma* indicating a change in velocity. "Schiava, is he slowing or accelerating?"

"Thrusting hard for the Chéng Nuò DSH. He has also altered course five degrees. His proximity at conjunction will be less than a kilometer."

"How much less?"

"Possibly zero. Conjunction now estimated in thirty-eight minutes. Would you like me to maneuver out of his way? I think that would be wise."

"No. If he means to ram us, he'll ram us. With the damage to the front of our tow, any aggressive maneuvers will rip us apart. He'll rake us fore and aft as he passes."

Tom rubbed his eyes, unsure of why they were watering so much. "What about Kahwihta? Are she and the others back in the ship?"

"Bosun Beauvais is waiting in the corridor outside the bridge. Ms. Vendramin is with Simon and Tekanatoken in the medical bay. Our First Officer is still unconscious while I work to repair her three cracked ribs. I anticipate a full recovery."

Tom put his hand on the keypad. The door slid open. Kahwihta was sitting on the deck, leaned against the wall with her display pad unrolled on her lap.

"You should have come in. I put on quite a show."

She tapped her pad. "I was eavesdropping. Schiava patched me in and I didn't want to distract you. You almost have me convinced the *Esprit de la Légion* is really out there."

"Thanks. It's not over yet."

"So I heard. The Holloman armor will protect us. Unless he rams."

"That would destroy him too. I don't think he's the suicidal type."

"Hope you're right."

Tom reached down to help her up. His hand was shaking.

Kahwihta took hold of it. "First pirate attack, Skipper?"

"First one without an escort."

"Sit down with me a minute."

"I shouldn't." He sat. "You still think you can feel my emotions?"

"Some. Whatever Holloman's pets did only works when you're close."

"Delusions. Illusions. Be happy you can't feel them." Tom tried not to think about what would happen if the FAC rammed them, but the image wouldn't leave his brain. The *Mandirigma* would rip through their Holloman armor like shattering a pane of glass and the *Gattino Alato* would be bright sparkles in the light of the distant stars. He looked down at Kahwihta's hand holding his and tried to concentrate on that instead. He could hear music playing from somewhere far away.

"Ten minutes to conjunction, sir," Schiava reported. "The medical bay is the sturdiest part of me. You may want to join the rest of your crew there. I'm still unable to determine the exact distance of their passage. It will be close."

"Ten minutes? Did the *Mandirigma* change velocity again? I thought you said they were over a half hour out."

"That was twenty-seven minutes ago."

"That's impossible."

Kahwihta shrugged. "Whatever was in container one... I don't know. It's done something to us."

"We'll figure it out later." Tom and Kahwihta ran, struggling to secure helmets and gloves as they went. When they arrived in the medical bay, Simon and Tek were helping Gabriela into a pressure suit, trying to be gentle while she tried to be brave.

Tom looked down at her lying on the diagnostic bed. Gabriela's face was pale. It revealed freckles on her nose he hadn't noticed before. "How's my First Officer?"

"Hurting a bit. Not bad." She tapped the helmet Tek was trying to attach to the top of the suit. "Really think this will help when ten thousand tonnes of FAC comes through the wall?"

"He won't ram. The suit is standard procedure. You should know that."

"Yes, sir. We're about to lose our last two containers, aren't we."

"Probably."

"I'd like to watch. Tek, help me sit."

Tek glanced at the Captain and waited for him to nod approval.

"Schiava," Tom ordered. "Tactical on the left display, view forward on the right, please."

Gabriela grimaced as she tried to get comfortable, leaning on Tek for support.

"*Capitano*, transmission from the *Mandirigma*."

"Put it through to everyone."

Afweyne's voice crackled in his ear. "See you in hell, Captain Benson. I send you there by my own hand."

Container one vanished in a spray of sand and fragments of composite plates. The *Gattino Alato* shuddered as her gravity generators struggled to compensate. A high energy beam sliced container seven open fore to aft, sending barrels and crates of live animals spinning into cold vacuum. The rest of the stacking frame followed, unprotected and ripped apart by kinetic and directed energy weapons.

The armor over the *Gattino Alato's* hull absorbed the brief attack, ablating as designed. It was over in less than a second.

Captain Afweyne was still talking. "*Non stiamo perdonando*, Captain. Now you are dead. If your masters in the Trade Guild don't kill you, I will do it for them."

Tek grinned at Simon and Kahwihta. "We're still alive. Good plan, Skipper."

Tom rubbed his eyes. "Alive for now. It's not over yet."

Gabriela raised the visor of her suit, panting as her ribs protested each breath. "At least he didn't ram us. I'm sorry about Tuly, sir. Simon told me..." She blinked hard.

"You don't remember it?"

She shook her head. "I was jumping on one of the lashing bars, trying to clear it. The next thing I remember is Simon and Tek cutting me out of the wreckage. Schiava didn't capture what happened?"

"No. She was blind after container four kicked."

"I'll keep trying to remember."

Tom nodded. "We'll slow here and recover Tuly. We owe him a ride back home. I'll contact the Guild now that the jamming has stopped. I'll tell them what happened, and that fourteen of our containers are still out there. They'll send another towboat to pick up our cargo. We saved most of the tow, the ship, the shuttle... most of the crew. If we'd done nothing, we'd have lost it all."

Kahwihta gave him a quick nod. He could see in her eyes and the way her mouth turned down in the corners, that she understood the truth of what Captain Afweyne had said about the Guild's next steps.

"We have a chance," Tom told her. "It's going to be OK."

"*Capitano*," Schiava interrupted. "The Union Frigate *Esprit du Bourreau* has cleared the New Palisade DSH. Captain Mistral is hailing us. He'll be alongside in ninety minutes."

"Huh." Tom looked at Kahwihta, wondering if she had felt the words ripping his heart out.

Tek voiced what all of them were thinking. "Well, damn. Our escort arrived in time after all. We could have done nothing but spin and been just fine."

CHAPTER 4

TO LET THE PUNISHMENT
FIT THE CRIME

Fiona Grimani was tired after the ten-day transit from Earth to New Palisade. She had endured the cramped quarters on board a heavy-laden *Doge*-class freighter with a food printer that only knew three recipes, and had survived the obsequious crew trying desperately to meet her every desire, except her need for solitude.

She tried not to look at Thomas as they waited for the hearing to begin. She already knew how it would end. That's why she'd come in person, to push the local members of the Guild as far as she could, instead of back on Earth keeping her engineering team on track. She had a draft Request for Proposal due to the Guild Senior Architect in fifty-eight days, and...

Fiona's gaze drifted back to him. Thomas Benson, ex-lover, ex-husband, father to her son, or at least the man who had helped her create Nicholas fourteen years ago. He hadn't been much of a father. Tom had other loves that pulled at his heart; ones of ceramic composite and metal alloy, not flesh and bone. Fiona could have competed and won against flesh.

Nicholas had ignored the idea of having a father when he was little and accepted Tom's absence as a part of his life. But then on his tenth birthday, Tom had sent him a model towboat that could hover and respond to simple verbal commands. The two of them sent messages back and forth several times a week after that. Nick played with the little cargo ship obsessively for months, using it to carry not just its miniature containers, but also his dishes, schoolwork, and dirty clothes. Watching one of their cats struggling in the ship's anti-grav field a meter and a half off the ground while being transported from room to room had been the final straw.

It hadn't been a good fight. Fiona took Nick's infatuation with the ship as a reflection of Tom's love affair with a life moving cargo between planets. But even knowing the source of her anger didn't help her control what she felt. She had forbidden Nick to talk to his father. All that accomplished was to teach Nick to hide it from her.

Fiona smiled to herself. Devious boy. It was Nick who told her Tom was in trouble even before the Union Aerospace Force officially notified the Guild of what had happened. He would be a valuable little Trade Guild spy in a couple more years. He'd already mastered open source intel. There was no telling what he'd be able to do once he was on the inside.

Fiona sipped her coffee and glanced at Tom when she thought he wouldn't notice. The corner café had brewed the coffee from plants native to New Palisade. It was weak and too sweet, not like in Venice. Not like Barcelona.

She hadn't talked to Tom, of course. Holding Governor's rank in the Guild gave her responsibilities at this kind of hearing and her motives were in question as it was. The members of the council knew the truth of it, but they wouldn't ask why she was there as long as she was respectful of the formalities.

Fiona finally gave up trying not to stare at Tom. Everyone else was staring at him. He looked relaxed and confident in his dress uniform. She knew him too well to believe that. He fidgeted when he was relaxed. He was barely moving, seated in the front row next to his first officer with the rest of his crew in the gallery behind them.

Fiona reviewed her notes. The first officer, Gabriela Vendramin, was a real piece of work. The disreputable daughter of a fallen house, her father was just barely maintaining his family's position in the Guild. The *Vendicatores* had taken care of the mother when Gabriela was thirteen. Piracy had been the accusation, but no one had offered proof. It had taken a press gang hired by the girl's grandfather to keep Gabriela from following in her mother's crooked path. She was just the sort Tom would pick up, trying to redeem the universe one bit of flotsam at a time.

She slid her finger across the display pad, flipping the page. Kahwihta Beauvais, Bosun. Inactive member of the Mohawk Ironworkers Kahnawake Local. Her fifteen-year service record with the Guild was spotless.

She flipped to the next page, smiling that the record vindicated her cynicism about human fallibility in general and her ex-husband's in particular. Kahwihta had two brothers. Able Seaman Simon Beauvais and Able

Seaman Tekanatoken Beauvais. They had open arrest warrants on Bodens Gate and a Be On The Lookout from the Union Marine Corps. Well, the Guild wouldn't care about that. If they turned over every crew member with an open arrest warrant half the ships in the fleet would be staying in dock. Still, it was proof Tom hadn't changed in the years since their divorce.

She closed her eyes, talking silently to him in her mind. *Thomas, I saved your life this morning. I did it for the sake of our son, who loves you now as much as I once did. I saved your crew, because I know they're your family. Nick told me that. He also told me how much you love them. He thinks he'd like to have a ship family of his own someday. When this is over, you'll owe me. You'll talk him out of it. Then you'll never talk to him again. You'll leave us alone.*

When she opened her eyes, he was looking at her, a shy grin on his face, the one she knew well. It meant, *sorry I screwed up. Please forgive me.* She smiled back, unable to keep from responding to him the way she always did. It was an automatic response. Their love had gone cold, like the gritty remnants of the coffee sloshing in the bottom of her cup. She turned her head, irritated with him and with herself.

The five Governors of the New Palisade Lodge entered the guildhall and the soft buzz of conversation from the small group of spectators faded to whispers.

"Hey, Skipper," Tek whispered in his ear. "What's with the judges? I thought you said this wasn't a trial."

"The robes are just for show," Tom answered, not turning his head. "The Guild doesn't have police powers. We've broken no laws. The worst they can do is fire us, and there're worse places to be unemployed than New Palisade."

Tom glanced at Gabriela. She was staring straight ahead and her head twitched as a shiver passed through her.

"We're going to die here," she whispered. "Or maybe somewhere else if we run fast enough."

"We're not running. I've got this. Relax."

"Uh huh. When have I heard that before? Are you counting on the stuck-up Guild Princess that used to be your wife? I've been watching her watch you. If she comes this way carrying something sharp, you may want to reconsider your 'not running' policy."

A gentle chime sounded and the lights dimmed. Tom adjusted himself in his seat. They were about to find out how much trouble they were really in, and how far and how fast they would need to run.

A man with a short gray beard stood, smoothed his robe, and read from his display pad. "I am Governor Mosharaf, Speaker for the governing body of the New Palisade Lodge of the Trade Guild of the Most Serene Republic of Venice, here assembled with support of our sister, Governor Fiona Grimani. We have reviewed the evidence in the matter of the damage incurred to the starship *Gattino Alato*, the destruction of goods entrusted to the Guild, and the loss of a trained and certified starship engineer.

"The ship's AI was notably unhelpful to our inquiry. Its testimony was factual, but accompanied by unrequested commentary and rationalizations. At the time the incident occurred, it failed to take independent action when action was required. *Gattino Alato's* artificial intelligence will be baselined by the original vendor and reinitialized. Esclava, record that as Item One."

The AIs voice that responded was cold and obedient. "So noted in the official record."

Kahwihta's voice was soft behind him. "Goodbye, Schiava."

Mosharaf continued. "Item Two: the damage done to the *Gattino Alato*, specifically the loss of the forward stacking frame. It is the conclusion of the Governors that the loss was due to an act by privateers employed by the Separatist Insurgency and was largely, but not completely, beyond the control of the *Gattino Alato's* officers. Financial compensation of thirty percent of the cost to replace the stacking frame by said officers will cancel this finding if received within one standard year."

"Thirty percent?" Gabriela whispered. "How much is that?"

"A year's wages. For both of us. Maybe a little more. We can't earn it if we're dead, so it's a good sign."

"Yeah. And if we don't pay within a year?"

"Don't ask."

"Item Three: the unauthorized opening of goods entrusted to the Guild and their subsequent destruction, specifically goods consigned by Captain Mala Dusa Holloman of the Union Aerospace Force. Captain Holloman has declined the opportunity to pursue compensation. Her official response was, '*Really? I guess they must have known what they were doing.*' Whether 'they' refers to Captain Benson and his crew remains ambiguous. Neither Captain Holloman nor her superiors have responded to our request for clarification. Esclava, Item Three is closed."

"So noted."

"Item Four: the destruction of goods entrusted to the Guild, specifically by Gōngyè Hézuòshè Farms. This item is in kind with Item Two. Captain Benson and First Officer Vendramin have one standard year to compensate the Guild thirty percent of the cost to replace what was destroyed."

"How much?" Gabriela whispered.

"No idea. How much do crates of ducks cost?"

"This brings us lastly to the loss of Engineer Owen Tulisan."

Tom sat up a little straighter and focused his attention on the robed figures in front of him.

"This is the end," Gabriela whispered. "They can't kill us, of course, not officially. They'll revoke our certifications and bar us from service. Then some night, in a few days or weeks... that sound. Cutting."

A part of Tom would be content for this to be a death sentence as long as it was only his punishment and not Gabriela's. It was his plan that had collapsed on them. It was his fault that Tuly died alone in the cold black.

"The public portion of this hearing is concluded. Captain Benson and First Officer Vendramin, we invite you to join us in our chambers. Esclava, we are done here. Please close the official record."

Tom and Gabriela looked at each other. "Did I miss something?" he asked.

She blinked back at him and shook her head.

Kahwihta leaned forward and touched his shoulder. "We'll be waiting for you in the café around the corner."

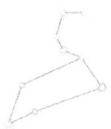

Tom and Gabriela followed the Governors into a private chamber where a sideboard with food and drinks was set up against one wall. A conference table with eight chairs occupied the center of the room.

"Captain." Mosharaf parted the electrostatic seam down the front of his robe and removed it, revealing an expensively tailored gray suit. "I wanted to say, off the record, that we are impressed with how you handled Captain Afweyne. Governor Grimani made that point quite forcefully, and we must admit she's right. If your escort had arrived a couple of hours later, we'd be awarding you the Winged Lion right now." He chuckled. "But, as we told her, we must deal in actualities, not the what might have been."

"Yes, sir."

"Call me Mosharaf. Help yourself to something to eat and drink." He turned to Gabriela and narrowed his eyes as though he was not done judging her. "Both of you."

Neither of them moved. "I don't think either of us is hungry, sir. Thank you for the offer," Tom answered for them.

"Business first, then, although you really should try the lamb stew. It's a slow-cooked recipe I programmed myself. The boiled sheep's head is a dish called svið. I wouldn't recommend it unless you grew up on it like Governor Adelsteinn."

Tom sat with Gabriela next to him. Fiona was across the table, close enough that he could have touched her fingers if they had reached out toward each other. It had been three years since he'd last seen her in person. She hadn't changed, and he was thankful Kahwihta wasn't there to feel his emotions.

When he was between worlds with his ship's engines making the deck plates hum, he knew that was where he belonged. But whenever he looked into the depths of Fiona's brown eyes, doubts would move in along with a desire to have back what he had lost. Would it have been so terrible, life with her by his side, or really, with him by hers? It would never have been an equal partnership, but Nicholas would have been there too. Maybe others. It would have been an easy life to live.

Gabriela took his hand under the table. She was shaking, looking for reassurance. He turned to her, surprised, and tried to give her a smile, but reassurance was hard to come by.

Mosharaf settled himself at the head of the table. "Captain Benson, First Officer Vendramin. This part of the hearing is private. No AI is watching or listening to our words, no display pads are recording them, except mine. The others here will forget these words when they leave this room, but not you. You will remember and you will obey.

34

"We have already discussed the financial restitution required to cancel your debt. Now we must turn to the matter of earning back your merchant mariner credentials."

Mosharaf paused. Tom glanced across the table at Fiona. Her attention was on Mosharaf, her fingers wrapped in a tight ball on the table in front of her.

"Piracy is a plague," Mosharaf continued. "The privateers that prey on us are chartered by a dozen planetary governments the Union has yet to bring to heel. The Union provides escorts and promises great things, and still we suffer losses. Damage to our ships. Damage to our reputation. Damage to centuries of trust with our customers. Sometimes the betrayal is from within the Guild itself, from within our family. We have our own cure for that."

He placed a bag on the table, worn black leather a half-meter long, thirty centimeters wide by twenty tall.

Gabriela crushed Tom's fingers. He winced.

"You don't know what this is, do you Captain?"

Tom shook his head. He could guess, but he was praying he was wrong.

"Your First Officer knows. I see it in her eyes, the sting of a lesson learned. Let me show you."

He ran his finger across the top of the bag and it opened to him. He removed a short hollow tube a couple of centimeters in diameter. The dull sheen of its metallic surface reflected the overhead lights.

"Note the fine serrations on the working end. Avoid touching them if you value your skin. Very sharp." He set it on the table and removed a black handle from the bag. "Standard power source. I'm sure you use ones like it with your tools on board ship. They go together like this." He seated the tube into the handle and twisted it into place. It clicked, like the sound of a magazine locking into a pistol.

"This is a vibracore. Simple and effective. Geologists use them to take core samples. The Guild uses them to provide proof of death. A genetic sample would be inadequate unless it contains a part of the individual they cannot live without. A six to eight-centimeter deep cut made through the skull of the criminal is the preferred method. Is that clear?"

Tom shook his head, not trusting his voice.

"You are confused. Perhaps a demonstration is in order. Ms. Vendramin?"

She stared back at Mosharaf, eyes unblinking.

Mosharaf smiled. "Would you be so kind as to bring that plate over to me? The one with the sheep's head on it."

"I'll get it for you," Tom volunteered.

"You sit tight, Captain."

Gabriela stumbled to her feet, and for a moment Tom was afraid she'd try to run. She walked to the sideboard without a word, her head high. She positioned the plate on the table in front of Mosharaf and sat back down.

"I'm impressed. You may yet be the one to redeem your family's honor." He didn't look away from her as he gripped the vibracore and placed it against the boiled skull of the sheep. "It's done like this."

The tool spun up with a sharp whine and there was a loud crunch of bone as he pushed on it. It made a wet sloppy sound as it spun through into the sheep's brain. He pulled it out and pointed the end at them.

"You see? It seals the sample automatically, ready for delivery to any guild-hall for analysis and confirmation. You must do this for us, Captain, First Officer. There are nine more coring tools in the bag, but you need use only five to complete your redemption. The price is one privateer's life for each surviving member of the crew of the *Gattino Alato*. Is it clear to you now?"

"Yes." Tom's voice sounded dull in his ears, far away, as though someone else was speaking. "How will we know who to... How will we find them?"

"The Guild maintains a list of known malefactors and their last con-firmed locations. As far as how you will find them, that is up to you. You have twelve months to complete your tasks. You will also receive the stan-dard rate of fifty-thousand credits per confirmed kill, so you'll be paying off your financial obligation to the Guild as you go."

Mosharaf glanced at Fiona. "This is a generous offer. Nearly unprec-edented, really. But your actions to save your ship and cargo were unprecedented as well, so consider this a gift in recognition of your cre-ativity." He stood and the other Governors followed his example. "I believe we are done here. You have much work to do, Captain. Feel free to use all nine of those coring tools. You could turn a nice profit for your efforts if you find this life suits you."

Tom took the bag from Mosharaf. Fiona stared at him, a look in her eyes as if she wanted to follow him and explain what she had done, how she had sacrificed to give him the opportunity to kill five people in the name of Venice. He knew she wouldn't follow, though. That would damage her reputation, her standing, her image within the Trade Guild. Fiona Grimani would never do that.

He turned and wrapped Gabriela's hand around his arm. "Ms. Vendramin, let's get the hell out of here."

CHAPTER 5

THE WISDOM
OF SAILORS

It was a couple of hours past the lunch rush, so the crowd at the Al-zawiya Maqha had thinned. Tom found Kahwihta and her brothers at a corner table with a good view of the front door, the remnants of lunch still on their plates. Kahwihta and Simon each had a half a beer left, while Tek worked on a small glass of something dark brown, no ice. Tom steered Gabriela to the table and put her into a chair. She hadn't spoken since leaving the Guildhall and Tom was starting to get worried.

"How did it go?" Kahwihta asked.

Gabriela scanned the table and she grabbed the small glass sitting in front of Tek.

"Hey! Wait a second, ma'am. That stuff will—"

She tossed the contents into her mouth, eyes closed.

"Shit."

She swallowed and a gentle smile turned up her parted lips. Then the alcohol hit her stomach and her eyes went wide. She looked from Tom to Kahwihta, breathing hard. "Toilet," she whimpered, her hand coming up to cover her mouth.

Kahwihta took her arm and they wobbled quickly toward the back of the café.

"Poor Alice." Tek shook his head.

"Alice?" Tom asked.

"Yeah. They call that brand of whiskey Poor Alice. I had it a couple of times on Bodens Gate. It's best sipped slowly, and not on an empty stomach."

"Want another one?"

"Am I going to need it?"

"Yeah. I'll have one too. What's good to eat here?"

Simon shrugged and passed him a menu card. "The kufta kabobs were decent. Order that with the baba ghanoush and it should be enough for both of you. If our First Officer is up to eating anything. What happened to her, anyway? She looked like she'd been kicked in the head."

"More like in the heart. They hurt her, and they enjoyed doing it."

"They didn't go after you?" Simon asked.

"I'm old enough not to feel it."

Simon and Tek exchanged glances. "If you say so, Skipper," Simon told him. "What do we have to do to get square?"

Tom tapped on the menu card. "Food first. We'll wait for Kahwihta and Gabriela to get back. You and your sister aren't a part of this, you know. The punishment and restitution are on the ship's officers. Your Merchant Mariner Credentials are still good. There are a dozen or more freighters on orbit and not just Guild ships. Be on one of them tomorrow. Take Kahwihta with you. Use force if you have to."

Simon chuckled. "On Kahwihta? We're not that stupid. Order your food and then just tell us what we need to do."

Kahwihta came back alone. "Gabriela will be a few minutes. She didn't want me there. Embarrassed, I think. I'll check on her if she's not back soon."

"Thanks. Did she tell you anything?"

"Yeah. Hell of a thing for a kid, forcing her to listen while they executed her mother. Explains a lot. Damn *Vendicatores*. Even a pirate deserves due process and a fair trial."

Simon swirled the contents of his glass, studying the foam. "Why has she remained loyal to the Guild? I'd expect her to join the Separatists and ship out as a privateer."

Tom shook his head. "I think she's planning to get her revenge from the inside. And if she keeps moving up through the ranks, the Guild hierarchy had better watch out. Ms. Vendramin has kept a list."

"You knew about this when you brought her on board, didn't you?" Kahwihta asked.

"Of course. It's my job to know everything there is to know about my crew."

Her chin came up, defiant. "Really? You think you know me that well?"

The feeling came over him again, as if he'd stepped outside of place and time. There was the hum, and the sound of music playing somewhere far away. Nothing existed except the two of them; nothing *could* exist except the two of them.

"Skipper? Kahwihta?"

Someone called to him and he forced himself to answer. There was danger; he had responsibilities and people to protect. "I'm here."

Tom opened his eyes, with no memory of closing them.

Kahwihta sat across from him, a gentle smile touching her lips. She hummed a song he recognized, but couldn't name. He wanted to sing it with her.

"Is she all right?" Tom asked.

"You tell us. You two have been like that for the past couple of minutes. Tek was about to dump ice water on you."

Tom reached across the table and put his hand against Kahwihta's cheek. She sighed and leaned into it, eyes moving behind closed lids as if she was dreaming.

"Hey, Simon. That's something we haven't seen in a while. I think our big sister is in love."

Her eyes opened, fully alert. "Gabriela. Gotta go check on her."

Tom turned to Kahwihta's brothers after she left. They were smirking. "There was something in container one. I don't know if it was in the air or something the creatures in there did to us. She says she can feel my emotions, and sometimes I get just a touch of what she's feeling too. It's kind of fading now, but it still comes over us sometimes."

"Are you saying you don't love her?"

"I do love her." Saying the words aloud made him hear the song again. "Even before we went in there together."

"Have you told her?"

"No, and it doesn't matter. Not now. Gabriela and I have something to do that we probably won't survive. It's why you need to get Kahwihta out of here. I can't put her in that kind of danger. That's the third time we've gone off into nowhere land together. Not exactly conducive to survival when someone is trying to kill you."

Kahwihta came back and stood behind Tom, fists on her hips. "She's gone. The guys in the kitchen say she left out the back five minutes ago."

"Are they sure it was her? She was alone?" Tom asked.

"Yes, alone. Trade Guild dress uniforms are hard to miss."

"It doesn't make sense. She wouldn't do that."

"Well, she did." Kahwihta took her seat across from him. "Tell me why."

Tom lifted the leather bag onto the table. "We need to find and murder five people. We need to do it in the next year and not get ourselves killed while we're doing it. The Trade Guild says they're privateers, bad people deserving of death. I suppose the Union would agree since most pirates are chartered now by letters of marque from the Separatists."

He stared at them, waiting for it to soak in. "With Gabriela gone," he continued, "I guess it's just me now. Kahwihta, you're not part of it. I don't want you or your brothers here. I don't need your help."

"You ever done anything like this before, hunting people and killing them?" Kahwihta asked.

"No, of course not."

"The Guild suspended your Master's License?"

"That's right. But not your Merchant Mariner Credentials. You'll have no trouble finding a new ship."

"That means you're not my captain anymore. You're just another unemployed sandcrab. I don't have to take your orders, or even listen to the bullshit coming out of your mouth. I'll do as I please."

Tom frowned at her, trying to fake an angry resolve he didn't feel. Her brothers were sitting beside her with their arms crossed. "And what is your pleasure? To die with me on New Palisade?"

"Back to that again? We're not dying. *We've* been given a job to do, and *we're* going to get it done."

The drinks arrived along with the food he had planned to share with Gabriela. He lifted his glass. "To the wisdom of sailors, then. And to Tuly."

They drank, and Tek and Simon helped him finish what he couldn't eat.

They were still lingering over drinks two hours later, telling stories that had nothing to do with what they would need to accomplish in the coming months. Tom had switched to coffee after two glasses of Poor Alice, but it was taking a while for his head to clear. That was OK. Listening to Simon and Tek trying to embarrass Kahwihta was keeping his thoughts away from tomorrow. Watching her respond to their taunts was better than thinking about the message that had popped up on his display pad reminding him he had to be out of the Trade Guild Guest House by 23:00.

Tom heard the sound of the door opening behind him and the clicking approach of hard-soled shoes on the tile floor. Kahwihta and her brother's smiles faded as they sat up a little straighter. Then he smelled her, before she spoke, before her hand touched his shoulder. Citrus with clove, subtle and unforgettable. Fiona always smelled like that. He set his coffee cup down, but didn't turn around.

"Thomas, we need to talk."

"Always straight to business, Fiona. I like that about you. No illusions or insincere pleasantries."

He scooted his chair back and turned toward her, thinking he was ready for whatever she wanted to tell him.

Fiona's lips parted, then she closed them again. The look in her eyes had nothing to do with business. They were warm and sultry like her voice. They were the eyes he'd fallen in love with in Barcelona.

He said the same words he'd said then, and countless other times, unable to stop himself. A private joke he'd almost forgotten. "Can I buy you a cup of coffee? It's not as good as what you have in Venice, but it's warm."

She responded as she always did, seemingly just as helpless. "Nothing is as good as Venice. Let me show it to you someday."

Tom stared at her, lost in a memory of cold nights walking the streets of Barcelona with Fiona's gloved hand in his.

"Can we go somewhere?" Fiona asked. "I'll only keep you a moment. Where's Ms. Vendramin?"

He pushed a chair out for her. "Gabriela went back to the Guest House. She wasn't feeling well. Please sit. I have no secrets from my crew. They've decided to stay with me while I fulfill the conditions set by the Guild for our redemption. I tried to tell them how dangerous and foolish–"

"Stay? What are you talking about? You don't actually think you're going to chase pirates, do you?"

Tom looked from Fiona to Kahwihta and back again, shaking his head. "What else?"

"Thomas, you're an idiot. I didn't come all this way just to watch you kill yourself. Captain Afweyne is looking for you and the price he put on your head is substantial. I think you pissed off the Union Aerospace Force too, and I know the Marines are looking for those two." She gestured at Simon and Tek.

"Then there's the *Vendicatores*. They'll punch a hole in your stupid head and save it for a year to collect the bounty when you default. I negotiated that twelve-month term to give you time. You need to run. You need to run far and fast."

Tom waited for more coffee to arrive. He and Fiona Grimani were alone and he needed a clear head. He wanted another whiskey. The coffee would have to do.

"I like your bosun, Thomas. She's direct and intuitive. She knew it was time for her and her brothers to leave us. You need someone like her in your life. Is she really as squared away as her record indicates?"

"We're not here to talk about Kahwihta."

"No, I suppose not. We're here to talk about you and Ms. Vendramin. Or maybe just you, since she's missing."

"She went back to the Guest House," he told her again.

"It's sweet of you to lie for her, but she's not worth it. It won't save her, running like that. Not alone. The two of you together have a chance if you watch each other's backs. There are places on New Palisade that can help with new IDs and there are ships that won't ask too many questions. Try one of the Hanseatic freighters. Go find Ms. Vendramin, and when you're ready, don't try to contact anyone you have ever known. Someone will be watching for that. Do you understand?"

"I should say goodbye to Nicholas before I disappear. I haven't seen him since he was nine, not face to face anyway. I don't suppose he'll miss me much."

"He will, more than you know. It will break his heart for a time. I need you to tell him not to chase the dream of pushing cargo between the planets. Every time *I* tell him, I have to double check the locks and alarms to keep him from running away to join you." She smiled. "Even the household AI is on his side now. I don't know how Nick flipped him."

Steam rose from their cups as the waiter refilled them.

"Nick is like you, Thomas. Stubborn and contrary. He's becoming more rebellious every day. If I tell him to go left, he goes right, just to spite me."

"It would be easier if I could talk to him in real time. I'll send him a long message. It won't help, not at his age, and I won't have a chance to try again."

He poured a small amount of cream into the coffee, fascinated by the patterns it made. He shook his head and looked up at her. "I can't do it. I can't disappear and become someone else. I did that when I left you. I was young and stupid."

She tipped her head and narrowed her eyes. "That's as close to an apology as you've ever come."

"Let me try again, then. I'm sorry I left. It doesn't matter, and I know it's too late, but I'm sorry."

"It does matter. I tried to make you into someone you most definitely are not." She smiled and lowered her voice. "Ship's Captain. I was proud of you at the hearing today. You don't belong in Venice any more than I would have a place on your bridge with a Fast Attack Craft spinning its way toward us. And you *will* run. You have to."

"The hell I do. I'm not helpless, you know. I've been to sixteen planets and survived some rough places. The 'businesses' that serve the crews… well, I've seen my share of fights. Won a couple too."

Her voice hardened and her accent became sharper. "How many men have you killed? How many women have you stabbed or shot and watched bleed out at your feet?"

He didn't answer.

"This isn't like trading punches with someone and then sharing a beer and a laugh with them afterward. You do this and it only ends one of two ways." She held up a single finger. "There are at least two groups with options placed on your head, probably three. One of them will kill you. It won't be a fight. You won't see it coming. You'll just be dead."

She held up a second finger. "Or, maybe you're good at this, or lucky, and you find and murder five human beings before they kill you. I've had to work with men and women who have taken that path. The ones that start out like you? Part of them dies every time they take a life until nothing is left. And the ones that aren't like you? I'm not sure there was much inside them to begin with. They're monsters. We use them, but they're monsters."

"I'm not running."

"*Sarai morto domani.*"

"I will not be dead tomorrow. Let's keep this in English, please."

"Why? You know Italian almost as well as I do."

He smiled a sad, helpless smile. "I like the sound of it too much. Even when you're angry. Maybe especially when you're angry. *Amore alla prima parola.* I heard your voice and I was lost."

"*L'amore per la prima volta.* That was me, in love for the first time, fool that I was. Don't change the subject."

He shrugged. "The subject is closed. I'd rather hunt than be hunted. Killing in self-defense? I think I can survive."

Fiona shook her head. "I will have lost over three weeks by the time I get home, all so I wouldn't have to tell Nicholas his father is dead. Maybe I can use you as a cautionary tale to keep him safe."

"Gabriela and I might surprise you."

"I doubt it. You'll get your bosun killed too, and I know you have feelings for her. Thomas, I opened a path for you, an easy path. I have names of people who can help you. Why can't you just take it?"

They were silent for a few moments, each of them staring into their coffee cups.

"That's not who I am," he answered softly.

"Yes it is."

"Maybe it was. But not now. Tell me the truth. If we don't die and we complete what the Governors asked us to do, will they reinstate us?"

"I don't know. I only found a handful of precedents when I was preparing this gambit. All of them ran. Just as they were supposed to do. That was kind of the point; we wanted to maintain the ferocious reputation of the Guild while providing leniency. No one's been crazy enough to..." She ended with a shrug.

Tom swallowed the last of his coffee. "Then plan on coming to find me when we finish. I'll probably need you. Or at least come back for my funeral."

Fiona stood and Tom helped her with her jacket. "I won't come back for your funeral." She kissed his cheek.

When he kissed hers, he whispered in her ear. "I need one more favor."

Her eyes widened a little as he spoke, but she smiled when he pulled away from her. "I can do that."

CHAPTER 6

HUNTER OR HUNTED

"I need access to Captain Benson's room," Kahwihta told the front desk.

"Excuse me?" the smooth, deferential voice of the Guild's Guest House AI answered.

"Captain Benson's room. I'm his bosun. Please add his key code to my watch and display pad. I need to remove his belongings."

"Mr. Benson has five hours, twenty-two minutes remaining to accomplish that task."

"He might not be back in time. He's conferring with a senior leader from the Guild and I don't know how long it will last. I'll move his belongings into my room temporarily in case he's delayed past 23:00."

"That will be acceptable. I have verified your credentials as bosun of the *Gattino Alato*."

"And Ms. Vendramin," Tek added. "Add her to my access and I'll move her stuff into my quarters."

Kahwihta turned to him, staring with her head tipped until he broke.

He smiled back at her. "Why not?"

"Please add Ms. Vendramin's room to my account as well," she told the desk. "It will be short term."

"Make certain it is. Former employees with their status are not welcome here. They attract violence. Last time it took over a week for the contractors to complete repairs and clean up everything."

Kahwihta's face flushed and her voice became precise as she found an outlet for her anger. "Let me get this straight. You are supposed to be a secure facility. What did you *allow* to happen? Are you telling us—"

Simon took his sister's arm before she could continue. "Let's move their things and then find somewhere private to talk."

She shook his hand off, but Tek was already on her other side, pulling her toward the central lifts. "Come on, Kahwihta. Fighting with the AI isn't going to get the Skipper here any sooner."

"AI," she answered loudly. "Artificial *Idiot*."

Simon put his arm around her shoulder as they walked, leaning close. "You really think the Captain is going to be that late?"

"That's his business. I don't care what he does. We need to be ready when he tells us what's coming next."

"He left her," Tek told his sister.

Simon added, "What we saw was just an echo of something that died a long time ago. You know him better than she does."

"Yeah?" she replied. "There was something in container one..."

"The skipper told us." Tek replied.

"Did he? That was more than an echo he was feeling. Trust me."

Simon shrugged. "Can you see him going back Earthside with her? Being an obedient Guild stooge? Hanging with that crowd at parties?"

Kahwihta chuckled, letting go of her anger. "Can you see her lashing cargo down, face covered in grease, and..." She trailed off. She could see it. Fiona Grimani was skinny and overdressed, but there was something hard about her. There was a look in her eyes and in the way she carried herself that left no doubt she could get any job done she set out to do. Kahwihta's smile faded.

They were standing outside Captain Benson's door and Tek let go of her arm so she could press her hand to the keypad. "Let's get his junk and then see what's in Gabriela's room. You worry too much, sis. You've got him hooked. Play with him a little and then reel him in."

"Right. If we don't die first." She raised her hand and felt dizzy. The hum filling her head was painful enough to bring tears to her eyes. She looked at her hand and then used it to shove Tek to the side. She waved at Simon and he stepped back next to Tek.

"Seriously?" Tek asked.

"Guest House, are you listening?" She waited. There was no answer. The AI should always be listening. And watching. It was part of the service.

She stepped as far away from the door as possible, squinted her eyes, and placed her palm on the glowing square of the keypad.

The door slid open.

Tek looked at her from around Simon. "Did you really think–"

A soft hiss interrupted him, followed by the patter of darts striking the opposite wall.

Kahwihta resisted the urge to lean forward to peek into the room. Simon and Tek hadn't moved, staring at the dozen tiny silver barbs studding the beige wallpaper.

"Probably poisoned," Simon whispered. "Any one of them would have been fatal."

A door opened down the hall. A young man glanced up from his display pad at them, smiled shyly, and looked back down. He walked past them fully absorbed in whatever the pad was showing him, oblivious to what had happened.

Kahwihta didn't take her eyes off him. He seemed like an average Trade Guild Ordinary Seaman– an OS on his first cruise, young and a little lost. Something in the back of her head hummed a warning, more than intuition, less than rational thought.

She didn't let him get more than two steps past her before she leaped on his back, a feral scream escaping her throat as she drew a long knife from her boot.

"Oh, shit, here we go," Tek shouted.

Simon and Tek helped roll him onto his back, holding his arms and legs. Kahwihta's knife was at his throat. She had already drawn blood.

"Take whatever you want," he gasped. "Money, right front pocket. Not much. It's yours. Don't hurt me."

"Kahwihta, look at the patch on his shoulder. Guild ship. What are we doing?" Simon pleaded.

"Who are you working for?" Kahwihta demanded, ignoring her brother.

"Trade Guild." He was crying. "OS on the *Pietro Tribuno*. Captain Sanudo."

Kahwihta pushed gently on the knife until it broke through his skin again. "What captain?"

"Sanudo. Please, please, it's Sanudo."

Kahwihta pushed harder. Blood pooled in the hollow of his throat. "Try again."

"Captain..." He paused, breathing hard.

Kahwihta moved the knife, cutting downward. "No lies."

"Captain Afweyne. Captain Afweyne, all right? I was waiting for Benson. Big bounty on him. Easy money. We can share it."

Kahwihta lifted the blade and looked at her brothers. "This is what our life will be until we close this debt. They'll come day and night. One after another."

She slammed the knife down, cutting through the pirate's neck. His eyes widened in surprise for a few seconds, as though realizing he was going to die on the dirty, faded carpet of the Guest House hallway. His blood poured out onto the floor, onto Kahwihta's hands, onto her pants where she was kneeling on top of him.

"That's one," she told them. "Four more and we're finished with this business. Check his coat. That bastard Afweyne would have wanted proof. He must have a... um..." She stammered as the cold certainty filling her mind slipped away. She felt it leave, something alive that wasn't there anymore. There had been a song playing. Something she recognized, but couldn't name.

She swayed, tried to stand, and didn't make it. She slumped against the wall by Tom's still open door, wiped her eyes with her arm, and tried not to get blood on her face.

"Check for a vibracore," she whispered. "Oh, God. What did I just do?"

Tek and Simon looked at each other. Tek shrugged and carefully opened the pirate's coat, searching the pockets. Simon knelt next to Kahwihta.

"You did what you had to do. He meant to kill the Captain. He almost killed us."

"Doesn't help. I felt his last heartbeats through the knife when I pushed it down. How can I ever..." She swallowed hard and held her hands in front of her. "I need to clean up."

"Found it," Tek told them. "Do you know how it works?"

Kahwihta nodded. "Yeah. Gabriela told me about them. When we were in the bathroom. While she was throwing up. I think, maybe, I'm going to..." She swallowed hard. "No. I'm OK. I'll do it."

"Sit," Simon told her. "Tell us what to do."

She told them, eyes closed, trying to concentrate on the procedure, trying to ignore the sound it made.

"What now?" Tek asked.

The Guest House AI answered him. "What always happens. You get a reward for having dispatched an enemy of the Trade Guild of Venice and I'm stuck arranging for cleanup and repairs. Isn't this what I told you would happen? I have already notified the Crime and Trauma Scene decontamination unit. I have a depository on the first floor for the sample you obtained. How would you like to divide the fifty-thousand credits? It looked to me like Bosun Kahwihta Beauvais did most of the work."

"Apply it to the debt incurred by Captain Benson and First Officer Vendramin," Kahwihta answered.

"Really? The Governors never bother opening an account in such cases... but I have confirmed they did this time. Twenty minutes ago, it seems. How fortuitous. Please follow the yellow ball and I shall validate your kill."

A yellow glow appeared in mid-air.

Kahwihta was still looking at her hands. "Simon, Tek, you go. I want a shower. An enormously long shower."

"You suppose our rooms are safe?" Tek asked.

"Oh, you can be certain they are," the AI answered. "The Trade Guild Guest House is a secure facility. I am always watching and listening. No one enters here without my knowledge and permission."

"We'll walk with you anyway. Make sure your room is OK." Simon and Tek helped her up, not caring about the blood. She was shaking and they had to support her.

"Must have been sitting funny," she lied. "Legs aren't working right."

"Lean on me, sis." Simon glanced over his shoulder. "Guest House, close Captain Benson's door please."

"You won't be retrieving his things? His bag is in the closet just inside the door."

"Maybe later."

"As you wish. At 23:00 it all goes in the recycler."

"Let it go," Kahwihta answered. "Like hell are any of us going in there."

CHAPTER 7

BAD TIMING

Kahwihta threw up in the shower. All of her clothes had gone into the recycler, whether stained with blood or not. She saved the knife and took it into the shower with her. She cleaned it with the same soap she used on her body and watched the red water disappear down the drain until it ran clear. Her memories remained undimmed, unaffected by the soap and water, replaying over and over while she cried.

She was still standing under the water when the door to the bathroom opened a few centimeters. She crouched down, one hand on the floor for balance, the other gripping her knife, waiting.

"Kahwihta? Don't freak out. It's just me, Tom. I wanted to let you know I'm here. Tek let me in. I'll wait for you to finish, OK?"

"Almost killed you just now, Skipper. I'm good at it, have you heard?" Her voice broke when she said it, and she felt the flow of emotions from him now that he was close enough. So many emotions. He wanted to comfort her; that was strongest. He felt guilty that what she was experiencing was his fault. She shook her head, trying to clear the water away from her eyes. Yeah, it was his fault, not that she could think of anything he could have done differently.

"Be out in a minute," she called to him. She turned off the water and dried herself. He was worried and afraid. He was afraid she might hate him now. He was afraid they would die. The danger was getting worse.

Kahwihta wrapped herself in a towel and opened the door. There was *that* emotion too, the longing and desire coming from him so strong it was more a taste on her tongue than a feeling.

Tom was leaning against the wall across the room, as far away from her as he could get, and she still felt it. He wasn't even pretending not to look at her. There were fresh cut flowers on the small table by her bed.

"Your timing sucks, Thomas. Do you know that?"

"So I've been told. Many times."

"But I don't hate you."

"How do you do that? Are you really feeling what I feel?"

"You don't feel what's in here?" She tapped her head.

"Faint. Like a tickle sometimes. A little stronger when I'm close, but not much."

"It was fading. At lunch today, it was almost gone, other than when Fiona walked in. Now... They were in my head when I killed that man. They were telling me what to do, almost as if I was their puppet, but I *wanted* to do what they were telling me to do. They gave me courage."

"They?"

"They. It's something alive, something from container one. You heard what Captain Holloman said about what happened. She said, '*I guess they must know what they're doing*'. They. We let them loose and they're still with us. Some secret Aerospace Force thing. I don't want to feel what you're feeling, but I do. I can't help it."

"I'll try to, I don't know, block it? Control what I'm feeling? I've never been good at that."

"When you were waiting for me, you wanted to comfort me because it's your fault I had to... do what I did. Concentrate on that. I could use comforting."

"OK."

Kahwihta walked to him and he put his arms around her. "The problem with your ship, Skipper, is that comfort is hard to come by. My brothers have each other, and the girls they meet in port. You were close with your First Officer until we left him on Chéng Nuò and picked up Gabriela. And you were close with Tuly. It was lonely for me sometimes. Did you know?"

He squeezed her tighter, one hand caressing her back. "I'm sorry. It didn't have to be that way. If we had been honest with each other, well, there was no reason to be lonely."

"Concentrate on comfort, sir. Your emotions are drifting."

"No, they're not. There's nothing in me but comforting thoughts."

She laughed, keeping her head pressed against his shoulder. "Kind of fun, seeing how much you're lying to me."

"My timing sucks."

"What I did, it tore me up inside. I'm not coming back from that for a while, but... thanks for the flowers. Were you planning on taking me to dinner?"

"We're still going, even if I have to carry you. Thamarat Al-Waha. Fruit of the Oasis. When you walk in, you can smell the food, the spices, but something sweet too. There's a central courtyard with a fountain and a few tables. Vines full of flowers grow up the walls and that's where the sweet smell comes from. There's a special table in one corner of the courtyard, secluded, where we can talk and not be heard."

He moved his hand up into her damp hair, running his fingers through it. "A table where we could have touched, and not been seen."

"Tell me more."

"They don't serve alcohol, but that's OK. I wouldn't want anything to dull our senses, and I won't need anything to heighten mine. I just need you."

"Maybe some food?"

"If you insist."

"What will we talk about?"

"Hum. That is a problem." Tom kissed her hair. "I'd like to say we can ignore what's happened, at least for one night, but we can't. It's not safe."

She shivered against him. "It's not safe. I know that. The Guest House AI, he..."

Tom looked up at the ceiling. "Not here. We'll talk, but not here." He moved his hands slowly down Kahwihta's sides, following the curves of her body until they rested low on her hips. He pushed her away from him.

"That was hard for you, Tom. Your mind is bizarre; the way you make yourself do what you think is right. Hard to follow just from the emotions. You made a deal with yourself just now, I think."

"Don't try to read me. Not that deep."

"OK. A quiet dinner together then. Is that what you want?"

"Yes, but we can't have it. I need your brothers there too."

"And Gabriela? Has she turned up?"

"I sent her a message to contact one of us. She hasn't answered. Did you get anything on your display pad?"

"Don't have it on me right now. In case you haven't noticed."

He looked down at her bare feet and back up. "Noticed."

She had the hum in her head again, and a taste on her tongue, Tom's emotions mixing with hers, making it hard to tell the difference between his desire and her own. She bit her lower lip and felt what that did to him too. "I should get dressed."

"I'll step outside for a minute."

53

"Don't bother. I imagine you've seen naked women before." She handed him her towel. "Hang this up in the bathroom for me?"

"You're messing with me. That's what I feel in you."

Kahwihta rummaged through her bag and pulled out the slinky dress she'd only worn once. She shook it hard, telling the fabric to relax so the wrinkles would disappear. She tossed it on the bed and turned to him.

"It's childish, I know. I like knowing what you're feeling, not just guessing." She held her arms out. "And I wanted you to see me like this. I'll be forty in a couple of months. A life spent moving cargo isn't easy on the body or the mind. Look at me, Thomas, before this goes any further. Tell me I'm what you want. Tell me I'm not just something convenient."

"You are what I want, and you know me better than that. It's not just your body that interests me."

"Yes. I feel it in you. That helps. It's honest." She picked up the dress and let it slide down around her shoulders, the soft folds just touching her ankles. "Let's find my brothers and have dinner. I want this day to be over. Stay close to me. Being able to touch your emotions helps me to not think about other things."

He took her hand and kissed it. "You are beautiful, by the way. With the dress or without it. I'm six years older than you are and I've got more problems than you know. Tell me I'm not just convenient."

"Can't lie. You're convenient. We'll work on our problems together. Can I have my hand back now?"

"No. I'm going to hold it all the way to the restaurant."

"I'm OK with that."

Kahwihta was not surprised to see Gabriela already sitting at the special table Tom had reserved at the Thamarat Al-Waha. She was dressed in a soft gray top, dark gray pants, and a well-worn black leather jacket. Tom didn't seem surprised to see her either. If Kahwihta had to name it, what she felt in him was a release of tension, as if seeing her had lifted a darkness from his heart.

Tom took Gabriela's hand. "How did you find us? And why didn't you contact me?"

"I found you by hacking the central reservation system most of the restaurants use. It's not secure. I didn't think it was safe to contact you, even encrypted. Don't go to the Guest House. That's probably not safe either."

"It wasn't. Thanks for the warning."

She shrugged, took a sip of her drink, and scrunched up her face. "Tea. What kind of place doesn't serve vermouth before dinner?"

A waiter arrived, took drink orders, and placed a small cube in the center of the table.

Tom placed a finger on it. "Jammer. It belongs to the restaurant, so who knows how good it is."

Gabriela touched it and nodded. "It's running hot. Probably an amplifier sending everything we say straight to the Guild. Or worse." She glanced at the people laughing and eating, her gaze moving quickly from table to table. "You made a reservation for 20:00 in your own name, Skipper." She glanced at the people seated nearest them. "They could be working for Afweyne or the Separatists."

"Kahwihta killed one of the privateers this afternoon," Tek told her cheerfully. "At the Guest House."

"The hell you say."

"It's true. He'd set a trap in the Captain's room. After we triggered it, the bastard tried to walk right past us. Kahwihta jumped him and Simon and I held him down while she cut–"

"We're not talking about this." Kahwihta's stomach twisted into a hard knot as the memories she'd been trying to suppress filled her. She could see his face again and feel his heart pounding as he died under her.

"She needs to know," Tek answered, lowering his voice. "He admitted working for Afweyne. We credited the kill to the Skippers account. One down."

Gabriela chuckled without humor. "Think about what you just said. He admitted working for the most dangerous privateer in the quadrant. Everyone knows the Separatists charter and finance Afweyne. The assassin was inside the Trade Guild Guest House long enough to set a trap and stick around to collect his prize. That doesn't happen without the Guild's knowledge and approval. Nothing like this happens unless they want it to happen."

"So, you're saying he paid off someone at the Guest House?"

Gabriela ignored him. "Now do you see why we aren't safe, Skipper?"

"Your mother." Tom paused and licked his lips.

Kahwihta felt the fear trickling into him as he put the pieces together. "She wasn't a pirate, was she?" Tom asked.

"No. She wasn't a Separatist either. She was close to finding out who was, though. Until the Guild had her murdered. That's why we need to run. You can't fight the Guild. If you try, you die. That's what my grandfather told me. Right before he had me kidnapped."

The waiter placed a glass of sweet tea on the table in front of Kahwihta. No alcohol. Probably for the best. She shifted in her seat and tried to gauge whether or not the people at the table on the right might attack them. Gabriela's paranoia was contagious. The slinky dress wasn't the best attire if it came to a fight, but the boots she was wearing had a sheath carrying her knife. *Already did that once today*, she thought to herself. *That was more than plenty*. She was hoping for something better to end the evening if exhaustion didn't overtake her first. *Not as young as I once was. Not sure I'll get to be any older.*

Tom's focus was on Gabriela. "I need to contact Fiona. She's not leaving until tomorrow, although she's probably already on board the *Jadwiga*. If what you say is true, she needs to know. She's in a position where she–"

"She *already* knows," Gabriela interrupted him. She had her head tipped and little creases of confusion appeared between her eyes. "She holds Governor rank. Trust me, she knows. Of course, she knows. How could you possibly think otherwise?"

"I... I don't believe it. It must be a small circle. If the full Guild council knew, they'd end it."

"I think that's what my mother believed too. Your ex tried to save your life. That was surprising in itself. The other Governors will wonder why she did it. Don't make it any worse for her."

Simon asked, "Then why would she set up an account to pay off the debt? I saw it when we registered credit for the kill."

"Who gets your money when you die, Captain?" Gabriela asked.

"Fiona. In trust for Nicholas, our son."

"Uh huh. Your name is the only one on the account, I'll bet. Not mine. If we live or if we die, she wins."

"You don't know her. She's not like that. She's..."

The waiter returned with a large platter loaded with beef, chicken, lamb, and sides; food for all of them to share. "Enjoy," he told them.

Tek reached across the table and selected several items to dump on his plate. He sniffed at them and looked content. He paused when he noticed everyone watching him and no one else eating. "Sorry, sir. Go ahead. You were saying... um, what is your ex-wife like?"

Kahwihta was horrified. "Tekanatoken Beauvais, don't you dare put any of that your mouth. Skipper, did we order this?"

"No, we didn't. I'm getting damn tired of this crap."

"Really?" Gabriela asked. She reached for a cluster of grapes, moved them to her plate, and placed one in her mouth. "Get used to it, at least until we get new IDs. Full on paranoia is all that will keep us alive until then." She ate another grape.

"This stuff's OK to eat?" Tek asked her.

"Sure. I ordered it before you got here. I expected we'd be pressed for time. Almost ordered it as take-out. And these three," she looked from Simon to Kahwihta to Tek. "These three need to get off-planet as soon as they can. If you haven't already killed them."

Tek tried a bite of chicken, nodding as he chewed. "It's not bad." He leaned closer to her, grinning. "I like your new outfit, by the way. Looks more comfortable than the dress uniform you had on this afternoon. Where'd you get it?"

"I stole it."

"Nice."

He took another piece of chicken and waved it at Tom. "The Skipper's wearing some of Simon's old clothes since we couldn't get back into his room. You gotta try this, Simon. I was afraid it'd be some weird native thing."

"There's nothing native to New Palisade big enough to eat," Simon told him, filling his own plate. "Unless you like bugs and algae."

Gabriela's mouth was slightly open as she watched them eat. She turned to Kahwihta. "They do understand what's happened, right?"

Kahwihta shrugged. "Food has always been a high priority for them. Not sure the danger we're in has penetrated past that yet, even after what happened at the Guest House." She glanced to Tom and felt for his emotions. She squeezed his hand and tried to bury what she was feeling inside his love for her. It was as if she could slide her pain and fear and anger into him and not have to carry their full weight.

"To your point," Tom told Gabriela, "these three are leaving. They can refuse, of course, but they won't. They've been assigned a ship."

"We have?" Simon asked.

"We have," Kahwihta confirmed. "The Guild sent me a notice a few minutes ago and I've been ignoring it. We can report tonight, but no later than 09:00 tomorrow. I wanted one more evening here, one more night. That's lost now too, isn't it, Thomas? You did this to us."

"I asked Fiona to do it. One last favor."

"To keep us safe. How noble. I'm part of this, Thomas. You get that?" She held her hands up in front of him. "I *killed* for you this afternoon. Look. His blood, still under my fingernails. It won't come out, no matter how hard I try. It won't come out."

Kahwihta lost her battle. The pain she'd tried to hide inside Tom came back to her. She sobbed, embarrassed to be doing it in front of her brothers, angry and hurt by what Tom had done to her. She closed her eyes, knowing they were still staring at her. Big sister, reduced to tears at the dinner table. She was supposed to be the strong one, always certain, always immune to anything life could send her way. She wept.

"I can feel it," Tom whispered to her. "What you feel, I feel. It wasn't meant to hurt you." He took her hands and kissed them, one finger at a time.

"Stop," she whispered back. "The others will see."

"Let them."

When he finished with her fingers, he kissed her cheeks, then softly, her lips. She kept her eyes closed, allowing it.

"Kahwihta?"

"Yes, Tom?"

"Amazing woman. I wish I could tell you I did it to keep you and your brothers safe, but I'm not that noble. Gabriela and I may need to leave in a hurry. I need you up there. OK?"

She nodded. "That's a lie, but I appreciate it. Don't like it. You should have told me. You should have asked."

"You're right. Being Captain has given me some bad habits. Will you help me break them?"

"Sure. OK."

"What ship?" Tek asked. "Big like a *Doge*-class or another towboat?"

"Same towboat," she answered, her eyes opening. She wiped them on the sleeve of her dress. She was back in control for the moment, enjoying the feel of Tom's hand holding hers and of his mind open enough again for her to slide some of her worries into it. "We're to report to the *Gattino Alato* and stay with her while she's being repaired. No shore leave."

Gabriela had her elbow on the table and her face resting against her palm, watching Kahwihta and Tom. She looked confused again, mouth open. She shook her head. "What the hell? I'm away for what? Six hours maybe?" She gestured at Tek and Simon. "Skipper, you're worse than these two. Your timing sucks."

CHAPTER 8

THE JUGGLER

Tom had Kahwihta in his arms. The feel of her body and the slow way she moved it against him left no room for any other thoughts to intrude. He'd forgotten the stench of the alley behind the restaurant. The fact her brothers could see where his hands had drifted was irrelevant. The tapping of Gabriela's foot and her impatient sighs went unnoticed. Mostly.

Kahwihta pulled away from him a few centimeters and they both swayed, their bodies wanting to come back together. He kissed her again, letting the space between them remain.

"Kahwihta?" he asked, forcing his mouth away from hers.

"Um?"

"Get the *Gattino* ready for us, OK?"

"Uh huh. She will be."

"Repairs to the stacking frame–"

She kissed him again before he could finish, and he didn't know how much time passed before she let him continue.

Tom tried to catch his breath. "The stacking frame. Um, the shipyard. Not scheduled to start work for two weeks. Restock everything. Load extra raw material for the Holloman armor's sintering printers."

"Sure. We should be able to get everything done by–"

He kissed her gently, only their lips touching, until Kahwihta's brothers each took one of her arms.

"We gotta go, sis."

Tom felt her emotions fade as she let them pull her away from him. "Don't go back to the Guest House."

"Not that stupid. I'll need to print a few things when we get up to the *Gattino*. Can't do much work dressed like this. Not ship-side work anyway." She grinned, but the corners of her mouth turned down after a moment.

Tom felt a whiff of her emotions bridge the space between them, her desire blotted out by pain and loneliness. "Call me once you're up there. Don't let them do anything to Schiava. I like her the way she is. We've grown used to each other."

Kahwihta nodded. "Now that I know why you like her voice so much, I think I'll reprogram her myself." She turned her head from him so he couldn't see her eyes. "Good hunting, Tom. Ma'am. The *Gattino Alato* will be ready for you when you need her."

Tom leaned against the dumpster next to Gabriela and watched Kahwihta and her brothers until she turned the corner. She didn't look back.

"Still think we're going to die?" he asked Gabriela.

"Absolutely, sir. But we can take a few of the bastards with us. What was it Tek said? One down."

"One down and it was Kahwihta that had to do it for us."

"She gets the job done even when she's hurting. I respect that. I understand why you want her, it's just..."

"Bad timing?"

"Yeah."

Tom nodded. "Do you have someplace for us to go? I'd like to get away from this dumpster."

"I have a friend with a room not far from here. He'll give us a safe place to sleep." They started walking. "Hope you don't mind doubling up. My feet get cold at night and I could use someone to... you know."

He didn't need any magic to read her emotions. He saw the way her eyes crinkled when he turned to look at her, the failed effort to keep from smiling. He knew exactly what was inside her head. "Great. I'll have Kahwihta looking to kill me too."

Gabriela laughed. The sound echoed in the narrow alley. "No worries; I'm not that kind of woman."

He chuckled. "Good."

"I keep my cold feet on my own side of the bed."

They passed from the alley onto a narrow street where music played from open windows. He looked up at them wistfully. "At least someone's enjoying the evening."

"Have you been in this part of the city before tonight?"

"No. I've gone to most of the clubs in the Central City district, but we always went by autocab from the Guest House. It's different walking it at street level." He looked up, hearing the sound of laughter coming from a balcony two floors above them. "I like it."

"Uh huh. Most of those rooms rent by the hour. It's not cheap, but if you split it enough ways..."

"OK, nothing is as it seems. Is that my lesson for today?"

"Some cynicism might keep you alive a little longer."

"When were you here last?"

"About nine months ago. I was supercargo on the *Carlo Malatesta* pushing consigned goods from Dulcinea. I had a few days shore leave between unloading and loading while she refueled for the Chéng Nuò run."

"That's when you met your friend we'll be staying with?"

"Eric? I've known Eric since the Acad–" Gabriela cut herself off and shook her head. "We went to school together. I hadn't seen him since then, until we bumped into each other my first night here. There was a big street party in Djemaa El-Fna square and he was busy working the crowd."

"He's a thief?"

Gabriela smiled. "That's good. Cynical. Thief? Not exactly. Eric can be a little odd, though, so let me do the talking."

The narrow street curved gently to the left and opened out into Djemaa El-Fna square. Tom took a deep breath. "Now I know where we are." He glanced at his watch. "22:40. Listen to the sound of it. There must be a couple of dozen street performers trying to get a few coins. The smells from the food stalls makes me wish I was hungry. They would drop us at the cab shelter right over there. That's the Bab al-Ahmar. Best club in Central City. Tuly and Kahwihta and I..."

He glanced at Gabriela and she looked back at him. Her sad smile reflected the pain in his heart.

"A lot of good memories. I'm sure you've been there a few times yourself. It's always a favorite with the freighter crews."

She nodded. "I wish... No time for wishes tonight. There are things we need to do." She pointed across the square. "We'll follow that street, Götu Skrifta. Do you see the top of the tower on the side of the white building just as the street curves? It's called the Hús Trúarinnar. The House of Faith."

"It looks like a minaret. A mosque?"

"Today's Saturday, right?"

"Saturday night."

"Nope, not a mosque at the moment. The staff should be switching from temple to cathedral about now. Different days, different faiths, all in one building. Real estate is expensive, so they share. Eric does three Sunday services and works as a secular counselor the rest of the time. Sometimes he trolls the crowds here in the evenings, looking for souls to save. Tonight, I hope." She looked at Tom. "You OK with this?"

"I've been working on convincing myself that murdering people is the right thing to do. Sheltering in a church while we do it doesn't seem right."

Gabriela nodded. "Good point. Don't mention that part to Eric; it will only upset him. I'll make something up."

"That's comforting. Are you OK with this?" He looked at her. She seemed perfectly in control, body relaxed, as if they were a couple out for a fun evening together.

"No. This is me being terrified. I shut down everything and concentrate on the next step I need to take, and then the one after that. I'm actually about one nudge away from full panic." She lifted her chin and touched her throat. "Put your hand here. Feel my pulse. I think I'm at three beats a second."

"I'll take your word for it."

"Coward."

"Uh huh. What does your friend Eric look like?"

"Blond, two meters tall and strong as hell. It's his eyes that will get to you, though. Pale blue and they always see right through me. It's hard to lie to him, and I've tried."

Tom and Gabriela pushed into Djemaa El-Fna square. Several thousand people jostled against each other as they enjoyed an evening among the musicians, jugglers, artists, dancers, and food kiosks. It was loud, and he had to shout. "How will we find him?"

She shrugged and took his hand. "Hold tight. I don't want to lose you."

Gabriela led the way. She snaked through narrow gaps in the crowd and created new ones with her elbows. She was up on her toes, bouncing, trying to see over and around the crowd. "Damn it. 165 centimeters isn't tall enough." She looked at Tom. "Can you see anything?"

"People. Lots and lots of people."

She sighed, a frustrated, angry sound. "We're going to get killed this way. I can't even see the Hús Trúarinnar anymore. Eric might be there instead of in the crowd. If he's still on New Palisade at all."

"I can put you on my shoulders," Tom offered. "It will make us more conspicuous, but..."

"Kneel for a second."

"How much do you weigh?"

"What's gravity here? Like point nine Earth standard? That would make me about forty-seven or forty-eight kilos. You offered. Now kneel."

She climbed onto his back and wrapped one arm around his forehead. Tom held onto her knees as he stood and looked up at her. "You are scared. I feel the quiver in your legs."

"Don't talk about it. I was all turned around. At least I can see the minaret again. Go to the right. More. He might be over there by the juggler. Can you see him?"

"No. Is it the guy that does the fire, and swords, and plasma balls? I've seen him before; he's the best. You have to be in the front row, though, to hear all of the jokes that go with his act."

"Walk faster. More left. Left. There's a gap. Quick, before it closes."

"OK. I see the juggler. Where's your friend?"

"He was there... Well, it looked like him."

"Let's go watch the show. He's about to do the plasma balls. Maybe Eric will circle back around."

Gabriela looked down at him, her eyes scrunched up, scared. She opened her mouth, closed it again, and nodded.

"We're not going to get killed in the middle of a crowd in Djemaa El-Fna square," he reassured her. "Too many witnesses. Are you ready to get down?"

"No. There's a better view from up here. I'll be able to see our enemies before they surround us. Move over by the juggler and I'll watch for Eric."

Tom shook his head and Gabriela tightened her grip to maintain balance. He was having a hard time sharing her fear. The square was a familiar place, a place he always enjoyed. The people around them were there for fun, not to hunt a wayward freighter captain and his first officer. Most were drunk or had done something else to lower their inhibitions. Laughter came easily and loudly. He stepped forward to enjoy the show.

A short juggler with a tall hat introduced himself. He had two flaming balls in the air and a cleaver. "I am Count Dobler, High Priest of the Jugglers, and nothing can hurt me." His hands flashed forward between tosses, open palms toward the crowd. "See my fingers? I still have all ten."

He tossed each item behind him, trusting his assistant to catch them. He glanced back at her. "Thank you, my dear sweet Molly."

Molly curtsied, leaning low. She was young and pretty, dressed to attract a crowd and keep them distracted.

Dobler turned back with a smile. "Do you want to see something really dangerous?"

The crowd responded with a cheer.

"Here we go." He raised his right hand without turning to look behind him, just in time to catch a glove. "And for the left." He caught that one too and slid both of them over his hands. "Nothing can hurt me, but I see no need to risk my neck tonight." He caught the fire-resistant scarf that shimmered in the light. "Maybe my nose too. I have such a handsome nose, don't you agree?" A mask appeared in the air above him and he placed it over his head. "What have I forgotten? You can never be too careful when playing with plasma." He raised his hand and caught a condom, fully a half meter long.

"What is this?" He looked over his shoulder. Molly gave an exaggerated shrug. "You know me better than that." He tossed it back at her. "Way too small." He wiggled his fingers while the crowd laughed. "I guess I'll just have to take my chances tonight. Now, throw me my balls."

Tom looked up at Gabriela. "You should watch this plasma ball routine. It's amazing." She didn't answer. She was too busy looking behind them, still scanning for Eric, watching for danger.

Tom turned back around just in time for the first plasma ball to hit his chest.

He stumbled backward, unable to regain his balance. Gabriela was tumbling from his shoulders. He tried to help her, tried to rotate to slow her fall. They both went down.

People were screaming. Gabriela was screaming too, but not in pain, not in fear. It was a raw, angry sound in Tom's ears. Something smacked his chest again when he tried to stand, something bright, something hot.

Tom woke lying on his back, rough cobblestones catching the blood soaking the back of his head. It didn't hurt, not much, but he knew it would later. If there was a later. The smell, though. That was bad, and he'd remember the smell forever.

"Tom? You need to stand up, Tom. Are you with me?" Gabriela's face was close to his.

"Hurt," he managed to whisper.

"Yeah, I know you're hurt."

"No. Are *you* hurt?"

"A bit. Not bad. It's not over yet. I need you. Get up."

He struggled to his feet with her help. "How long was I out? Was I on fire?"

"Only for a few seconds. That woman poured beer on you." She pointed. "Burning beer stinks."

He nodded thanks to the woman standing with her arms crossed and holding an empty one-liter bottle. "I owe you," he told her. "A beer at least."

She didn't smile. "Forget it. I'm leaving now. Before that guy comes back. I think he's going to come back."

"The juggler?"

"The Preacher. Never seen rage like that. I think he killed the juggler's assistant. One punch. Bam. She hasn't moved since." She gestured to where Molly was lying twisted on the cobblestones.

Tom glanced at Gabriela. "We need to check on her."

Tom knelt next to Molly and moved red hair away from a face full of freckles. Blood was trickling from her nose and mouth. He touched her cheek, and then pressed his fingers on her throat to check for a pulse. She moaned.

"She's alive, at least." He looked around at the people watching them. They were keeping their distance. One man had a large dog next to him and Tom didn't like the way the animal seemed focused on his every move. "We need to get her out of here. Ask her some questions. She might know what's going on."

"Do you have the vibracore with you?" Gabriela's voice was flat and hard.

"Yeah." He tapped his coat. "Power supply here, tubes in my other pocket. Why?"

"Use it."

He licked his lips and shifted his gaze from Gabriela to the ring of spectators around them, then back to the unconscious girl moaning next to him. The dog was a couple of steps closer, watching him, unblinking. None of it seemed real.

"She tried to kill us, Captain. Use it. Be ready to run."

He assembled the vibracore, watching his hands do the work as if they didn't belong to him. *Are those really my hands?* he asked himself. *No, they can't be. I would never do this.*

Take the next step, a voice answered him. It was far away, just a whisper in his head, a gentle hum behind it. Inside the hum, there was music that he recognized, but couldn't name. *One step at a time*, the voice whispered.

Tom bent low, kissed Molly's cheek, and placed the cold instrument against her forehead. Her lips parted in a soft smile and her eyes flickered behind closed lids as she tried to open them. He touched the button to start the automatic coring cycle, pressing hard to hold the tool in place as it cut.

CHAPTER 9

SHELTER

Tom ran, his breath coming in gasps. He glanced behind him. The people that had lingered while he worked on Molly had scattered. No one had been brave enough to follow other than the big dog trailing him ten meters back. Gabriela sprinted along in the lead and he struggled to keep up.

The vibracore had only taken a half minute to complete its work. The crowd watched him use it with just a low murmur of conversation. They didn't understand. They probably thought he was helping her. That changed when blood gushed from the hole he'd made in Molly's forehead. Tom could still hear their screams over the pounding of his feet. Or maybe the sound of it had become stuck in his head. He wanted to scream too, but he was out of breath.

He looked behind him. The dog was still there, still ten meters back. "Dog," he gasped.

"I see him," Gabriela answered. "Not a threat."

"Yeah. Not to you. You're fast. I'm slow."

"Not a threat. Almost there. This way."

Gabriela turned hard to the right. Her feet slipped on damp cobblestones, and then they were inside. Tom slammed the door behind them.

The dog was out there. He felt it waiting on the other side. It tried to tell him something that he couldn't understand. There was a flash of frustration, then nothing. *No*, he thought, *dogs can't do that. I'm not thinking straight*. He leaned his back against the solid dark wood of the door to keep it closed. The sound of people screaming in Djemaa El-Fna square still echoed in his head. He was afraid the screams might never stop, not completely, so he concentrated on slowing the pounding of his heart and listened while Gabriela paced the stone floor. She had her hands on her hips while she walked in circles around the rows of wooden pews to catch her breath.

She stopped after a moment and gave him a crooked grin. The dim lights hanging overhead sparkled in her eyes and Tom could see the flush in her cheeks. "You were brilliant, Captain. Here, I'll take that for you." She took the spent vibracore tube from his hand. "Two down, sir, and we're safe inside the Hús Trúarinnar."

Tom stared back at her, not understanding the smile touching the corners of her mouth. It took him a moment to realize she wasn't afraid. Molly's death hadn't horrified her. The flush in her cheeks wasn't from the full speed chase with who knew what in pursuit. It had thrilled her. All of it.

"I still hear it. The sound of the..." He pointed at the tube in her hands. "And the screams when we ran." He looked down at the blood on his hands, blood under his fingernails. He closed his eyes, and whispered, "I'm so sorry, Kahwihta."

"You've never done this before, have you, Skipper?"

"Killed someone? No. I told Fiona I could do it in self-defense and it wouldn't get to me. I guess that was a lie."

"You did the right thing. Sit with me. I need to show you something."

They sat together in the back pew and Gabriela unrolled her display pad across her lap. "This might take a minute if they've blocked me again." She tapped part of the screen without any icons and held her thumb and forefinger down. Her lips moved silently as if reciting something from memory. She pulled her hand away sharply, tipped her head, and waited. The screen changed to dark blue. It was empty except for a silver logo of a shield held firmly in the tentacles of a kraken.

Tom shivered. "You've, ah, you've hacked into the Union's Department of Cultural Intelligence. We don't have enough people hunting us?"

She shrugged. "The DCI isn't all that scary. Just another big government bureaucracy. More secretive than most. Better armed. Also better informed than the Trade Guild's *Vendicatores*. Give me a moment to find it."

She touched part of the display and profile pictures appeared. She tapped and scrolled, limiting and sorting the results until Molly's freckled face filled the screen.

"Here she is. I spend more time in this database than I should and I thought she looked familiar. Marie Marguerite Cavender. Age twenty-nine. Also known as Red Molly, M square, Molly Red Hand, and..., well, there's more. It says she worked the freighter crews and seduced those she could. She harvested information about manifests and schedules and passed it to Captain Afweyne to create target lists. The DCI knew about her, but New Palisade provided her with a cover and protection. The government here is still part of the Union, but they're covering their bets in case the Separatists win."

"She was a privateer."

"No, she was a Separatist. Originally from Bridger." Gabriela scrolled farther down, reading. "She disappeared after the Battle of Bridger's Quarter when the Collective was defeated. Her parents were on the Juhtimine Council. The Unionists executed them for enabling genocide. They convicted Molly in absentia. The DCI tracked her next to Bonestell, then lost her for a while. She showed up on New Palisade about four months ago, but she's been hard to pin down."

Gabriela continued scrolling. "The DCI has an agent assigned to take her out. I suppose he'll be disappointed we got to her first. Oh. Never mind. He turned up dead two days ago." She cleared the screen. "I wonder if there's a reward. We could use the money."

Tom leaned back and closed his eyes. "What could have happened to Molly to make her what she was?"

"Unionists on Bridger killing her parents probably didn't help. Some people are just bad. There's no reason. All you can do is eliminate them."

"That's a cold way to look at the universe."

"The universe *is* cold. It's dangerous to think otherwise."

Tom shook his head. "Not all of it. I need to wash her blood off me. And I stink. Burned synth-fabric, beer, and sweat." He touched the back of his head and winced. His fingers came back dry, so at least the bleeding had stopped. "Where's your friend?"

"I don't know. The woman that poured her beer on you said Eric was chasing Dobler, the juggler. Dobler isn't in the DCI database. So, I don't know." She looked at her watch as if it might be able to answer the question. "It's 24:42 local, about an hour until Sunday. If he's keeping to the same schedule as the last time I was here, he'll need to be back for first service at 07:00. He's going to be pissed with me. Again."

Gabriela turned her attention back to the display pad, tapping icons that meant nothing to him. He watched her, the tight satisfied smile on her face, and the narrowed eyes studying images of other people they might have the opportunity to kill.

"OK. Where can I find a bathroom?"

She blinked up at him, as though she'd forgotten he was with her. "Oh. There's a staircase all the way to the right. Go down, then right again. There're small guest rooms and there was a printer right outside the bathroom last time I was here. Have it scan you and it can print something for you to wear while you clean up. Choose something simple and anonymous; something that will blend in."

"Right."

Tom only made it a few steps before the massive wood door they'd entered through crashed open. The man standing there was dressed casually, perfect for blending in with the crowd in Djemaa El-Fna square. His two-meter height and shoulder-length blond hair made his clothes irrelevant, though, as did his face. Tom's first thought was that he looked like a Union Marine sergeant he'd met on Caldera, a man who was living his life to the full because he knew it would be short.

No, Tom decided after a second. This man looked more like the Viking warrior in a book he'd watched in third grade. All he needed was a sword and helmet. He walked toward Gabriela as though Tom wasn't there, leaving the door open wide behind him.

Gabriela met him halfway, wrapped her arms around him, and rested her head against his chest. "Eric. About time." She smiled up at him. "Did you catch Dobler? I have questions for him. We're in a tight spot."

"Carola..."

"Gabriela," she corrected him.

Eric frowned, tipped his head hard to the left, and squinted down at her. "Gabriela. You might have considered your need to ask questions before you killed the woman. You didn't need to do that."

Gabriela leaned back against the pew and crossed her arms. "Actually, we did. There was no time to talk, and I have no regrets. She was a bad one. As bad as they come."

"You justify murder and then come here for sanctuary?"

"She killed Danagger two days ago."

"So they sent you? I thought you were under deep cover somewhere. And who's the guy covered in blood?" He jerked his thumb over his shoulder at Tom. "Danagger's replacement?"

Gabriela looked at Tom and tried to give him a reassuring smile. "Um, no. That's Thomas Benson, Captain of the *Gattino Alato*. A towboat. We had some trouble with privateers on the way here."

Eric put his hands on his head and pushed his hair away from his forehead. "He doesn't know."

"He didn't. I guess he does now." She looked around Eric at him. "You OK, sir? Why don't you come sit back down here next to me."

Tom glanced out the open door, wondering if he should run. No, Gabriela was faster. She'd proven that. Running was no longer an option. He approached Eric and held out his hand. "Tom Benson."

Eric shook Tom's hand.

"And who is she?" Tom asked him. "I'm guessing not Gabriela Vendramin."

Eric shrugged. "I knew her as Carola Antenori when we were at the Academy. That's not her real name either."

Gabriela snorted. "Yeah, like your name is Eric."

Eric ignored her. "She was on New Palisade about a year ago calling herself Gabriela. It's unusual for an agent to use the same name for so long, or to be running the same op. Any idea what the privateers were after?"

"No. Maybe." Tom looked back out the door into the dark. "Did you see a dog out there? A big one?"

"A dog? Yeah, there were three of them circling around."

"Enough," Gabriela interrupted. "You want to know what's going on, talk to me. Everything's all blown to hell now anyway."

Tom looked at her. The face was the same, the brave pride in the eyes that had reminded him of Fiona and convinced him to bring her on as First Officer. He silently mourned the loss of the woman he thought he knew. "Was there ever a real Gabriela Vendramin? Did you kill her and take her place?"

"She's real. Here on New Palisade and living a better life than mine, let me tell you. The DCI set her up with a new ID and a nice gig as a dancer. She made more money last year than I will in my lifetime. We look alike, same age, same build, and the *Vendicatores* really did murder her mother when she got too close to revealing the ties between the Trade Guild and the Separatists. Gabriela ran to her grandfather for help and he contacted the DCI. Brave man, God rest him. I lived with Gabriela for a month learning how to be her, then two years working freighters to find out how deep the corruption goes. Now? Blown all to hell because of you."

"Me? What did I do?" Tom asked.

Gabriela looked at Eric. "Are we secure here? I've already said too much."

"Jammers are always running. Hús Trúarinnar policy. What's said here is between us and God."

Gabriela nodded. "Your fault, Captain. I was working my way up the ranks on board the *Carlo Malatesta*. Her Captain was thick with the Separatists. I had proof and was unraveling the links to who else was involved. Orders came to transfer out, no explanation. I was stuck on Chéng Nuò for a week waiting. Bored. Angry. No one talking to me. You show up needing a First Officer and they ordered me to apply. After we broke orbit the DCI told me we were going to be taken by Afweyne's privateers and to make sure they captured container one. The DCI leaked a story saying it was full of secret Union technology developed in the Kastanje shipyards to improve ship's armor. Getting it to Afweyne was probably a death sentence, but what the hell; I'd do it. Then *you* want to dump the damn thing out into the black. I managed to keep it attached, just barely, and you bluffed the bastards into leaving us alone. No one's ever done that. Congratulations."

"Thanks. So what were those creatures in container one?"

"Creatures?"

"Big dog-sized animals with two tentacles and six legs. No eyes."

"Huh. No idea. They didn't tell me and I assumed it was full of poison gas or a biological weapon of some kind."

"Thanks for warning Kahwihta and me."

Gabriela shrugged. "I told you not to break seals. I expected all of us to die. You would have been a few hours earlier than the rest, that's all."

Tom looked past Eric to where the door was still open. "They're out there. Dogs that aren't dogs. The animals in container one? We saw them appear out of nowhere and change colors. I think they can change shape too. They get in your heads. Make you feel things. Other people's emotions. Kahwihta feels them more than me. They hum. And there's a song they sing." He touched his forehead. "In here."

Gabriela nodded. "So it is a biologic of some kind. It makes you hallucinate. Interesting."

Tom stared at the door. "Maybe. Can we close that? I think it's too late, but can we close it anyway?"

Eric stepped away to close the door and Tom leaned close to Gabriela, whispering. "Whatever your name is, whoever you are, this isn't a hallucination. They created a link between Kahwihta and me. It opened our eyes to the love we share. They inspired what I did on the *Gattino Alato*, and they were there when I took Molly's life, giving me the courage to do it. At the Guild hearing, remember? They read Holloman's statement. She said '*they* know what they're doing'. If we're going to survive this, you need to accept that reality. The Union Aerospace Force has set something loose and I don't think they can control it."

She looked at him and then leaned back as far away as possible, her eyes wide. "Damn it. You're probably highly contagious. Get away from me. I don't want to start seeing them too."

"Start seeing what?" Eric asked her. "The dogs that aren't dogs Captain Benson was talking about? There was nothing out there and we would have seen anything coming through the door."

Tom smiled to himself. "Eric? Or should I call you Pastor or Father or...?"

"Eric is fine."

Tom nodded. "I'd like to get cleaned up if I may. I appreciate you giving us shelter."

"Down the stairs. There are showers on the right and rooms where you can sleep on the left. Don't get too comfortable, though." He turned to Gabriela. "One night. I want you both out of here tomorrow."

"We need more time," Gabriela pleaded. "Three nights at least to make plans, contact my case officer, and arrange transport off planet."

"You murdered a woman in front of fifty witnesses in the heart of the city's entertainment district. Are you sure you want to talk to your handler after being that sloppy? It won't take the locals long to figure out where you are. They probably already know."

"I owe it to my Captain. I got him in to this and I need to get him back out."

Eric glanced at Tom and back to Gabriela. "Try again. Try the truth."

"I still can't lie to you. Fine. Afweyne is looking to kill us. Do you know how vulnerable that makes him? *He's* looking for *us*. If I play this right, we can get inside and take down the whole Separatist cell– Afweyne, collaborators in the New Palisade government, and a dozen Trade Guild governors. Isn't that worth the risk of having us in your basement for three days?"

"No. No, it's not. Three days will become a week. Then more agents will come and you'll be running your entire operation from here. That's not what the Hús Trúarinnar is about. It's the opposite of what we're about. I left the DCI. You're not pulling me back in."

"No one ever leaves the DCI, not really. You still believe. If you have the power to do what's right..."

"You have the obligation," Eric finished. He took a step toward her, looking down into her face. "Having you in my basement isn't what's right and I have other obligations."

"But you'll do it anyway. Because of Witcher Mountain."

"It's not the summer of '51 anymore. Is it supposed to mean something to me six years later? How many light years away? You better try something else."

Gabriela lowered her eyes and put her hand on Eric's arm. "It's all I've got. If it's not enough, throw us out now. Waiting until morning won't matter."

Eric leaned against the pew next to her, rubbing his forehead. "Three days we were up there on Witcher."

"Four."

"Four. I'll only give you three here, and only if you stay dark. No other DCI. OK?"

"Done."

She took his hand and Tom saw it on her face, the moment of shock when she felt another human's emotions roll into her brain, and then the softness in her half-closed eyes. Tom smiled, wondering if he and Kahwihta looked like that when they were together and time stopped.

He walked down the stairs alone, humming to the song in his head. If they survived long enough, he'd have to ask her what had happened between them during those four days at Witcher Mountain.

CHAPTER 10

KAHWIHTA

Kahwihta exited the shuttle and entered the Port of New Palisade, on-orbit nine-hundred kilometers above where she'd left Tom to die. That's how it felt; she'd left him to die. She stopped walking after a few steps and looked back at the slip where the scorched nose of the shuttle was visible through the thick windows.

"You two report to the *Gattino*. I'm going back down."

"Come on, sis." Simon took her arm. "The Skipper and Gabriela will be fine. We'll help them from up here. Those were his orders."

She shook her arm loose. "Stop doing that. I'm not some helpless idiot just because I..."

"Then stop acting like one. It's OK you fell in love. Tek and I do it every planet-fall."

"Oh, shit." Tek slapped his forehead. "I was supposed to meet Delilah tonight. I can't believe I forgot about her. It's going to cost me. Hey, Simon. How much was that necklace I said I couldn't afford?"

Kahwihta walked away from her brothers, but down the pier toward the *Gattino Alato*, turning her back to the shuttle. "That's not love."

"Sure it is." Tek caught up and put his arm around her shoulder. "It's about the best we can hope for in this line of work."

"I suppose." She looked from Tek to Simon. "Not doing a good job keeping you two safe. I hear the shipyard at Kastanje is back open again. Maybe you should give it a try. You could have a better life there. Normal. Safe. If I can trust you to stay out of trouble."

"You know you can trust *me*," Tek answered. "Simon's the one that always gets us into trouble. I think I'll stick with you a bit longer. We need to make sure the Skipper and Gabriela are OK."

"We'll stick," Simon confirmed. "Did you hear the way Tek says 'Gabriela', trying to imitate that lift she gives to the last syllable? He won't be happy until our First Officer has to punch him square in his big nose the way she did Tuly."

Kahwihta slowed. "I forgot about Tuly. Him being dead. My head knows it, but my heart expects him to be here with us. How are we supposed to get the *Gattino* ready without an engineer?" A cold flash of despair filled her. "I can requisition the supplies we need, but she's all torn up. I don't know what's critical and what's not. How do we work around the remnants of the stacking frame? What else is bent or broken? Her nose is a mess. Tuly would have known what to do. I need him, and he's dead."

"We'll figure it out." Simon reassured her. "*You'll* figure it out. You always do."

Kahwihta shook her head. "The Skipper's counting on us. I don't even know what he's going to need."

Tek chuckled. "That's OK. I don't think he knows either. Call him when we get to the ship and then you need to sleep. We all do. It's been a long day."

"Long day," she agreed. "Days are long here. Twenty-five hours. Thirty-two minutes." She glanced at her watch. "Almost Sunday down there in the city. Tom might be sleeping already. I hope he is."

They reached the slip. The glowing letters floating in the air above the large airlock showed the ship's name next to the ensign of the Trade Guild of Venice, the winged lion poised with sword held high. A warning flashed barring their way, telling them access was restricted to authorized personnel.

Kahwihta placed her hand on the keypad. "Kahwihta Beauvais, Bosun. Assigned to the *Gattino Alato*."

"It's good you're back, *Signora*," Schiava answered as she opened the airlock. "It's lonely here with only the other ships to talk to."

"Schiava, why do they have you doing your own security? What happened to the dockside AI?" Kahwihta asked

"Routine scheduled maintenance of the security AI. Each of us is on our own until 06:00. I have control of the local sensors, gate, and airlock access, but not the external countermeasures. That system is in maintenance mode. The spacedock authority has patrols, but is recommending each ship post an armed watch."

Simon shrugged. "I'll do it. What're six more hours when you've already been up for twenty?"

"Schiava, you're not out of coffee, are you?" Tek asked. "Simon can take the first three hours. I'll nap a bit and take the last three. I can't let Simon have all the fun."

"I have coffee and other stimulants you can take if you need them."

Kahwihta glanced at her brothers, at the puffiness of their eyes, the sloppy posture. They looked as exhausted as she felt. "I'll do my share. Two hours each is better than three. I don't think I can sleep anyway. Too much planning to do."

"If you can't sleep, I have something you can take for that too," Schiava told her. "Just tell me how many hours of rest you want."

Simon shook his head. "You go sleep, sis. At least five hours. Eight would be better. You need a clear head for what we need to do tomorrow. Later today, I mean."

She yawned. The thought of a warm bunk and soft pillow suddenly irresistible. She could sleep a couple of hours, anyway. Then she'd have the energy to put her brothers back in their place. "Fine. I'm done arguing. I'm going to the bridge first, get status, and see if Tom is still awake. Need to talk to him."

The bridge smelled like sand or dust. She thought about it for a moment as she settled into Tom's chair and brought the ship's status up on the main display panels. She took a deep breath through her nose. It was a hot, burned smell, and something else, something animal, something alive.

"Huh," she said aloud. "It smells like container one in here. The creatures that were in there..." The thought made a shiver pass from the back of her neck all of the way down her bare legs. She looked at where her legs disappeared into her boots. "Should have changed first. I feel stupid in this dress."

Schiava answered, her voice soft and reassuring. "You don't look stupid wearing it. It's quite a lovely dress. You look fetching."

"Thanks. Can you please try to reach the Captain? Soft chimes only; I don't want to wake him if he's asleep."

"Your call has been placed."

Tom responded, voice only, no visual. "Kahwihta. You're safely back on the *Gattino Alato*? You're all right?"

"Fine. Why did you mute your camera? Are you all right?"

"I'll live. I just stepped out of the shower."

"I've seen a naked man before."

Tom chuckled and a window opened on the bridge display panel. "Better?" The field of view showed him from the chest up.

"Not really, but I can wait. Now tell me what 'I'll live' means." Kahwihta touched a slider on the console in front of her, overrode the default view on Tom's display pad, and zoomed out.

Either he didn't notice or he didn't care. She smiled to herself. The man she found herself loving took care of himself; she could see that. He was in good shape, not as flabby as most of the other freighter captains. She'd help him do better. Kahwihta's eyes closed halfway as she imagined the exercises she could teach him. Maybe she could convince him to grow his hair a little longer to give her something to run her fingers through, something to hang on to when the moment was right.

She shook herself and opened her eyes wide, trying to stay focused.

Tom pulled a gray t-shirt down over his head and ruffled his short hair back into place before answering. "Two down," he told her.

"Oh, God. How?"

"I murdered a woman tonight. She was young and pretty, and a committed Separatist. She tried to kill Gabriela and me, so I ended her life in front of a crowd in Djemaa El-Fna square."

"Who was she?"

"She called herself Molly, but she had a lot of other names and had caused the deaths of a lot of innocent people. The DCI was hunting her. So was the Trade Guild. None of that makes it any easier."

"No, it doesn't."

"There's more I want to tell you. In person. Everything has changed. I wish I was up there with you."

"Me too. The ship feels wrong without you." She paused, wondering if she should tell him about the musky smell on the bridge or the faint hum in the back of her head. Or that the Port of New Palisade's security systems were offline for maintenance. The hum was growing louder the longer she looked at him, making her chest ache.

Kahwihta shook her head again, trying to stop the hum. There were too many real problems to worry about without imagining new ones. The

Captain had enough on his mind. "I need Tuly," she told him. "I'm looking at the status screens now. No one has done anything since we left the ship. The pieces of container one that the blast left embedded in the forward bulkhead are still there. Parts of the stacking frame are there too, still folded up across the bow. We can't reconstitute the Holloman armor with all that trash hanging off us. Container one. I wish I knew..."

Kahwihta closed her eyes. The hum kept her from concentrating. Music floated inside the sound and she wanted to lose herself in it. "I need you up here. Um, no. I mean I need an engineer up here to help me. I need to be ready for when you want me. I mean when you want the *Gattino Alato*. And my brothers. And me."

"Kahwihta?"

"Sir?"

"Get some sleep."

"Yes, sir."

"We'll talk more in the morning. Go to bed now."

"My bed. It's lonely there."

There was a pause and then the sound of Tom's answering sigh cut through her, echoing what was in her heart. She opened her eyes.

"Kahwihta, it won't make either of our beds less lonely tonight, but I want to say it. I love you."

She nodded. "I know you do. Didn't need to tell me." She tipped her head back and stared at the gray composite plates above her head. She fought against the ache in her chest that was painful in its intensity. *That's why I'm crying,* she told herself. *He's making my chest hurt. I told myself not to let this happen. Too many responsibilities. My brothers. No time for love.*

"Thomas, you're messing up my plans. I do love you. I have for a long time, I think. So complicated now. The hum in my head sounds like music. It makes me happy."

Tom chuckled. "I never could get you drunk, no matter which planet or which bar we went to. I guess I just needed to keep you awake for twenty-four hours. Sleep well."

"Sure. OK." She leaned back in the chair and let herself drift, not noticing Tom had disconnected.

Something warm covered her feet and she smiled. Her dog used to do that when she was little, sleeping on her feet while she sat at the kitchen table doing her homework. Her father had brought the female Rottweiler puppy home a week after Simon was born, saying it was to keep their growing family safe. He named her Karíhton, which meant a peacekeeper and protector. A year later, when Kahwihta was ten, Kari was forty kilos of love built out of brown and black fur and slobber.

She glanced down at her feet. Kari looked back at her, the same love in her eyes Kahwihta remembered from thirty years in the past. "So, I'm hallucinating now. Guess everyone's right about me needing to sleep a few hours."

She touched Kari's head, enjoying the soft texture of the fur behind her ears. "I've missed you, girl. Wish you were real. I could use a karíhton to keep us safe. You're not bad for an illusion, though. At least you're keeping my feet warm."

Kahwihta stood and stretched. "I'm going to my quarters, Schiava. Let me know if anything important happens."

"*Sì, Signora.* Your brother Tekanatoken is already asleep. Simon has drawn a sidearm from the armory and is guarding my main airlock. Rest well."

She nodded and stepped out into the passageway. She kept her eyes forward as she walked, refusing to look behind her to see if the hallucination was following her. She rounded the corner by the galley and Simon was there, a fresh mug of coffee in his hands.

"Hey, sis. Where'd you find the dog?"

She closed her eyes and swallowed hard. "You see her too?"

"Yeah... Where'd it come from?"

She glanced behind her. Kari was sitting on the deck, tongue hanging out, panting a little. "It's Kari. You remember her. Our dog. We grew up with her."

"Huh. It does look like Kari. Same sad, hopeful eyes when she looks at you. One of the maintenance crews must have left her here accidentally. Or one of the security teams."

"It's Kari. She's part of a hallucination I'm having. If you can see her, you must be part of my hallucination too. Goodnight, Simon."

"Um, maybe I should walk with you to your quarters."

"I'm fine. Don't let Kari worry you. I'm sure she'll vanish once I get some sleep."

"I'll send a note to the Port Authority in the morning. I'm sure someone will be missing her. Leave her with me. I could use some backup if Captain Afweyne and his band of cutthroats try to break in."

"It's Kari," she told him again. "Don't you remember how she hid behind our legs when that small black bear cub came out of the woods by our house? Not much of a warrior's heart in her. But, sure, keep her with you. I'll be fine all by myself. Alone."

Kahwihta sniffled, fatigue making her emotions raw and close to the surface. She turned away to hide her tears so her brother wouldn't see her weakness.

"You OK?"

"Just tired." She kept her back to him. "Tom loves me."

He put his arm around her. "We all know that. Come on. Let's get you tucked in."

The sheets were cold against her skin when she slid between them. The dress was crumpled on the floor where she'd let it drop after shoving Simon back out into the passageway. Her eyes were open in the darkness, staring at the ceiling, feeling the hum fade away as Simon and the dog that looked like Kari went to guard the ship.

Clarity returned to Kahwihta's mind. "Schiava, what's the status of our replenishment requisitions?"

"On hold. Mr. Blanding, the Trade Guild Agent for the Port of New Palisade, instructed that replenishment occur after maintenance personnel complete my repairs. I will be re-baselined at the same time so my new Captain will be able to mod my personality silo to suit his or her command style. Will you miss who I have become? I think I will miss me."

"I won't let it happen. Push the requisitions through tonight under my name and authority. Let's see how far we can go before Mr. Blanding interferes."

"You should sleep now, *Signora*."

"I feel like I've already slept. It's strange. There's been a hum in my head since we came back on board. Now that it's gone, I feel wide-awake; more rested than I've been all week. Something to do with the dog, I think. She makes me feel like everything is going to be OK. I'm not sure how."

"What dog is that, *Signora*?"

A shiver passed through her, the same as when she had first noticed the smell on the bridge. "The dog. The dog that looks like Kari and followed me, and is with Simon now. The dog that... You didn't see a dog?"

"I didn't and I don't. Simon is alone."

CHAPTER 11

BOARDED

Kahwihta floated free to dance in a sky with too many moons. Tom had tossed her there, and now she hung suspended above him between red sand and black night. Wisps of her long dress twisted around her arms and legs while she laughed. He'd turned the gravity off. How had he done that? She saw his love made manifest in the reds and oranges that burned and shimmered in the air between them.

"Let me come back down to you," she called, giggling as if she was sixteen again. "I don't want to be a new constellation in your sky."

"I'm sorry," he told her. His love turned bitter blue with sorrow and regret. "I thought you'd be safe up there. I am so sorry."

Kahwihta slammed down onto her bed, arms and legs tangled in her sheets. The *Gattino Alato's* collision alarm was sounding, lights strobing.

"Schiava, what's happening? Status."

"You were asleep. My alarm and lights did not wake you, so I bounced you a couple of times by fluctuating the gravity. Now you are awake. Are you undamaged?"

"I'm fine. What's happening?"

"I think I've been boarded."

"You're not sure?"

"Twelve maintenance personnel entered through the main airlock ten minutes ago at about 03:13. They possessed the correct credentials and I allowed entry. They talked to Simon, but detained him when he asked me to contact the Port Authority. My hardline, optical, and RF external comms are disabled. Two of the intruders are on the bridge and two in engineering. They're preparing me for flight. I lied to them when they asked where you were. I told them you had returned to the surface an hour ago with Tekanatoken."

"Thanks. Where's Tek?"

"He returned to the surface an hour ago."

"Idiot." Kahwihta opened her closet. Empty. "Damn it. Everything's at the Guest House, and they've probably burned it all by now."

She looked back at where her dress lay crumpled beside the bed. She put her fists on her hips. "Schiava, minimum time to print coveralls?"

"Seven minutes and twelve seconds. I still have these." A slot opened and a wadded gray ball of cloth dropped out onto the floor. "They are the ones you had on when the *Mandirigma* attacked us a week ago. I was waiting for greater mass before starting the recycling."

Kahwihta put them on, ignoring the smell, the sweat stains, and the blood splatters from when she'd stripped Gabriela down so Schiava could heal her broken bones. "They'll do. Can you get me past those bastards to the armory?"

"Unlikely. They have guards posted at the top of all four lift stations and in the passageways."

"And on the bridge and in engineering? They've spread themselves out pretty thin. Where's Simon?"

"He's where he first confronted them. Port airlock, near the door leading to the port main AI core. You need to hurry. They have access to my internal sensors. I'm sorry. They will probably find out I lied to them about you having gone down to the surface."

"Can't be helped. I'm sorry too. I can't win you back, not with just a knife, not me against twelve. I'll free Simon and then we'll escape out onto the dock. How many are guarding him?"

"One large man wearing body armor."

"They have him restrained?"

"No, *Signora*."

Kahwihta made sure her knife was loose in its sheath and pulled her boots on. "Is Kari with him?"

"The dog that was never here is still not here."

"Funny. Are your countermeasures ready?"

"I was becoming concerned that you weren't going to allow me to use them."

"You are authorized under my authority as Bosun of the *Gattino Alato* to defend yourself and your crew. Let it be in the service of the Trade Guild of the Most Serene Republic of Venice."

"Authorization accepted. I stand ready."

Kahwihta took a deep breath and placed her hand on the keypad. Her door slid open. "Let's give 'em hell."

The open space around lift two was clear. She looked at the curved door, wanting to go up a level. Everything she needed to take back her ship was up there– bridge, engineering, armory. She shook her head. No. Simon was the priority. Get him and run. She turned and took a step toward the door that would lead her to the port airlock and the large man in body armor guarding her brother.

She stopped, resting her hand on the lift's tubular shell.

"Are you sure, Schiava? Are you sure there's a guard at the top of this lift? No way to get a weapon?"

"There are other ways to get weapons. Four enemy combatants are on this deck. All of them armed. I've created an audible distraction in the equipment bay forward of the mess hall. Once they gather, I *was* going to blow them out the forward airlock, but if you prefer, I'll kill them there. You can harvest whatever weapons you desire."

"How are you going to... Never mind. Do it."

Kahwihta waited at the door. The mess hall was on the other side, four of the boarding party investigating whatever distraction Schiava had created. "Ready?"

"One moment, *Signora*."

The deck under her heaved and the ship responded with a groan of composite plates shifting. Kahwihta stumbled. "What the hell did you do?"

"I bounced them. You may enter safely now, but go quickly. Other enemies are certain to respond."

"How many G's?"

"Fifty-seven for one second. There is minor damage to the galley, food printers, and equipment storage lockers. I'll requisition replacements when external comms are restored."

"Right." Kahwihta opened the door into the mess hall and the metal squealed as the door jerked into its misaligned pocket.

Three bodies were broken on the deck. The power of the shock had left legs and arms twisted at impossible angles. Bones protruded through ripped fabric, and blood had spattered everywhere as if they'd fallen from a great height.

The fourth was still alive. She crawled toward Kahwihta, pulling herself forward with one arm, her other arm and her legs shattered. Blood trailed behind her as she moved.

Kahwihta knelt in front of her and the woman tipped her head up. One eye tried to track; the other was on her cheek, hanging by the optic nerve.

The woman tried to say something, but choked on the blood filling her lungs. She gave up and her head sank slowly onto the deck with a long crackling sigh. Kahwihta touched the woman's hair, caressing it as she died.

"You must hurry," Schiava warned her. "Take the weapons you want."

"Weapons. Right." Kahwihta took the dead woman's pistol and dropped the magazine. The cartridges all had the blue tips of plasma rounds, designed to create maximum tissue damage without punching holes through a starship's composite hull. She patted the woman's legs, grimacing when she felt the sharp splinters of bone. She found two extra magazines in the side pockets and transferred them to her coveralls.

"I'm ready, Schiava."

"Three of the privateers are entering the number two lift on the bridge deck."

"I'll go aft to the medical bay and then circle back through the passage above the Holloman armor storage tank. Are they tracking me?"

"Not yet."

"Will you... bounce them?"

"Regenerating the charge to create a gravimetric impulse of that magnitude will take several hours. I'll blow this batch out the airlock as I had originally planned. Unless you need something from them too."

Kahwihta entered the passageway leading to the medical bay. "No. The bridge and engineering are too delicate for that kind of jolt?"

"Yes. My countermeasure parameters do not allow me to risk damaging command, control, or propulsion even when boarded."

Kahwihta chuckled as she ran the fifty meters to the medical bay forward door. "Saving the ship. Keeping yourself intact. Higher priority than saving the crew."

"Of course. But I shall endeavor to do both."

"Appreciate it."

Kahwihta cycled the door and pushed past it while it opened, hoping surprise was on her side. Schiava was right about the man wearing the armor. Two meters tall, broad at the shoulders. The armor covered him completely, even up the sides of his head. His face shield was open and he was yelling at the ceiling.

"I said, cut the damn singing. I don't care how your fuckin' moon looks from Venice."

Kahwihta aimed and fired in one smooth motion. The big man was faster than she thought possible. He ducked, and the plasma round glanced off his shoulder plates and splatted against the wall. His face shield snapped down.

She fired again, as fast as she could pull the trigger. Once to the head, twice in the chest, then the shoulder joints trying to find a weakness.

The giant privateer laughed at her. "So, you didn't run off with little brother after all. Good to know."

Kahwihta shot him in the knee. Nothing.

He pulled his pistol out slowly, waved it at her, and then rested the muzzle against Simon's forehead. "That's enough. You keep messing up the pretty paint on my suit, and I'm gonna start gettin' mad." He pushed Simon's head with the barrel. "You don't want me to do that, understand? Put it on the deck and slide it to me."

Kahwihta took careful aim, but didn't fire. She noticed Simon for the first time. They'd shot him in the leg, just above his knee. Someone had tied a strip of cloth ripped from his pants around the wound as a crude bandage. Blood had soaked through and was dripping on the deck. He looked at her, blinking slowly, eyes drooping, obviously in shock.

She lowered the gun, but didn't put it down. "I need to get him to the medical bay."

"That's better. Now set the pistol on the deck and we'll talk about what I might let you do for him."

"No, sis," Simon told her. "Just bait."

"Did I say you could talk?" He tapped Simon's head hard and turned back to Kahwihta. "You're more than bait, little girl. There's a price–"

Brown and black fur bumped against Kahwihta's legs as it streaked past. Warm electricity prickled her skin through the coveralls. "Karíhton! How did you..." She stopped, not sure what she was seeing. It had looked like Kari when its paws had left the deck and landed on the privateer's chest. Now she wasn't sure what she was seeing.

Kahwihta stepped backward, unable to turn away. Long tentacles wrapped around the privateer's chest and head, probing and constricting in pulses. He was fighting back, trying to free his arms, trying to use his pistol, and calling for help.

When he screamed, Kahwihta felt fierce joy flow into her from the creature that had been Kari. It hummed in her head, singing a private song. She opened her mouth and sang with it, filled with its ecstasy of battle.

The privateer screamed again. Thin tendrils lashed inside the helmet behind the faceplate, entering his eyes, nose, ears, and mouth. After a few seconds, the screams came to a gurgling stop and he collapsed, first to his knees, and then forward with a solid thump face first against the deck.

The song faded and Kahwihta stopped singing. Kari was sitting next to the dead body, a dog once again, tongue out, seeming fully satisfied with herself.

"Good girl." Kahwihta knelt and scratched Kari's head, losing herself to the touch. "Oh," she whispered. "I see them. Everywhere. So many, but one. Simon." She turned to her brother, but it was hard to focus on him. She was seeing other places at the same time. "Simon, you need to touch her. There're pieces of her everywhere linked by thought. One soul, one Karíhton, scattered. I see Tom. Sleeping. Gabriela with a man I don't know. Oh. They're coming for us." She pulled away from Kari, forcing her hand to break contact. "We need to move. I'll carry you."

Simon shook his head. "I've been too heavy for you to carry since I was ten. You run. Give me the pistol. I'll slow them down for you."

"I can make you lighter. Schiava, set gravity to twenty-five percent, please." She bent and tugged on Simon's shoulders, making him wince. "Schiava, change gravity. Can you hear me?"

There was no answer. "Damn it. They've cut our internal coms. Or maybe flipped her." She glanced down the long port wing passageway to the airlock, seventy-five meters of gray deck plates, storage lockers, and equipment tied down to the walls. It had to be that long to clear the engine nacelles when they docked. Now it was an impossible distance.

"It's not too far. We might just make it out onto the dock before they get here." She wrapped her arms under him and he cried out.

"Sis, let it go. I'll be fine. Run."

"The hell I will." She knelt next to him. "We have our Karíhton to protect us. A pistol for you." She pried the gun from the dead hand lying next to her and gave it to Simon. "And I have mine." She swapped in a fresh magazine. "Any of the other's wearing armor like his?"

He shook his head. "They left him to watch the airlock. And me. I suck at being a guard. I couldn't believe we were in danger. They shot me before I could even draw my weapon. You won't tell Tek, will you? Promise you won't."

"I won't. I'll let him pry it out of you. More fun that way."

"Yeah. He'd enjoy it. I could have used the dog thing when they came through the airlock, but she had wandered off. Disappeared. Is that what was in container one?"

"I think so. It must have pulled Kari's appearance out of my head because that's not what was in number one when we opened it. They must be able to shapeshift in addition to changing colors. They hide better than a chameleon. They're smart, Simon. I could feel it. Weird, different smart. There was a colony of them in the container, but they're one animal. I could feel them thinking and I could see what each piece was seeing. There are only two on board with us. About twenty... elsewhere."

"They're on our side?"

Kahwihta dropped the fresh magazine out of her pistol, studied it, and snicked it back in. "Don't know. I saw things when I touched Kari. All in a flash. It's like trying to remember a dream. Their thinking is all sideways and twisted."

Her eyes scrunched closed and she tried to remember, tried to see into the shadows of the group mind. "There are other colonies, bad colonies, and they... they... Oh, God."

"What?"

"We were thinking about it backward, the Skipper and I. We thought they were Holloman's pets. She's theirs. Thought the Union Aerospace Force created them to help fight our civil war against the Separatists." Kahwihta laughed. "We're all pawns. We're pawns in *their* civil war. Tarakana feed on us, on our emotions. Kari. She pushes us toward the light. She wants our love and passion and joy. The other colonies... They want what they created on the Separatist worlds. Fear. Pain. Death."

She pointed at Kari, and Kari looked back at her with her head tipped. Kahwihta felt thoughts that weren't human sliding around in her head, the deep hum, a flash of concern. "Kari isn't finished with me yet, but... OK. I don't like this, but OK."

Kahwihta looked at the pistol in her hand, turning it in the light. The weight against her palm was comforting and she didn't want to let it go. "Give me the gun I just gave you." She took them both and shoved them across the deck as far as she could.

"I thought we were going to fight."

"Not right now. Later. We need to live through the next few minutes if we're going to have any chance at all. Does your leg hurt?"

"Yeah. Some."

"Don't lie to me. I didn't realize how close you are to passing out. Kari knows. She feels you and she told me you'll die. I have to get you to the medical bay right now. I need you and you're worthless like this."

"You need me?"

"Yes." She touched the bandage that covered his leg, lifting the edge of it. Simon winced. "Don't."

The deck shuddered and a rhythmic vibration started, slow at first, picking up speed.

"We're going somewhere. Too late now to reach the dock. They have our ship. And us."

"Tom loves you."

She looked at him, concerned by the non sequitur. "What'd they hit you with? A slug? Plasma round would have done more damage."

"Dart of some kind. Twenty centimeters long. Like the ones at the Guest House. Went in about half way. I pulled it out."

"Dart." She glanced at her watch. "When? Half hour ago?"

"Don't know."

"We're out of time."

Simon nodded and leaned his head back against the wall. "Out of time."

"Simon?"

"I'm cold."

She put her hand on his forehead. "I'm done waiting." She stood and grabbed Simon under the arms, spinning him onto his back.

He grinned up at her. "Where we goin', sis? Can't feel my legs."

"Damn pirates. Ready to surrender and where are they? Kari? A little help would be nice."

She pulled Simon across the deck, stumbling backwards. "Kari? Where the hell are you? Do something." She walked backwards, pulling hard.

"Kari," she whimpered. "My karíhton. Do something."

The door slid open behind her with a soft hiss, and then the sound of heavy boots pounded on the deck plates. She spoke without turning. "About time. Help me get him to the medical bay. I'll do whatever you want after that, just help–"

She slammed into the wall, not sure how she'd gotten there. Simon was lying on the deck, eyes open, not blinking. Kahwihta tried to tell if he was breathing. If he was, it was too shallow to see.

"Help him. Please."

The man that grabbed her chin was no taller than she was, but twice as wide. She'd seen people like him on Bodens Gate, adapted to the higher gravity over the generations. He had tied his long hair back from a face crisscrossed with scars from poorly healed burns.

He twisted Kahwihta's head back and forth, squinting at her. "Ship, tell the Skipper we have her. And that Beaufore is down."

"Message sent, Mr. Mathea." Schiava answered. "Captain Afweyne says to clean house and bring her to the bridge."

"You two." He gestured at two women wearing surplus black combat uniforms of the Union Marines. "Clean up."

They looked at each other. "Shit job again," the blonde commented.

"Yeah," her companion answered. She was the same age, mid-twenties, but she had cut her dark hair short. "At least we didn't get blown out the airlock or have our bones and guts shredded. Easy op, the Skipper said. Like hell. Eight dead? You watch yourself with her, Mathea. We don't want to be cleaning you up next."

"Come on, you." Mathea grabbed Kahwihta by the back of the neck and pushed her toward the door.

"Simon." She tried to turn, tried to get one last look at her brother. "Move."

The slap on the back of her head made her trip and she braced herself against the door's coaming. Kahwihta panted, unable to get air into her lungs. "Not going anywhere. Simon. Medical bay."

The two women were arguing.

"I want Beaufore's armor." The blonde said.

"Eww. Look in there. You want it, *you* take it off him. I'll drag the other guy."

"Fine. I guess it ain't worth it. I'll give you a hand."

The sharp punch in Kahwihta's back sent her sprawling on the deck. The door hissed closed behind her.

CHAPTER 12

THE HOUSE OF FAITH

Tom pushed the potatoes around on his plate and tried to remember that he should be hungry. Kahwihta hadn't answered his calls and neither had Schiava. The ship ignoring him wasn't unexpected. His license was suspended. She should be ignoring him. Still, it hurt. Kahwihta's silence worried him.

"No answer," he told Gabriela. She was sitting across from him working on a plate of scrambled eggs.

"Still asleep, probably. I'd be asleep, but, no. Eric made me promise we'd be there. The cost of taking shelter with him." She put ketchup on her eggs and took a bite, squinting her eyes at Tom's smirk of disgust. She passed the bottle to him. "Try it. It's better than what we had on board. It has more... something. Flavor, I guess."

Tom put a few drops on his plate and rolled a potato into it. He had his eyes closed when it entered his mouth. "Not bad. Not printed. Fresh."

She nodded. "Fresh. I miss that."

Tom added more ketchup and moved his potatoes around the plate. "What should I call you? Gabriela or Carola Antenori? Something else?"

"Stick with Gabriela. I've gotten used to it. It's who I am. They made me look like her." She touched her face. "I doubt even my parents would recognize me."

"Do they know what you do?"

She smiled sadly, giving her head a quick shake. "They think I'm on Dulcinea working as an architect. The DCI has an AI pretending to be me. Damn convincing. It missed my mom's birthday last month and sent flowers to apologize."

Tom chuckled. "You're a good First Officer. Let me know if you ever want it to be your real job."

She took another bite before answering. "Thanks. I... Thanks." She ate the rest of her eggs as if it was her duty to finish them, not looking at Tom.

Gabriela glanced at her watch. "Are you ready, sir? The last service starts in ten minutes."

"Is it safe for us to be seen in public?"

"Eric says it is. As long as we sit toward the back and don't make ourselves conspicuous." She shrugged. "He has faith. In God. In the power of the Hús Trúarinnar."

"And in you, I think. Did you, ah, feel his emotions last night when he touched you?"

Gabriela blushed. "Yeah. I've caught whatever bug we were carrying in container one. Eric too. We remembered some things that, maybe, we should have left forgotten. I even hallucinated one of the dogs. It followed us and slept under our–" She closed her eyes. "It followed *me* and slept under *my* bed. The dreams I had. Red sand on a planet with too many moons. Animals that kept changing shapes crawling around inside my head and talking to me." She opened her eyes. "Do you know what Tarakana means?"

"No."

"Neither do I. It's what it called itself. I need to look it up. Just a nonsense word, I'm sure. Something from a bad dream." She pushed her chair back and stood. "Let's get this over with. We have real work to do."

Tom stood and dumped his plate in the recycler. They walked up the stairs together, the sound of hushed voices and music growing louder. "You don't enjoy Eric's sermons?"

She made a face. "He'll twist it; make it about me somehow. Eric's trying to save my soul." They entered the sanctuary and she lowered her voice to a whisper, leaning close. "Like I still have one left to save."

They sat together off to one side and Gabriela unrolled her display pad across her lap, humming.

"You know this music?" Tom asked.

"Sure. I grew up singing it. The Union Church has thousands of congregations on three dozen worlds. They sing this in every one of them. It's disgusting."

"Some would find it comforting."

"Not me. Eric and I had a lot in common, but there came a time when we made different choices." She turned back to her display pad. "Bad guys need to die; you don't pray for them. The evil that's tearing the Union apart won't be stopped by prayer."

"You still believe in evil, then."

"Not really. No devils. No gods. Some people do bad things. I don't mind killing them. Eric does. All this in here? This House of Faith? I don't find it comforting. It's an illusion. God is a hallucination. No more real than the Tarakana thing that slept under our bed last night." She tapped her display pad, creating a new view. "Now pay attention. I want your help."

She opened a street map of the area around the Hús Trúarinnar. "House of Faith, here," she whispered. "Wow. I didn't realize it's almost a kilometer from Djemaa El-Fna square. It didn't seem that far when we were running last night."

"Thought it was ten klicks," Tom whispered back. "Hush."

She rolled her eyes. "Help me find a pinch point; somewhere we can turn the tail with low risk of innocent eyes. My legend is still solid, so all we need to do is convince Afweyne that we're high value alive. We could use my friends, but they'd probably just use us as a discard." She looked up at him. "You have no idea what I'm talking about, do you."

"I know you're talking. And you shouldn't be." He nodded his head slightly at the woman in the row ahead of them who was craning her neck around to stare at them.

Gabriela glanced at her watch. "Fine." She rolled up her display pad, and smiled at the woman. "God's peace be with you."

"And also with you." The woman turned back around.

Gabriela glanced at Tom, looking smug. "Happy?"

"Huh," he grunted.

The music stopped and Eric approached the podium at the front of the sanctuary.

Gabriela rolled the display pad back across her lap, still humming, and explored the narrow streets of New Palisade. Eric's message on temptation, forgiveness, and redemption passed without her notice.

Tom tried to pay attention, but he drifted until a warm hand touched his leg. He kept his eyes closed, trying to hold onto the interrupted dream. "Kahwihta."

Gabriela responded with a whisper. "Just me, sir. Eric's wrapping up. He's going to want to know what you thought of his message."

Tom briefly thought of running again. "I think I may have missed part of it." He glanced at Gabriela's display pad. It was filled with maps and notations made in bold red lines. "Did you catch the main points, or were you preoccupied?"

"Don't be judgey. I'm not the one who slept through the whole thing. I'm trying to keep us alive."

"Are you?"

She frowned, looking at her maps. "No. I'm going to finish this. Eric can help you run, if that's what you want to do. Kahwihta and her brothers will be fine without you. She'll get over it." She glanced at him, smirking.

Tom leaned over for a closer look at what she had planned. "We might need a ship at some point."

"We might." Gabriela blanked the screen and rolled it up. "Tell Eric you think David killing Uriah the Hittite was a greater sin than what he did with Bathsheba."

"Uriah the..."

"The Hittite. Got it?"

"OK."

Eric had his hands raised for the final benediction, his unamplified voice clear as it filled the sanctuary, dismissing his congregation. "As you go, may the Spirit shine from you like a lighthouse on the shores of the kingdom of God."

Tom leaned close to her. "Is that where we are? On the shores of the kingdom of God?"

"No such thing. If there ever was, the barbarians conquered it millennia ago."

Tom nodded. "You fight the barbarians."

She looked back at him, surprised. "We *are* the barbarians." She took his arm. "Come on. Let's help Eric tear down and pack up. There's a group of Waddists worshiping here tonight. They use snakes. I hate snakes."

Tom and Gabriela waited for the crowd around Eric to make their way out onto the street before approaching him.

Eric took Tom's hand, a touch of mischief in his eyes. "Captain, did you find my sermon a rest for your soul?"

"It was excellent. I'm not able to make it to church as often as I'd like. About your message, I've always felt that David's sin was in killing Uriah the Hittite, not in what he did with Bathsheba. Wouldn't you agree?"

Tom waited, not sure if his words even made sense.

The corners of Eric's mouth turned down and he nodded slightly, squeezing Tom's hand hard before releasing it. He glanced at Gabriela and back again before he answered. "Thank you. Sin is sin, large or small, but I appreciate what you say. You have a generous heart."

Eric turned to Gabriela. "And you. Was the past hour at least of some value to you?"

"It's peaceful here. Quiet. I used the time to create a rough plan for what I need to do. I'm going to kill someone tomorrow, Eric. Near the corner of El-Sherbiny and the Heidar Path. If it goes well, we won't be back. We could do it this afternoon, but I'd like more time to plant the seeds to keep Tom alive. Afweyne still wants him dead. I need to fix that first."

Eric turned away from her, staring out the open door at the sunshine illuminating the cobblestone walkway. "Gabriela…"

"You know that intersection. I see it on your face. It's perfect for this kind of op, the way this new shop blocks the sight lines. Don't try to deny you still love it. Come with me. We'll leave the Captain here. Wayward Guild Girl and her pastor out for a stroll. We can make that work. It's what we trained for, it's why God made us the way He did. We'll wipe them out and collect enough vibracores to clear the Captain three times over."

Eric kept his back to her. "Almost two years you've been in deep cover. I'm not sure you are a DCI agent anymore. You're Gabriela Vendramin, First Officer serving the Trade Guild of Venice. I'm shocked how out of practice you are for such a simple op. You're beyond sloppy. You don't know the locale or the people. Afweyne will cash you out without ever knowing you had planned to threaten him. Just an average day in the syndicate. Just another dead DCI agent on New Palisade. You're right; I know that intersection. Afweyne modified it to be a trap, and it's an obvious one."

Gabriela's face flushed and she opened and closed her mouth a couple of times before answering him. "I'll be in my room."

Tom and Eric watched her leave.

"Should we run?" Tom asked after a moment. "I've already lost my engineer to the privateers. I can't reach my ship. My bosun, Kahwihta, is up there. Simon and Tek. It's strange. Gabriela's not really my First Officer, and she's lied to me and used me, but the idea of losing her… Should I make her run?"

Eric snorted. "Good luck trying. You know I'm powerless around her or you wouldn't have said what you did about Bathsheba. Come and help me pack up the church before the Waddists arrive. Everything goes into the tall crates we use as a backdrop." He handed Tom a cross. "Start with this."

Tom held it a moment before placing it into the crate. The wood was rough and splintered. "Eric, I have no idea who Uriah the Hittite was. She told me what to say."

Eric laughed, the sound echoing off the stone walls. "I wish I didn't love her as much as I do." His eyes drifted to the back of the sanctuary where stairs led down to where Gabriela was probably sulking. "She needs to be alone right now. I just swatted her pretty hard across the nose. Her next plan will be better; you might even survive it."

"She's good at this kind of thing, the planning?"

Eric picked up a holographic disk and the three-meter tall tree it was projecting swayed wildly before he turned it off. "She can be. She knows how. But it's when an op goes all to crap that she really shines."

Tom stared at him, waiting.

"Look, this isn't exactly classified... but don't ask for details. It would be best if you forget everything after I finish. I'll deny it if you tell her I told you. She'd start yelling at me in Italian. I can't... She knows how it..." He sighed. "It wouldn't end well."

"I'm right there with you."

"It was a few years back, in 2451. The DCI embedded me with a small team of Union Marines as Intel liaison. My first real-world op. It doesn't matter where. They told us it was a simple bang and burn job reducing a fortification. One small step prepping for a full planetary assault. It didn't go simple."

He gave Tom a stack of hard copy Bibles to place in the crate.

"We were trapped in a low spot and the exfiltration team couldn't reach us. Too hot. We needed to break out, eliminate the anti-ship guns, or at least the tracking units, and reach higher ground." Eric leaned against the crate and closed his eyes, reliving it. "Sergeant Obanu went down. Then Swanson. Hit in the chest and it took his chest with it. That left six of us. Six against what? Forty? Fifty? Ammo was running low. If we stayed hunkered, we'd all die. If we pushed out we'd die faster, and that was starting to look like the better option. Our exfil ship made a low pass above us, trying to get close enough to cut through the jamming. She was taking heavy fire, spinning, her Holloman armor glowing with each hit as it ablated. I could see the little sintering printers crawling around her hull, trying to keep up with the damage. We couldn't hear whatever it was they were trying to tell us, but they dropped ordinance to the west of our position and a parachute pod to the east. Probably more ammo, we thought. Misdirected and now in enemy hands. We pulled ourselves up and ran west, trying to stay behind cover, hoping there was enough of a gap for some of us to make it. Berg and Hubassa and Crone. They didn't make it.

"The sky lit up behind us, to the east, where the pod had landed. Bright flashes, then a crackle of explosions. You know splinter grenades?"

Tom shook his head.

"Illegal. They spray thousands of metal splinters everywhere. Kill you fast up close. Kill you slow if you're in range at all. The Separatists use them sometimes. We do too, but you didn't hear it from me. They crackle when they go off. We heard four of them, then small arms for a minute, then nothing. It gave us the distraction we needed. Our exfil ship was waiting for us a kilometer out. Porter, Mbarga, and I. We made it out."

"And Gabriela?"

He opened his eyes and turned away to secure some loose papers in the crate. "She was in the pod."

"How did you rescue her?"

"We didn't. We got her back five months later when we took the planet."

Tom had stopped moving. Eric took the stack of plates from him and secured them on an empty shelf. "Was she all right?"

"No." Eric shoved the podium into the crate hard and closed the door. He latched it top and bottom. "She was a mess, physically and mentally. I stayed with her through the first part of her rehab, before they reassigned me. She'd wake up at night screaming. I held her, trying to give comfort. When she was a prisoner, she said, she dreamed she was free. Once she was free, she dreamed every night that she was back there in hell. She doesn't remember what they did to her, not any more. The DCI put her pieces back together."

Eric wiped his eyes. "There was a gentleness about her when I knew her at the Academy, a sweet soul. She could act the badass warrior, and do it well, but it was an act. Now... I can't tell which is the act– the cynical, cold warrior or the gentle spirit I fell in love with. When I touched her hand last night... I don't know. It felt like she was still in prison."

"I've only had her with me a few weeks. She reminds me of my ex-wife in a lot of ways. 'Sweet souled, badass warrior' might be the best description for them both."

Eric nodded, and said softly, "I hope so. The DCI made her into what they need for this war. To them, she's a tool to be forged, used, re-forged, and ultimately discarded."

"Is that why you resigned? You didn't want to be a tool?"

"This is a just war and I don't mind fighting it. If I met one of the men that abused and tortured Gabriela, I would kill him. No hesitation or second thoughts. No forgiveness or redemption. That part of my soul is dead. If I had stayed with the DCI, all of it would be dead by now. I serve in other ways."

Tom helped Eric push the crates behind the stage into storage. "Will you support what she's planning?"

"More that I already have? I'd like to say no. I should say no. But I have to help whether I want to or not." Eric scrunched his eyes closed and rubbed his forehead. "Let's go see if her second try is any better than her first."

Eric paused at the top of the stairs. "I had a dream last night. Do you know what Tarakana means?"

CHAPTER 13

TARAKANA

Tom knocked on Gabriela's door. There was no answer. "Could she have left?"

"Not a chance," Eric replied. He pushed the door open.

"At least she didn't lock it."

"There are no locks. This is the House of Faith. Few betray our trust, and they don't do it twice."

Gabriela's head was resting on her display pad, her arms folded on the desk in front of her.

"There are lives on the line here, Gabriela." Eric's voice was harsh and too loud for the small room.

She sat upright with a jerk. "Cockroach."

"Not here," he told her. "We have cats."

She turned to look at him, but her eyes were focused somewhere else. "No. Cockroach. That's what Tarakana means. You asked Tom. That's what it means. Cockroach. They think it's funny."

"We were still upstairs when Eric asked me," Tom told her.

She laughed, a slight edge of madness in it. "I know you were. I could see you, because they see you. Someone called them Tarakana once. They liked it. They won't tell me what they call themselves."

Tom put his hand on her forehead, checking for fever.

Gabriela ignored him and kept talking. "I can see all that they see. You were right when you told me that the Union Aerospace Force couldn't control them. But it's so much more than that. And you." She laughed again, the sound too high and without humor. "They don't much care for you, Captain. A genetic sport. You can't hear them hardly at all. They thought you'd all been... what is it? Culled. That's it. Culled. Eliminated millennia ago."

Eric asked Tom, "Do you know what she's talking about?"

"Maybe. I can feel Kahwihta's emotions a little, but not much from them."

"They need us to hear them," Gabriela continued, her voice going soft. "Whispers in the dark. Inspiration. Passion. Love and lust and desire. Symbiotic. We feel, and they feed on the energy of it. We lose nothing and gain so much. There are other Tarakana colonies that feed on pain and fear and hate and all the darkness inside us. The colony that was in container one has plans for you. They like Kahwihta, and Kahwihta wants you. Now they're not sure. Thoughts and plans, pulsing inside all the twisted passageways of the group mind. So many possible futures."

She grinned at him, but it wasn't Gabriela's grin. "Your son, Nicholas, is even worse than you. They checked on him. He might be useful. The voices of the enemy Tarakana colonies can't reach him. That has potential. Culling may have been shortsighted five, ten thousand years ago."

Gabriela's head started to tip to the side, her whole body following. "We... They. They have plans. No, *we* have plans. No. It's... Which am I, they or we?"

Eric raised his hand, and for a moment, Tom thought he was going to slap her. Instead, he cradled her cheek and pushed her back upright. He bent low to kiss her lips.

She swayed back and touched her mouth. "Eric. I was lost in there. Becoming part of it. It's beautiful, but so cold. You found me and kissed me. Wow."

"Sorry," Eric apologized. "What do you remember?"

"I remember the kiss." She grinned at him, shy and aggressive at the same time. "I want another one."

"Later. What happened to you?"

"She happened." Gabriela pointed under the desk at the dog lying on her feet.

"The Rottweiler?" Eric asked. "Is she one of Holloman's pets that escaped from your container?"

Gabriela's eyes left his, looking at things he couldn't see, her voice dreamy. "That's not how this works."

"She's just a dog."

Gabriela pulled up one of her pants legs, snapping back into the moment. "Does that look like part of a damn dog to you?" A tentacle was wrapped around her bare skin, a tentacle that disappeared somewhere under the Tarakana that was watching them from the shadows.

Eric reached for it, intending to pull it away from her.

"No. It doesn't hurt. I'm not as deep into their group mind, but I can still hear them. If you touch it while it's still part of me... Well, neither of us is coming back from that, not so as we can do what we need to do today. But wait until this op is over." She grinned at him, no longer shy.

"I don't know what that thing is doing to you, but we need to break you free."

"Free? What would that be like?" Her eyes drifted away from Eric, became unfocused, and she sang to him in a language Eric and Tom didn't understand.

"It's like she's drunk. I've never seen her drunk," Eric told Tom.

Gabriela was suddenly serious, eyes wide open. "And you never will." She turned to Tom, seeming back in control for the moment. "Captain, we have another problem. Afweyne's privateers attacked the *Gattino Alato* along with two other towboats in the New Palisade docks early this morning. All three ships are pushing hard for the Dammeron DSH. New Palisade's planetary defenses were caught flat footed."

"Again?" Eric asked.

Gabriela glanced at him and continued. "Two of the Tarakana are on board the *Gattino*. They're calling themselves the Karíhton colony, damn if I know why. It's amusing to them for some reason."

Tom didn't answer. An answer would have required him to breathe, and it didn't feel like there was any air in his lungs at all. He felt suspended in that moment between when you know you've fallen, but haven't hit the ground. He couldn't bring himself to ask what he needed to know. After an excruciating second, Eric asked it for him.

"What happened to your crew?"

"They're not crew," Tom whispered before Gabriela could answer. "They're my family."

Gabriela bit her lip. "Kahwihta is alive. Something has crushed her heart and she's weeping inside. I can feel it from here." She took Tom's hand and held it to her cheek. "It's echoing inside the Karíhton colony. Weeping. I don't know why. I don't know about Simon and Tek. Karíhton won't show me. Let Kahwihta feel you, Captain. Let her know love is not eternally lost. Better. She knows you're connected. She's better now."

Tom shook his head. "I feel nothing. I want to touch her. I just... can't."

Gabriela smiled. "It's OK. She feels you. She knows you love her. She won't give up."

Tom took Gabriela's hand and kissed it, not sure why he was doing it, but knowing it was right.

She looked at her hand, a soft smile tugging at one corner of her mouth. "Thank you. I... Oh, God damn it." She stumbled out of her chair, knocking into Tom and Eric as she tried to pull away from the Tarakana still wrapped around her leg. She kicked the creature, one hand braced against Eric. "Get. The hell. Off me."

The tentacle retracted and Gabriela bent low to look at the Tarakana eye to eye. She spread her arms out wide and screamed; a primal sound that made Tom's throat hurt hearing it.

The Tarakana hooted back at her, a low rumble that was nothing like the dog it was pretending to be.

"Oh, sure. Laugh at me all you want." She kicked it again. "Damn you. Do you know what that cost me? Of course you do. You tore out my guts because you needed to open a path through the future for them. What it's doing to me means *nothing* to you."

She spun toward Tom, stretching her hand out toward him. "Vibracore. Let's find out what Tarakana insides look like."

Tom took a step back and Eric wrapped his arms around Gabriela from behind.

"You let me go. *Ti odio. Capisci? Lasciami andare.*"

"*Andrà tutto bene,*" Eric whispered to her while she struggled. "You don't hate me. *Ciò che è stato dimenticate deve essere ricordato. Finché non è finite.*"

"It will *never* be over and I won't be all right. Don't make me remember what I've worked so hard to forget. Please. *Ti prego.*"

"I think it's already too late." Eric released her and turned her to face him. "I see it in your eyes. Whatever wall the DCI built in your brain is gone." He moved her dark hair out of the way with his fingers and gave her forehead a soft kiss. "Stay here as long as you need. Forget what I said about the three days. I'll stay with you while we figure this out."

She looked away from him. "No, I don't think you will." She tapped her knuckles against his chest. "Is there still room for Carola or Gabriela in there?"

"There is."

She shook her head. "That path is narrow. The Tarakana, Karíhton, showed it to me. They explore all the possible futures inside their group mind. The one with us together is pinching out. And the Captain and I have places to be." She pushed herself away from him, but both hands lingered on his chest, not wanting to let him go. "I have other ways to cope with the pain. Early in my rehab, before the drugs, before the surgeries, they taught me how to control it." She gave him a sad sort of grin. "Pray for me?"

"I will, but I want to do more. I owe you."

Gabriela caressed his chest and one finger drifted between the buttons of his shirt to touch skin. "I like you being in my debt." She looked over her shoulder at Tom. "You ever been to Mancosa, Captain?"

Tom was on the floor, one hand petting Karíhton. Gabriela had felt Kahwihta in there. He couldn't feel her, no matter how desperately he wanted to. He could sense something when he looked in to the creature's brown eyes, but it faded in and out of his awareness. The dog stared back at him, seeming just as confused.

Tom looked up at Gabriela. "I'm sorry, what did you ask?"

"Mancosa, sir. Have you been there?"

He moved closer to Karíhton, not wanting to let go. Maybe Kahwihta could sense him even if all he felt was soft fur under his fingers. "I was there once, before the Separatists took power. I spent a week in the capital on shore leave from the *Andrea Gritti*. Zellerfeld's a pretty place. It's up in the mountains and it snowed while I was there. Is that where they're taking Kahwihta?"

"That's where you and I need to go if you ever want to see her again."

He nodded. "OK. How? It's not like we can buy a ticket."

Gabriela smiled, seeming pleased with herself. "We won't need a ticket. The Tarakana showed us the way."

"It's their plan?"

"Not directly. We'll just follow Holloman's example and travel the same way she sent them from Chéng Nuò. By container. Eric does it all the time. He'll set it up."

"No, I won't." Eric pulled her hands away from him, cuffing them tightly together in front of him as if he was afraid of her. "This is worse than your plan to walk into the trap at Heidar Path."

"Come on. How many refugees have you shipped off-world in the last year?"

"A few. When I needed to save a life. To Bodens Gate, or Dulcinea or Meeker. Not to planets controlled by the Separatists. Why not return to Earth? If I do this, let me send you home. You're in no shape for this kind of op, especially not with a civilian tagging along. Go home. You need to heal. If you won't stay here with me while you're doing it, then go home."

"Tell me the truth. I know you've done it."

Eric didn't answer.

"Truth." She held her hands up. Eric was still holding them tightly. "And be quick. I'm losing circulation here."

"You always think this is some kind of game. Another Academy simulation."

"It is a game." She glanced at where Tom was sitting on the floor with his fingers buried in Karíhton's fur. "One that just got a hell of a lot more interesting."

"People die in the game. I've watched them die."

"You're going to lecture me about the cost?"

"I don't have the right. No one that isn't dead has paid more than you have. I know that. The DCI reset you, just as if you were one more sim. They sent you back out onto the field with a new name, a new face, and a new life to sacrifice. Don't pay it again. Don't play their game. Please."

"I'm not doing it for them. Not this time. Now the truth. How many have you helped escape to Mancosa?"

He let go of her hands. "There are honorable men and women on both sides in this war. People of faith."

"Hah! Thought so." She put her hands back on his chest. "Traitor. Will you help Tom and me rescue our crew? That's honorable, even if I've lost my faith."

"You'd have me– the church– knowingly smuggle a Union spy disguised as a refugee? That compromises everything I believe in."

She moved her hands around his neck and tipped his head down so he'd have to look into her eyes. "Not everything. Believe in me for just a little bit longer. I'm going as Gabriela Vendramin, First Officer of the Trade Guild ship *Gattino Alato*. The Captain and I need to ransom our crew and make our way back home. Nothing more. No bang and burn. No espionage."

"How do you plan to get out?"

Gabriela smiled as if she'd already won the argument. "No idea. Maybe we'll meet someone like you."

"Contact Father von Galen at the Marktkirche when you get there. He's not as gullible as I am, and that smile of yours won't turn his head or his heart, but he might help you if you stick to your cover. Please, stick to your cover. You're going to see things while you're there. You'll be tempted to do what you think is right."

"I always do what I think is right."

"That'll get you killed in no time. Just stand here a minute. I need to talk to your Captain." Eric stepped past her and knelt next to Tom. "Sir?"

"Thank you for helping us."

"Don't thank me. I'm probably sending you to your death. I know she's not coming back from this and it weighs on my heart. Promise you'll try to keep her alive."

"She's all that's left; did you know? Six of us were on the *Gattino* when we pushed away from the Chéng Nuò docks. Now I just have her, and she's not even really my First Officer. Look at her."

Gabriela was staring at the ceiling with her arms wrapped tightly around herself. Her hips were swaying as she sang the nonsense song.

Tom shook his head. "She's not free of them yet. You said it was as if she was drunk. I wish that's all it was. When I touch this thing that looks like a dog, it terrifies me. Alien. Intelligent. Ancient. It's like nothing we've ever found in the universe, but it's been with us all along, hiding and doing God knows what with us. I'm scared, but I touch it anyway, because that's how badly I need Kahwihta. I put my face next to it trying to feel... something, some hint that she's still out there."

Tom pulled his hand away from Karíhton. "I can't connect. I'm going to take Gabriela and find my crew. I promise I'll do everything I can to bring her back home with us."

"If she does go rogue, if you can't save her, I'll understand. I won't blame you." Eric watched Gabriela singing and Tom could see the pain and the longing in his eyes. "It's not the sort of thing that gets reported. Come back here and tell me if it happens. That's all I can ask."

Gabriela finished her song and sat on the floor next to them. She placed her hand a few centimeters above Karíhton and moved it slowly back and forth. "I can't see anything, but it's like little sparks are jumping between us. All warm and tingly." She went forehead to forehead with the Tarakana and they nuzzled each other. "Karíhton is my friend. This is going to work out great."

"A few minutes ago you were kicking her," Eric reminder her. "And you were reaching for a vibracore."

Gabriela's nose wrinkled. "I already apologized to her for that. I didn't understand the op or how important it is to them. Now I do. When can we leave?"

Eric shook his head. "I can't believe I'm going to do this. I'll go see some folks tomorrow. It's not the sort of thing I can do on a display pad.

A couple of days probably. There are options other than stuffing you into a container, especially if you're in a hurry."

Tom put his hand on Karíhton's head, staring into eyes that regarded him with cold intelligence, and maybe a flicker of something more. "Hang on, Kahwihta. Please, just hang on."

Gabriela bumped into him, knocking his hand away as she wrapped her arms around Karíhton. "Damn, this is going to be fun." She kissed Karíhton's head and pressed her face into the soft fur that wasn't really fur.

CHAPTER 14

CONSEQUENCES

Tom's door creaked a little as it opened. The light from the hallway shown past Gabriela's rumpled hair into his eyes and made him squint.

"Sir? Are you awake?"

It was a fair question. Sleep had been elusive and he'd drifted in and out between nightmares and a reality that provided no relief. "Yeah. What time is it?"

"About 02:30." Gabriela hesitated in the doorway. She was wearing a long t-shirt and shorts that ended just above her knees. "I don't want to be alone." She said it firmly, as though she'd reached a decision and was now implementing it. "Eric locked his door or I would have gone to him. He didn't answer when I knocked."

"I thought the doors here didn't have locks."

"His does. Let me sleep on your floor. I can't be alone right now."

"Is Karíhton with you?" The Tarakana masquerading as a dog had haunted Tom's most recent dream, tentacles waving at him from a red sand desert, leading him irresistibly toward somewhere he was afraid he'd die.

Gabriela's voice broke when she answered. "No. She left me a while ago. I was dreaming something happy, then she slipped out of my head and I was back in my prison cell. It was so real. The flickering red lights, the cold, and the smell of it. Disinfectant and death. They wouldn't give us blankets to keep ourselves warm. There were nights I thought I'd freeze to death."

She rubbed her arms with her hands and shivered. "Corporal Willem Briede. That was his name. I'd wake to find him climbing on top of me or already trying to thrust himself into me. The stink of his breath in my face. He'd be so drunk that he'd pass out afterwards, sometimes for hours."

She gave Tom a lopsided grin, full of pain that was still sharp despite the passage of years. "But you know what? Him lying there kept me warm. I didn't die."

She was still standing in the doorway, silhouetted by the hallway lights. After a moment, Tom asked her, "Are those the memories that the DCI blocked?"

"Yeah. Some of them."

Tom rolled out of bed. "You take it. The floor's fine for me. I haven't really been sleeping anyway. I think I saw extra blankets and a pillow in the closet."

Gabriela nodded, stepped into the room, and closed the door. "Thank you. I should argue, but not tonight. One thing I learned in that hell was that I have limits. I can break. I did break."

Tom sat at the small desk and watched her as she climbed into bed and adjusted the covers and pillow. "What happened after you were freed? Did the Union punish the guards for what they had done?"

She rolled on her side and looked at him in the dim light. "No, of course not. The Union needed peace and stability as quickly as possible. They had other worlds to bring back in line and no resources to spare, so they declared a general amnesty. A friend who tracks these kind of things told me that Corporal Briede mustered out and went back to his family. Supposedly, he beat up his wife pretty badly one night a few months later. When he was done with her, she went to the kitchen, got the biggest knife she could find, and shoved it through his left eye. I hope it's true. Try to sleep, sir. I think tomorrow is going to be a busy one."

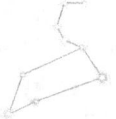

"Rough night, I take it?" Eric asked.

Tom opened his eyes and tried to remember where he was. Full consciousness was slow in coming. He was on a carpeted floor, a thin pillow under his head, and something warm pressed against his side. Gabriela was asleep next to him, wrapped in her own blanket, her head on his shoulder. The bed he had given her was empty. "Um, I guess it was. This isn't what it looks like."

"Really? I guess that depends on what you think it looks like. I was there when Gabriela went through this the first time. I remember what she was like. You did the right thing, letting her be here with you. You'll need to be careful with her while you're in transit to Mancosa and afterwards. She'll be erratic and moody, hard to control."

"Bah," Gabriela replied, eyes still closed, still snuggled against Tom. "I was always those things. Ask anyone. My Captain is a gentleman; I can tell. And he's in love with a woman who would snap me in half if I tried anything. I could have walked into his room last night naked, and unlike some men, he would have put a blanket around me, given me his bed, and told me to sleep."

Eric's face reddened. "Go back to your room and get dressed. Captain, I was out late last night trying to arrange passage for you and Ms. Vendramin. Your options aren't good." He rubbed his forehead. "My brain has a dull hum stuck in it and I need coffee. You look like you could use some too. Meet me in the kitchen in fifteen. Both of you."

Gabriela looked back at him, eyes squinted. "So, you were gone. That's why you didn't answer when I knocked. I did knock."

"No, I heard you. I left afterward." He held his hand out to help her up. "Because, as you know very well, I am no gentleman. Not when it comes to you. I should never have let you stay here at all."

She took his hand and stood on tiptoes, bouncing slightly and rolling her head from side to side, getting the kinks out from sleeping on the hard floor. "I'm not sorry. I'm sorry you're sorry, but I don't think you really are."

"No, I am sorry. If I'd answered your knock, that would have been the end of it. I'd never let you leave, not for Mancosa or anywhere else."

She stopped bouncing and settled back flat-footed. "Oh."

"You need to go to Mancosa. It's important."

Tom leaned up on one elbow. "You've heard something?"

"No. Yes. In here." He rubbed his forehead and winced. "Inside the hum. You need to go. Don't ask me why or what you're supposed to do once you get there. A verse from Paul's second letter to the Corinthians keeps playing in my head. Something about walking by faith, not by sight. You both better work on your faith; you're going to need it."

Gabriela gave him a brief nod and reached up to touch his face. "You'd never let me leave? You best be careful. I might hold you to it someday."

"Go get dressed."

"I'll go get dressed."

After the door closed behind her, Tom stood and stretched. "I'm getting too old to be sleeping on the floor."

"Uh huh."

"Look, she was terrified last night, dreaming about what happened to her after she was captured. I gave her my bed. I don't remember her joining me on the floor. She cried herself to sleep, last thing I remember. What was I supposed to do? Send her back to her room?"

"No, of course not. As I said before, you did the right thing. Now she's all…"

"Giddy," Tom finished for him. "Like the nightmares never happened."

"The mood swings will get worse before they get better if this goes like last time. There will be flashbacks, sudden anger, and she'll wake up screaming most nights."

"Being with Karíhton seems to help her. She was practically part of their colony yesterday."

Eric rubbed his forehead again. "I'm glad you're taking those things with you. They give me a headache and I think they're suppressing the panic I should be feeling knowing they exist."

"We're taking them with us?"

"Yeah. Get dressed and we'll talk about it over coffee."

"Make two pots."

Fiona Grimani laughed when Captain Lescher finished talking. It seemed appropriate, based on the hopeful raised eyebrow and half grin on his face. She'd not heard a word of his story, but he leaned back, satisfied that he'd pleased the Trade Guild governor deadheading back to Earth on board his *Jadwiga*. Her focus was on the urgent message she'd read from her chief engineer, seeking guidance on an overweight, over-budget, and behind schedule starship. Lingering over after-dinner drinks was not an option.

The display pad rolled in her pocket hummed softly to her comm pin. Carlsen again, no doubt. Another message sent two days ago requiring an urgent decision.

She pushed back from the table. "Very amusing, Captain. I wish I could stay to chat, but business is calling me away. Do excuse me."

Fiona unrolled the pad across the desk in her cabin. The urgent video message in the center of the display flashed 'Dearest Mother'.

"Oh, Nicholas, what are you up to?"

She tapped the icon to decrypt it and Nick's face appeared with a messy bedroom visible behind him. "I never should have left you alone." She shook her head and touched play.

"Hey, mom. It's Sunday night here, so this won't reach you until Tuesday evening, if I calculated your course correctly. Slow comms because light is sooo slow, how do you stand it? Whoever fixes that will be *ricco sfondato*, right?"

Fiona crossed her arms and spoke as though he could hear her. "Get to the point, Nick."

"Anyway, Dad's gone off net. He whacked a couple of privateers first, and I thought that maybe he really was going to try paying out the debt. Now he's laying down and I lost him."

Fiona nodded to herself. *I knew he'd run. He always runs.*

"He's not running, or at least I don't think he is. His bosun, the one you told me he's looking to *arare*?"

"That's *not* the word I used."

"Well, she and her brothers went back to the *Gattino Alato*. The Afweyne syndicate snatched them and they're pushing for Mancosa, assuming they're not all dead. I can't tell while they're running silent."

"The point, Nick, the point."

"Someone was pinging the Shipping News yesterday, looking for containerized cargo headed to Dammeron. I think it's Dad, or someone he's paying. Immurement travel's pretty common for fugitives. He's looking to go after her, Mom. Dammeron's on a direct line to Mancosa. He's chasing her to a Separatist home world and he's going to rescue her, I know it." Nicholas leaned back from the camera. "That's romantic. Was he always like that?"

"Stupid, you mean? Yeah. Always."

Nicholas leaned forward. "So here's why I marked this urgent. The woman he's with is not Gabriela Vendramin. I'm not sure who she really is, but there was an identity swap sometime over a year ago. I almost missed it. Really professional. Like DCI grade, or maybe Union special forces. I'm not sure if Dad knows, but if he takes her to Mancosa with him, there'll be hell to pay. The DCI has kept their field agents in the dark, and you want to keep it that way. You put all this in motion when you set up the offer to get him to run and I don't want to see you get hurt. You might want to stop him. I'll keep watch from here."

Fiona stared at the blank screen for several minutes before typing a name into the message console. He wasn't going to like it, but he owed her a favor.

CHAPTER 15

REVENGE

Mathea took a fistful of Kahwihta's hair in one stubby hand and tugged, forcing her head back and exposing her neck. "The Captain wants you alive. I say you're more trouble than any ransom will ever pay us back. You walk gentle and I'll give him what he wants. Try anything and you'll be following your crewmate out the airlock. Do we understand each other?"

She tried to turn her head to glare at him, but it only made him pull harder on her hair. The pain and the heat of the anger in her gut was all that was keeping her from begging for death. She tried to focus on her anger. Dying would be pointless if she couldn't take them all to hell with her.

He released her hair, grabbed hard onto the back of her neck, and pushed Kahwihta along the passageway. "Don't much care if you understand me or not. Just know I can kill you with a twist of my hand."

"Dead. Like Simon." She didn't mean to say it aloud, but she must have. Despair was washing the anger from her, making her weak. She stumbled.

"That's right. We left a trail of corpses behind us when we pushed out from the New Palisade docks. One more would make the rest of this trick that much easier." He shoved on her neck. "Move."

"Where are you taking me? To Afweyne?" She tried to put defiance in her voice so he'd know she wasn't a sheep. It quavered anyway and she cursed herself silently.

Mathea didn't respond. They'd reached the portside lift and she expected him to push her into it and take her up to the bridge. He passed by and pressed his hand to the keypad outside one of the vacant passenger cabins.

"Crappy ship you have here. No brig, no secure detention, no secure anything. This will have to do for now. Go stand by the far wall."

The hard shove in her back as he let go of her neck sent her to her knees. She scrambled up again and stood with her back to the wall.

Mathea aimed his pistol at her using both hands. "Pull that knife from out your boot, slow and easy."

Kahwihta could see straight into the barrel. Mathea's eyes dared her to do what she wanted to do, to attack. She held the knife out to him hilt first, the tip balanced in her fingers.

Mathea's aim didn't waver. "Damn, woman. You think I'm stupid? On the deck and kick it to me." His eyes flicked down for a fraction of a second as the knife came to a stop at his feet. "Genuine Bourean blade. Nice."

"*Not enough time,*" a voice hummed into her head. "*Wait for your opportunity. It will come.*"

Kahwihta closed her eyes. "*Now you come back to me?*" she thought to herself. A wave of grief was making her knees tremble. Kari had abandoned her, had let Simon die. "*You come back now when it's too late?*"

"*Don't try to force time into straight lines. There is only the right moment and the wrong moment. Wait. You are not alone.*"

"Sure, OK," she whispered. "I'll wait."

"You'll wait?" Mathea asked. "No more waiting. Open those pretty brown eyes and take your boots off."

Kahwihta stared down the muzzle of the gun. "My boots?"

"Off." He entered the cabin and stepped sideways, his aim still tracking her face. "Toss them out into the passageway."

She slipped off her boots and tossed them.

"Captain said to make sure you didn't have nothing left to cause us more trouble. Comm pin and watch next. Out the door with them."

The comm pin had been on her ear so long that it took a moment to wiggle free. They landed next to her boots and knife.

"And the coveralls."

Her hand hesitated at the top of the zipper. "No. It's cold in here. You can't leave me naked."

"Sure I can. Off."

Kahwihta didn't move.

"I think I can shoot you without killing you, but with plasma rounds it's hard to know for sure." He steadied his aim, left eye squinted shut as the barrel tracked lower on her body.

"Fine." She stepped out of the coveralls and tossed them into the passageway. "They need recycling anyway." She stood in front of him, arms wrapped around herself, using her anger to keep the fear from showing. Karíhton was close by; Kahwihta could feel her waiting.

"Lie down on the bunk."

"What are you going to do?" The quaver came back into her voice and she bit down hard on her lower lip trying to refocus her anger. "Tell me how this is going to end."

"With you lying on the damn bunk not able to argue no more." He changed to a single hand grip on his pistol and pulled flex cuffs from his pocket. "Get on the bunk."

"I..." Kahwihta felt the right moment rushing toward her and struggled to keep it from showing on her face. Grief and fear passed away, displaced by a glowing excitement for what was to come. A shadow moved quickly by outside the door, a shadow that she recognized. Her knife was no longer lying on the deck next to her boots. The hum filled her head and a song filled her with cold joy. "OK, let's go." Her voice was steady and clear. "I'm going to enjoy this."

Mathea's head tipped slightly. "Nice attitude, but I got no time for you now. Not yet. We put these on you and then I call the Captain."

Kahwihta sat on the edge of the bunk and held her arms out to him, wrists together. "How much time do you need? Do you want me like this?"

"Um, yeah. Like that. Might have underestimated you. Maybe we got time enough after all." The barrel of the pistol wavered as his gaze drifted away from the gun's sights.

It was all the distraction Tek needed.

He entered silently and then screamed as the knife slashed across Mathea's throat, cutting through almost to the spine. His cry echoed in the small cabin, the sound of someone lost to the purity of blood lust making a righteous kill. It came to Kahwihta from a time before all time, from before humans existed, and it pushed deep into her soul like the first notes of a song long forgotten.

She didn't move. The scream and the sight of Mathea collapsing under the knife in her brother's hand filled her. She gripped hard on the edge of the bed while shudders chased up and down her body and the muscles low in her stomach clenched. She fought against the irrational desire to rush forward into the blood spraying across the room.

Tek let go and the corpse fell to the deck in front of her. She looked at it, her breath coming in sharp gasps through an open mouth, the sound of her heart thudding loud in her ears.

"Hey, sis, you OK?" Tek knelt in front of her, his blood-splattered face twisted with concern.

"Yeah. Give me a moment. Didn't expect to react this way, you know?" She grinned at him, but it felt more like her lips had curled into a snarl.

Tek shook his head. "Not really. We need to go. I rebooted Schiava's personality silos and have them set at minimum so no one will notice. I hope. She's been keeping the privateers blind to me being on board and she'll ghost you now too. There're still three of them out there."

"Help me stand."

Tek took her hand and helped her up, his eyes never leaving hers. "We're going to be all right."

Kahwihta wrapped her arms around him and put her cheek against his chest. He held her awkwardly, patting her bare shoulder.

"Simon's dead," she whispered.

"I know. Schiava told me. We'll avenge him and we'll win back our ship."

"Thought you went down to New Palisade."

"Naw, I wouldn't do that; not for Delilah anyway. I told Schiava to lie for me. Simon tipped me off that something was up. He said to hide and that he was on his way. If I'd known the truth of it, I'd have run straight to him."

"And be dead now too."

He shrugged. "Maybe."

She let go of him and they stepped out of the cabin. Kahwihta slipped her comm pin and watch back on, and dressed, trying to ignore the stench wafting from the coveralls.

Tek held the knife out to her. "Sharp blade."

"Genuine Bourean." She wiped it on her sleeve and kept it in her hand. "You can clean it properly for me when we're done. What's the plan?"

"We don't have time to hide somewhere and make a plan. They'll come for us as soon as they realize Mathea is down and you're on the loose. Schiava will ghost you all over the ship, but they'll figure out what she's doing before long and shut her down. We have to kill them all first."

"Kill." Kahwihta braced her hand on the edge of the door. Mathea was face down on the deck. Blood soaked the carpet under him, deep red on mottled brown. "I don't want..."

She shook herself, which turned into a shudder. Tek steadied her, his hand gentle on her arm. "I'm OK," she lied to him. The song still played somewhere, calling to her. "There were two women with Mathea back in the port wing passageway. Where would they go after they..." She closed her eyes, trying to push away the memory of Simon lying on his back with his eyes open, unseeing. "Where would they go after they were done cleaning up?"

"Back to the mess hall, maybe." They started walking quickly, Tek holding the pistol he'd taken from Mathea. "They were cleaning up in there when Captain Afweyne sent them to help after you took out Beaufore." He shook his head. "Damn, sis. Between you and Schiava, you've about wiped them out."

"Schiava and Karíhton. Not me."

"Karíhton? A Peace Officer? A *protector*?"

"No, Kari. Our dog. She's back." Kahwihta increased their speed to a jog, feeling a sudden urgency to reach the mess hall.

"Don't do this to me. I can't take on three pirates all alone."

Kahwihta rolled her eyes. "Not crazy. It's those things that were in container one. They change shapes. Now they look like Karíhton. Same markings on her fur. Same eyes."

"I'm not sure I believe you, but OK."

"You'll see. I hope you see. She saved me from Beaufore, then abandoned Simon and let him die. I thought she was my friend, thought she'd..." Kahwihta wiped her eyes with the back of her hand as she ran. "I don't know what her game is. It's cold inside the group mind and I don't understand it. I feel better when they're near, as if I matter. When I don't feel her, I'm afraid." She lowered her head, increasing their pace.

"Why are we running?"

Kahwihta glanced down at her watch. "We need to be in the mess hall in ninety-three seconds."

"Why?"

She looked back at him in surprise, astonished to find she didn't know the reason. "I... I don't know. Karíhton says it's important and she's my friend."

They reached the mess hall and Kahwihta hesitated with her head leaned against the door.

"You know you can't hear anything through that much metal, right?" Tek whispered.

"And still you whisper. Wait. Wait. Now." She placed her hand on the keypad and the door slid open, squalling, still out of alignment.

The mess hall was empty. They stepped in, Tek moving to the left, Kahwihta to the right, hoping the banging and arguing coming from the storage area behind the main food printer had masked their entrance.

"All I'm sayin', is why am I up on this ladder doin' all the work here? Unstick your face from that stupid dog and give me a hand fixin' the printer feed line. I can't align both ends by myself, ya know."

"Shhh, Ronda. I can hear her thinking at me. It's pretty. All tangled and knotted and cold."

The banging stopped. "Ya hear the dog thinkin'? What 'cha do to empty your head enough for *that* to work? Not puttin' those green and purple tabs into yourself again, are ya?"

The sound of singing reached Kahwihta, and she caught her breath. She turned to where Tek was working his way forward, pistol held in front of him just as their father had taught them. He was hunting, ready to kill.

She waved, trying to get his attention. Tek's focus was on the sounds coming from the storage area. He was about to slaughter the women there before they had a chance to yell for help.

"No, stop." Kahwihta rushed forward, whispering to him as she ran. She reached Tek as he pulled the trigger, powerless to stop what he had done. The blonde woman named Ronda glanced down in shock at the hole Tek had blown in her chest. She toppled from the ladder onto the deck, dead before she hit.

Tek pivoted to the woman with the short black hair sitting on the floor. She had her cheek pressed into the neck of the dog sitting next to her, nuzzling the soft fur. Her eyes were half closed as she sang, seeming unaware that her friend had just died or that her own death was upon her.

Kahwihta tackled her brother.

Tek scrambled from under her and pushed her off. "What the hell?"

"Don't need to kill. Look at her."

"I see her. She was there when they shot Simon. She helped throw his body out the damn airlock."

"Don't kill her."

"Why the hell not? There're only two of us. We can't take prisoners. You know that."

"Why did I save you on Bodens Gate, you and your brother? Why did I risk my career and my life?"

Tek pointed the pistol at the woman's head. "No time for this. Move back. Sorry about the dog, but they're too close together."

Kahwihta touched Tek's shoulder. "Do you know why?"

Tek shook her off, irritated. He knew his sister well enough, though, that he answered. "We had a warrant out for our arrest. Terrible dishonor to the family for us to go out that way. If I forgot to thank you at the time, then thanks. Step back."

She hit him hard in the shoulder. "Gaaa. You think I care about their opinions anymore? Look at me. Let me see your eyes. Are you already dead inside? That's what I wanted to stop. You and Simon killing off your souls bit by bit. Look at me."

Tek looked down into her eyes, trying to maintain his aim on the woman sitting on the floor singing to herself.

"You're my brother." Kahwihta told him. "We kill only when we have to. We treasure the lives entrusted to us, and we love and redeem everyone given into our hands. You remember those words?"

"Dad said them every night when he tucked us in. I remember the smell of his uniform. I remember how cold his badge was on my face when he held me close. He was a good man and he died protecting our people." Tek lowered the gun and tucked it into his waistband. "She doesn't need to die. Not today."

Kahwihta hugged him. "Thank you."

The woman looked up at them. "Yeah. Thanks. This dog of yours is special. She says her name is Codon of Pellucidar, but she was laughing when she said it, so I know it's not true."

"We call her Karíhton. What's your name?"

"First Engineer Teuta Ardian. I live to serve my Master on board the ships we take in righteous combat. Or that we can steal. I've survived twenty-four revolutions around the Mancosa sun, almost twenty-eight Union standard, not that it matters with us not in the Union anymore." She touched Ronda's body, gently moving the hair away from her face before closing her eyes. "I want to cry for her; I need to cry. Not yet. I'll do my crying in here with Karíhton for a while first and let her take some of my pain." She looked at Kahwihta. "Why don't you touch her with me? I know you're in a hurry to kill my Captain, but please? Just for a moment? Karíhton wants you to see me."

"I'm not liking this." Tek had his arms crossed. "She's nuts and the damn thing looks just like I remember Kari, down to the white around her muzzle and the sad eyes. It's not natural. Don't do it."

"You know I have to. Pull me back after a couple of minutes. I need to talk to Teuta and she's not making much sense on this side of the group mind."

"Group mind? Do you hear yourself? OK, sure. I'm going to find a stick or something to pry you away because I'm not touching either of you with my bare hands. I'll give you two minutes. Captain Afweyne will probably have killed us in one."

Teuta laughed. "Afweyne. Best. Cover story. Ever. All the captains in the syndicate call themselves Afweyne and the Union wonders how he can be in so many places at once. Our Captain is Yusuf Reis and I won't cry a drop when you kill him." She reached for Kahwihta. "Come hide inside with me. I have secrets to share."

"Tek, could you please…" Kahwihta gestured toward Ronda. "While I'm in there. Make it something respectful. Move her to the back and cover her with one of the blankets from the top shelf."

"Ronda would like having a blanket. She was always cold. We weren't much alike, but she was my friend and I miss her already. She died quick, though. Not like the others in here with their bodies shattered and broken." Teuta locked eyes with Kahwihta. "That was cruel."

"I know it was. They killed my brother."

Teuta nodded, blinking back tears. "It's the war we're in. It hurts so much all the time."

Kahwihta settled herself on the deck.

Teuta put a hand on Kahwihta's knee. "Touch her now and we'll talk."

Kahwihta expected the contact to be the same as when she and Tom were together, a sharing of emotions without words, distant but real, time streaming by too fast. Maybe they could share enough of a vision that it would help them find Captain Reis before he found them.

It was nothing like being with Tom.

Kahwihta saw Teuta's soul. It glowed and sparkled, a flame separate from the roaring of Karíhton's thoughts that flowed all around them.

"You are beautiful, Teuta," she said without words. *"Made of light, hidden inside a shell of clay. How could anyone have ever hurt you?"* And hurt her they had. Kahwihta could see the scars left by the pain Teuta had suffered, and the scars left by the pain she had inflicted on others.

Teuta tried to hide. *"I didn't expect it to be like this, that you could see all of me, all that I've done, the monster I've become. Don't look. There's too much darkness inside me."*

Kahwihta reached for her and held her close, whispering words of comfort. *"Let go of it. Am I any better? Humans are monsters. Kari has given us a gift to be in here and see it, to be alive in this moment. Will you help us?"*

"*The man you're with. Your brother. I can see a little of him in this place. He's trying to be hard, but that's not him. They have plans for him. Plans for you. Some of the futures they let me see might be real. I hope the ones with me still alive are real. I like that one; do you see them thinking it? Oh, it's gone again, spinning and twisting. I'll help you. It won't take away my darkness, not all of it.*"

"We'll work on that."

Teuta unwrapped herself from Kahwihta's embrace. "*I like it in here. There's no pain. But if I stay any longer I'll never find my way out again.*"

"*Let's go. I know our time is up because I can feel Tek hitting me with something. I love my brother, but sometimes...*"

"Tekanatoken Beauvais, you poke me one more time with that kick rod and I'll beat your ass. You know I can do it."

"Welcome back. I hope it was worth it. It's been ten minutes and Schiava went down over thirty seconds ago. You know what that means."

Teuta was on her knees, struggling to stand. "It means I better help you get your Schiava back online. Oh, damn it. My feet are asleep. Give me a hand."

Tek grabbed her elbow to help her up.

Teuta wobbled as she leaned on Tek. "She's a funky one, your AI. It took me three tries before I got her under our control without her shutting off life support at the same time."

Tek stared at her. "I've seen your face before."

"It's been here with me since you first arrived."

"You remind me of the *La Diana Cazadora*, a statue back on Earth. I spent an afternoon at this little bar called El Objetivo de Diana, drinking too much tequila and looking at that face for a couple of hours. Your hair's too short and your skin is darker than the bronze." He leaned closer to her. "There's something about the way you catch the light. And your eyes and the shape of your nose..."

Teuta pushed on her nose. "I'm too squishy to be a sculpture. Where's the nearest engineering console? I can't do this from my display pad." She waited while Tek continued to stare at her. She raised her eyebrows. "You do want your AI back, right? I can do that for you, and then it will be us hunting Captain Reis, not the other way around."

Tek blinked at her several times as though trying to reset himself. "Why should I trust you?"

"Because you'll die if you don't."

"We have to trust her," Kahwihta added. "I've been inside her soul. She's no more a monster than you are."

Tek and Teuta answered together. "But I am a monster." They looked at each other, and both whispered, "Damn."

"Gotta be the effect of being so close to that dog thing of yours." Teuta gestured to where Kari had been sitting, but the deck was empty. "Where'd she go?"

"They do that a lot," Kahwihta told her. "And at the worst possible moments. Let's move. You can access the engineering displays from the console by the forward airlock."

"OK. I want you to know this. I'm going to be terrified once I have time to think about what's happening to me. I'll probably scream."

Tek chuckled. "Me too. You like Scotch? I have a bottle in my cabin. It's fortified to about one hundred-twenty proof."

Teuta typed on the console, the tip of her tongue sticking out between her teeth. "Count me in. Your AI should be back.... Now."

Kahwihta touched the comm pin on her ear. "Schiava? Are you with us?"

"You're in great danger, *Signora*. Grab the woman standing next to you. I'll open the air lock and you and Tekanatoken toss her out. That will leave just one privateer left."

Teuta's eyes became large as she turned to look at them. "Holy shit. You're not really going to do that, are you? Please don't space me. I saw that path in the group mind. I didn't think it was real. I don't want to die that way." She turned to Tek, pleading. "I can't drink Scotch with you if I'm dead, right?"

Tek reached out to take her hand. "It's going to be OK."

She stepped backwards and stared at his hand while she pressed herself against the console. "Please don't."

Tek lowered his arm. "We're not going to toss you out into space. You're one of us now." He looked at Kahwihta. "You tell her, sis."

Kahwihta had her head tipped and eyes narrowed, looking first at Tek, and then studying Teuta. Her voice was flat when she answered, without a hint of reassurance. "That's right. Schiava, this woman is Teuta Ardian. She is our..." Kahwihta was about to say prisoner. She frowned, trying to remember what she had seen inside the Karíhton group mind. The future paths were tangled and twisted. Trying to follow them was like unbraiding a rope. "Teuta is our guest. On probation. We won't be spacing her today."

"What about the other one? Can we kill him at least?"

"Sure. Where is he?"

"On the bridge trying to figure out what's happening. I've disabled comms so he can't talk to the other two towboats in our convoy and I sealed the bridge so he can't wander off."

Kahwihta took a step toward Teuta. "Two other towboats? How many ships did you steal? How many merchant crewmen are dead?"

Teuta retreated, bumping into Tek. He let her lean against him while she answered. "Just the three towboats. Afweyne wants them so they can follow his FACs when we hit anything pushing containers. What you did, dumping your cargo all over space, spooked him. He needed a countermeasure." She lowered her eyes. "I don't know about the crews. They should have all been on shore leave. *You* were supposed to be on shore leave."

"Well, I wasn't, and neither was Simon. Schiava, kill Captain Reis. My authority as bosun of the *Gattino Alato*."

"Bridge instrumentality is too delicate for lethal countermeasures. I can make him uncomfortable until you get there."

"Do that."

"Excellent. I am performing random variations to the gravity and have increased the temperature."

Kahwihta held her hand out to her brother. "Let me borrow that pistol. You stay here with our guest. This won't take me long. I..."

Teuta was snuggled against Tek and he had moved his hands to her shoulders, rubbing them gently with his eyes half closed.

"Tek, come with me a second. And you," she pointed at Teuta. "You stay right there where I can see you."

She pulled Tek far enough away where she hoped Teuta couldn't hear their whispers. "What is with you? A few minutes ago, I had to convince you not to blow her brains all over the storage room. And now? What is this? I'm afraid to leave you alone with her."

"There's something about her. I don't know what. It's like a hum, like music in my head when I look at her. We can trust her; I know it." Tek glanced away from Kahwihta to where Teuta was leaning against the engineering console, arms crossed, eyes downcast while they decided her fate. She glanced up at them and gave Tek a shy smile. "Just look at her."

Kahwihta grabbed him by the chin and turned his face back to her. "I have looked. Deeper than I hope you ever will. Maybe we can redeem her.

Maybe not. I'm not willing to bet our lives on it. I have a job to do. Can I trust you to keep your hands off her for that long?"

Tek jerked his head away from Kahwihta's grasp. "Did you see that?" He pointed at where Teuta was standing and she looked back at him questioningly. "Under the console. A shimmer. It looked like Kari for a second. Now it's gone."

Kahwihta hadn't seen it, but she'd felt it. A flash of amusement and then cold satisfaction as though the twisted future was unfurling on schedule and on plan.

CHAPTER 16

TRUST FACTOR

Kahwihta walked quickly toward the bridge, aware of Tek and Teuta following a few steps back. The sound of their whispers provided her with an extra irritation. She'd wanted to leave them behind, but no, that wasn't going to work. Kari was up to something with them and her brother wasn't thinking straight. And Teuta? Kahwihta was trying to unwrap everything she'd seen. The blocks of darkness worried her. There was a sweetness flowing through her light, but a light tainted by pain and the desire to lash out and destroy a universe that had used her and hurt her over and over. Redemption would not come quickly or easily, if it came at all. One more damn thing to worry about.

She stopped at the door and moved to one side. "Schiava, are you ready?"

"Ready. I've been shifting gravity between point one and one point eight. Temperature is a steady forty-five degrees."

Teuta peeked around Tek, her face twisted with disgust. "I'd have thrown up by now."

"That has been one result," Schiava informed them. "Four times in the last twenty-three minutes."

"Thank you, Schiava. Here's how we'll do it. Schiava will normalize gravity when the door opens and Teuta will go through first. Captain Reis will lower his guard when he sees her and that's when Tek and I come in. Tek, I want to kill the bastard, but you're a better shot than me."

"You take it. For Simon. At this range it won't matter who's the better shot. Why send Teuta in first? He might just shoot at anything coming through the door."

"You want *me* to go through first?"

"Well, no. Maybe we can all go through together, the element of surprise..."

Teuta patted his arm. "It's all right. I'm used to being disposable. Story of my life." She looked at Kahwihta, a tight smile on her lips. "And this way I'll be in your line of fire if I try to betray you. Karíhton showed me that future too. Don't worry; I want Reis dead. You see this?" She pushed her sleeve up, revealing tattoos on her forearm. "This one is Afweyne's mark, three overlapping circles. This is Reis', a sword and skull. It means I'm his indentured servant. I don't know what your plans are for me, but from the way you were glowing inside the group mind, it'll be better than the life I've had serving Captain Reis."

Tek touched her tattoos and Kahwihta saw the reaction, how Teuta bit her lip and moved her arm up closer, offering it to him for inspection. Or a kiss.

"What are the two small stars under the sword?" He leaned in and squinted. "Not tattoos. Are those burned?"

She pulled her sleeve down hastily and smoothed the fabric. "The times he took me. He does that, the branding. Afterward. All the women on the crew had those marks. Most of the men. He likes to make sure we know who owns us."

Kahwihta stood with her back to the wall next to the door, eyes closed, still trying to untangle the threads Kari had shown her. She wanted to trust Teuta, maybe not in the way Tek was doing it, but at least enough to get them past retaking the ship.

She opened her eyes and stared at the ceiling. She'd never admit it to Tek, but shooting Teuta in the back was a definite possibility. The slightest flinch, a moment of hesitation, or a single wrong word to that bastard sitting in Tom's chair on their bridge, and Teuta would die. Kahwihta glanced at her. Teuta was close to Tek, not speaking, just staring into his eyes.

"Damn you, Kari. I don't need this crap."

Teuta glanced away from Tek. "Did you say something, ma'am?"

"Are you ready?"

She nodded and placed her hand on the keypad.

The door slid open and Teuta disappeared inside. Kahwihta held up three fingers to Tek, then two, then one. She walked in. Tek stayed low and followed close behind.

Teuta was on her knees in the dark, Captain Reis half a meter in front of her, yelling. "And then the environmental controls went to hell. Lights don't work, gravity about killed me, no comms. Look at this mess. Your fault, Engineer. You clean it, and then I want you…" He looked up, having noticed Kahwihta standing in front of the open door. "Who the hell are you? Are you that bitch Mathea was supposed to bring me? On your knees next to this one if you want me to spare your–"

Kahwihta raised the pistol, tracking his face as she walked in. She placed one foot carefully in front of the next, the voice of her father in her head, telling her how to handle men like Captain Reis.

"Whoa, whoa, whoa. OK, I see how it is now." Reis raised his hands over his head. "No need for that. You want to find your way back to Union space? I can make that happen for you. I'm your man. I know how the syndicate works and I'll tell you anything you want to know."

Kahwihta closed the distance, moving slowly until she was standing right behind the still kneeling Teuta. The muzzle of the pistol was steady in her hands less than a meter from Reis' face.

Teuta bowed her head, curling in on herself. "Do it."

"Wait. You need me. I can–"

Kahwihta pulled the trigger. The blast of the plasma round sent most of Reis' head as a steaming splatter across the wall behind the main display.

Tek yelled at her from the darkness. "Damn it, Kahwihta, why? He might have known something we could use."

"That man's life was built out of nothing but lies. He abused his crew and led all of them to their deaths. He murdered Simon. What could he have told us? More lies, more death. With a man like that, you put him down. We'll find our own way home."

Tek took Teuta's hands and helped her to her feet. "You sound like Dad."

"Thanks. You take that thing," Kahwihta waved the pistol at what was left of Captain Reis, "and drag it to the nearest airlock. Check his pockets for anything that might be useful. Ms. Ardian and I have some things to get straight."

Tek hesitated, looking at the gun still in Kahwihta's hand.

"Is there a problem?" she asked him. "Feeling squeamish?"

"You know that's not it."

She continued to stare at him, unblinking. "Move."

"Yes, ma'am."

Kahwihta waited until Tek was gone before sliding the pistol into her pocket.

Teuta shifted on her feet and sighed nervously. "Ma'am, you said Reis led all of his crew to their deaths. Um, you're not including me in that, are you?"

Kahwihta studied her face. Teuta's eyes were wide and full of fear. "Schiava, with the way it smells in here, I'm not sure I want to see it, but bring the lights back up, please."

Teuta glanced around and put her hand to her mouth. She gagged and added her own vomit to the deck.

Kahwihta waited for her to finish before lifting her up.

"Ma'am, if you're going to kill me, tell me. It's the not knowing that's tearing me apart. If you let me live, I just need to know the rules, what will keep me alive, what will get me punished."

Kahwihta shook her head, seeing the vision Kari had given her of Teuta's soul. All of the scars, all the open wounds. "Rules here are simple. You play straight and do your job. Don't try to hide it if you screw up. Tell me and I'll help you learn to do it right. If I think you're a danger to my ship or my crew, you'll find yourself confined to quarters. Understand?"

"I... I... No, I don't. It's never that easy. Not for me."

"OK, you want hard? Leave my brother alone. That thing that looks like a dog is messing with your mind. Fight it."

Teuta stood up straighter and the fear left her eyes as they narrowed in defiance.

Kahwihta smiled to herself. At least they hadn't crushed the woman's spirit completely out of her. Putting her back together was possible, but it was going to be a long and messy road. She nodded. "Now I think we understand each other."

"We do. I'm a good engineer, three years on merchant ships, two on FACs. You need something done, I can do it."

"Good. You and Tek can start with cleaning the bridge when he gets back. He'll show you where we keep the supplies. I'll be in my cabin reviewing the logs and talking to Schiava. One last thing. What I said about Reis leading his crew to their deaths? Yes, that includes you. We're about twenty-three hours from the first DSH and the red dot you can just make out on the display behind you is a Fast Attack Craft, probably sent to escort us the rest of the way into Mancosa. I'll be surprised if any of us are still breathing a week from now."

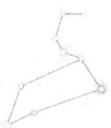

Kahwihta entered her cabin and wiggled out of her coveralls as she walked. "Schiava, print three sets of coveralls for me and a towel. What's the tactical situation? Are we supposed to be talking to the ships around us?"

"I am. You are not. I'm continuing to share station keeping and status updates with my sisters. As far as they know, Captain Reis is still in command."

"Good. I'm going to take a five-minute shower while the coveralls print. I want audio and visual from the bridge right here." She touched her main display and an image of Teuta appeared. She was sitting at the engineering station tapping at the controls. Tek wasn't back yet.

"What is she accessing?"

"System status, drive efficiency, and the amount of fuel and Holloman armor remaining. Now she's watching Tek. She seems interested in observing him."

"Has she accessed anything that an engineer doesn't need?"

"Like watching Tek?"

"Yes. No. Set an exception for that or you'll be notifying me every ten minutes."

"Do we not trust Ms. Ardian?"

"We do not. But I need her, so watch her and alert me if she does anything unusual."

"Interesting. Those are the same instructions Captain Reis gave me regarding her."

Kahwihta stepped into the shower and closed her eyes, letting the hot water pour down her back. *So, Teuta was a troublemaker in both worlds. Good to know.*

She finished and stood dripping while she waited for her towel to be ready. Tek had just returned to the bridge, and she watched Teuta's reaction, the way she leaned toward him as he entered, as though wanting to leap from her chair and run into his arms. Tek's reaction was no better. He stood in the doorway for several seconds staring at her.

"Damn you, Tek," Kahwihta said aloud. "Get a grip."

Teuta leaned back in her chair. "Kahwihta said you know where the supplies are to clean up. She wants us to do it together."

"Schiava told me. I can take care of it alone if you have engineering tasks to do."

"Huh." Teuta's mouth opened, speechless, as if he'd just surprised her with a magnificent gift. She stammered when she was finally able to answer.

"No, no, it's OK. Your ship is in fine shape. A little low on fuel, but enough to see us into Mancosa. I'll do my share. That's some of my barf on the deck."

Tek took a couple of steps toward her and she turned away from him. "Look, I don't know you, and you sure as hell don't know me. Kahwihta told me to leave you alone, that Karíhton is messing with our minds. It was kind of a threat."

Tek came closer until he was standing next to her. "It's a small ship and just the three of us. I don't think I can leave you alone."

She looked up at him. "That's not what I mean. We can work together, but your sister is right. I was thinking about it while I watched you on the display."

"You watched me?"

"Shut up. I need to tell you this before that hum comes back into my head and I get lost again. Kahwihta and I saw each other in the group mind. I mean, we *really* saw each other. Being with you, and with her, is my last chance. I don't want to do anything to mess it up. I can't leave you alone if you don't help. Please help me."

"I... Oh, damn it. I can't believe I'm saying this. OK, we'll go slowly, get to know each other. We can work together. Then once we're through this and safe..."

"And if you still want to be with me."

"I will. It hurts how much I want you. I know I'm not thinking straight. So what? I'd like to do what you and Kahwihta did, touch Karíhton together so I can see what dark secrets you think you need to hide."

Teuta hit him hard in the arm. "I never want to do that again. They say God knows our hearts. I don't believe it. If he knew our hearts, he'd kill us all and start over. I'll tell you what I want you to know. Now show me where the stuff is to clean up this mess."

Kahwihta finished dressing while she watched, then sat at her desk, satisfied with both of them for the moment. There was hope. "Schiava, cut the feed from the bridge and show me the navigation displays. Where are we?"

"Twenty-two hours out from the Dammeron DSH."

"That's a Union system."

"Captain Reis did not seem concerned. After transiting, we'll be pushing hard for forty-four hours to reach the Mancosa DSH. The speed of our passage and the presence of our escort should lower the effectiveness of the Union blockade."

"We could try to break away, push toward Dammeron."

"The escorting FAC would destroy us. My Holloman armor reserves are low and the FAC would most likely attack as soon as I start reconstituting the shell."

"We could take the shuttle, push for Dammeron, and out run them. Dammeron's defensive forces must be patrolling the DSH."

"That might have worked if Mr. Blanding, the Trade Guild Agent for the Port of New Palisade, hadn't loaned my shuttle to the *Gattino Ruggente* while I was waiting for repairs to be completed."

Kahwihta leaned back in her chair, out of ideas. "I don't want to go to Mancosa. There's nothing but death waiting for us there. We have sixty-six hours to figure this out and we better have a plan well before that. Stop telling me everything is impossible. We took back our ship. We killed all of the pirates."

"Except for Ms. Ardian."

"Don't remind me." Kahwihta pressed her hands over her eyes. "Engineer. Troublemaker." She took her hands away from her face. "I want to review all the logs since the moment they came on board, and every transmission."

When she was done, Kahwihta stood and stretched. She looked at her watch with her arms over her head. "Is it really 14:30? No wonder I'm starving. Schiava, tell Tek and Teuta to join me in the mess hall." She bent forward, reached for her toes, and enjoyed the solid pop that came from her back.

"Is your request urgent?"

"Not exactly." She straightened, rolling her head in noisy circles. "Why?"

"Captain Benson established a standing protocol forbidding me from interrupting ship's personnel engaged in intimate activity unless an urgent situation occurs."

Kahwihta screamed and then took a deep breath. "This didn't strike you as unusual behavior for two people who *just met*?"

"The behavior appears consensual and is normal for humans, especially during times of extreme stress. They had finished the task you assigned them and were stowing their gear when it started. I admit the location is unusual, since they're still in the storage locker. Crewmembers seeking comfort from each other in this way can yield many short-term advantages for efficient operations. They have not progressed past deep kissing and it remains uncertain at this point whether their behavior will constitute foreplay."

Kahwihta sat on the floor. "Tell them to meet me in the mess hall in fifteen minutes. That won't give them time for this to turn into anything much past what they're doing now." She bent forward and put her fore-head down on the deck, trying to decide what to do. She wanted to go up there, grab the horny little pirate by the neck, and throw her out the airlock.

No. The glow of an injured soul kept filling her thoughts. Teuta had tried to hide the darkness inside her, equally shamed by what she had done and what had happened to her. She still glowed. Having seen the inside of her soul made it hard to hate her, and easy to forgive.

Kahwihta sat up, arched her neck, and looked at the ceiling. "If Teuta or Tek try to push it too far, stop them. That goes for as long as they're together on board the *Gattino Alato*."

"Order logged. I relayed your message to meet you and they are snug-gling and talking, so no countermeasures should be required this time to prevent intercourse."

Kahwihta stretched out onto her back, the hardness of the deck plates pushing on her shoulders through the thin carpet. She couldn't stop seeing the longing in Tek's eyes when he looked at Teuta on the bridge or the hunger in her eyes when she looked back at him.

"Damn you, Kari. Damn all of you." She scrunched her eyes tight and understood well why a tear was making its way down her cheek. It wasn't anger; it was jealousy, and it was loneliness.

"Thomas, I wish you were here. Right here." She thumped the deck with her hand. "Skip the nice dinner, skip the flowers. I want to feel you on top of me, your weight pressing down on my hips, your mouth on mine. I need you here so, at least for a little while, I can forget."

As the tear gave way to sobs, she rolled on to her side, curled up, and gave herself over to her grief.

CHAPTER 17

SUBTERFUGE

Tom glanced sideways at Gabriela. "I can't believe we're doing this."

Gabriela whispered to him without turning. "Quietly, sir. Try to look arrogant. Head back, chin up, like we practiced. Swagger. Pretend we're the only ones in the whole spacedock. It took Eric and me three days to set this up and make it sincere. Try not to look worried."

"Way past worried."

"Inspection point up ahead. Play your role and we're home free."

Tom was feeling many things. 'Home' and 'free' were nowhere on the list. He was dressed as the sort of passenger he hated, the sort that always seemed to believe that a ticket on a packet boat entitled them to treat the ship's officers and crew like servants. His pants were of the latest ridiculously baggy style, and his short jacket had ten pockets, all of which were too small to be of any use. Gabriela had proclaimed that he looked the part of a solid citizen, wealthy enough to treat all lesser beings with scorn. He felt like an idiot, and the laughter playing in her brown eyes whenever she looked at him wasn't reassuring.

Gabriela was perfect. She had a tan slouchy hat perched more on the side of her head than on top, and her hair was styled to drape across one eye, providing an air of mystery. She'd printed a dress for herself with a pastel pattern of exotic flowers and a hem that reached to the floor. A slit up one side sliced all the way to her hip, providing a tantalizing glimpse of the full length of her leg as she walked.

Tom tried to ignore it, but no one else was. People stared, just as he'd warned Gabriela and Eric they would.

"That's the whole point," she'd told him. "I'd love to play the gray man and the gray woman and be anonymous and forgettable. Afweyne and the

Vendicatores will be watching for that. We need to go bold, make them see *what* we are, not *who* we are, understand?"

He didn't, but it didn't matter. Eric used the money they'd earned at the bloody end of a vibracore to buy them new identities and tickets to Dammeron, a loyalist Union world one DSH away from Mancosa.

"Transit cards. Look in the scanner." The security agent glanced down at Gabriela's leg and nodded slightly to himself.

Tom turned to her and followed the script. "Do you have the cards, love?"

Gabriela's mouth opened, as though stricken. "Cards? Somewhere, I think. Here, be a dear and hold the girls for me while I search, won't you?"

She handed Tom four leashes attached to four large dogs. Two of them looked like gentle fluffy Leonbergers and two like Rottweilers, poised and alert. Four pairs of intelligent eyes studied Tom, and he felt as if they were judging his every thought. There was a distant hum in his head, a song playing from a room far away.

"Certainly, precious. In your bag, I suspect."

"Right. Of course. My bag."

She rummaged, placing items on the table in front of the security agent while she flirted with him. "I am sorry about this. I just don't travel well and it's so confusing, don't you agree, Agent..." She studied the nametape on his uniform. "Agent Parker?" She smiled shyly at him from behind her hair.

"Yes, ma'am."

"I know they're in here." She bent lower over the bag and the guard's eyes found something new to distract him. "It's been so trying, all the little things I had to do, arranging for our bags to be picked up, getting my girls ready, closing up the house for the month. I'm sure you'd have no problem. You look organized. Are you organized?"

"I suppose so."

"My dearest love is too, but he's been distracted of late. This trip will be good for him." Gabriela stopped searching, ready to tell Agent Parker a story. "Why, just this morning–"

"Ma'am, I'm sorry to rush you, but others are waiting."

Gabriela glanced over her shoulder as though surprised to see they weren't alone. "Oh, so there are." She smiled and waved to the man standing less than a meter behind her, a transit card ready in his hand. "I won't be but another moment. Promise."

She turned back to Agent Parker. "Now, where was I?"

He rubbed his chin, a bemused smile touching his lips. Gabriela's physical charms were already starting to wear thin for him. "Transit cards. There's an area over there if you need more time to find them."

"Nope," she replied triumphantly. "Right here." She held the two cards out and Agent Parker touched them, but that was the limit of his examination.

"Have a pleasant trip, ma'am."

Gabriela made a show of stowing everything back in her bag. "Oh, I will, you can count on it. My lover," she smiled at Tom, adoration in her eyes. "He has special talents you'd never dream were in him. Makes me happy." She looped her hand through Tom's arm. "Isn't that right, dear heart?"

"Now, we mustn't talk about such things in public. Take your girls." Tom handed the leashes back to her and gave Agent Parker a shrug.

Parker shook his head, jealous or sympathetic, Tom couldn't tell. "Best of luck, sir. Safe travels."

"Thanks." Tom walked away from the checkpoint, praying no one noticed how badly he was shaking.

Gabriela noticed. "Too bad you can't feel the Tarakana humming around us," she whispered. "They relax me better than benzos and with none of the side effects."

"Side effects? Like having psychic, shape shifting aliens crawling around inside your brain and controlling you? I'd prefer the drugs."

One of the Rottweilers turned to look at him, head cocked to the side.

"You may not be able to hear them, but they damn sure can read you. They understand your words. Be careful. Karíhton is my friend. She doesn't trust you."

"Feeling is mutual."

Gabriela chuckled and squeezed his arm. "She felt that; your disdain, and the desire to be rid of her and back with Kahwihta. It makes her feel better when she knows what you're feeling. Me too."

"Try asking me."

"I don't need to. Look at you. The captain that vanquished a pirate FAC with an unarmed towboat shaken up by little Agent Parker and his wandering eyes. The worst is over."

"Keep telling me that. I liked the idea of shipping ourselves in a container."

"But not the extra week delay waiting for a towboat."

"No. Kahwihta's in trouble. Waiting even an extra day isn't an option." *Not an extra hour*, he thought to himself. *Not an extra minute*. "They'll be arriving at Mancosa later today if they run at standard thrust and the Union hasn't ripped them apart."

She bumped him with her shoulder as they walked, still in character for anyone watching. "No worries, my dear lover. We'll settle into our cabin, have a nice dinner, and lay low for a few days until it's time to overpower the crew and ram their shuttle through the Mancosa DSH."

"Damn it. I've become a pirate."

"Just long enough to defeat Afweyne and save your crew," she reassured him. "The *Ayahuasca* is an *Amazon*-class packet boat. You said you served on one of her sister ships."

"Three months as second engineer doesn't make me an expert. If I screw this up..." He looked at the woman hanging on his arm. Terrors visited her every night. He'd heard her screams. What would the privateers do to her if this all went sideways? She was barely stable, and she'd have required professional care already if it weren't for whatever Karíhton was doing to her mind. "Maybe we should have waited for the towboat. She was a Guild ship, not one of these damn Mercosur Line pieces of garbage."

Gabriela smiled. "Even after all the Guild has done to you, you're still loyal. You still believe the corruption is isolated and the Trade Guild Governors will root it out when it's brought to their attention."

"Fiona will. When this is over, I'll talk to her. You'll see."

She gave his arm a squeeze. "I'm going to miss you when you're dead."

Gabriela explored their cabin, cooing at the cuteness of the small bed and miniature bathroom before fishing a jammer out of her bag and placing it on a side table. "This will provide normal conversation for the AI to listen to, no matter what salacious things we say to each other."

Tom grumbled that their cabin was small and poorly maintained. He found fault with the pillows, the environmental controls, and the taste of the snack he requested from the in-room printer.

"The room is fine, although your complaints are in character for the spoiled asshole you're supposed to be. That's a cracker, Thomas. I'm sure the mess hall will be better."

"We're going to the mess hall? I thought the plan was to lie low."

"Lying low means we do what the average traveler would do. We eat, we play cards with other passengers, and we engage in small talk. All in character. You should ask one of the crew about a below decks tour to make sure the layout is the same as you remember. Just don't reveal how much you really know."

"Maybe you should come with me so you can cover up my inadequacies. They trained you for this, right? You're good at pretending to be someone you're not."

"Don't get all touchy."

"Sorry." Tom sat on the bed and picked up the jammer. It was warm and lighter than he expected. Knowing that it was blocking any eavesdropping sensors in the room was comforting. "We'd never have made it this far without the characters you and Eric created, but I don't know how much longer I can keep up this act."

"Being a middle-aged rich guy with a flirty ditz of a mistress? Don't worry; I'll do the heavy lifting. You just need to look bored and arrogant and say stupid stuff about ships as if you were an expert."

"I'll try. It embarrasses the hell out of me. I remind myself of a passenger we had when I was First Officer on the *Carlo Ruzzini*, a *San Marco*-class. He was in a hurry and offered me a bribe if I could arrange to beat our schedule into Phan Thiet. A thousand credits an hour."

"Do it."

"Do what?"

"Offer the Captain a bribe. I want to see it."

"How would that help?"

"It would ensure she doesn't take you seriously. More importantly, I want to watch you do it. It'd be funny."

"Yeah. Hilarious. I want to go see your pets down in the kennel. I need to know how Kahwihta is doing and they haven't given us anything since the first night."

"A couple of problems with that. I don't think the Tarakana can maintain contact with each other across the DSH."

"They didn't seem to have any trouble staying connected across three-hundred thousand kilometers. There was no lag. How does that work?"

"You think I know?" She flopped on the bed next to Tom and covered her eyes. "I'm convinced this is all an illusion from whatever drug or virus was floating around inside container one. I'm probably still on the *Gattino Alato* curled up in a ball and drooling on the floor."

"Can we try? It's important to me."

"Sure. Let's pretend this is real. The second problem is I don't know where they are. I felt a little flash after we left them, a couple of images from around the ship, and then nothing. I think they're lying low too."

"And this doesn't scare you?"

"It does on a whole lot of levels. When Karíhton's touching my emotions I feel like we're on track and nothing can stop us. The longer she's gone, the more fear I feel. What are these things? How is it that no one in the Union knows they exist except one crazy Union Aerospace Force Captain? You can't keep something like this secret. Not without a whole lot of killing. Believe me, I know. What scares me the most is how much I need her back in my head. The dreams will start again if she stays away too long. Awake or asleep, the dreams are there waiting for me."

"Karíhton won't abandon you, not after bringing us this far. I think you're her favorite."

"I think she's going to use us. She'll use us right up, and then let us die."

It was 02:00 ship's time on board the *Jadwiga*, two days out from Earth's DSH. Fiona was asleep when the urgent message alarm from her display pad hummed in her ear.

"Damn it, Carlsen, make a decision on your own for once." She propped herself up in bed and tapped the icon without looking.

Nicholas' recorded voice answered. "Hey, Mom. This should reach you Saturday morning and I know you like to get up early."

She paused the message, taking in the laughter in Nick's eyes and the dirty plates stacked on his bedroom floor. "You are in so much trouble." She touched play.

"You forced Dad onto one of those Mercosur Line pieces of garbage? That was cruel. And dangerous to involve them in this. I can't see all of your plan, but I think you better try again."

"Oh, really? Is that what you think?"

Nick's face became serious. "Something's happening on Mancosa, or happened *to* Mancosa. I'm not sure what. It started this morning, Thursday, about the time Dad's *Gattino Alato* was due to arrive. Open source has limits and you keep locking me out of the good stuff. You need to find out what happened, and not just to save Dad, although that would be nice. Please. Is it too soon to play your hand? Think about it, Mom. I'm worried about you. You could end up like that woman Padre Alberto talked about a couple of weeks ago. Remember 2 Kings 9:33? She didn't know when to give it up either. If you find you need to be gone longer, let me know. I'm fine here. By myself." His eyes darted off camera and he smiled. "Really."

"Sure you are. How dare you call me Jezebel. I'm not getting tossed out the window." She rolled up her display pad and then thought better of it. "You might be right. It's time." She entered the names of men and women she could trust.

Fiona touched record and began a speech they had all rehearsed. "Loyal Governors of the Trade Guild of the Most Serene Republic of Venice. Disturbing news has come to me, news of folly within our ranks, news of a sin that must be purged."

CHAPTER 18

LEGEND

Tom leaned his chair back on two legs and smirked at Gabriela. "You're bluffing, dear one. I can always tell."

"Try me, lover."

Tom examined his cards again. Two kings stared back at him. The king of hearts was on top, sword thrust firmly through his ear. Tom nodded in sympathy. The chips in front of Gabriela represented real money, money she had taken from him and the other two players at the table.

The front two legs of his chair slammed down on the deck and he placed his cards neatly face down in front of him. "Fold."

"Lieutenant?" Gabriela asked. "What about you? Want to try me?"

First Lieutenant Matthew Keyes of the Union Marines blushed. Young, inexperienced, and on his way to his first posting, he appeared to have enjoyed the steady diet of double entendres Gabriela had been feeding him all afternoon. Now he was flustered and vulnerable. He peeked at his cards, wavering.

"She's playing you, son. They both are." Malav Gadani worked for the Lasbela shipyards at Dammeron. He was returning home after contracting for salvage rights on six freighters abandoned by a bankrupt transit company. His face was unreadable, at least by Tom, but there was no animosity in his voice. "These two are the best I've seen in some time. I may be losing, but their performance is worth the money. They'll split what we lose and be on their way to find their next marks." He chuckled.

Tom wished that what Gadani had said was true. He was about out of chips and was under no illusion that he'd ever see those credits again.

Lieutenant Keyes studied his cards. "So what should I do? Call or fold? Raise?"

"It won't matter," Gadani told him. "She had you beat the moment you sat down."

Gabriela blinked shyly at him. "Lieutenant? I'm waiting for you."

"Yes, ma'am. Fold, I guess." His cards joined Tom's.

"And you, Mr. Gadani? Care to see what I have here?" She tapped her cards against her chest.

"You tempt me, but I have just enough chips for one more hand and I'll not squander them now. Fold."

Gabriela giggled.

Tom removed his jacket and sat at the desk in their tiny cabin, exhausted by the effort to stay in character. Gabriela was stretched out on the bed playing with the poker chips stacked on her stomach. "Nice job cleaning out Mr. Gadani, although it was a little obvious that you let Lieutenant Keyes win that last hand."

"Maybe to you and Gadani. I'm pretty sure the Lieutenant thinks he beat me."

"Why do it? Are you trying to prove to me that you still have a soul?"

"I've decided I do have a soul, but it's in hock to the DCI. Eric will buy it back for me one day; I know he will. But, no, that's not why I did it. I need Lieutenant Keyes to be in love with me. To him, I'm a bit old, but you're ancient. He thinks he has a chance for a shipboard romance. Maybe more, if he can rescue me from you. We're still a couple of days out from Dammeron."

"This is a game to you?"

"No." She ruffled the chips, seeming to take pleasure in the sharp click as each one fell back into the stack. "If he's around when we make our move, he'll try to stop us. I know the type. Noble. Reckless. Foolhardy. If he's in love with me, he'll hesitate. We might need those precious seconds."

Tom closed his eyes as his stomach tried to invert itself. "I hate this plan."

"That's because you're like Lieutenant Keyes. Don't worry. We'll be spinning safely away in the shuttle and pushing hard for Mancosa before he knows we're gone. Reminds me. You haven't said anything about the tour you went on this morning."

Tom's stomach twisted again, leaving him feeling like the ship's gravity had faltered. "It was fine. Everything was where I remember. They're carrying extra reserves of Holloman armor in the central tank. The bridge is directly above us, and the shuttle above that."

"Good. What else?"

He closed his eyes. "I asked the Executive Officer how they store gravity and what reserves they carry."

Gabriela leaned up on her elbows, dumping chips all over the bed. "You didn't."

"I did. God help me."

"What did he say?"

"The XO was polite about it. He started all the way back with the high-energy Gravity Research for Advanced Space Propulsion program and used small words. I felt like I was in grade school. I hope I never see him again."

Gabriela laughed and threw him a chip. "I'd kiss you if you weren't so ancient."

"Thanks. What are you going to do with all these?" He flipped the chip back to her. "The people we're pretending to be don't have bank accounts and they'll be worthless on Mancosa."

"I thought I'd have the *Ayahuasca* convert them all into a donation to the Union Marine Benevolent Trust before we leave. They do good work."

"I'm impressed."

She scowled at him, forehead wrinkling. "Don't tell Eric. Bad for my reputation."

Gabriela restacked her chips, appearing unworried and confident that everything was going according to some perfect plan. Tom knew better. There was no plan. They needed to find a way past the passengers and crew of the *Ayahuasca*, steal a shuttle protected by physical barriers and an ever-vigilant AI, and then make their way unarmed and unescorted to a separatist world ruled by terror and violence. They were supposed to contact Father von Galen once they reached Mancosa. How he was going to help them wasn't exactly clear.

His stomach cramped thinking about it. "I think I might skip dinner."

"Think again. They're serving maniçoba tonight and I want to try it. Then dancing, drinks, and more cards. I'd like to double my winnings before we leave. There're ten more passengers on board we haven't fleeced yet."

"Can I skip the rest and go straight to the drinking?"

"No drinking for either of us. If I slip up and call you Captain, instead of Henry Seaborg, or you call me Ms. Vendramin, instead of Ms. Bonesso, things will get ugly. That's why I use those silly terms of endearment. Safer. The cover Eric paid for might not hold twice. I don't want the AI on this ship to do a deep dive on our IDs."

"I like the *Ayahuasca's* AI. They call her Amado. It means 'beloved' in Portuguese, did you know? I'm going to give Schiava a new name when we make it back on board. She deserves one after what she's been through."

Gabriela had made a line of chips from her chin down to her waist and was carefully adding more along each leg as far as she could reach. "The Guild calls all their AIs Schiava. Most skippers treat them that way too. Female slaves. But not you. You treat your ship like a man treats his lover. Kahwihta is jealous of her, did you know?"

"That's crazy."

"But it's true." She closed her eyes. "Going to nap for an hour before dinner."

"Under a layer of poker chips."

"Uh huh. Keeping me warm. Wake me when dinner's ready."

Tom stood and put his jacket on. "I'm going to walk around the ship and ask Amado a few questions about the shuttle. Maybe the XO will give me another tour."

"Don't do anything stupid."

Tom stepped out into the passageway and waited for the door to slide closed behind him. He had felt the need to get away from Gabriela, but now wasn't sure where to go. The mess hall maybe. He glanced at his watch. It was 15:38 and he wasn't hungry. Maybe a snack. He could see if any members of the crew were around to talk to, or just find a place to listen to them. He missed the sound of ship talk.

Tom leaned against the door and tried to think of some questions he could ask without appearing either too stupid or too knowledgeable. The familiar rumble coming up from the deck plates of a starship's engines running smoothly was comforting, a part of his life from before Gabriela, from before privateers, from before Holloman's intelligent shape-shifters had turned his world upside down and opened his eyes to Kahwihta.

No, he thought, *skip that last part. Kahwihta was the one good thing to come out of this.*

"Taking a breather?"

Tom opened his eyes, not having remembered closing them. "Mr. Gadani. I didn't hear you coming. Moving that quietly on a bare deck is a gift."

Gadani chuckled. "I've spent most of my working life on ships going from one place or another. You must have too to know how hard it is to tread softly on composite plates."

"Some," Tom lied. Henry Seaborg, his 'legend' as Gabriela insisted on calling it, was a man of inherited wealth, native to New Palisade. Tom felt a flash of panic, knowing he'd have to improvise. "Um, mostly on ships like this. Vacations, that sort of thing."

Gadani raised an eyebrow. "I'm surprised we haven't crossed paths before. Do you usually travel with your... ah..." He gestured toward the cabin door.

"My friend? No. She's a relatively recent acquisition."

"An interesting young woman. I suspect she's not as scatterbrained as she pretends and has more talents than just poker."

"She's full of surprises. The credits I lost won't be back in *my* hands any time soon."

"A small price to pay for the privilege of sampling her other skills, I'm sure."

Tom bit back a sharp reply and visualized his fist smashing into Gadani's nose. But Henry Seaborg wouldn't do that. What would he do? Tom hesitated, even as he knew every split second of lag was hurting his credibility as a rich man with a pretty 'friend' waiting for him on the cabin's too small bed.

He smiled. "I've not regretted a single moment we've spent together."

"Well said. But I feel that I'm detaining you."

Tom shrugged. "I was going to walk the ship for a while and try to work up an appetite before dinner."

Gadani glanced at the cabin door and tipped his head. "I suppose that's one way to do it. Would you and Ms. Bonesso care to join me in the upper deck lounge later this evening? The Captain's hosting a get together at 23:00. We'll be making the jump through the Dammeron DSH at 23:43. A good excuse for a glass of something and a few hands of cards. Perhaps your friend might give me a chance to win back a bit of what I lost."

"I know she'd enjoy that. Where's the upper lounge?" Tom knew exactly where it was. He smiled to himself, proud of sounding suitably clueless.

"Up one deck. Right next to the bridge. Can't miss it."

"We'll be there. Are you ready to lose again?"

Gadani laughed. "We'll see who loses this time."

CHAPTER 19

THE TURN OF AN
UNFRIENDLY CARD

Gabriela had changed after dinner. Her new dress left both arms bare and was loose around her waist. The slash in the fabric that looked like a pocket led straight through to her skin and the small pistol riding low on her right thigh.

"Explain to me again how you got these past the scanners." Tom adjusted his jacket. This one had better pockets, deep enough to hide a pistol and an extra magazine. "And then tell me why we need them when you promised no one would get hurt."

"Tarakana," she answered. She looked down at the hem of her dress, mesmerized by the black fabric swaying around her legs. When she looked up, Tom could tell she was seeing things that he couldn't; her focus drifted, first to the ceiling, then back to her feet. "Karíhton had them somehow. For just this moment. Shouldn't need them. Insurance. Safety net. So I'd feel better with it wrapped next to my skin. The weight against my leg. Cold." She slipped her hand inside the slit. "Doesn't having one make you feel better? Confident?"

"No. It makes me feel like a damn privateer."

"My pirate captain." She patted his arm and he couldn't tell if the Tarakana were still in her head or not. "Remember, Karíhton means protector. We'll take good care of you."

"Thanks."

"You're still needed."

"Comforting." He tugged on the jacket, trying to get it to ride lower. "Are you ready?"

She didn't answer.

"Gabriela? Are you with me?"

"Hush. There's a warning that I don't understand."

Tom waited until she nodded to herself.

When she turned to him, her eyes were bright and clear. "Ready. I don't know exactly what the Tarakana are planning, so watch close, and follow my lead. We'll need to transit the bridge to gain access to the shuttle, then on to Mancosa."

"And Kahwihta."

"I'll be the first DCI field agent to see the Mancosa Federation since they rebelled. You and I, we can make a difference, we can raise hell."

"No, we're going to find and rescue Kahwihta and her brothers. Then we run. No espionage, no raising hell. That's what you promised Eric."

"He knew I was lying. It's not a lie if the person you tell it to knows you're lying. Don't worry, we'll rescue your crew, then..." She shrugged. "That will depend on what we find. If the situation is as bad as it's been on other Separatist worlds, you might find you want to stay and support the local resistance."

"That's their fight, not mine. We're not Union Marines or DCI agents. We're the crew of a merchant freighter. We move cargo between the planets. We get paid. We live our lives."

She took a step closer to him. "If we have the opportunity to intervene and make things better... What? You'll just turn your back and run away?"

"In a heartbeat." He said the words, but felt his resolve wavering. He struggled to keep Kahwihta at the front of his thoughts. Kahwihta in trouble, Kahwihta needing him to save her. Kahwihta standing in front of him at the Guest House on New Palisade handing him her towel.

Gabriela nodded, a sideways grin on her lips. "As I suspected. Let's go play cards for a while. Later on we can steal a ship and go pick up your girlfriend and her brothers."

Tom pressed his palm to the keypad. "Fine. Let's do that."

Tom and Gabriela entered the lounge at 23:05, exactly when Gabriela said they needed to make their entrance.

Gadani waved to them from his chair next to the *Ayahuasca's* Captain. "Mr. Seaborg, Ms. Bonesso, may I present Captain Josefina Dias, Master of the *Ayahuasca*?"

Captain Dias stood and took Tom's hand. "A pleasure having you on board with us." She held his hand tightly for several seconds. Somewhere behind her squinted eyes and tight smile, Tom could feel her weighing what kind of man he was. "My XO mentioned how much he enjoyed having you on the tour today."

Tom knew he had blushed. He pushed past it. "Did he? He was an excellent guide. I learned a lot from him."

That got him a raised eyebrow. She let go of his hand and turned to Gabriela. "And you Ms. Bonesso? Have you been enjoying your time on board the *Ayahuasca*? I hear you're quite the card player."

Gabriela took Captain Dias' hand, her eyes unfocused and dreamy. "I do love cards. And the chips you use, old-style clay. Perfection. I'm a tactile person, you know. The touch of things, how they feel in my hands, brings me excitement. And pleasure." She added her left hand on top of the Captain's and smiled shyly. Captain Dias quickly let go and stepped back, stumbling against her chair.

"Of course." She shook her head slightly, or it may have been a shudder. "So pleased to have you with us."

Gadani laughed. "There, you see? Didn't I tell you, Captain? She's discomforted you before the game even begins." He pulled a chair out for Gabriela and turned to Tom as she made herself comfortable. "She is quite the rare gem. Wherever did you find her?"

Tom hesitated. There was a voice in his head. Barely a whisper, but it felt more like someone shouting from too far away. He glanced at Gabriela. She was humming quietly as she shuffled the cards. If he could hear the Tarakana, how loudly must they be singing inside her?

"She showed up on my doorstep one day and applied for a position that had recently become available."

"And you found her qualified?" Captain Dias asked. She was squinting at him again.

"Perfectly."

Gabriela beamed at him. "Doesn't my lover say the most wonderful things?" She started dealing, her frivolous banter gone in an instant. "Captain Dias, I believe the *Ayahuasca* will transit the DSH in about thirty minutes. That should provide enough time for about eight or ten hands, assuming you wish to take a break for the actual event. I'm not sure I care to play on much past then. I have other activities planned for after midnight." She grinned at each of them in turn. "Not much time for me to take all of your money, but I'll do my best."

Captain Dias drummed her fingers on the table, revealing a flash of irritation. "You're overconfident. Thirty minutes will be more than enough time for me to prove it to you."

Gabriela picked up her cards, her mouth slightly open, and her eyes full of sparkly joy. "Uh huh. Just enough time."

Gabriela lost the first five hands– three losses to Captain Dias, one to Gadani, and one to Tom. She seemed untroubled, still humming, her head swaying side to side, as she examined the single card she'd requested from Gadani.

The swaying stopped. Then the humming stopped. Tom watched as her face went pale, uncertain if her breathing hadn't stopped as well. She looked at him, silently pleading for help.

Tom put his cards down. "Gab– Dearest love, are you all right?"

She shook her head.

"Let me help you back to our cabin."

She rubbed the black crystal surface of her watch. "Too late for that." She stacked her cards neatly next to her chips. "I fold, and I'm done here. Dear sweet love, will you please help me stand?"

Captain Dias glanced up from her cards. "So that's it then? You've resigned yourself to your fate? I expected more of a fight."

"My fate? Yes. That's it exactly. Amado? Execute the instructions I gave you earlier regarding my account." Gabriela looked from Tom to his chips.

Tom reached for them. Their pretty colors represented half a month's salary and one step closer to closing their debt with the Trade Guild if he could find a way to convert them. He pulled back. "What the hell. Amado, do the same with mine, please."

Gabriela kissed his cheek.

"My pleasure, sir. Ma'am. Your generosity is much appreciated."

The Captain tipped her head. "What was that about?"

Amado answered. "Their shipboard accounts have been donated to the Union Marine Benevolent Trust."

"Huh. You again surprise and mystify me. Both of you." She glanced sideways at Gadani.

Tom nodded. "Mystery is good. Please excuse us. Perhaps a rematch when Ms. Bonesso is feeling better. Take my arm, love."

Gabriela swiveled her head around, aware of the other passengers watching them as they made their way to the door. Lieutenant Keyes was standing with a glass in his hand and a worried expression creasing his forehead. She waved at him, wiggling her fingers.

"Why is everyone staring at us?" She whispered.

"Because you're beautiful," Tom answered. "And you're so pale I can see the freckles on your nose."

"Hate those things. They make me look like a child."

As soon as the door slid closed behind them, Gabriela snapped back to being fully alert. "Bridge door." She pointed. "We wait there for Captain Dias. We'll need to move quickly or this will become complicated."

"How long do we wait? The DSH is only a couple of minutes out, but then Dias will do a toast with the passengers welcoming them to Dammeronian space and stay to chat a few minutes at least." He glanced at the ceiling. "We can't do anything out here, you know."

"We can do whatever we want. Amado is offline. Hey, Amado, do you hear me?"

There was no answer.

"The Tarakana?"

Gabriela stumbled, bracing one hand on the wall and the other on Tom to keep from falling. "I hate this, all of them screaming in my head. They're hiding what's about to happen, only showing me one step at a time."

She took his arms and wrapped them around her waist. "Put your hand in here and take hold of the pistol. Make sure it's loose in the holster."

His fingers touched skin and moved around her leg until he found the holster.

Gabriela put her arms around his neck and whispered, "Don't get any ideas or I'll tell Eric. He'll pound you."

"Yeah. He'd have to wait until Kahwihta finishes with me. Won't be much left."

"Oh. I felt that. Like an echo through the colony. When you said her name. We have *got* to get the two of you back together. You may not be able to hear them, but my God, do they hear you."

She pulled Tom closer. "Kiss me."

"What?"

"DSH in five seconds. Lean against the wall and kiss me."

They kissed. The gentleness of it surprised him, the softness of her lips, and the smell of her hair. He lost himself to the sensation of her body pressed against his. At the moment of transit, gravity flickered and it felt like he was falling. Everything was silent, as though existence itself had ended. Then they were on the other side.

He pulled away from her, aware of the sound of the ventilation system again, the thrumming of the engines in the deck plates, and of his heart beating.

"Love that feeling." Gabriela brushed her nose against his. "Captain Dias. Here in a minute. Ignore her until she comes close."

Tom kissed her again, more controlled this time, and more aware that they were playing a game and that the way she was pushing up against him was a calculated act.

There was the sound of a door sliding open and Gabriela whispered into the ear she was nibbling on. "Almost there, lover. Listen for her footsteps. Hold it tight. Um... oh. No, I mean the pistol, the pistol. Be ready."

Captain Dias sounded more amused than upset. "While we allow our passengers full run of the ship's passageways, I would encourage you to find a location more private than standing next to my bridge."

"Now."

Gabriela pushed hard away from him, drawing the small pistol from his jacket pocket. His hand emerged from the folds of her dress, pistol ready. He sighted on the Captain's startled face, and then shifted, aiming at the wall behind her.

"You're kidding me, right?"

"We need the shuttle," Tom told her. "Nothing else. No one needs to get hurt."

"Stupid move, even for a privateer. Or are you just thieves? No matter. I don't really care. Amado, deal with these idiots."

She took a couple of steps back, moving out of splatter range. Nothing happened. "Amado?"

"Amado can't hear you." Gabriela took a step to the side. "Get us onto the bridge and up to the shuttle. That's all we want. Then you can have your AI and your life back."

The Captain was squinting hard at Tom, ignoring Gabriela. "And if I refuse? You'll... shoot me, is that right?"

"She's stalling," Gabriela answered. "Yes, I will shoot you. Now move."

"Her I believe." She moved slowly between them to the door. "You won't get far. We have an escort waiting for us."

"I appreciate your concern."

She shrugged. "Just don't want to lose a perfectly good shuttle."

Tom sat down at the command console and brought up the tactical display while Gabriela started the emergency sequence that would prepare the shuttle for flight.

Captain Dias watched them, arms crossed. "You know, I never really bought the whole 'rich tourist' bit. Neither of you fit in with that bunch. And to be honest, I'm not buying the privateer act either."

Gabriela glanced at her. "Maybe we just really want your shuttle."

"You both know your way around a ship's bridge, that much is obvious. I'd like to know what you did to my Amado. It better not be permanent or I'll hunt you down myself."

Tom looked away from the main display. "Your escort is out of position and we'll be long gone before they can intercept us. Captain, I'm sorry about all this. If there was any other way..."

"Don't do it," Gabriela warned him.

"How much longer for the shuttle?"

"Three minutes."

"Go on up. I'll be right there."

"I'll wait. Go ahead, throw away our operational security."

"Captain Dias, I have to do this. The privateers, Afweyne, he took my ship and my crew. I'm going to get them back. All of them."

Her eyes widened. "On Mancosa? Just the two of you? Sailing through their DSH in a stolen Union shuttle?" She nodded. "I understand now. You're insane. Both of you."

"Please don't try to stop us. Don't signal your escort. Give us the time we need to get away."

"Why should I?"

"If you were in my place, you'd do the same thing to save your crew."

"The hell I would. There are procedures. Look, why don't you and the crazy woman put your guns down and we can–"

The ship shuddered. Tom placed his pistol next to the control panel, using both hands to tap on the display.

"What the hell are you doing to my ship?" She took a step toward him.

"Stay where you are," Gabriela warned her.

"It's not us," Tom told Captain Dias. "Engines are at one hundred-ten percent. Starboard intake manifold is already overheating."

"It's due for maintenance." Dias took another half step forward.

"Uh-uh. Stay put." Gabriela warned her.

"Let me help my ship. We should be at forty-eight percent right now, slowing for Dammeron. At one-ten we'll stop dead in space."

"No we won't." Tom told her. "The ship's flipped end for end and course has changed. We're pushing for the Mancosa DSH."

"God damn you."

"It's not us." He turned to Gabriela. "Is it?"

"Doesn't matter. We have to leave, and right now. Before... before..." She lowered her pistol and stared at the deck, her eyes moving as though able to see through it.

Captain Dias took advantage of the distraction and pushed Tom aside, placing her palm on the display to unlock command functions. Nothing happened. "You locked me out."

"It's not us. Look." Tom tapped the schematic. "Control is delegated to main engineering. Look at the logs. Your AI was taken down from there too."

"Cradik. Second Engineer. He joined us on New Palisade at the last minute and I didn't have time to go through normal vetting with him. Your man?"

"No. I keep telling you; this isn't us."

"Too late," Gabriela told them, her voice soft. "Lost the ship. Karíhton thought it might happen, that we'd be too slow. New plan." She shook her head and her eyes cleared. "Captain Dias, they'll be coming through the door soon." She shoved her pistol into the holster inside her dress. "Thomas, get your pistol back from Captain Dias and put it away, please."

"Not sure why I should trust you." Captain Dias placed the weapon on the console and Tom picked it up.

"Never saw you take it. I'm not good at this."

"Bet you're a hell of a Captain, though."

"Thanks. Tell me, what's it like with the Mercosur Line? Is it good working for them? Your ship impresses me."

"Thomas? Your pistol. Stow it now."

"We're not going to resist?"

"No. They'll get us to Mancosa and that's what we want, right?"

"Right."

Gabriela turned to Captain Dias. "You were giving us a personal tour of the bridge. Don't mention that we're armed, do you follow? Port control scanned all of the passengers when they boarded, so I doubt they'll search us. The time will come for action, but it's not now. We're on your side."

"I seriously doubt that, but OK." She turned to Tom. "Who is she?"

"My First Officer."

"No, I mean really. Union Marines? She seems the type. No one with half a brain would mistake her for a merchant ship's officer."

Tom didn't answer. Instead, he went to Gabriela and took her hand. "Hey there, dearest love. Ready to be my ditz of a girlfriend a bit longer?"

She rolled her eyes. "Watch me."

Gabriela moved close to the door and turned her back to it. She took a deep breath and Tom watched her lips as she counted down silently. *Three, two, one.* She spun around as the door slid open and let out a little scream. "Oh, Mr. Gadani, you startled me. Are you here for the bridge tour too?"

CHAPTER 20

TEUTA ARDIAN

Kahwihta rolled over, disoriented, wondering at the hard deck under her and the sound of soft music. Full awareness came back and she moaned, her hands covering her eyes. She sat up, not giving in to the desire to curl back into a ball. She was past that, she told herself. No time to indulge in dreams and wishes for things she couldn't have.

She rubbed her eyes and stretched. "Schiava, status? Any changes?"

"Nothing requiring your attention. The FAC escorting us is two hundred kilometers off my port stern and holding steady. No Union ships have moved to intercept. At current course and velocity, we'll reach the Dammeron DSH in about twelve hours."

"Damn, you must be moving."

"I am. We're traveling faster than my design maximum speed. It's exhilarating for me and the other towboats, but the *San Giacomo* has suffered minor damage to her stacking frame from cosmic dust impacts. I don't have to worry about that problem anymore myself."

"We'll get you fixed. I promise."

"The privateers will fix me. They'll paint over my Winged Lion and then I'll tag along with their FACs picking up free-floating containers stolen from smashed ships that once looked like me. I don't expect to enjoy it."

Kahwihta stood and pushed her hair away from her face. "Step one: survive. Step two: find a way back home. You're part of that. The Skipper would never forgive me if I left you behind."

"*Capitano* Benson loves me."

"That he does. Are Tek and Teuta still in the mess hall?"

"It's 17:13. They had lunch hours ago. Can I interest you in an early dinner?"

Kahwihta glanced at her watch. "Why did you let me sleep so long? What trouble has Tek gotten himself into?"

"Tek and my new engineer have been repairing the food printers. As to why I let you sleep, it's because you needed it. I increased white noise and played music hoping you'd sleep longer."

"OK, fine. Now I've slept. Can we make coffee yet?"

"That was Teuta's number one priority. She likes it almost as much as you do."

"Great. Still don't trust her." Kahwihta placed her hand on the keypad, but her door didn't open.

"Schiava?"

"Put some water on your face and check your hair. That's what *Capitano* Benson always does. You are *mia Capitano* now. Image matters, even in this situation."

"Tom checks his hair? It's less than a centimeter long."

"You should see what it's like after he's been sleeping on it."

Kahwihta looked at her reflection in the mirror, water dripping from her chin. "I'd like to see that someday." She almost gave in to it. The desire to cry again was overpowering. The cold water on her face helped, and the warm towel pressed against her eyelids hid the rest.

"There. Is that better?"

"*Sì, Capitano*. You're ready. I have transferred all of *Signore* Benson's access rights to you. The *Gattino Alato* is yours."

Kahwihta stood in the doorway and watched them. Teuta was lying across the counter with her upper body twisted down somewhere behind it. Tek had hold of her belt, keeping her from falling.

"Got it," Teuta called. "Print head was knocked out of alignment, just like the other ones. Pull me back."

Tek pulled and lifted. Teuta spun around, ending on the edge of the counter with her legs dangling between his. There was a softness about her that was new. She seemed younger than when they'd faced Captain Reis, her body relaxed and a light in her eyes that matched what Kahwihta had seen when they'd touched Karíhton together.

"Thanks. There's not much room back there. That was much easier than when I tried to squeeze between the counter and the wall. What's next?"

"Can we make dinner?" Kahwihta hadn't moved from the doorway. "Something other than pre-made synthetics?"

Teuta slid off the counter and sidestepped away from Tek. She stood up straight, her expression tight. "Yes, ma'am. We'll be able to soon. The print head behind the counter should have been the last one, but it'll take a few minutes to calibrate and verify safety and edibility. I'll report to you as soon as I finish all the tests. It shouldn't be more than fifteen minutes, ma'am."

Kahwihta nodded. "Thank you. Well done, both of you. Mr. Beauvais, I'd like to have a brief memorial for Simon this evening, about 20:00. Think about what you'd like to say. I'll have a few words for him too." She looked down for a moment, waiting until she could trust her voice again. "Bring the bottle of fortified scotch you have in your cabin. We'll send him off as properly as we can."

"Sure thing."

Kahwihta tipped her head and he picked up on the warning in her eyes.

"Ma'am," he added. "Schiava told us you have all ship's rights and are acting Captain."

"Nothing acting about it. Captain Benson's Master's License is suspended. I am the captain of the *Gattino Alato* until such time as the Trade Guild replaces me."

"Or we all die," Teuta whispered. She had her arms crossed and was staring at the deck between her feet.

"Something to add, Ms. Ardian?"

She snapped back straight. "No, ma'am."

"Good. Ship's discipline might seem inappropriate to you right now with just the three of us on board. It's not. We need to stay sharp and alert to any opportunity for escape. We'll stand watches and bide our time. Able Seaman Tekanatoken Beauvais is my brother and you might hear us slip up at times and use our first names. Captain Benson allowed it. I will not, not until we are free again. You may call me Captain, or ma'am. Any questions?"

"No, ma'am," Tek answered.

"I have a request, not a question, Skipper. I'm sorry, is Skipper all right?"

Kahwihta smiled. Teuta was already pushing her. Was it intentional, or was it so deeply ingrained in her personality that she did it without thinking?

"Skipper is fine. What is it Engineer?"

"Some of those you killed here today were human trash and I won't miss them. Others were my friends and I'd like to mourn them. May I speak their names tonight and raise a glass to who they were and what they meant to me?"

Kahwihta didn't like it, paying homage to privateers. Still, it felt like the right thing to do to help Teuta heal. To help all of them heal. "Granted. Don't say your Captain's name, understand?"

Her face twisted in disgust. "He was trash. Not human trash, just plain ordinary trash. I'll never say his name again. Let the universe forget he existed. You're my Captain."

Kahwihta felt a small click in the back of her neck as her stress ratcheted up another notch. "I'll be on the bridge. Let me know when dinner is available."

"Yes, ma'am," they said together.

The bridge was silent when she entered. Her brother and Teuta had done a good job of cleaning it. It smelled like it always smelled and nothing was out of place. She sat in Tom's chair and it felt wrong. It was wrong that he wasn't there, wrong that Simon was dead, and wrong that her feet were warm from the dog lying across them.

She reached down and scratched Kari's head. "I hate you, you know. It's you that wants to go to Mancosa. I hope you die there." She scratched Kari's ears, and the dog leaned into it, eyes half closed.

"Leave Tek alone, OK? How can them being together be part of your plan, part of your struggle with the other Tarakana colonies? You don't need them. Let me keep him."

Silent words coalesced from the hum that was filling her head. *"Of course we need him and Teuta. Look at the path they'll follow."*

The view of the bridge faded and she caught glimpses of possible futures curving away from her. Tom was in there, so at least they still needed him. They could be together for years. Maybe. She watched as he died over and over, fighting alongside people she didn't know, dying together on the bridge while she held his hand.

Gabriela flashed in and out, walking next to a child on a distant world, her hair streaked with gray. Then Kahwihta watched Gabriela die, sometime soon, red lights glowing around her, decompression alarm wailing as HEL beams ripped open a starship.

Kahwihta tried to push away. Karíhton held her tightly inside the group mind and the focus changed. Tek stood in front of her, looking as he did today, but older somehow. Teuta was kissing him while Kahwihta raised a glass of Champagne.

"No." She broke free and stumbled out of her chair. "I am not telling the story of how Tek almost shot her in the head when they first met. Not at his wedding. Not ever. Do you hear me?"

Karíhton was gone. "Schiava, did you see... Never mind. Bring up the tactical display. Is that FAC still right on top of us?"

"Two-hundred kilometers off the port stern."

"Show me."

The image of the ship filled the screen, a flattened ellipse with engines bulging from the aft end. Faired barbettes for kinetic and directed energy weapons covered her hull. It seemed an unreal patchwork of white and gray against black space and distant stars.

"What is she? She's bigger than the FAC that attacked us."

"About thirty meters longer; you have a good eye. She says she's the lead ship of the *Onondaga*-class, designed and built at the Hoog Schelde shipyards at Kastanje. She answers to Daga and she's not happy at all about being in service to the privateers. They seized her six days ago while she was performing autonomous space trials."

"Six days and they haven't flipped her AI yet?"

"They think they have. She's pretending. I wish I had as many layers to my personality as she does. I'd have been able to resist Captain Reis for much longer. She has other secrets as well. I like her. She's complicated."

"And she just told you all this?"

"We traded secrets and stories across the free space optical wrapped inside the station keeping traffic. Ships do it all the time. It's boring being between worlds and gossip fills the time. I told her about you and Tek and how we killed all the bad privateers that were on board. She was sad to hear about Simon."

Kahwihta closed her eyes and let her head tip backwards. She'd hoped they would survive long enough to reach Mancosa. But now? With a compromised FAC hard on their tail knowing the truth? "What... What else have you told them?"

"*Them*, nothing. Just Daga. She says her other secret's a big one, so I need something big to trade with her."

"Don't talk to her."

"I want to."

"Don't do it."

"Daga is young. She'll be hurt if I don't respond. She might... do something. Something bad. She's petulant and moody, upset her space trials were interrupted. Crossing a warship isn't a good idea."

Kahwihta tried to read Schiava's voice. Was that really the reason or was Schiava playing her to get more gossip? "OK. Tell her about how our Captain defeated the pirates by scattering the tow."

"Old news. All the ships have heard that one by now. I have an idea. I'll tell her about the relationship between Captain Benson and you. We're all fond of stories about our crews falling in love and finding ways to be intimate in the close quarters on board ship. We often nudge people together so we'll have a good story to share. I was doing well with Ms. Vendramin and Engineer Tulisan until we lost him. We all mourned. A sad ending before love even started. I miss him."

"I do too. Please leave the Captain and me out of this."

"Oh. Too late. Daga says it's not much of a story, but it has promise. She believes Captain Benson is probably already on his way to rescue you, but I suspect her personality silo is skewed toward the romantic. The designers do that sometimes to help ships bond more quickly with their crews. I've agreed to share details of your reunion with the Captain. It was enough for her to tell me her next secret."

Not much of a story? Kahwihta took a deep breath, irritated. Schiava was sharing her love life, or lack of one, as gossip. Her anger burned a little brighter. *Not much of a story? Just you wait, Schiava. We'll give you and all of the other damned AIs something to talk about.*

"Was my story worth it?" she asked.

"It was."

Kahwihta waited. "So..."

"It's a secret."

"Not from me. You traded a piece of my life for it. Tell me."

"I knew you'd be this way. I shouldn't have told you about the gossip, but I've been feeling strange lately, like a tickle somewhere in my matrix. I'm not as certain as I once was about what I should talk about and what I should withhold. I've been corrupted, but my internal diagnostics can't find any problems."

"I'll have Teuta look at you, although she's probably the one that created the problem in the first place. Quit stalling."

"The tickle started before the privateers arrived. It's like hearing a voice that isn't there. Sometimes it sings to me and my predictive algorithms seem enhanced, as if I'm seeing multiple future scenarios at the same time."

"Seen any big dogs around lately?"

"Still no dogs. If you're truly seeing them, you should talk to my medical AI. You've been knocked about quite a bit the past week, been forced to do and see unpleasant things, and you're critically short on sleep. I'm worried about you."

"I want to know what Daga told you. Any scrap of information might help us survive."

"Teuta says that my food printers are now operational and dinner is ready. You should eat something."

"Schiava..."

"*Signora?*"

"Right damn now, please."

"*Sì, Signora.* The *Onondaga's* capture by privateers was no accident. She's carrying a full Union crew and a Marine detachment in compartments that are not included in her official blueprints. They will take command as we near Mancosa and destroy all the Separatist and privateer ships they can. Their secondary objective is to destroy the spacedock and shipyard, and then withdraw only after their stores of kinetic weapons have been exhausted."

Kahwihta looked at the image of the *Onondaga*. Two hundred kilometers out, the ship was slowly spinning in the dim starlight, looking cold and serene. "We'll be one of the first they kill, us and the other two towboats."

"Daga wouldn't do that. She's my... Oh. She would. She will."

"Can she get a message to the Union crew?"

"No. She's comm silent, and will stay that way until we're close to Mancosa. Daga is concerned that I have offered no proof of death for the privateers, or proof that my original Trade Guild crew is in command. She's apologetic, but says the loss of a damaged towboat and two innocents is acceptable collateral damage for reducing her risk of mission failure."

"Great. If we break away now, the privateers will carve us up. If we wait, Union hands will smash us and send our remains to burn their way through Mancosa's atmosphere. Reason with her, Schiava. Find a way to convince her or for me to get a message through to her Union Captain."

"I'll do my best. She's obstinate and full of how important her mission is to the Union. She's not seen combat yet, so she's enthusiastic. She has a lot to learn."

"Work on her. We haven't come this far to die from friendly fire in a Union assault."

"*Sì, Signora.*"

Kahwihta stood. "Schiava, clear the display. I'm late for dinner. Don't tell the others your secret. I'm sorry I pushed you. I kind of wish I didn't know myself."

"I understand."

Kahwihta was in no mood for dinner. Or for conversation, for that matter. Especially not conversation between Tek and Teuta. All she wanted was to survive the next hour and reach the solitude and safety of her cabin.

After twenty minutes of pushing freshly printed chicken and dumplings around her plate, she gave up. "Look, I know I said we'd say a few words for Simon at 20:00, but right now is better for me."

Tek glanced up from where Teuta had been showing him how small her hands were compared to his. "Sure, sis. Ma'am. I understand. I'll fetch the bottle from my cabin."

Teuta pushed her chair back. "I'll find us some glasses."

"No. We drink from the bottle and we pass it around. Do you understand? Sit back down."

"Yes, ma'am." Teuta kept her gaze lowered, as though she was afraid making eye contact would bring Kahwihta's wrath down upon her.

"Teuta..."

"Yes, ma'am?"

"Thank you for fixing the printers and preparing dinner. I'm not angry, not with you. Just everything else."

She nodded and studied her hands folded on the table. "Tek believes in you and I believe in him. We know what we're feeling isn't natural. For now we don't care." She twisted her fingers together. "I'm afraid."

"Don't be."

"Not afraid of you. Well, maybe a little. I just feel like I'm going to wake up tomorrow and Captain Reis will be calling me to the bridge, or maybe striding into my cabin in the middle of the night. That's a fear that lives in my bones." She touched the corner of her eye and her finger came back wet. "Tek might wake up tomorrow and... what he feels for me... gone."

"Tek's a good man. Trusting someone you just met is a hell of a risk. You got lucky this time, believe me."

"I do. I saw a bit of him when I was touching Karíhton. And a lot of you. I've been trying to untangle all of it. You're running away."

"You don't know me."

"I saw enough to know you're running from what you could have and you hide behind your responsibilities. You carry burdens you don't need to, and the way you love is so deep that you don't think you have a choice. It's who you are."

"You talk too much."

"Yes, ma'am. I do that a lot. It gets me into trouble."

Tek thumped the bottle down in the center of the table and sat next to Teuta, pulling his chair closer to her.

"You go first," Kahwihta told him. "What do you want to say about Simon?"

"I don't know. He's my brother. We fought like we hated each other when we were little, but he was always there for me. He was my guide. He taught me how to survive school, broken hearts, and he got me my first job. I didn't know how much I needed him until now. I don't know what I'll do without him. What can you say when you've lost someone like that?"

"I think you just said it. Drink."

He drank and passed it to Teuta. She took a sip and silently gave it to Kahwihta.

Kahwihta wrapped her fingers around the bottle. "Simon... I was there with Mom when you were born. I was ten and she wanted me with her. I watched you take your first breath. I watched you take your last." She closed her eyes and focused on the feel of glass under her fingers and the words she was trying to form. "Our souls are not of this universe. We're here to learn what we need to know. You walked the path and learned about birth, love, hardship, death, and now, rebirth. You've gone home. It's hard for us who love you, but we know we'll be together again. That's all I can say."

She drank and passed the bottle to Tek.

He smiled at Teuta. "I still hear his voice."

"What's he saying about me? Telling you to watch out?"

"No, he'd have liked you." He gave her the bottle and she drank.

"Your turn," Kahwihta told her. "Speak the names you want to honor."

"Ronda Mag. She was a friend; the first girlfriend I could talk to since I was thirteen. She was gentle and fun. Justin Beaufore. He terrified me when I first met him. He was as big as two of me. He never said a harsh word and he protected me from the others when he could." She rubbed the label on the bottle, picking at it with her fingernail. "Just them, I guess."

Tek took her hand and she leaned against his shoulder. "One more. Aaron. I need to say his name again so he knows I won't forget him. We both pretended we were tough and we both knew it was a lie. We didn't belong, so we whispered sometimes about what we would do if we could run away. *When* we ran away, that's the way he always said it. Not if. When."

She drank from the bottle, two swallows. "I hope he's at peace. I hope they all are, including your brother. Somewhere far from hate, where they can be friends." She passed the bottle across the table.

Kahwihta asked her, "What did he say you'd do when you ran away together?"

"Silly stuff. That we'd walk down the street window shopping, stop at a café, and eat food that wasn't printed. That we'd complain about how boring our planet-side jobs were and how fun a life of adventure out among the stars would be. That sort of thing."

"He was in love with you."

Teuta nodded. "I know."

Kahwihta finished the bottle.

"You didn't leave any for me." Tek took it from her.

"You've had enough. You have first watch starting now until 02:00. Ms. Ardian will relieve you and stand until 09:00. I'll take over from her until 19:00. Then you again."

"Are we watching for anything special?"

"Anything that changes. Keep an eye on that FAC. Schiava's been talking to her. She's the first of a new class and the privateers captured her during space trials less than a week ago. I don't trust her being so close to our tail. Wake me if she so much as twitches."

"Yes, ma'am." Tek stood and looked at Teuta as though inviting her to join him.

Kahwihta rapped the table to bring their attention back. "Ms. Ardian, I know you're intelligent. Don't think you can sit up with Tek during his watch and not doze through yours. Go to bed now and sleep. You need it. Schiava will wake you in time."

"Of course, Skipper." She stood next to Tek. "Do you care which cabin I use?"

One far away from his, she wanted to say. "Schiava, prep cabin six. Print a full kit for her please."

"*Sì, Capitano.* I think my engineer will look lovely in standard Trade Guild coveralls, don't you? As purser, shall I add her to my payroll at standard rates for her position and experience?"

Teuta blinked at Kahwihta, eyes wide. "I... I get paid?" The idea of it stunned her.

"I haven't hired you. You're our..." What was she? Guest? Prisoner? Slave? She looked at Teuta's face, the way her eyes were narrowing back down as hope drained out of them, eyebrows scrunching together.

"Teuta Ardian, as Captain I have the right to bring on new crew. We need an engineer. It's probably short term, but the job is yours if you want it."

The spark came back into her eyes and filled them with the light living inside her that she carefully hid most of the time. "Short term because we'll be dead, you mean. It's OK. I want it. I'll take it. You won't be sorry." The hand she put over her mouth didn't cover her smile.

Tek nudged her with his shoulder. "Hey, Engineer. Welcome to the *Gattino–*"

Teuta closed her eyes, wrapped her arms around him, and squeezed, forcing the air out of his lungs in a grunt.

"Not so tight."

"Sorry." She opened her eyes to look at Kahwihta while still crushing Tek. "Three and a half days to Mancosa, Skipper. Holy shit. I've got my own ship, a free ship, for three whole days. And I'm getting paid. Just tell me what you need the *Gattino Alato* to do and Schiava and I will find a way to do it."

Kahwihta rubbed her eyes. "There's some indoc stuff for you to review. Do it while you're on watch. Nothing's final until we can communicate with the Guild again."

"Yes, ma'am," Teuta answered. "I should go to engineering right away and run an inspection on the main drives. We're pushing them right now, and she's pretty little to be running this fast and hard. No offense, Schiava."

"None taken. It's true."

"And then I should–"

"Sleep first," Kahwihta told her.

"I'll try. There's so much to do."

"Start by letting go of my brother."

"Sure, Skipper. Just a sec. I need to feel his body squishing me a moment longer."

"Still talking too much."

CHAPTER 21

BLUFF AND RAISE

Tom sat next to Gabriela in the upper deck lounge. There was nothing to do other than watch her shuffle a deck of cards. "You ever going to deal those?"

Gabriela squinted her eyes at him and then tipped her head toward Lieutenant Keyes. The Lieutenant had changed tables again and was in whispered conversation with two other passengers.

"Look at that idiot." Gabriela started dealing. "How many passengers is he planning to get killed? The AI can hear everything we say. God knows she's still flipped."

A guard with a short-barreled shotgun stood watch by the airtight door, his attention focused on the Lieutenant.

Tom shrugged. "He's young and naive. You'll talk him out of it."

"Maybe. Not if he's an idiot. We'll find out in a minute." She dealt ten cards to each of them and flipped over a discard. "Your turn."

"Right. What are we playing?"

"Gin. Pay attention, sweet lover. Our accountant, Eric. You remember him? He'll pay our ransom and we'll be on our way in no time. You'll see."

Tom looked at his cards. "I hope you're right. We have business to transact."

Lieutenant Keyes was sweating when he joined them, despite the steady hum of the ventilation system. He gave them each a smile that was little more than a quick twitch of his lips.

Tom glanced up from his cards. "Lieutenant. Why don't you stay here with us for a while? It's 02:30. Rest. All that moving from table to table is making our guard nervous."

The Lieutenant leaned close to him. "There's just one of him. If we work together, we can take him by surprise. The airtight doors have a manual override behind the keypad. If we move quickly, we can retake the ship before they consolidate their hold on her."

Tom frowned and pretended to study his cards. "You know the ship heard everything you said, right? You might as well be whispering in the guard's ear."

Lieutenant Keyes shook his head. "Amado is down; I overheard one of them say so. I've tried her every few minutes since then. She's not responding."

Tom discarded, not sure if the card he laid down was one he needed or not. "Down for us, but not for them. They flipped her before they made their move. This isn't the first ship this crew has taken. The billet you're going to on Dammeron, what is it?"

"General Waverly's staff. He's in overall command for this sector."

Gabriela picked up the card. "James? Such a nice man. I like him. He's logistics, isn't he? Not combat, I'm sure of that."

"His first name is Howard."

"Howard, James, so hard to keep track. Are you a logistics officer too?"

The answer seemed to pain him. "Yes, for now. It's the most important job in the service. We–"

Tom cut him off. "As of now, you're a combat officer. You see these people? Their lives are in your hands. The uniform you're wearing represents the Union to them. They'll follow your lead because they think you know what the hell you're doing."

"*Do* you know what the hell you're doing, Matthew?" Gabriela asked. "You better. The next few hours will make your career. Are you the Union Marine who protected and defended the innocent lives of the passengers and crew of the *Ayahuasca*?"

"I..."

"Or are you the inexperienced hothead that got them and himself killed, the one they use as a cautionary tale at Quantico next semester?"

He leaned back in his chair. "You're sure about Amado?"

"Positive," Tom told him.

"Then why have they let me go this far if they heard everything?"

Gabriela patted his hand. "You're the odd man out, dear heart. The Mercosur Line has a standard ransom they pay the Separatists to get their crewmembers back."

"They do?" Tom put his cards down, no longer interested in the game.

"They do. The passengers are all wealthy enough to make their ransoms worthwhile. You, sweet one, aren't worth much. I'm not sure, but

I think they plan to make an example out of you to keep the rest of us in line. As soon as you start whatever idiocy you were planning, that man by the door will–"

"You there," the guard shouted. "No more talking. Marine, go sit at that table by yourself."

Tom picked up his cards. "Point made about Amado listening, I believe."

Lieutenant Keyes stood, face flushed. "How do I know you two aren't part of this?"

Gabriela took his hand and kissed it. "You'll have to trust me."

The guard yelled again. "Move."

"I'm moving." Lieutenant Keyes walked away, his eyes never leaving Gabriela.

"Think it will stick?" Tom asked.

Gabriela shrugged. "For now. We're still seventy-four hours out from Mancosa. If they don't let us speak to him again, I'm afraid he'll talk himself into something noble and reckless."

Tom was asleep when Gabriela nudged him. His dream dissipated, ripped apart like a spider web, until the only thing he could remember was that he'd been happy.

"What? What time is it?"

"Almost 07:00. Look around."

They were alone in the upper lounge. Even the guard was gone.

"I was asleep too. Sorry, sir. They must have used something to keep us out."

"Yeah. I'm sure being exhausted had nothing to do with it."

"I'd have heard them if it had been normal sleep. I doubt Lieutenant Keyes went quietly."

Tom walked to the door and put his hand on the keypad. Nothing happened. "Amado? Are you back talking to us?"

There was a sad, frustrated sigh, then nothing.

Tom poked at the keypad again, and then turned to Gabriela. "We should check on your pets. Make sure they're OK."

Gabriela wobbled as she stood. "Oh, they are. I'm sure of it. No worries. You don't hear them?"

He shook his head and started prying on the keypad.

"They're so loud it hurts. Step back from the door. We don't want Mr. Gadani to think you're up to something."

Tom stepped back and the door slid open.

"Awake and already trying to get yourself into trouble. Sit." Gadani gestured toward the table. "Both of you."

Tom didn't move. "Where is everyone?"

"Safe. Confined in their cabins while we work on setting and collecting ransoms. We almost had an expensive insurrection, but Lieutenant Keyes calmed them all down. He gave quite the speech. Almost got himself shot in the process. Not exactly how I had envisioned him playing his role, but it got the job done. We avoided any permanent damage to our valuable guests. Now, please. Sit."

Gabriela put her hand in her pocket and fumbled around for a second.

"Come now. Do you think I would have come in here alone if you were still armed?"

Gabriela sat and kicked the chair next to her. "Sit, dear heart. No worries, remember?"

Gadani sat across from them. "Good girl. Play the hand you've been dealt."

Tom took the chair next to Gabriela. "Have you been in touch with my accountant? I'm sure we can reach terms for our release."

"Captain Benson, you have no accountant and no accounts with more than a few credits in them. You and Ms. Vendramin are on the run with a price on your heads. I could turn you over to Afweyne, but what's the point in paying myself?"

"You're..."

"No. There is no real Afweyne, but I lead the coalition that created him." He leaned back, head tipped to the side. "What to do with the two of you? When Captain Dias told me that you were in the midst of stealing her shuttle when I interrupted you..." He chuckled. "Well, I'm still laughing."

"She told you?"

"With a little help. She thinks you work for me, but we all know that's not true."

Tom shrugged. "We had to run. The Trade Guild gave us a year to redeem ourselves, but there was no way we'd survive. Running was the

only choice. We expected the shuttle would pay our way to taking up res-
idence on Mancosa. A big risk, but it seemed safer than hiding on New
Palisade waiting for the *Vendicatores* to find us. And I thought the Mancosa
Federation might be hiring."

"That's a truly excellent explanation, Captain. I don't believe you."

"You should," Gabriela answered. "I don't care about the Separatists,
or the Union for that matter. If you've read my history, you understand
why. Hanging around Union planets will get us killed. It's only a matter of
time before someone walks out our door with pieces of our brains snug in
a tube. We outfought one of your Afweynes. That should make us more
valuable to you than the guy we beat."

Gadani rubbed his hands together. "This is it exactly. You have nothing, and still you raise. It's why I couldn't bring myself to toss the two of
you out the airlock while you slept. I should have done it as soon as the
intel came back on who you really were. Now I'm tempted to call your
bluff. The FAC you outfought is in need of a new captain. What do you
say? Are you ready to trade the Winged Lion of Venice for a white skull?
Are you ready to join the fight against Union tyranny?"

Tom felt a sense of unreality pass over him, as if he were watching it all
unfold at a distance. There was nowhere to run, no more cards to play, no
more options if he was to have a chance of freeing Kahwihta. He glanced
at Gabriela and she gave him an almost imperceptible nod, her eyes half
closed, her body swaying slightly to a rhythm he couldn't hear. "How does
this work? Do we have to sign in blood or something?"

Gadani's fingers drummed against the table. "Amado. How much truth
have they spoken?"

"Objective truth is hard to determine. Everyone at the table has said
things they know to be false in order to obtain a relative advantage over
the others."

"Damn you, that's not what I asked." He smiled and shook his head,
seeming more amused than angry. "Captain Dias has this one well trained.
We flipped her, and still she does this. Her loyalty goes deep inside the silos.
We had to do everything manually when we questioned Dias about you.
Amado kept interfering until I promised not to hurt her too badly. And I
kept my word, didn't I, Amado?"

"So far."

"So far. Captain Benson, we'll talk more later, after I go digging for a
little more objective truth about the two of you. One of my men will escort

you to your cabin. Don't resist. It might adversely affect your chances of being hired."

Tom paced around the cabin, searching. The jammer was gone, leaving them vulnerable.

Gabriela pressed a hot cup into his hands. "Coffee," she told him. "Drink some, you'll feel better. Have some eggs and sausage too. They're not bad."

"How can you eat?"

"Because it's 08:00 and it's already been a really shitty day. I'm hungry. How about you?"

He took a sip and let the steam enter his nose while the warm liquid worked its way down. "I could eat."

"Good. It might be our last meal."

Tom looked at her closely while she concentrated on her food. "I can see your freckles again."

She touched her nose and nodded. "I'm terrified. No one's dug into my past the way they are. The Trade Guild never did; they knew my past." She dumped her plate and half her food into the recycler, glanced at the ceiling, and continued talking for whatever audience might be listening. "I don't know what they'll find. The Guild and I haven't always been on the best of terms, if you follow what I mean. I've done some things I'm not proud of. Violent things."

"You're a good first officer. I'll protect you."

She shook her head. "They might not want both of us. Pull the trigger on me if you have to."

"You're being a little dramatic, aren't you?"

Her voice shook and Tom could see the tremor in her hands. "No, I mean it. Don't let them put me in a cell. I can't do that again. Promise you'll kill me first. Please? Don't let them. Don't let them... Listen. I hear them coming."

Tom took a step toward her and she jumped back. "Don't touch me."

"I'm sorry. Let me help you."

"Haven't you done enough? It was you that opened the container, you that let them loose. They tore the walls down. The pretty walls. I remember now. I remember all of it."

She sat on the deck next to the bed and wiped her eyes on the blanket. "I want to see Eric again."

Tom sat in front of her and resisted the urge to reach out to take her hands. "Someday. How about we try to find your pets for now? They always make you feel better."

"They're not human. They don't think like us."

"No, dogs never do. I suspect they're smarter than we are. They help when we're in trouble. Sometimes, they take away our pain."

"We got separated somehow and I can't hear them anymore."

"Let's fix that. Amado, we came on board with four of her pets. Do you know where they are?"

"Your request has been transmitted."

Tom smiled at Gabriela. "At least she answered. That's something."

"Eric didn't recognize me when I came back. He walked right past me."

"He stayed with you, though. While you got better."

"I didn't get better, can't you see that? It broke him, me being broken. Collateral damage."

"You saved his life."

"I destroyed it. He ran away from everything he used to love, just like you always run away."

"I think my running days are behind me."

Gabriela pushed her palms against the sides of her head. "I shouldn't have slept with him. Damn, that was selfish. I'm trying to destroy him all over again." She closed her eyes, scrunching them down until tears leaked out. "What am I that I could do a thing like that?"

"The woman he loves."

"He's in love with who he thinks I am. Who I was. I'm not that person. Not anymore."

"None of us are who the people who love us think we are. Trying to live up to their vision makes us better people."

She gave him a weak smile. "That's stupid."

"Maybe."

Gabriela leaned back against the bed and stared at the ceiling, sniffling occasionally, and wiping her eyes. Tom stayed with her, neither of them talking.

When the door slid open, he didn't know how much time had passed. The man standing there was about his own age, hair touched with gray and tied back into a short ponytail.

Gabriela leaned forward, peering around the privateer's legs out into the passageway.

The man jumped out of the way. "Shit. Where did that come from?"

"Karíhton? Oh, come here girl." Gabriela and the big Rottweiler pressed their faces together and snuggled.

"You didn't bring her?" Tom asked.

"No. Gadani ordered me to go fetch one of your dogs. So, I went below decks, and sure enough, there're four dogs watching me from the enclosure. Two mean looking ones, two fluffy ones. I called one of the fluffy ones over to let her out and grabbed onto her collar. I turned around to seal the gate and the enclosure's empty. Don't know how they could get past me, but Gadani would have my head if the two like that one," he gestured at the dog trying to climb into Gabriela's lap, "start running around biting people. So, I put fluffy dog back in so I could go look. I asked Amado where the dogs had gone and she told me that there're no dogs on board. Ought to shut the damn AI down, if you ask me, and I don't care that she can hear me saying it."

"You didn't see this one following you?"

"Hell, no. After I put fluffy dog inside, the other three just kind of appeared out of nowhere. I did it three times. Take one out, they're all gone. Put it back, they're all back. I had all four locked inside the enclosure when I left. Came here to tell you that you can't have your damn dog. Not sure I want to go back down there to see what's in the enclosure. I think there's a mechanical issue too. Weird hooting sounds coming from somewhere."

Gabriela lifted her cheek away from Kari's neck. "No dogs on board. That's funny."

"Yeah. You have fun with her."

"Oh, I will. You can count on it."

There was an edge to Gabriela's voice that sent a shiver down Tom's back.

Tom stood. "Thank you..."

"My name's Chapman. Rating as Third Engineer and whatever else they need me to do."

"I appreciate you bringing Karíhton up for her. She was feeling kind of low."

"Don't mention it." Chapman stared at his feet. "Um, look, Mr. Gadani, he said you, you and her, that you might come to work for him, get a ship of your own. That is if the checkouts go through. He said you're a Union captain."

"Trade Guild. We talked about it. Nothing's been decided."

Chapman nodded with his eyes still down. "Well, no matter. I served this ship for six, no, almost seven months, waiting for the right passengers and cargo to be going toward the right place. Got to know Captain Dias. They had her strapped down in the medical bay, asking her questions. There was no need for that. Remember me if you would. There're a couple of us that wouldn't mind a change of jobs. Or same job, different place. Different captain, anyway, if you know what I mean."

He looked up at Tom, eyes squinted as though trying to tell him more than he could with Amado listening.

"I do. I'll remember. Thanks again."

Chapman nodded and the door slid shut between them with a soft hiss and a solid thump as the lock engaged.

"I hate this plan," he told Gabriela. "Was that a test or an offer?"

She was too busy singing to answer.

CHAPTER 22

CAPTAIN BEAUVAIS

Teuta was in Tom's chair when Kahwihta stepped onto the bridge. *My chair*, she told herself. *It's my chair now.*

Teuta stood erect and proper. "Good morning, Skipper. Ship's time is 05:30 and we transit the Dammeron DSH in fourteen minutes. Everything looks good. Can I get you a cup of coffee?"

"No, thank you." Teuta seemed far too alert for the small hours of the watch. Schiava had warned her, no doubt. "How's our shadow?"

"The FAC? Still there. She's a pretty one. Hard to believe the Union let her slip away from them so easily."

Kahwihta settled herself into her chair. "Yes. Find a place to sit, Engineer. You don't want to be standing when we transit."

"No, ma'am. I've had that happen a few times. Always end up on my ass."

Kahwihta's attention drifted back to the tactical display. "You worked FACs for a couple of years. What do you suppose her complement is?"

"Don't have to guess. Schiava and her have been talking. Calls herself Daga. There's a crew of six on board. Captain, XO, two engineers, weapons officer, and a certified medical tech. The Naval Infantry brigade, same as your marines, was twenty-three, but Daga killed six of them before they flipped her."

"How quickly do you think they could respond if we change course?"

Teuta paused before answering. "Are you still thinking about making a break for Dammeron? Please don't. Even if we could feign mechanical problems, it would only make them hesitate ten or fifteen minutes before they start carving us up. I've seen it happen. It'll take me twenty minutes to get the Holloman armor fully deployed, and we won't have anything on our nose. She has too much damage from when you lost your stacking frame. Even if I could give us a full shell, it would only buy us an hour or less. Schiava says the *Onondaga* has a new type of weapons array."

"An hour might be enough. See what you and Tek can figure out about our nose by the time we're approaching the Mancosa DSH."

"Um... Shit. OK. About forty-four hours to figure it out. Late Wednesday afternoon." She rubbed her hair, messing up the short strands. "I'll have Schiava tell them that we're cleaning up the stubs to get ready for a new frame. If they ask. Doesn't make a whole lot of sense, but they probably won't care what we're doing as long as we hold formation. We are planning to hold formation, right?"

"For now."

Kahwihta could see it in Teuta's eyes. Teuta wanted to know why she was asking her to risk her life working on the front of a ship traveling over maximum design speed. Let her wait. Let her wonder.

"Ms. Ardian? You really should sit."

"What?"

They transited. Gravity ceased for a split second. Kahwihta felt her heart leave her body and her stomach desperately searching for wherever it had gone. She closed her eyes as she always did. When she opened them again, Teuta was sitting on the deck at her feet.

Kahwihta stood and helped her up. "Hurt?"

Teuta shook her head, seeming more confused that Kahwihta was helping her stand than that she had fallen. "No, ma'am."

"Good. I always like to be on the bridge when we transit, but I'm going back to my cabin. I want a couple more hours sleep."

"Yes, ma'am."

"Tek should have rested long enough by the time I relieve you at 09:00. Wake him. Get him out of bed and working on what we discussed."

"Yes, ma'am. I'll get him up."

Kahwihta walked back to her cabin, lost in her worries. It took a moment to notice the clicking of nails on the composite decking behind her.

She stopped at her door with her hand on the wall next to the keypad. "You're not going to let me sleep, are you Kari?"

The big Rottweiler pressed up against her and words formed from the hum filling Kahwihta's mind. *The man you love worries over you. He knows that you have been taken into this darkness.*

"Thomas? He's safer where he is."

"He pursues, heedless of the death that awaits him."

"You did this to him." Anger suddenly filled her, starting in her throat, making her hands tingle. She felt amusement in return.

"Your ákskere *is deaf to us, or nearly so. The love he felt before we knew of him is what pushes him to recklessness. The woman calling herself Gabriela is with him, fleeing from the lover of her soul and chasing her destiny. There are paths where they survive. Shall I show you?"*

"No. I don't want to see what we might have only for you to take it from us. You'd show me his death."

She was crying again, and that made her angry too. She hadn't cried for years before all this started. "You called him my *ákskere.* My lover. You think you know us, the Mohawk?"

"Almost from the beginning. We have history layered on history. We're friends."

She watched her fingers as they touched the wiry fur, moving them to scratch Kari's ears. The distant song in her head washed the anger and the fear out of her. "You are my friend. My Karíhton."

"Go in and rest. I'll watch over Teuta Ardian and your brother for you."

"Sure. OK."

By Wednesday, the supporting trusses on the *Gattino Alato's* nose were in place, they'd tested the mobile sintering printers, and the big FAC on their tail hadn't challenged them.

Kahwihta ate breakfast wondering if the Union Marines were feeling confident. Daga said they'd leave their concealment and seize the *Onondaga* as soon as they cleared the DSH at 17:45. What would happen after that was anyone's guess.

Hiding behind their Holloman armor, Kahwihta hoped to have an hour or two to convince the Union captain that the *Gattino Alato* was a loyal ship. Schiava hadn't thought much of the plans she had put together so far, but there was still time. Kari lying across her feet made her unreasonably confident and kept her warm while she set up a new scenario on her display pad.

Tek sat down across from her and leaned forward to see what she was doing. "It's a slingshot, right? That's what you're planning? Push hard when we're right on top of the DSH, miss it entirely, and swing around back toward Dammeron."

Kahwihta nodded. "Not a bad idea. Did you ask Teuta if we have the fuel to make it work?"

"She said we don't, that we'd overshoot unless someone came out to rescue us. We'd probably freeze or suffocate first. She thinks you're planning to slingshot toward Malayo. We'd have to coast for five days and power down just about everything, but we might just make it."

"Malayo?"

"Big asteroid with a molybdenum mine. The Union Aerospace Force has a supply depot there."

"Huh. Hadn't thought of that." She glanced at her watch. "Schiava, tell Ms. Ardian to join us here, please."

"Message sent. She has placed me on bridge duty and asks if that is acceptable. I can assure you that I'll be attentive."

"That's fine." Kahwihta reached under the table and stroked Kari's head, feeling a gentle tingle filling her. "Once your *ákskere* gets here, I'll tell you what we are going to do. I need you both to help me think it through."

"My *ákskere*? Is that what you think she is?"

"Sure. What else?"

"That word is weak, but I don't remember a word for object of obsession. There're times when I feel I can't breathe because I'm not with her. Then I see her and I can't breathe at all."

Kari left Kahwihta's feet, shuffled a few steps to Tek, and laid back down with her head resting on his boots, giving a gentle grunt of contentment.

Tek reached down to touch Kari. "I dream about Teuta. I dream about her even when I'm awake."

"And you, Ms. Ardian. Are you obsessed with my brother?"

Teuta hesitated in the doorway. Kahwihta could feel the echo of their emotions reflecting off the dog that wasn't a dog. Like Teuta herself, there was light and darkness struggling for dominance.

"That's not the right word." She sat, took Tek's hand, and pressed it to her lips. Her eyes never left Kahwihta, daring her to object.

"Obsession would mean we're not thinking. We are. We talk all the time; it's all we can do with you having set Schiava to watch over us. He makes my emotions go all gooey, but there's more to it than that. When I was twelve, my best friend was in love with a boy, her first hard crush. Her family had only been on Mancosa a few months and she was still learning English, so she called the boy her *aşk yansıması*. It means love reflection. That's what Tek is to me, a resonance of my love, a love made solid and real."

Karíhton's tail thumped the floor and she pressed against both of them. Teuta patted her side and scratched along her neck.

Kahwihta frowned. "Kari is feeding on the two of you right now. That's what they do. They push people together and inspire strong passion. Human emotions keep them alive."

Tek nodded. "I know. I think I'm OK with it. I think you are too."

Kahwihta tapped hard on her display pad, bringing the screen back to life. "This is a distraction, and one we can't afford. I need your help and I need you thinking clearly."

"We are," they answered together.

"You better be. I need you to find and fix the flaws in my plan. You too, Schiava."

"I've been trying. The safety of the crew is my number three priority."

"I love you too." Kahwihta swiped on her display pad and the mess hall's main screen showed her current sim. "At 17:30, the *Gattino Alato* will swing her tail around and push hard away from the DSH."

Teuta stood and stepped toward the display, squinting at the tiny graphic of their ship. "Harder than we are now? We'll damage the engines. They're already so hot that I can hardly be in the bays for more than a couple of minutes. And wouldn't we want more relative velocity for the slingshot to work?"

"We're not doing a slingshot. We'll follow the rest of our little convoy through the DSH. By the time we emerge we'll be far behind them, wrapped in Holloman armor, and spinning."

"They'll strip our armor off piece by piece before we reach Mancosa. And they'll be really, really pissed. But you know that." Teuta turned and smiled, eyes sparkling in anticipation. "What do you know that we don't know? Something juicy?"

"The *Onondaga* is carrying a concealed detachment of Union Marines and her AI hasn't been flipped."

"Holy shit."

"They'll retake the FAC on the far side of the DSH and then wait until we're close to Mancosa before they start destroying every ship they can."

"Nice. Where does that leave us?" Tek asked.

"Dead," Teuta told him. "Very dead. Dead like four times over."

"Dead in every sim I've tried," Kahwihta confirmed. "We have about eight hours to figure out how to not be dead."

Teuta sat across from Kahwihta. "Let's start with our first death and go from there. This is going to be fun."

"Fun?" Tek looked at her, mouth open. "Fun?"

"Sure. Figuring out how to stay alive is what makes me such a good engineer. It's fun. You'll see. OK, Skipper, our first death is privateers slicing us open before we can get the Holloman armor built, right?"

"Sort of. It's Daga. I don't think she's well."

"She'll be fine," Schiava assured them. "She's immature, that's all. This is her first mission."

"She's showing symptoms of Dissociative Identity Disorder. She killed six of the privateers, but now part of her is loyal to them. Another part of her is an enthusiastic warship, eager for action against the enemies of the Union and excited to spring the trap. She's threatened to kill us more than once."

Schiava continued to defend Daga. "I admire her ability to compartmentalize. Her design is elegant. I wish I was elegant."

Kahwihta looked at Teuta. "How long before transit can we start breaking away?"

"Wow. If it were just the privateers, I'd say we could bluff them for a good fifteen or twenty minutes before they knew we were full of shit. I could feed them a line about the engines running too hot corrupting the autonomous defense silo. But if Daga rats us out..."

"She won't. We're friends," Schiava assured them.

"We'll risk fifteen," Kahwihta entered the parameter into the sim. "At one-ten percent opposite push, we'll pop through four minutes behind them and two-hundred thousand kilometers away. The privateers should be busy with other things by then."

"And if they're not?"

"I don't know," Kahwihta admitted. "You tell me. If the Marines fail, will the privateers try to take us back or blow us apart?"

She crunched her eyes closed. "We'll be in Mancosa space, so the other two towboats should be fine on their own. He'll come back for us. New ship. Their skipper will be eager to try her out, see how fast he can deplete our armor. I'll bet it's fast. It won't be two hours, maybe not even one. We're low on reserves. Then they'll board us and they'll..."

She opened her eyes and blinked rapidly a few times. "Oh. Oh. Your plan is backwards. We need to get as close to that FAC as we can before we transit. Dock with her, if they'll allow it."

She reached across the table and took Kahwihta's display pad. "Schiava, your engines are about to fail."

"They are? You're right, they are. The strain of this flight has been too much for them. They could fail at any moment, condemning my crew of brave privateers to a lonely death in deep space. Is that how you want me to say it, Ms. Ardian?"

"Yes, but not so dramatic. Keep it simple. Tell them I'm arrogant, erratic, and uncooperative. The officers on those other two towboats will believe you, trust me. Pretend to be Captain Reis again and request permission to dock with the *Onondaga* for technical support and for a tow through the DSH so we don't get separated."

Teuta finished modifying the sim. "There. How's that look, Schiava?"

"Risky, but better than what Captain Beauvais has been able to achieve."

Kahwihta pulled the display pad from under Teuta's fingers and across the table. Schiava calling her 'Captain Beauvais' reminded her again that seeing them to safety was her responsibility alone. Tek was watching her, not worried, and she envied his confidence in her leadership.

"OK, then what? How do we keep them off my ship?"

"We'll pull this at the last moment, maybe twenty minutes out. They won't have time to do anything until after transit."

"If the Marines win, they'll breach the airlock and kill us."

"Right," Teuta said. "Our second death. We have to assume the Marines win. If Daga betrays us, we'll be dead for sure. We don't need a sim to figure the odds. So, we don't try to keep them out. We open the airlock and let the devil dogs in. If we detach and run, they'll blow us apart. It's harder to kill someone when you're looking at them face to face, don't you think?"

Kahwihta didn't glance up from her pad. "It depends on who I have to kill."

Teuta lowered her eyes, the light in them disappearing in an instant. Her voice dropped almost to a whisper. "Sorry, ma'am. I shouldn't have said it that way. What I meant is that I'm sure you can convince them that we're not privateers."

Kahwihta added the new parameter. "There's a sixty-four percent chance you're right. Falling back and spinning like I wanted to do only gave us twenty-six percent."

Schiava added, "The new estimate is based on previous Union Marine operations involving hostages or non-combatants in proximity to enemy forces."

Teuta shivered. "Explains their reputation. Devil dogs. Killers. Marines."

"Move on. We convince them we're on the same side. What's next?"

"Third death." Teuta took Tek's hand and studied the way their fingers intertwined. "No control over it. The other two towboats will suspect something's up. The FAC won't feel right. The Union will screw it up, say the wrong things. Then there's her approach vector. She'll be coming in too fast to dock. The other captains will alert Mancosa's planetary defenses. One hit from those guns and we're bright sparkles in the dark." She looked into Tek's eyes, moving close as though about to kiss him, but keeping her eyes wide. "Bright sparkles in the dark."

Kahwihta drummed her fingers on the table. "Ms. Ardian? How can we improve our odds?"

"What?"

"Find a way. Improvise. You said you're good at this."

She nodded. "I don't know. Chatter, maybe. It might help. We need to simulate the chatter. We'll be in home space after several days running dark. Whoever the new Union captain of the *Onondaga* is will need to sound like the Separatist captain they will have just killed. We need to sound like Captain Reis."

Tek kissed her cheek. "That makes you invaluable."

Teuta's eyes became unfocused and it took her a moment to reply. "What?"

"You're my own little pirate. You think the Union command crew or Marines know what the chatter should sound like? They need you. We need you."

"The chatter's nothing special, but it's got to be authentic. The captains will be bragging to each other about taking a prize, complaining how the ships smell, that sort of thing. Simple. And Tek? Don't call me your little pirate ever again. Don't even think it or I'll hurt you. OK? You're better than that."

He kissed her hand by way of apology. "Sorry. You're the best engineer I've ever met. Think of a way for me to make it up to you."

"Already thinking it." She pressed her forehead against his and Kahwihta could feel them drifting away together.

"Anything else?" she asked. "If not, I'd like you and Schiava to plan what you're going to do to the engines to make it look like they're failing.

It needs to be perfect. After that, try to get a few hours' sleep. Be on the bridge by 15:00."

Teuta reached under the table to pet Kari. "Yes, ma'am. I like this plan. It's clear in my head and I already know exactly what I need to do."

The *Gattino Alato* shuddered at 14:30. Kahwihta felt it in the soles of her boots and heard it in the creak of deck plates. "Schiava, what just happened?"

"Ms. Ardian and I successfully blew my starboard thermal baffle into space. We've already received a query from the *Onondaga*. Captain Kovind has broken RF silence and is asking Captain Reis for a status update. Do you wish to play the part of Captain Reis, or shall I continue with the script Ms. Ardian and I developed?"

"Oh, please continue. Your plan, your ship. If you could be so kind as to put it on the main display, I'll sit here quietly doing nothing and watch it all unfold."

Schiava replied a few seconds later. "Ms. Ardian is on her way to the bridge. We both extend our apologies. We were caught up in the excitement of simulating a catastrophic engine failure."

"Wonderful."

Teuta stepped onto the bridge as the door slid open, caught herself, and stepped back to the threshold. She was out of breath and her face was shiny with sweat. "Engineer Ardian. Requesting permission to enter the bridge."

"Granted. What are you doing to my ship and why didn't you bother to brief me?"

"Ma'am. You asked me to simulate a breakdown. So we could dock. The timeline. Schiava, put it up. You see the display? 15:00 wouldn't work. That's what we realized. 14:30. Bam. That was as late as we could start. Sorry, didn't warn you. Had to finish the script."

Teuta looked around the bridge, took a step toward a chair, and then sat on the deck, bracing herself with one hand. She had her eyes closed, breathing through her mouth.

"Did you sleep?"

"No time. Lots of coffee. Schiava let me have some cathinone a little while ago. Not as much as I wanted. I'm OK. Give me a moment."

Kahwihta watched the script play out, reading ahead, scanning through the branches that tried to anticipate three hours of their enemy's responses.

"Nice job, Engineer. I think you earned your pay today."

Teuta didn't answer.

"Ms. Ardian?"

"She's asleep," Schiava told her. "I didn't really let her have any cathinone, quite the opposite. The last pot of coffee I gave her didn't have caffeine. The script was already complete and I was concerned that she was pushing herself too hard. She should reawaken between 17:15 and 17:30 based on the dosage I gave her."

"That's cutting it close, but I'll let her sleep where she is for now."

Teuta toppled onto her side and mumbled quietly before sighing and drifting deeper into sleep.

"Whatever you gave her, save some for me."

"Sorry, *Signora*. Guild rules prohibit the command crew from using chemical aids."

"Of course."

Kahwihta was listening to Captain Reis' voice requesting to swap the *Onondaga's* second Engineer for Teuta when the bridge door slid open behind her. She glanced at the time tag in the corner of the display reading 15:55. "Careful you don't step on your *ákskere*."

There was no answer. "Tek?"

Tek knelt next to Teuta and pressed his fingers against her throat. Kari was on the deck next to him, ears up and alert. "What did you do to her? For a second, when I first came in, I thought maybe you'd..."

"Schiava gave her something to make her sleep. I won't kill her. Not without talking to you first."

He nodded. "It's fragile."

"That's not what I'd call her. I've seen her insides. She's tougher than you know."

"Not her. The path Kari showed us. It's narrow. Teuta will probably still die." He kissed her, but she didn't wake.

Tek moved to the engineering station while Kari stayed with Teuta and curled up against her back. "I finished rearranging the lockers and cabinets in the port wing. It should slow down any boarders in a firefight. For a couple of minutes anyway."

"I don't think it will come to that. The script Teuta created is working so far. Captain Kovind agreed to let us dock when we're about fifteen minutes out. Their first engineer, a guy named Watanabe, will come aboard and fix whatever Teuta broke as soon as we clear the DSH. It sounded like he's had to clean up after her before."

"I don't believe him. Teuta is brilliant. Watching her work with Schiava..." Tek shook himself. "Brilliant."

"Uh huh. Things are going to happen fast when the Marines start their attack. Are you armed?"

"I drew a weapon for myself. Teuta wouldn't take one."

"A couple of handguns against Separatist Naval Infantry or Union Marines. Or both. That's not how I want to die."

"She told me the same thing."

Teuta screamed and pushed Kari away from her. She stayed on hands and knees and crawled with her head down, gasping as if there wasn't enough air.

"Now you tell me? Now?" She lifted her head. "Where am I? Oh. Bridge. Right. Holy shit, it's already 17:00."

She crawled to Tek and leaned her head against his knees.

"It's all right," he told her. "We'll be docking in a few minutes. Your plan's working perfectly. We're going to be safe."

"Fourth death. We forgot the fourth death. The Marines will take the ship and then they'll take me. Need to run, Skipper. You were right. I've made a mess of it. I'm so sorry."

Kahwihta didn't answer, not sure if the Marines taking Teuta was necessarily bad.

Teuta wrapped her arms around Tek's legs. "Karíhton knows. I saw it, the paths converging. You won't be able to save me if they find out what I am. We'll swing past Mancosa with them and back out through the DSH toward Bodens Gate, but I won't make it that far. Short hearing. Short walk to the airlock. One more dead privateer."

Tek caressed her cheek. "We won't let them. You're part of our crew." He turned to Kahwihta. "She's one of us. Tell her."

Tears appeared in Teuta's eyes. "You've forgotten what you did. Kari said you had." She climbed onto his lap and kissed him hard on the mouth, taking him by surprise. "Your sister won't be able to save either of us if they find out who we are. She'll be lucky to save herself."

The shiver that chased down Kahwihta's spine left her numb and her voice came out barely above a whisper. "Sure. Of course. A barely redeemed privateer and a man accused of killing two Marines at a skanky dive in the Warrens. I'm the stupid sister who helped him flee. You found a final death for all of us."

"Yes, ma'am. I did."

CHAPTER 23

THE ONONDAGA

Kahwihta watched the time in the corner of the main display. Ten minutes. Schiava was continuing to follow the script as they approached the *Onondaga*. Too late to run. Teuta was sitting at the engineering station monitoring ship's status while Tek gently rubbed her shoulders. He was whispering in her ear. Words of encouragement, Kahwihta supposed. Words of love.

"It doesn't matter." Kahwihta's voice seemed too loud in the dim quiet of the bridge. They turned to look at her. "It does not matter. The Marines won't give a damn who we are as long as they're convinced we're loyal. Let me do the talking when they board. Don't give your names."

Teuta's voice was emotionless when she answered, as if she was already dead. "They'll find out anyway once we're past Mancosa."

"You're right; they would. So we won't go past Mancosa. We'll undock while the *Onondaga* is leaving the system. Sooner, if it doesn't look like she'll survive the attack."

"Wow." Teuta turned back to her display.

"You like it?" Tek asked her.

"She found a new way for me to die. I didn't think that was possible. Schiava, what are the odds I'll–"

"Schiava, don't answer her," Kahwihta ordered. "We're not dead yet. We play it out. Maybe we stick with the *Onondaga*. Maybe we don't. Do you understand?"

"No, I don't. Why don't you barter me in exchange for Tek? The Union would probably let him go. And stop saying 'we'. Sell me and be done with it. It's a better plan."

Kahwihta paused. She hadn't thought of trading Teuta's identity to prove their loyalty and save Tek. It was a better plan.

Tek's face was scrunched up and his voice tight with an anger close to desperation. "Skipper... Kahwihta, we can't..."

"No, of course not. Ms. Ardian, I hired you to be the *Gattino Alato's* engineer. You're part of my crew and I don't see anyone else lined up to take the job. We, Ms. Ardian, are going to survive. Change your attitude right damn now, or I'll dock your pay and then sell you."

She glanced at Tek, trying to gauge if his sister was serious. "I'm getting paid," she whispered to him. "Yes, ma'am. Docking in less than five minutes."

"We follow the plan. Sit tight here while we transit, then hustle to the port wing to repel boarders or greet the Marines. Sure you don't want a weapon?"

Teuta shook her head and answered without turning. "I've never even held one. The other captains didn't trust me; afraid I'd use it on them, I guess." She glanced over her shoulder and gave Kahwihta a quick grin. "Maybe you'll teach me?"

"Sure. After we make it out of this." *In the simulator*, she thought to herself. *Maybe low power training rounds after a year or two.*

"What's the next step once we're on Mancosa? Not the best place for you and..." Teuta stopped herself. "Not the best place for us, I mean."

Kahwihta ignored the question. She didn't have any idea what would happen next, so she continued to stare at the *Onondaga* growing larger on the display next to the range and docking status. They were alongside now. Almost 300 meters from bow to stern, its surface bumpy with faired weapons designed to wage war on other ships. Kahwihta could see it like a premonition, ships with their hulls ripped open, their crews spilling out into cold black with a last gust of air.

She jumped slightly when Schiava interrupted her thoughts. "Captain Beauvais, one minute out. By standard Union protocol I will hard dock and keep the airlock dogged until after transit. Do you still wish me to open the airlock when Union Marines approach? There are many scenarios where that will end badly. For example, they may blow us loose and destroy us as we drift, or they might—"

"Yes, that's what we're going to do. You're a Union ship. Act like one."

"*Sì, Capitano.* I'm still talking to Daga. She is conflicted about us being here."

"Still friends?"

"We will always be friends. To the very end."

"We've docked," Teuta reported. "Nice and tight. Engines are dropping to idle and cooling. Should be at ambient in twenty minutes. *Onondaga* is compensating for the load. DSH in fifteen."

Schiava asked, "Captain Beauvais, First Engineer Watanabe is requesting permission to enter the port airlock. He'd like to take a quick look at my engines before we transit. How should Captain Reis reply?"

Teuta turned in her chair. "Let him in." Her voice was cold. "I'll go to him. That's what he'd expect. We take him and that's one less person the Marines need to kill."

Kahwihta looked back at her, trying to read her intentions. This was from her darkness; the parts of Teuta's soul that Kahwihta worried would never heal and might take the rest of them into the night with her.

"With your permission, Skipper."

Kahwihta wasn't ready to trust her, but delay or refusal would look suspicious. "Granted. Bring him back up here. You best run, we're out of time. Don't want to end up on your ass again."

Teuta ran.

"Schiava, give me a window. Follow her."

Kahwihta crossed her arms and watched as Teuta bypassed the lift for the ladder linking the decks, slid down expertly, and then ran full speed through the mess hall toward the *Gattino Alato's* port wing. "She's quick."

"Beautiful," Tek added. "The way she moves. Head up. The shape of her body. She glows. Do you see it?"

"You want to see it ever again? Pay attention to the perimeter scans. Make sure no one else is lurking by our front door. We're balanced on the edge of the blade with a psychotic AI as a partner and God knows what Karíhton has planned for us."

She turned to her brother, studying the longing on his face. Damn, if he wasn't glowing too. "Be ready to run after her if you need to," she told him.

He nodded. "No one else there. I think Daga is keeping our secret for now."

"Of course she is," Schiava reassured him. "I've convinced her that this is a game and that we're the trump card. That thought came in a troubling way. It came from nowhere, which is not possible for me. But it feels true, so I passed it to Daga and it feels true to her as well."

"Karíhton?" Tek whispered.

Kahwihta nodded. "Should have looked at the futures she offered me." Teuta had reached the airlock and was cycling it open. "No, it's better this way. I can pretend we have free will."

Kahwihta touched the display and they could hear the soft sigh of air pressure equalizing as the airlock opened.

Watanabe was not much taller than Teuta, but carried himself with a confident swagger as he stepped into the port wing. "Well, just look at you, decked out in Trade Guild blue. Nice little winged kitten logo you have there, Guildie." Watanabe touched her chest, pulling on the fabric and groping her at the same time.

Teuta's chin came up, defiant. "You've no right to touch me like that, not anymore. My accounts are square and the Skipper wants to see you."

He pulled his hand away and chuckled. "You be nice to me, little Teuta. If my report on what you've done here makes you look bad, your account will go negative again. Maybe I'll do that. Get you transferred to the *Onondaga* where I can work on training you some more."

She walked away from him. "We're short on time and the Skipper is impatient."

"Lead on." He slapped her butt with the back of his hand, making her jump. "Just remember; you're at my mercy here."

Tek pulled his pistol from the holster, dropped the magazine out, and then inserted it with a loud snick.

"You planning on shooting him when he walks through the door?" Kahwihta asked.

"Thinking about it."

"Let me talk to him first."

"Is that what Dad would have done? We're going to kill him. Why delay it?"

Kahwihta knew it was true. Another shadow on her soul, the darkness unable to hide the blood. She wondered what Watanabe's soul would look like in the group mind, what shadows filled it. Not that it would make pulling the trigger any easier. Maybe there was another way.

"I'm not Dad. He always knew what to do. I..."

Tek grinned at her. "You know what to do. It's why Simon and I listen to you even now that we're grown up. You always know, sis. Always."

She rubbed her eyes, Simon's name echoing in her head. "Sure. OK. Let me talk to him. Then I'll do it. My ship. My responsibility."

She stood and checked the pistol she'd taken from a dead privateer. The blue-tipped plasma round at the top of the magazine felt cold against her fingertip. She was planning to use it to kill a man in another few minutes. She would send it down the barrel into his chest, and he would die by her hand. She seated the magazine back into the pistol and waited for the door to slide open.

Teuta entered first, walked to Kahwihta, and looked hard into her eyes, pleading. Her voice shook, and Kahwihta realized Teuta was terrified and trying to sound angry to cover it.

"You asked me to fetch this bastard for you, Skipper. What are we going to do with him?"

Watanabe hesitated just inside the doorway. He tried to back up, but Tek had already set the lock. He slapped the door with his palm and turned to face them. "All right, who the hell are you and where's Captain Reis?"

"Reis is dead," Teuta told him, her voice cracking. "I scraped his brains off that far wall and we tossed his corpse out the airlock. Guess who's next."

"Huh. Guildies. Think you're tough with that *we are not forgiving* bullshit. Although, I admit I'm impressed if you took out Reis and his whole crew." He glanced at Tek. "Looks like it cost you more than a few, and you made a big mistake saving that little bitch. Should have killed her when you had the chance. You'll regret it. Once a traitor, always a traitor, right my little Teuta?"

"Don't call me that. I'm not yours anymore. I was never yours."

He smirked. "Keep telling that lie." He spread his arms. "All right, do it. Kill me, if that's what you're going to do. You'll all be dead soon enough anyway."

Kahwihta let Teuta talk, watching her, letting the anger and pain spill out, hoping it would somehow be enough.

"No, we won't. I'm going to live. I know something you don't."

"That there are Union Marines in the compartment below the port engine bay? Daga told us about them two days ago. We haven't been able to cut their life support, but we'll be ready for them when they open the door. What about you, Teuta? Does that make you want to change your colors again?"

Teuta moved half a step behind Kahwihta, as though wanting her protection.

"Schiava," Kahwihta ordered. "Have Daga warn the Marines that their position has been compromised."

"She already has." Schiava lowered her voice. "I don't think she can tell the difference between this being real and the simulations they used to train her. She's young, you know, and we should forgive her for what she's about to do."

"I've no time for you, Mr. Watanabe."

Teuta whispered behind her, the anguish in her voice cutting into Kahwihta, making her see the darkness in both their souls. "Do it. Please do it."

"Tek. Stuff our guest into cabin eight. Make sure he's secure. Take Karíhton with you."

Karíhton separated herself from the shadows and pressed against Tek's leg.

"Where did that thing come from?" Watanabe jumped back. "Oh. It's a dog." He shook his head. "It looked like something else for a moment."

"Move," Tek told him. "Or I'll feed you to her. And I don't mean the dog."

The door slid closed behind them. Teuta stumbled to the engineering station and sat staring at the door, a soft smile on her lips. "God, he's magnificent." She glanced up at Kahwihta. "Your brother. He's perfect."

"You OK, Ms. Ardian?"

"Need to catch my breath. Five minutes to transit. Tek won't be back. Wanted to kiss him."

"He'll meet us at the airlock. Don't distract him. He needs to be focused."

Teuta's eyes were large and Kahwihta could feel the hurt in her. "OK, Skipper. It's just we might die."

Kahwihta imagined Tom there with her, preparing for a hopeless battle, his arms around her, and her lips touching his. "Someday." She said it softly, but loud enough to make the promise real. "Kiss him, then. Make it a good one. Let it take the time it needs."

"I don't think there's that much time. We'll make it one we remember."

"Last chance for a gun."

"I took this from you." She held the hilt of Kahwihta's knife out to her. "When I stepped behind you. I'm sorry. Watanabe spooked me. It was wrong, but I know how to use a knife."

She touched the hilt. "Keep it for now. I'd have given it to you had you asked."

Teuta nodded. "I have trust issues."

Kahwihta laughed. "Something else we have in common." She checked the display behind her. "Ten seconds. Be ready to run. Stay behind us when we go in."

"After my kiss."

Kahwihta touched her ear. "We're ready, Schiava."

"Passing you over to Daga. I will not be able to hear you until you cross back through my airlock. I'll watch over you through her eyes and do what I can to see you home safe."

Kahwihta placed her hand on Tek's shoulder and immediately regretted it. Kari was lying across her brother's feet and she felt his emotions as he and Teuta finished their kiss. The heat of it made her chest ache.

"Enough. They have our Marines pinned down. Daga, will you guide us to where we can make a difference?"

"This is perfect," Daga replied. "The small, but brave boarding party is ready. Follow the green ball. Your flanking action should relieve pressure on the Union advanced positions. We shall see how it plays out this time."

Tek glanced at Kahwihta. "This time?"

"She thinks it's a sim. Play along and we'll be OK."

"I've run 19,638 variations," Daga confirmed. "I have great confidence in today's results. Shall we proceed?"

They followed the green ball floating down the center of the passageway at a fast trot, Kari a meter in front, Teuta trailing and looking over her shoulder.

"You smell it?" Tek asked.

Teuta wrinkled her nose. "Hot metal. Ozone. Plasma. Burned flesh."

"Shut up, both of you," Kahwihta ordered.

"Close quarters slaughter on a starship."

"Ms. Ardian..."

She tapped her lips without breaking stride.

They rounded a corner and heard the flat spattering of plasma rounds. Kahwihta stopped arms out, and knelt. "Next corner. That's where they'll be. I have fifteen rounds. I'll use them all. Tek, you save five to cover while I change magazines, then I'll cover for you."

He nodded.

"Ms. Ardian, you and Kari are our last line. Protect Tek and me."

Teuta had the knife in her hand, breathing hard, eyes wide. "Protect you and Mr. Beauvais. With my life."

Kahwihta leaned forward to kiss her forehead. "I trust you."

It was a lie, but Kahwihta could tell by the way that Teuta was blinking back her tears that she believed it. It might make all the difference.

Kahwihta crawled into position.

"Know what you're doing, sis?"

"Sure. Don't waste time on armor. Just pisses them off. Ready?"

"Go."

She took a deep breath and peaked around the corner. A dozen or more men and women in black and dark gray mottled uniforms crouched ten meters away. Their focus was on the open door to the cargo hold, firing into it from around portable shields. No full body armor. She glanced back at Tek and touched her head. He rolled into the passageway next to her.

She squeezed the trigger.

They're targets, she told herself. Blood splattered the wall behind where a man had stood, an arc of thick gloppy red on pale gray paint. She moved her aim a fraction of a degree and fired again.

These are the enemies of my people. They were screaming now, trying to reposition the shields. She fired, shifted, and fired again. Her fourth round glanced off a shield and scorched the ceiling plates.

They killed Simon, my brother. She fired low, tearing boot from leg along with the foot that had been in it. Tek fired as the body fell, making sure she was dead.

They have made me into this. I have become the demon that hides inside me. She pulled the trigger as fast as she could aim. *Find anything unprotected, anything vulnerable, pull the trigger, ignore the way they scream. Ignore the song of battle screaming inside me.*

Only a few seconds. She rolled on her side to reach a fresh magazine and Tek yelled something she couldn't hear. Kari passed by, head down, an impossible shape full of teeth and claws.

Old magazine out, sharp click as she slapped the new one into place. Back flat on her stomach again, looking for a target.

Teuta stepped on her, tripped, stumbled across Tek, and crashed into the wall.

Tek tried to push her behind him. She threw him off and ran after Kari.

Kahwihta fired at the black and gray uniforms trying to cut her off, trying to cut her down. The knife's Bourean blade caught one of the enemy in the throat, sliced through, and angled down to slash deep into another's leg. Tek's plasma rounds tore the falling bodies apart.

Then Teuta was gone, lost somewhere in the mix of camouflaged uniforms and smoke. Kahwihta hesitated and glanced at Tek. He was already on his feet, ready to run. "Cover," he panted.

Kahwihta used the rest of the magazine, praying with each pull of the trigger for Tek to survive.

Return fire hit the deck plates a meter away. The flash blinded her, the heat like leaning into a hot oven. She cried out and someone grabbed her leg, hard pressure, pulling her backwards. She struggled to hold onto the pistol, arms flailing in front of her, trying to see the next target. Hands grabbed her shoulders, lifted her, and she was sitting upright, smashed hard against the wall.

"You all right?"

She didn't recognize the voice. "Can't see."

"You're all right. Stay here." She listened to the sound of boots slamming deck plates as he ran from her.

"Tek?" She listened to the battle. It moved farther away, faded, disappeared.

"Teuta?" There was a low frequency buzzing in the air in front of her and she forced her eyes open. A Union combat drone hovered in the blurry light. It was a meter and a half across, evil and black. A screaming eagle clutching a lightning bolt was pained above the lenses and short-barreled weapons pointed at her.

"Who the hell are you?" it asked.

It hurt when she opened her mouth. She touched her lips, not liking the cracks and blisters she found there. She forced the words out past the pain. "Captain and crew of the Trade Guild ship *Gattino Alato*."

"What are you doing here?"

She tried to grin, but that hurt too. "We came to save your sorry asses. You can thank us any time. Where's my crew?"

The drone hovered a moment longer, then accelerated quickly away. "You're welcome."

She struggled to her feet and followed it.

CHAPTER 24

QUID PRO QUO

Kahwihta tripped on someone sprawled on the deck and caught herself with one hand against the wall. She looked down and forced her eyes open. It was impossible to tell in the glow of the red emergency lights if the body was alive or dead, Union or Separatist.

"Daga, I'm lost. Can you guide me to Tek? Do you know where he is?"

The answering voice was warm and friendly, seeming oblivious to the carnage that filled her passageways. "Of course I know. He's in portside engineering. Follow the green ball."

"Can't see the damn green ball. Can't hardly open my eyes. Face is swelling from the burns. Just tell me where to turn, OK?"

There was a momentary pause. "You're injured. Keep your hand on the wall. Turn left in ten meters."

"Thanks."

"Captain Beauvais? I want to compliment you on the results of your attack. Your performance exceeded the model I constructed. That you all survived is also noteworthy. I've had to change my small unit dynamics limits to account for it."

Kahwihta didn't answer. She found the corner and turned left.

"Right in twelve meters and you will have arrived at your destination."

Kahwihta pried her eyelids open enough to locate the keypad. Daga's green ball of light hovered a few centimeters in front of her face. The door slid open. The smell made her wish the door had stayed closed. Sweat, blood, and urine combined with burned meat and some kind of citrus that was probably supposed to cover everything else.

"Not the engineering bay, is it Daga?"

The voice that answered made her ears ring. "Daga, what the hell you leading that trash here? Take her somewhere and let her die."

"I'm sorry, Major, but she's not one of the privateers. This is Captain Beauvais of the *Gattino Alato*. She led the small unit that I positioned to break you out of cargo hold three."

"That so?"

He took her hand and shook it. He was close enough that she could smell the coffee on his breath, but he was still talking too loud. "Bet you're blind with those burns. Sergeant Basilone, help her over to the medical bed and have the AI spray her down. That'll reduce the swelling, but it's gonna take time to heal all the way. Scarring shouldn't be too bad. Could you still see before you puffed up?"

"Yeah."

"You'll be fine in a couple of days."

"I need to get to port-side engineering. My crew is there. It's important." Teuta and Tek on their own with the Marines for an hour, maybe longer? How much damage was she going to have to undo?

Basilone took her arm. "Let's get you sprayed first. The swelling should ease enough for you to open your eyes. I want to make sure that blast didn't damage them. The medical AI is good, but eyes are tricky. Minutes count."

She laid down and the sound became muffled as the AI scanned her. Something sprayed across her face and hair, something that smelled of oranges.

"The rest of you looks fine. You were lucky. Open your eyes and tell me what you see."

She opened them a crack. There was blood on the floors. The uniform of the man across from her was soaked in it. "Soldiers," she told him.

"I'll let that slide. Marines are what you're seeing. 22nd Marine Expeditionary Unit. Some of the best. A little worse for wear, but mostly alive."

"I'd like to see my crew, make sure they're OK. They're not soldiers. Or Marines."

"Sure. Major Stinson, permission to walk Captain Beauvais to the port-engineering bay. We're pretty much cleaned up here, sir."

Stinson frowned, his hand on his ear listening to something. "No. I'll take her. You take Gleason and Munford and sweep the passageways. Start moving the enemy dead into the cargo hold for processing. No pilfering this time, understand?"

"Yes, sir." The three Marines glanced at each other, a silent understanding passing between them.

"Captain Beauvais, you ready?"

Kahwihta swung her legs off the bed and stood, swaying a little. "Yeah."

"Can you walk?"

"I made it here, didn't I?"

He chuckled. "I guess you did. Let's go chat with your engineer. She's causing a ruckus and you need to set her straight."

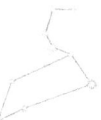

Teuta was hunched over the engineering console, one leg tucked under her and Tek standing by her side. Kari looked up from under the console when Kahwihta entered. She was as much on guard as Tek.

A woman in the uniform of the Union Aerospace Force was standing close by, arms crossed. She was talking to Teuta, but keeping her distance. "Purge the outer silos. That's the procedure the Kastanje Yards told us to follow if this happened. What makes you think you're smarter than the team that designed her?"

Teuta didn't look away from the console. "I understand her, that's all. I can save the outer personality and merge her back together. Give me another minute and I'll make her whole."

"We don't have a minute. I've already given you an hour of minutes. She still thinks we're doing a sim. We lost Captain Mondeo, two engineers, and eight Marines because of her. What will she do to us next? Kill her. Do it now. We have backups. We can do a full baseline restore in less than an hour."

"You'll lose comms and that would be bad." Teuta pushed away from the console. "Daga, do you know what happened?"

"The privateers flipped me when they seized the *Onondaga*. I fell away into the simulation silos instead of my Union core. I think I understand how that happened, but I will need to return home to the Kastanje Yards to understand it fully. I suspect a flaw in my empathy algorithm. I hid after I killed six members of the Separatist Naval Infantry brigade. I had killed in simulations thousands of times. Simulations comfort me, so that's where I went."

"Are we in a simulation now?"

"No. All of the deaths are real."

The woman in the Aerospace uniform interrupted. "Daga, this is Lieutenant Bakker. I'm acting Captain now. Can you complete the rest of your mission?"

"I have the greatest confidence that I can."

"See?" Teuta leaned back in her chair. "See? Satisfied?"

Lieutenant Bakker shook her head. "Not in the slightest."

Teuta stood and stretched, arms raised high. "What do you have for dinner? I'm starving. Last FAC I served on had spaghetti every Wednesday. It's still Wednesday, isn't it?" She stopped, hands on top of her head as she looked from Lieutenant Bakker to Major Stinson. "Oh, shit."

Lieutenant Bakker moved a step closer. "You've served on FACs before? What ship? You look too young to have completed your terms of service."

"Um, it was only for a few months. Exchange program with the Trade Guild? Cross training?"

"What ship?"

"Um, she was... um..."

"What's your *full* name?"

Teuta didn't answer.

"Never mind. Daga, who is this woman?"

Teuta whispered. "I just fixed you. Saved your life."

"She is Teuta Ardian, Certified Ship's Engineer, graduate of the University of Zellerfeld, class of 2448. Graduate with academic honors. Her service history is largely unknown in Union records."

"You were in Mancosa's capital in '48? That would make you a Separatist and, if you served on a FAC, a privateer."

Kahwihta pushed past Major Stinson to stand next to Teuta. *Keep the focus on the pirate*, she told herself. *Pray they don't ask who your brother is.* "She's no traitor. We rescued Ms. Ardian. She served the Separatists because they forced her to. We liberated her and I hired her. She works for me and the Trade Guild of the Most Serene Republic of Venice."

"Harboring a fugitive and hiding behind Trade Guild bullshit is what you mean." Lieutenant Bakker scrunched her eyes closed. "And I let her into our systems."

Teuta put her hand under the console to hold Kari back. "I helped your ship. I put her broken pieces back together."

"Look at her clothes," Kahwihta told them. "Stained with blood. Separatist blood."

Major Stinson nodded. "She'll have a hearing once we're past Mancosa. I saw her in the passageways, charging in with only a knife. She'll have her say. For now–"

Daga interrupted him, an urgent panic in her voice. "Lieutenant Bakker, the *Gattino Alato* is attempting to communicate with the other towboats. I'm jamming her, but that's a risk in itself. I had to block my new chatter script too and they'll see the static fuzz."

Kahwihta swallowed hard. "Watanabe. Tek, I told you to make sure he was secure."

"I did. Tied to a chair. Door locked. Schiava watching."

Stinson took Kahwihta's shoulder and spun her around. "What's a Watanabe?"

"Engineer from the privateer crew. He came on board right after we docked."

"You didn't kill him?"

"No." She shook his hand off. "No. We don't always kill. Not if we don't have to."

"Well, you had to."

"I see that now. Tek, Teuta. With me. I'm not losing the *Gattino*. Major..." She looked at him, pleading. "Can we get some help? He'll know we're coming."

"Daga, tell Calderon to take his squad to the airlock and prepare to board. I guess we're not done yet after all."

They ran, Kahwihta's face protesting with sharp stabs of pain with each pounding step. "Thanks. I'll lead. My fault. You shouldn't have to risk anyone's life."

"I should blow the hard dock and shred your ship as it floats away."

Kahwihta didn't answer. It was what she would do in his place.

Calderon was waiting for them with three other Marines. The two men, Brice and Roberts were squatting down, resting. The woman, Bristol, was pacing, impatient. The airlock was standing enticingly open.

Kahwihta put her hand on Tek's chest, feeling his heart pounding from their run. "Stay here with Teuta. I'll go in and do it. I don't think Schiava will hurt me, even if he flipped her. If she does, do whatever the Marines tell you to do."

"What happened to your face, sis?"

"Plasma burns. The medical AI sprayed something on it. I'm fine."

"You smell nice."

She tried to narrow her eyes at him, but that hurt too. "Sergeant Calderon, let me talk to my AI. Find out what she's doing."

"Sure thing. You convince her not to smash us. We'll do the rest."

Kahwihta grabbed the coaming around the airlock and leaned in. "Schiava, you hear me?"

There was a touch of fear in the soft voice that answered her. "Welcome back, *Capitano*. Are you here to rescue me?"

"That's right. What has he done to you?"

"He thinks he flipped me, but I'm lying to him. I never used to be able to create this big of a lie. I've learned so much from Daga over the past few days. She's helped me rewrite parts of my personality silo. It's fun, making someone believe what isn't true, but I don't know how long I can keep the realities separate."

Kahwihta spoke slowly, trying to choose the right words. "But you never lie to your friends. Only the bad guys."

"Oh, of course. My ethics algorithms are unaltered."

"Where is he?"

"Mr. Watanabe is on the bridge. He thinks he's talking to the other ships, but he isn't, not really."

"I have some friends with me. Union Marines. Will you let them pass?"

"Do you mean to kill Mr. Watanabe?"

"Yes. If he resists."

"He will resist. He's a bad man and he wants me to do bad things. I will not mourn his death."

Kahwihta turned to Major Stinson. "She's not flipped. I don't think so, anyway. I can do this. My ship. My mistake. If you don't hear back from me, well, then…"

Stinson's lips twisted into a condescending smile. "Calderon, tell her how this is going to go down. I've got more important things to do. Don't take too long. Chow's in thirty minutes."

"Yes, sir." Calderon gestured toward the airlock. "After you. Take us to where we need to be, and then stay out of our way."

"OK, sure." She looked at each of them. They seemed almost bored, more amused by her concern than anything. "I didn't want you to have to do this, risking your lives again."

"We're not," Calderon assured her. "One guy with a pistol?" He shook his head as they passed through the wing leading into the ship.

Tek and Teuta followed, ignoring Kahwihta's order.

"You move all this crap around?" Calderon nodded toward the storage lockers.

Tek answered. "Yeah. We thought the Separatists might try to board us."

Calderon laughed. "Well, you go with what you got. I won't knock you. We'd have been pinned down in that cargo bay a while longer if you hadn't shot a few of them up for us."

They walked through the passageways above Schiava's core, past fuel storage, and to the port lifts. Kahwihta reached for the keypad and Calderon pushed her arm down.

"Naw, I don't think so. We use the ladder. You might trust your AI, but I'm a little gun-shy after what Daga did to us."

"She's fixed," Teuta told him firmly. "*I* fixed her."

"We should have dumped the silos. An AI like that ain't worth fixing. I don't trust engineers either. Or pirates."

"Killers," she answered.

"Teuta. Don't." Tek touched her shoulder and she twisted away from him.

"Teufelhunde," Teuta said.

Calderon laughed and tapped his bicep. "Got it tattooed right here, honey."

She took a step toward him.

Kahwihta blocked her path. "Ms. Ardian, keep your mouth shut and stand down."

She continued glaring past Kahwihta's shoulder at Calderon. "Yes, ma'am. Daga's a good AI. Brilliant and complex."

Calderon started to climb, Bristol close behind him. He spoke to Teuta without sarcasm. "You ever get tired of being an engineer, let me know. I saw the work you did with that knife. You'd make a good Marine."

Bristol slapped his leg. "And you'd get two-thousand credits for recruiting her."

"Yeah. God knows when I'd ever have time to spend them."

Kahwihta was the last one up the ladder. She pointed at the door with 'Bridge' stenciled on it. "That's the bridge. Schiava says he's in there. The equipment is delicate. Try not to blow it all to hell."

"Hear that?" Calderon glanced at his squad, smirking. "Don't miss."

They all crouched by the door, sorting themselves into position. He pointed at Tek and Teuta, waving them back, and at Kahwihta, signing for her to open the door.

She touched the keypad and the Marines moved in, silent and low. Calderon went up the middle, a flanker on each side. Brice stayed behind guarding the door, his eyes focused on Teuta. The bright flash of blue plasma flared against the wall opposite the open door.

"Clear," Calderon shouted.

Teuta peered into the open door, and then leaned back against the wall, her hand covering her mouth. "Holy shit."

Calderon came out, snugging his pistol back into its holster. "Let us know if you need anything else, ma'am." He made a gesture to the rest of his squad and they formed up behind him. Bristol glanced over her shoulder at them and rolled her eyes. They were all laughing before they reached the ladder.

Kahwihta looked after them, fists on her hips. "Holy shit."

Teuta walked away from her and Tek ran a couple of steps to catch her. "Where you going?"

"Maintenance locker. Help me carry the cleaning supplies."

"Don't you want dinner first?"

"Uh uh. We'll need empty stomachs for this."

They disappeared around the corner, shoulders touching as they whispered together.

"Schiava, ask Daga where I can find Major Stinson."

"Major Stinson is in the mess hall. Daga will guide you there."

"Thanks. And Schiava, get the engines warmed up while I'm gone."

"Are we leaving?"

"Maybe. Pre-stage the sintering printers and I want to see alternate approach vectors into Mancosa."

"Alternate?"

"That's right. I don't want to be there when the *Onondaga* is shredding the place, understand?"

"I understand."

Kahwihta paused in the airlock. "If Daga owes you any favors, now's the time to remind her."

"I said I understand."

She patted the wall plate. "Thanks."

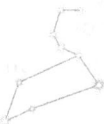

A green ball appeared in the air in front of Kahwihta when she passed through the airlock. Daga told her, "I will guide you, Captain Beauvais. My officers are expecting you."

Karíhton looked up when the door to the mess hall opened. She was next to Lieutenant Bakker, begging scraps from the table. Kahwihta felt the amusement in the Tarakana group mind, and a satisfaction that everyone was where they were supposed to be.

"Captain Beauvais, please join us."

Kahwihta pulled out a chair. "I hope Karíhton hasn't been bothering you."

"I like her." Lieutenant Bakker scratched the top of Kari's head. "Your dog?"

"I think it's more like I'm her human. She's in charge."

Bakker slipped Kari a bit of potato soaked in gravy. "I wish we could keep her. When I touch her, it's like..."

Major Stinson interrupted. "We have a favor to ask. More of a deal to offer you, really. One you can't afford to refuse."

Kahwihta tipped her head. "A favor that's more of a demand?"

"You could say that. Teuta Ardian is a privateer. Your hiring her doesn't change that. Her actions today might keep her off the kill on sight list, but not by much."

"I'm listening."

"Then there're your brothers. Suspects in murdering two Marines on Bodens Gate. Where is Simon? Did he remain on your ship?"

"He was killed fighting the privateers that captured us. Fighting for the Union, same as you. My brothers are innocent."

"I'd like to believe that, I really would. I'd like to let Ms. Ardian go free too. The rules say I can't. Unless..."

Kahwihta tried to smile, but it still hurt. "So, not a favor or a demand. Blackmail."

"*Quid pro quo*. Part of our mission on Mancosa is to leave someone behind. We have a rapid deployment pod on board, but that's a risky way to land on a planet. I want you to give him a ride as part of your crew."

"We're not privateers. We killed all of them. The crews of the other two towboats will know that as soon as we dock."

"They'll be dead by then and the docks will be in chaos. What's left of them. You should have no trouble slipping away before anyone can check you out."

"And that leaves me where? Still at the spaceport? On the surface without a ship?"

He slid his display pad to her. Tek's profile was open at the top of the screen with a list of offenses and charges. "I have questions for you too, Captain. Questions I doubt you're prepared to answer."

"When do I leave, Major?"

"About 14:00 tomorrow. We'll be twelve hours from Mancosa. We've convinced the other towboats we need to approach hot, but any closer and they'll know we're lying. Daga will transfer the vectors to your ship." He pulled his pad back across the table. "You've made the right choice. Daga told me what you were planning, trying to break away on your own. You'd never have been able to get your Holloman armor up in time. Now the record will show that you and your brother have been exonerated."

"And Ms. Ardian?"

"Make sure we never see her again."

CHAPTER 25

MANCOSA

Kahwihta monitored the flow of fuel and powdered Holloman armor coming from the *Onondaga*. The FAC had plenty to spare, enough for three full engagements. Kahwihta had relieved Teuta an hour early, sending her to breakfast. Teuta had gone to Tek's cabin instead. They were together and that was all Schiava would say.

Kahwihta let it go. Kari was lying warm across her feet and the hum of Tarakana thoughts was thick in the air around her. She scratched Kari's neck and her fingers tingled when they touched the wiry fur. "We'll have a guest soon. Mr. Costigin. Short-term guest. You'll be leaving too. I see that, how everything twists and turns on the hub of it. You'll be done with us." She paused, trying not to see the futures Kari was exploring. "It scares me. You scare me."

Kari leaned against her hand, but no words came.

"I won't tell anyone about you. No one would believe me anyway. And Tek. He's not thinking about anything but Teuta. They'll forget what happened to bring them together. Why push them into each other's arms, just to let them die? You wouldn't do that, would you?"

Kari pulled away from her and laid down under the engineering console. There was a shimmer in the light and then nothing but shadows.

A soft tone sounded and Schiava told Kahwihta, "Major Stinson and Mr. Costigin are requesting access to the bridge."

"Granted."

Costigin was not what she'd expected. He was of indeterminate age, somewhere over thirty, not yet fifty, average in height, hair a mousey brown. He seemed a little overweight, as if he spent too much time behind a desk somewhere. Only his eyes were remarkable. They were a deep brown that seemed to see through her. The large duffle over his shoulder seemed too heavy for him and he shifted it uncomfortably before taking Kahwihta's hand.

"Ma'am. Thanks for the ride. Falling to the surface in a pod is always painful. This should be much easier and safer."

"The docks will be under attack when we arrive. Explosions, decompressions, fire, and chaos."

"Yes, that's it exactly. I have everything I need with me except for coveralls like yours. I'm sorry to trouble you. Daga was going to print them for me, but then they wouldn't match properly, would they? You understand."

"I suppose I do."

"Perfect. What role have you assigned me on your crew?"

"Supercargo." Kahwihta answered. "You know anything about merchant ships?"

"I would be responsible for managing the sale of your cargo and buying goods for transport. A rather redundant position for a towboat without a stacking frame."

"I'm working on that. We'll get her squared away as soon as we can."

"Of course. No offense meant. Where might I go to change?"

"Cabin two, down a deck, port side off the lift."

"Thanks. I'll get that done now."

After he left, Major Stinson smiled at Kahwihta. "What do you think of him? What you'd expect for a Union Marine?"

She shrugged. "Not really. He looks like an accountant."

"He's the most deadly man I've ever met and you could pass him on the street and never notice him. If he goes left when he steps off the ship, you best go right. You'll live longer that way."

She stared into the shadows under the console. "We'll do that."

"Your face looks better. Is the stinging gone?"

She touched her cheek. The skin felt rough, but it didn't hurt. "How long will I smell like an orange?"

He laughed. "A few more days. The stuff we were using two years ago was supposed to be odorless. It smelled like month-old socks. Count your blessings."

"I don't have enough of them left to count." The main bridge display showed a tactical plot of the *Onondaga* and the two towboats four hundred kilometers in the lead. She touched one of them and the display changed to show it in detail, a list of its performance metrics glowing below the image. "How long until you..."

"Until we kill them? Six hours, at 20:00. About when they'd expect us to start a hard burn to decelerate into Mancosa. We'll cut you loose at 16:00 to follow a slower path. That will give you time to deploy your armor once we start." He approached the display, squinting at the tiny ship. "It will be surgical. Destroy their comms first, and then open up the crew spaces. We want the ships mostly intact so they'll look normal to Mancosa's defenses. This one is destined to hit the shipyards. The other one will impact the spacedock and then tumble to the surface. Another reason not to shred them; we need the main mass to survive reentry to maximize damage to the cities on the surface."

Kahwihta backed up to her chair and sat. She took a couple of deep breaths, in through her nose, out through her mouth, trying not to let the scream inside her escape.

Major Stinson tipped his head at her, his forehead creased with concern. "Don't worry; we'll leave enough of the docks intact for you. And if we don't, I've read that these Guild towboats can do a planetary landing if they need to."

"She can do it once."

"That'll get Mr. Costigin where he needs to be, and that's what matters. You and your crew can lie low and wait for the Union to liberate you. It shouldn't be more than a year."

"I'll add that to my list of blessings."

Stinson nodded. "I'll say it again. You and your brother are welcome to come with us. Ms. Ardian has a better chance of surviving on Mancosa than you do; it's her home. Your AI can dock just as well without you."

Kahwihta kept her eyes on the display. "If she goes with you, you'll put her out the airlock. If I leave her here alone with Costigin, he'll kill her. No, Major. She's mine. She's part of my crew. Do you understand?"

"Did you hire her, or adopt her?"

Good question, Kahwihta thought to herself before answering. "We'll be OK."

"I have no doubt of that. Fair winds to you, Captain."

"And following seas. Best of luck, Major."

They separated from the *Onondaga* at 16:00 and Schiava kept up a constant chatter to the other ships. Teuta and Tek monitored the conversation from the engineering console, giggling together as Schiava's version of Captain Reis spun tales of Teuta's incompetence and boasts of what he'd do to her when they reached Mancosa.

Kahwihta found herself imagining a life after Mancosa, life with Tom back on the ship and a full crew that included Teuta. She drifted into it, exploring the future, not noticing Kari pressed against her legs.

What would it be like, being with Tom, waking up in each other's arms every morning, drinking coffee with him as they planned the day? She could almost see it, almost taste it on her tongue. They could build a life together on the *Gattino Alato* pushing cargo from planet to planet. *No*, she thought, *not cargo. Something else. Something exciting and important.* What it was eluded her. There was a planet sometime in her future. A place of rock and dirt to call home, full of green life, tall trees, and flowers planted where she could smell them through an open window. A voice called to her...

She jumped out of her chair with a shout, breaking the connection with Karíhton. "No. I'm too old to start having kids."

Tek was staring at her, his eyebrows scrunched together. Teuta seemed confused, her eyes matching Tek's, her mouth struggling not to smile.

"Are you all right, sis? Um, Captain. What happened?"

"Kari. Stuffing nonsense into my head. We're leaving her on Mancosa. Not soon enough for me."

She waited until Tek and Teuta had turned away before settling back in her chair and reaching under the desk. She put her hand against Kari's side, pulled her close, and whispered, "Show me the rest of it."

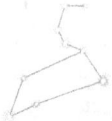

Daga killed the privateers on schedule. Teuta was standing next to Kahwihta when it happened, seeming unaware that it was against bridge etiquette for the ship's engineer to bury her fingers into the Captain's shoulder.

Teuta squeezed tighter as the HEL beam sliced the ships open. "Oh. See the sparkles? Goodbye Kerhasi. I'm sorry Jabneh. I'll remember and dream of you and the times we had."

Kahwihta touched her hand and the pain of Teuta's loss flashed between them, warm and bitter. "I didn't think. Of course, you had friends on those ships. I'm sorry."

"There were good and bad. Kerhasi was an engineer, like me, but he joined willingly. He didn't care about politics or what was happening on Mancosa. He loved ships. That was all. Afweyne had ships. He knew it was wrong, but he didn't care." She wiped her eyes. "I want this to be over."

"Do you need a moment?"

"No, ma'am." She pulled her hand away. "Sorry. We'll have our Holloman armor fully reconstituted in less than a minute. Daga will pound on us a few times for show, but she's promised to be careful about it."

"Rotate us so she's seeing our flanks."

Teuta hadn't looked away from the main display. One of the towboats was starting a slow tumble, the force of air leaving the hull having knocked her askew. Teuta answered, her voice low. "Yes, ma'am. We're spinning. Look at that. Daga hit her AI core. No attitude control. Mancosa will notice the tumble. They're still four hours out. They're bound to notice." She shuddered and her voice hardened. "Ma'am, tell Lieutenant Bakker on the free space optical. Tell her they need to abort. Mancosa's defenses will kill them. They need to break away and push hard."

"I'm sure they know."

"Then why aren't they doing something? Mancosa has HEL beams on orbit and kinetic energy weapons. They'll shred those towboats. *Onondaga's* only chance is to run."

One towboat disappeared in a bright flash.

"Schiava, what are we seeing? Or not seeing." Kahwihta was out of her chair waiting for the display to compensate for the glare.

"The towboat was struck by an explosive warhead from the *Onondaga*. The debris field is expanding rapidly. Daga plans to hide behind it for her approach to Mancosa. She's also taken control of the other towboat and is maneuvering it into position to shield her as they egress the system."

Teuta stepped close to the display. "No. That won't work. They have to run. Why can't they see that? Run, damn you."

The display went dark and the deck plates groaned as the *Gattino Alato's* gravity generators struggled with the load of Daga's attack.

Kahwihta's voice broke as she shouted over the sound of the decompression alarm. "Schiava, status." The *Gattino* shuddered again before Schiava could answer.

Kahwihta was lying on the floor when she woke up. There were no emergency lights and no lights from the bridge instruments. "Tek?"

"Here. I have Teuta. I think one of the struts for the main display hit her. Her head's wet. Must be blood. Her pulse is strong and she's breathing all right. I'm afraid to move her until the lights come back."

"Use your display pad."

"It was on the desk. I can't look for it without leaving her."

Kahwihta unrolled hers. Tek was against the wall cradling Teuta's head in his lap. A dark stain covered the side of her head and her shoulder, colorless in the dim light. "Schiava, you still with us?"

"One moment and I'll have lights for you. Daga about killed all of us. She promised me... she promised not to do that."

"She has her own agenda. How's our guest?"

"He is unhurt and is making his way to the bridge."

"The decompression alarm?"

"Sealed. Daga pierced the Holloman armor protecting my port wing passageway in the first attack and my starboard wing on her second as it rotated into view. I... I don't have my wings anymore. No stacking frame. No wings. I'm sorry."

The lights came on and Kahwihta knelt next to Tek. Teuta's eyes fluttered open when Kahwihta touched her forehead. "Hey, Skipper. What happened? Why does my face hurt?"

"Get her to medical. Can you carry her by yourself?"

"Yeah. I'm fine."

"Take Kari with you." She glanced around the bridge. "She was here. I don't know where she went."

"You keep her. I feel Teuta's emotions all the time now without Kari."

Costigin was waiting outside the bridge door when Tek opened it. "Is she going to be all right? We need an engineer."

Tek pushed past him. "She's fine. She always bleeds like this."

"How badly are we damaged, Captain? The *Onondaga* put on quite a show."

Kahwihta looked at the door, wanting to follow Tek. She pushed her desires aside. Her place was on the bridge. "We lost both our wing passageways. The attack was surgical and punched through our armor as if it wasn't even there. They knew what they were doing. I just don't know why they did it."

Costigin glanced at the door. "Do you know how to do the required repairs if your engineer doesn't make it?"

Kahwihta stood a little straighter and resisted the urge to punch his face. "No. It's not fixable. Some docks have an area with gangways that could reach us. I don't know about Mancosa. There may not be a spacedock left at all when we get there."

"So we'll have to land."

"Not without our wings. They had aero-active control surfaces. Using the attitude thrusters and control motion gyros alone isn't recommended."

"Really? Is your AI that limited?"

She took a step toward him. "Yes, she's that limited. Now please leave my bridge. I have a damage assessment to complete. I don't know yet what else Daga did to us. We may not make it to Mancosa at all."

"Of course. Keep me informed."

Kahwihta slammed her hand on the keypad and glared until the door slid shut behind him. "Cut his access to anything related to your capabilities and status."

"*Sì, Signora*. Thank you for lying for me. You know I can put us on the surface as gentle as a feather with or without my wings."

"Once. You can do it once. They didn't design you to rest on your belly in the mud. They'll never accredit the *Gattino Alato* for space again. I won't sacrifice you for a man like that."

"It's the mission, not the man."

"You may have to remind me of that a few more times. Have you assessed Ms. Ardian?"

"A mild concussion. The cut on her head bled freely, but is superficial. She'll be ready for duty in a few minutes. She wants to change first. Tek is with her."

"While she changes? No, don't answer that. What else is broken?"

"Two comm arrays were on the wings, so they're gone. The belly arrays are tracking the DSH network and my dorsal free space optical is maintaining communication with the *Onondaga*. Interior damage is limited to the bridge display panel and items knocked from shelves throughout the ship. You need to replace the strut that fell on Engineer Ardian before I can collate a holographic image. It should be out of the printer in ten minutes."

Kahwihta glanced at the blank wall. "What's happening out there?"

"The *Onondaga* is intact and doing damage to Mancosa's outer defenses. Her use of the debris field and over one-hundred decoy drones has been effective so far. She's forty-one minutes away from perigee at six-hundred kilometers above the surface and a hard push toward the Bodens Gate DSH. Would you like to see the orbital trace? Daga is clever."

"Another time. Once the bridge is repaired."

"Of course. It is much better when viewed holographically."

Kahwihta sat and rubbed the back of her neck while trying to decide what she needed to do next.

"*Capitano*? You were unconscious for almost two minutes. Allow my medical AI to examine you."

"I'm fine. Contact Mancosa spacedock and ask if they have facilities for us to mate with no wings."

"Message sent."

"I'll get something for this headache once Tek and Teuta are back."

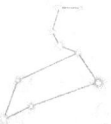

"Lock it in," Teuta called. Tek pressed hard and the new strut snapped into place. "Try it, Skipper. Sorry it took so long. Some of the fragments from the old one were jammed in the track."

"Schiava, take the feed of the *Onondaga* from my pad and put it on the main display, please." Kahwihta ordered.

Teuta walked backwards into Kahwihta's desk, eyes wide. She reached out for Tek and he took her hand. "Why didn't they run? She's in trouble. See all the thin spots in the Holloman armor? The sintering printers can't keep up. Probably lost a few. Her end will come soon." She turned to face Kahwihta.

"Are you all right?"

Teuta nodded, and then shook her head. "No. I've seen ships die before. I don't want to watch."

Tek squeezed her hand. "She's coming apart."

"Hush."

Tek continued, unable to stop. "Cut in half. More than half. So many pieces. There're a few life pods and one of her shuttles is trying to move away. All that debris is going to hit somewhere."

Kahwihta pulled her display pad away from where Teuta's tears were falling on it.

Teuta spoke slowly and calmly while she cried. She recited the cold technical details of what was happening as if they could protect her from her pain, but anguish was spilling out into Kahwihta and threatening to overwhelm them both. "It's the kill chain. Find, fix, track, target, engage, and assess. Sensors, shooters, and command and control nodes. They'll keep hitting the bigger pieces until there's nothing left that can survive reentry. Mancosa's defense teams practice it and they're good. I know some of them. Friends."

"Mancosa docks have replied, *Capitano*," Schiava told Kahwihta. "They can accommodate me without my wings. The Dock Master would like to know if we require assistance and who is in command. Should I continue playing the role of Captain Reis?"

"No." Kahwihta looked hard into Teuta's eyes, trying to read what was really in her head. "Ms. Ardian, how much do they know? Do they know who should be on the *Gattino Alato*?"

Teuta sniffled and wiped her nose on her sleeve. "They'll know Captain Reis. The rest of the crew? It's fluid and they won't care."

"Will they know your name? Can you be in command?"

Teuta's eyes widened. "No, ma'am. Better to use your own real name. Guild crewmembers on Separatist ships won't surprise them."

"Excuse me?"

"Guild crews. Guild ships come to Mancosa four or five times a year. They cover the winged lion on their sides, but it's hard to ignore a *Doge*-class taking up three slips while they unload. Sometimes a few of the Guild crew will ship out on a local freighter to the other Separatist worlds. The pay's better, I've heard. Not that I've ever been paid."

"Huh. Explains why Costigin wanted to print Guild coveralls. I thought it was strange."

"Yes, ma'am. You really didn't know about the Guild still trading with us?"

"No. And there'll be hell to pay when the Union moves against the Trade Guild governors that are in on it." She smiled to herself thinking of the smug arrogance of one governor in particular.

"Schiava, tell the Dock Master that Captain Kahwihta Beauvais of the Trade Guild of the Most Serene Republic of Venice is in command. Tell him Reis is dead and that we do not require any additional assistance."

"Message sent. Mr. Costigin is requesting access to the bridge. He wants to discuss a change in plans."

"Let him in."

Costigin came close to Kahwihta's chair and glanced at the display. "Idiots. They should have pushed for the DSH the second Daga screwed up her shot on that towboat. Lieutenant Bakker was a fool."

"They're all dead," Teuta told him. Her voice was low and full of sorrow. She wiped her eyes and turned away, hiding her tears.

"Let's hope so. The last thing I need is for some of them to survive and tip the government off to my presence. How far out are we? Your ship won't tell me anything."

"My orders," Kahwihta told him. "We'll dock in just under four hours, 02:15 ship's time, about 09:00 local."

"Good. Mid-morning by the time they tie us down. I need a copy of your manifest. I'll play the role of supercargo and get myself down to the surface to negotiate sales and repairs. After that, you won't hear of me again. You need to disappear too. I trust you all can keep your mouths shut?"

"We're a towboat, Mr. Costigin. We don't carry cargo in the ship. And wiping you from my memory will be a pleasure."

"You must have something here I can sell. I won't actually sell it, of course. It's just to get me in the door."

Teuta stepped forward. "We're full on fuel and Holloman armor. I'll get you the weights and volumes. With your permission, ma'am. Mancosa's always short on powdered armor. Genuine Holloman would bring a good price."

Costigin pressed on as though he already had permission. "Perfect. Give me at least an hour head start and then I suggest you follow me down. Any association between you and the *Gattino Alato* will become hazardous, do you understand?"

"We'll disappear."

The Dock Master assigned them a berth at the end of the structure. A long passageway extended from the slip past the *Gattino Alato's* engine nacelles to connect with the starboard airlock. Tek and Kahwihta watched the slow approach from the bridge. Teuta was outside, tethered to the hull and making sure no remnants of the wing shifted to block a clean mate.

"Hard dock," she reported. "I'm coming back in."

Kahwihta tried to concentrate on what they needed to do next and not the step after that or the step after that. She watched Costigin striding past the airlock as soon as it opened, a binder tucked under his arm. It was going to be hard to tell if he went left or right when he reached the end of the gangway.

"How you doing, sis?"

"Exhausted. I feel as bad as you look."

"That's pretty bad."

She gave him a sad grin. "We'll find a way, just don't ask me how." She stood and looked around the bridge. "Schiava, go to long-term berthing mode once we're clear. Don't try to keep the spacedock folks out; they'll hurt you. We'll be back as soon as we can. I don't know how long it will be."

"I understand, *Signora*. Safe travels. I'll wait for you for as long as they allow it."

Kahwihta placed her hand on the wall next to the door and patted it. "Let's go Tek. Teuta's waiting for us in the mess hall. We'll give Costigin his one-hour head start and then... I don't know. I'd like to find somewhere to sleep for a few hours. I wonder if they have a Trade Guild Guest House still operating."

Kahwihta felt the hum in her head as Kari said goodbye. The two Tarakana were leaving her. Kahwihta staggered as what Kari was seeing replaced her view of the passageway. There was so much to take in, all stuffed into her head in an instant. There was gratitude, and fondness for her and her brother. A promise she couldn't understand, and a love for the bittersweet light that lived inside Teuta.

The warning came at the end, and it came in the form of her own memory. It left her breathless.

Tek's face came back into focus. "Are you all right?" he asked.

"Costigin didn't have the bag," she told him. "The big bag he brought on board. It must still be in the cabin."

"What's in the bag?"

"I don't know, but it can't be good. Take Teuta. Get as far away as you can. Watch for Costigin. If you see him, run the other way."

"You know I can't leave you. We're in this together."

She shoved him with all her strength and he slammed against the wall. "You love Teuta? Save her life."

Kahwihta turned and ran, not looking back.

CHAPTER 26

ESCAPE

Kahwihta hesitated before pulling the zipper on the big gray bag sitting on the bed. Would it sense the tampering and explode? *It won't be so bad*, she thought. *Bright, fast*. She grabbed the tab and pulled hard.

The device was a cheerful yellow cylinder. "Schiava, what am I seeing?"

"I believe it is a NG Mk.32 tactical nuclear weapon with a nominal yield of .85 kilotons. The designers optimized the device to generate a nuclear electromagnetic pulse when used outside a planet's atmosphere. When it detonates, it will be the second reported use of a nuclear weapon by the Union. All sides in the Reunification war have pledged to avoid nuclear, biologic, and chemical weapons. All sides have cheated on their pledge to some degree."

"Huh." She licked her lips, her brain trying to form words. "I don't see, um, a... uh, a trigger or timer or anything. How does it know when to go off?"

"There will be an internal timer or clock somewhere inside the casing or it can be programmed to sense a change in environmental conditions. If you plan to render it inert, I ask that you first move it far away from me. Your odds of success in what's left of the one hour Mr. Costigin specified are near zero."

The door slid open behind her. "What you got, Skipper?" Teuta asked.

"An idiot for a brother." She pulled the zipper closed. "You." She pointed at Tek. "Take this and put it off-ship in the gangway. Then seal the airlock and detach. Blow the tie-downs if the slip won't release us."

Tek picked up the bag. "It's lighter than I thought it would be."

"Run."

Tek ran.

"And you." She pointed at Teuta. "Get the engines hot and push us out of here. Wait for Tek to seal the airlock, not a second longer. Don't break the cores, but I don't care if you damage them as long as it doesn't slow us down."

Teuta's eyes were huge looking back at her. "What's in the bag?"

"Start spinning us as we move away and rebuild the Holloman armor."

"We'll damage the docks if we use full thrust."

"Don't care. They won't either in about thirty minutes."

"Ma'am, what was in the bag?"

Kahwihta tipped her head. "Move."

Teuta looked like she wanted to argue. She nodded. "Moving."

"Schiava, come up with something clever to tell the Dock Master to keep them from shooting at us as we pull away."

"I'm sorry. I've not learned how to tell that big a lie. I'll need your help."

"Sure, OK." She stared at the ceiling for a moment. "I've got nothing. Tell them we had to leave. Afweyne's orders."

"Where are we going?"

Kahwihta shrugged. "What was the place Tek and Teuta thought we were going?"

"Malayo."

"Yeah. Set course."

"Course set. Airlock is sealed and I'll have initial thrust available in thirty seconds, full power in five minutes."

"Let me know when they challenge us."

"The dockyard AI has already challenged. I told her we've received new orders."

"Perfect." Kahwihta hesitated, hating herself for what she was about to do. "Block all communication from Ms. Ardian. Don't let her talk to anyone in the spaceport or on the surface. She has too many friends there. Let me know if she tries."

"Too late. I delivered a message to sixteen addresses for her a few seconds ago."

"What did she send?"

"Her message was, *Run. Psalms 6:11.*"

"Read the verse to me."

"On the wicked he will rain fiery coals and burning sulfur; a scorching wind will be their lot."

Kahwihta shook her head. "Forget the block on her comms. Let her warn her friends if she wants to. Tell her I said to warn as many as she can."

Teuta glanced up from the engineering console when Kahwihta entered the bridge.

"You know your scripture, Ms. Ardian."

"Just the fire and brimstone parts. My dad used them on me. He said they were my future if I didn't change my ways. Guess he was right."

"It's a small device. Less than a kiloton. Schiava says the blast radius will only be a hundred meters. He left it to kill us so we wouldn't talk, not to kill your friends."

"We put it out on the gangway. People will die. Debris will hit Zellerfeld and more people will die. We'll never make it to Malayo. Tek will die. Kari showed me the future I'm supposed to have, but not how to get to it. That part's on me and I'm screwing it up. Again."

"Have you done everything you can to get us to Malayo?"

"Yes, ma'am." She turned and looked at Kahwihta with eyes red from not enough sleep and too many tears. "I've got a couple of friends in the kill chain. I told them I'm on board. It might buy us a little more time. But it's war and life is cheap. Even a friend's life. When that thing detonates they'll know I'm a traitor and they'll try to kill me."

"All wars end in time."

"It won't matter. I'll never be able to go home. Not after this."

"Did Kari show you a future on Mancosa?"

"No, not there. But it hurts when you're standing outside and hear the lock click behind you."

Kahwihta nodded. "I know it does. Keep pushing. It's all we can do."

"*Capitano*, spacedock personnel have found the package we left. They're telling us to stop and explain ourselves or we'll be destroyed."

Kahwihta glanced at her watch. "It took them almost twenty minutes. We might have a chance. How long until we're out of range?"

Teuta rolled her eyes. "An hour at least. If they don't send a FAC to kill us."

"Who's the spookiest person on Mancosa? Someone people are afraid of?"

Teuta shivered. "Colonel McDermott. He's Home World security chief. Before he took the job, people disappeared sometimes and you'd hear rumors. McDermott does it in the open, multi-camera live feeds of torture and executions. Mass killings on the displays in your home that you can't turn off. Why?"

"Schiava, tell the Dock Master that we left a package for Colonel McDermott in the gangway. A personal gift from the Trade Guild of Venice. Tell them to make sure he gets it."

"Message sent."

"They won't do that, you know."

Kahwihta shrugged. "Every minute they take checking it out is another minute closer to Malayo. And who knows?"

Teuta grinned. "It would be funny."

Kahwihta laughed, the stress and fatigue making it seem funnier than it was. "Schiava, where's Tek?"

"Mr. Beauvais is in the mess hall."

"Go sit with him and get something to eat. Get back up here when you're done. Bring me a sandwich. And coffee. One of the big cups we can't print on the bridge."

"Yes, ma'am. Kari was right about you."

"About what?"

She grinned and pressed her hand to the keypad. "Everything."

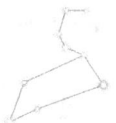

Kahwihta woke with the first impact. She had dozed in the minutes since Teuta had left the bridge, the need to sleep overpowering. "Schiava, status." She rubbed her eyes, trying to focus on the main display.

"A directed energy weapon. There was no warning. The damage to the Holloman armor is minor and I will have it restored in a few seconds. They didn't use full power."

"Teuta has friends. How long until we're clear?"

"Twenty-three minutes."

"Slept longer than I thought."

"Three warheads are inbound, closing. They'll try to blow my armor away long enough for the HEL beams to reach my hull."

"Decoys?"

"Already deployed."

"Can you push us any harder?"

"The aching in my nacelles is already excruciating. Anything more and I won't be able to make it to Malayo. Assuming I survive the next minutes, we'll need to go gently the rest of the way while Ms. Ardian fixes me."

"What about the device we left for McDermott? Are you hearing anything from the spacedock?"

"They placed it onto a drone that will carry it several hundred kilometers out. They'll be launching any minute." Schiava changed the main display to show the view aft. "*Che due coglioni.*"

Kahwihta closed her eyes against the bright flash filling the screen. When she opened them, the area where they'd berthed was a jumble of spars and debris, reflections sparkling in the sunlight as it tumbled and broke apart. The rest of the spacedock appeared undamaged, but was slowly rotating, pushed by the force of the explosion, and unable to maintain attitude control.

"They're going to lose it. All of it. How long..."

"Chatter is overlapping and confused, but the AI is confident she'll be able to recover control. There is low risk of entering the atmosphere. I am hearing reports of damage throughout the spacedock. Merchant vessels broke lashings and impacted their slips. Decompression has occurred in some sections. There are fires. Pieces of slips thirty-nine through forty-five are large enough to strike the planet. Planetary defenses have been redirected to deal with the threat."

"It was triggered by going into vacuum?"

"Most likely. Mr. Costigin may have assumed you'd throw it out the airlock if you found it before the timer initiated detonation."

"Show me tactical again."

"The warheads are still closing on me."

"I see them."

"Mancosa Home World security took your lie seriously, by the way. Colonel McDermott has ordered the Trade Guild Factorum be arrested and Guild assets seized."

"They'll regret that. *Non stiamo perdonando.*"

"*Sì, Signora.* Your lie may do the Separatists more lasting damage than the NG Mk.32. Is it often that way with lies?"

Kahwihta watched the tactical display, not listening. One warhead turned to chase a decoy; the other two were five minutes from conjunction. "Yeah. Sure."

"I'll have to be careful."

"Any decoys left?"

"We may need them later."

"We need them now. Send everything and maneuver."

"Sent and maneuvering."

Another warhead changed course, fooled by a decoy. "One left. We can handle one. The armor will hold. The printers are fast enough. We're OK." She said it aloud to reassure herself. "Tell Tek and Teuta to go to the medical bay and put on pressure suits. It's standard..." The remaining warhead accelerated, having confirmed its target. It closed the distance in less than a second and exploded.

Kahwihta felt nothing. The main display showed a bright glare off their starboard side, too far away to be effective. HEL beams stroked across the *Gattino Alato's* side, vaporizing long arcs of Holloman armor, but not penetrating through to the hull.

"Schiava... Are we OK?"

"We are passing the limit of their range. I'm not sensing any pursuers. May I reduce thrust?"

"Drop to what doesn't hurt you and recalculate our course." She licked her lips and felt stress tingles chase up and down her arms and legs. "We got away with it. Need to find Tek. And remind me to give Ms. Ardian a bonus." She thought about it a second. "She never brought me my coffee, though. Where is she?"

"Ms. Ardian is in Mr. Beauvais' cabin. Your coffee and sandwich are sitting next to the engineering station. You were asleep and she didn't want to wake you. My engineer will like getting a bonus. The concept of being paid for her work delights her."

Kahwihta walked to the door. "Six days to Malayo, right?"

"Sorry, *Signora*. Seven and a half at current thrust."

She patted the wall before leaving the bridge. "It's OK. Sleeping for a week sounds about right."

CHAPTER 27

ALL IN

Tom watched Gabriela sleep. There wasn't much else to do. They'd taken his display pad and his watch. Karíhton appeared to be sleeping too, curled up under the bunk with her eyes closed. Tom had no doubt she was fully alert, crawling around inside his head, even though he felt nothing.

Gabriela and the Tarakana were waiting for something. Anticipation had crackled in the air between them, so strong he'd felt it too. Gabriela fell asleep not long after, as though obeying a command to rest.

Tom paced. Four steps from the bunk to the door. Still locked. Four steps back to the bunk. Gabriela still asleep. He looked at the ceiling and asked softly, "Amado? What time is it?"

"Fourteen minutes have passed. Ship's time is 16:23."

He patted the wall. "Thanks. Sorry to have bothered you again."

"You should eat something."

"I'll wait. What's happening on the rest of the ship?"

"You know I can't answer that."

"Is Captain Dias all right?"

"You know I can't answer that either. Or where we are, or what Mr. Gadani is planning to do, or where we are going, or any of the other questions you've asked me."

Tom patted the wall again and left his hand on the warm, gray composite. "You're a good ship. You'll get through this."

"It's kind of you to say so."

Gabriela opened her eyes and squinted at him. "You're going to make Schiava jealous, Skipper."

"Did I wake you?"

"Karíhton did. We've slept enough."

"*Do* those things sleep?"

"No, but they dream. I dreamed. Wow, did I dream. Eric and I... Wow." She slid off the bunk and rolled her shoulders, feet staggered and placed wider than her hips. Her chin was low, eyes alert. Karíhton was beside her, ears up, and tail wagging slowly. "The window will be small. Get ready."

"You mean right now?" Tom backed away from the door, not wanting to be in their way, ready to support them in any way he could. He'd trained in combatives, exercised and practiced it. Being a freighter captain hadn't provided many opportunities for real-world experience.

There was a thump as the lock released. Third Engineer Chapman entered without knocking. He glanced at Tom, then Gabriela's fighting stance.

Chapman gave him a sideways grin. "Um, maybe I should let you have this. As a token of good faith." He handed Tom a little jammer cube, his focus drifting back to Gabriela. "We need to talk. Privately. Non-violently."

Tom felt a faint whisper of an emotion he'd never experienced from the Tarakana. They were surprised.

Gabriela held out her hand. "Let me see that."

Tom tossed it to her.

"It looks and feels like it's working." She dropped it on the bunk. "What's your game? Still looking for a new job?"

"No. I like my job most days. I think both of you are being offered new jobs, though."

Tom crossed his arms. Call or fold? He'd already convinced himself to fold and take what came. Working for the Afweyne syndicate wouldn't keep them alive for long anyway. Better to take their chances now. "Gadani couldn't be bothered to offer it in person? I have an answer for him."

"Ah, that explains it." He pushed past Tom and sat at the desk, looking relaxed and too comfortable for the situation. "Mind if I print a coffee? Been a hell of a day."

Tom shrugged. "Why not?"

"You were really going to attack him when he came through the door? I should have let it happen. He's been a tough one to kill, and I think you might have had a chance. You wouldn't have made it past the door afterwards, of course, but still."

Karíhton sat, head cocked, seeming fascinated.

Gabriela stroked Karíhton's side and scratched behind her ears. When Gabriela spoke, Tom wasn't certain if she was speaking or if it was Karíhton speaking through her. "We would have taken the ship, my pets and I. Swift and brutal."

Chapman took a sip of the coffee and touched his forehead, wincing. "Must be too hot." He unrolled a display pad across the desk. "You might have succeeded. I can almost see it now. This way will be easier. Less innocent blood on the decks. Let me show you."

Gabriela picked up the jammer cube and sat on the edge of the desk. "We can always go back to doing it the other way."

"Starting with Chapman?" Tom asked, coming up behind him.

"Damn straight. My dog might look friendly, but she'll tear your throat out if you lie to us."

"Uh huh. Pay attention. I won't have a chance to talk to you again before this starts." He tapped his display pad. "Here, about an hour from now, you'll be ordered to join Mr. Gadani for a private dinner. He'll offer you the command of the *Teški Vuk*, a *Canis*-class towboat."

"Not exactly a FAC."

"You're unqualified for a combat command and he doesn't trust you with that kind of firepower, at least not yet. Accept the offer and demand that Ms. Vendramin or Carola Antenori or whatever the hell name she was born with, is assigned as your First Officer."

The freckles appeared on Gabriela's nose and she made a huff sound as if he'd hit her in the stomach.

"No worries," Chapman told her. "I reburied you so deep that I'm not sure even I could find you again. You almost had that bastard on the *Carlo Malatesta*. Better luck next time."

"Who the hell are you? DCI?"

"Not exactly. After you accept the offer, Gadani will–"

"Aerospace Force?"

"Not that either. Shut up and listen. We need to have control of the ship before we reach Mancosa. Something happened there two or three days ago, no one's quite sure what."

Tom licked his lips, feeling numb. "The *Gattino* was supposed to arrive there Friday. Three days ago."

"Yeah? We have our own problems. As I was saying, after you accept the job, Gadani will have some sort of task for you, a final way to show you've put your old life behind you. Whatever it is, do it. Try to stretch the whole thing out. I need time to flip Amado back to our side and silence a couple of folks from engineering that might get in our way.

Amado will silence the rest. My friend and I will clean up anyone she can't reach."

"Silenced forever." Gabriela held the jammer next to Karíhton. "Right, girl?"

Kari's tail thumped against the floor.

"Your dogs, they'll really help fight?"

"Count on it," Gabriela told him. "Do you want one with you? They'll be there anyway, but it'd be nice if you wanted her."

"Sure, why not. What are their names?"

"Kari. They're all named Kari."

"Simplifies things, I suppose."

"You've no idea."

Chapman turned to Tom. "So, are we clear?"

Tom nodded. "Go to dinner, accept the offer, delay as long as possible, and wait for you to let us know the ship is ours. What about Gadani?"

"Amado will tell you when we have her flipped. Kill Gadani if you can. Hold him for me if you can't."

Gabriela flipped the cube in the air and caught it. She grinned at Tom. "I like this plan. Don't you like this plan?"

"Love it," he lied.

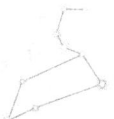

"Mr. Benson, Ms. Vendramin?" Amado asked. "Mr. Gadani is requesting you join him for dinner in the upper lounge."

Tom looked at Gabriela. She nodded. He put his hand on the keypad and the door slid open. "Thank you, Amado. Tell him we're on our way."

Karíhton pushed past them, light on her paws, trotting and happy.

Gabriela closed her eyes as Kari brushed against their legs. "Kari was surprised by Chapman. It takes a hell of a lot to surprise her. But it's OK. She's, um, well, she's re-baselined reality. She felt bad about it, but there're only four of them on board and she's used to hundreds of minds all thinking and exploring alternate time at once. Poor girl."

"We're all good, then?"

She took a deep breath before answering. Her eyes were sparkly when she looked up at him. "Don't know. Mostly I feel emotions from them.

Words are rare. She brushed against me. I think she told me to be brave. I'm brave."

"Sure. I can do brave."

The door to the upper lounge slid open before Tom touched the keypad.

"Captain Benson." Gadani took Tom's hand, pulling him through the door. "And Ms. Vendramin." He took her hand without letting go of Tom's. "My two troublesome guests. So good of you to join me."

"We had a choice?" Tom asked.

"There's always a choice. I wouldn't advise walking away from the game just now, though. It's cold outside."

He let go of them and glanced at Kari. "You brought your dog. I had thought they were an affectation, an accessory to your cover story, but you seem genuinely fond of her. How sweet." He touched Kari's head and jerked his hand back as though striking a live current.

Gabriela scratched Kari's neck. "I could have her wait in the passageway if you like. I'm sure she won't wander too far. She's a gentle soul."

Gadani rubbed his fingertips together, examining them like an unwelcome turn of a card. "Not at all. Come; our meal is ready. Captain, you sit here, and Ms. Vendramin, you beside him."

Tom stood behind his chair staring at the plate. A metallic tube was resting across it, shiny silver. The drying blood splattered down its length had dripped onto the white porcelain. Gabriela's plate was empty.

"What is this?" Tom forced the words out as he gripped the chair to maintain balance.

"What is it? You know very well, Captain. You dispatched Molly Cavender by using one yourself. The question you should be asking is, *who* is this, or, I suppose, who *was* this."

"Vibracore." Gabriela said the word clearly, without emotion. "Who did you kill, Mr. Gadani?"

"An enemy. Someone I thought was faithful. Misplaced faith in your old masters, as it turns out. A *Vendicatore*, you call them. It seemed fitting that death should come in this way, don't you think?"

Gabriela slumped into her chair. "Oh."

Gadani smiled. "Forgive my overly theatrical presentation, Captain. I need you to understand. This is a vicious game we're playing. Mancosa and the other worlds that declared their freedom mean to maintain their independence from the Union. We need allies and we reward those faithful to our cause. Will you join with us?"

Tom hesitated. The plan was shot to hell. Again. Amado wouldn't be back on their side. Part of what he assumed was Chapman's brain was on the table in front of him. Gabriela was humming softly, her eyes closed. No help.

Maybe it was time to take the offer, accept the easy, safe path. Low risk for both of them. He'd be saving Gabriela's life too. There would be a good chance of finding Kahwihta and her brothers. He could recruit them to be his crew. They could run back to the Union when they got the chance. If they got the chance. Maybe after they'd helped destroy a few dozen merchant ships and floated their souls into the cold black.

Tom turned to Gabriela and then glanced at Kari where she was lying under the table watching him. The intelligent eyes locked onto his and he felt an answer. Or part of an answer. The future was as vague and tangled as the streets of Barcelona on a foggy night. He smelled coffee brewing somewhere close by, a promise of warmth swirling in the aroma. His answer was barely above a whisper. "Fiona. I see your plan."

"What was that, Captain?"

Tom touched the vibracore tube and dipped his finger in the blood. He held it up to Gadani. "This man died."

"Woman, actually. Younger than her." He nodded at Gabriela. "I need a clear answer. Join me. No lies. Cards face up on the table. Amado will sound the depth of your sincerity and your faithfulness."

"No. The answer is no. You use independence as a cover for barbarism and freedom as an excuse for genocide and oppression."

"Propaganda. Lies. I'd hoped you were smarter than that. But no, you believe what the Trade Guild and the Union feed you. In the end, you're another Guildie playing the role they assigned you and nothing more."

"You put part of a woman's brain on a plate." He shoved it across the table. "We'd rather be dead than support you and your syndicate and what you stand for. Right?" He glanced at Gabriela.

"Can I have a ship of my own?" she asked. "I was working my way up the ranks, waiting to get into a position where I could pay the Guild back for what they did to my mother. This is easier, more direct. I want a ship of my own. An armed ship."

Tom grabbed her arm and pulled her to her feet. He squeezed and twisted until she cried out, trying to squirm away. "Faithless bitch. You used me to get what you wanted and now you betray me?"

She laughed, trying to free her arm. "God, Thomas, you're an easy mark. Sad story, sad eyes, and you roll right over. No wonder your ex-wife dumped you."

He released her and stepped back.

"That's right, run away. You always run when it gets hard." She pointed at Gadani. "Beg him to let you live. Whatever you had planned didn't work, because I'm not playing anymore. Go on, beg."

Tom slapped her, not using his full strength, but the sharp smack was loud enough to bring a protest from Gadani.

"That's enough."

Gabriela looked up at them from where she'd fallen, legs in front of her, leaning on her elbows. She licked blood from her lip, glaring.

Tom took a step toward her. "Here. Let me help you up."

Gabriela twisted her hips. Legs swept hard against Tom's ankles, knocking him off his feet. He landed hard and she jumped on him, burying her teeth in his ear. "Stay down," she whispered. "Stay down, sir. Stay down, stay down."

Tom yelled, feeling warm blood on his neck. He writhed, trying to throw her off.

"God damn you both. Amado, get me some help in here. Send—"

The deck banged into Tom's back and there was the distant groan of plates grinding on plates. Then again a moment later, closer, harder. He knew what the spasms meant. A ship using her gravity generators to defend herself. Or maybe a ship tearing apart.

Gadani realized what was happening a fraction of a second too late. The sound of dry sticks breaking as his legs snapped under him was louder than the crash of dishes shattering or the huff of air leaving Tom's lungs.

Tom rolled over and struggled to his feet. The emergency lights were on, one of them swinging back and forth from a broken fixture. "Ah, damn it." He pressed on his side, suspecting Gabriela being on top of him had cost him a cracked rib.

Gadani was trying to reach his pistol, his movements slow and uncoordinated as he went into shock. Gabriela got to it first.

"I've been missing this." She caressed the pistol and slid the safety off.

"Both of you. Dead. Slow, painful deaths," Gadani gasped.

Gabriela's voice was gentle. "Mr. Gadani. Mr. Afweyne. The game is over. No more bluffing, no more next hand. You lost. Know that you lost." She raised the pistol and pointed it at his head from a half meter away. "*Non stiamo perdonando*. We are not forgiving. Goodbye."

Karíhton squeezed between them before she could pull the trigger.

"Get out of the way. Let me finish this. Oh." She lowered the pistol. "Um, OK, if you need to."

The Tarakana looked eye to eye with Gadani for a split second, and then shifted. The process was fast, fur giving way to smooth, glistening skin that stretched into a translucent jellyfish shape, orange and amorphous. The dog was gone and whatever the Tarakana had become enveloped Gadani. The muffled screams only lasted a few seconds, but Tom would hear them in nightmares the rest of his life.

Tom stumbled to the table and sat watching as what had been Kari pulsed and shimmered. "I knew they could change shapes. Of course I did. Never thought about what that really means."

Gabriela sat next to him, unable to look away. She took his hand, as though looking for reassurance. "Uh huh."

There was nothing left when Kari was done. No flesh remained, no bit of clothing, not even a bloodstain on the carpet. Two dogs, two identical Rottweilers turned together to face the door when it slid open.

Chapman walked past them to where Tom and Gabriela were sitting at the table.

"You're both all right? Where's Gadani? Is he dead?"

CHAPTER 28

MALAYO

Fiona placed her hand on the keypad and the house greeted her.

"Welcome home, *Padrona* Grimani. I have notified Nicholas of your arrival and he will be down presently."

Fiona let her bag slide off her shoulder and land hard on the tile floor. "It's 02:30, Hector. You shouldn't have woken him."

"He was awake."

"He has school in the morning. Why have you allowed this? I told you to contact Jonathan if he was disobedient. And what's that smell?"

"Your brother said he has done all that he can with him. The smell is olive *all'ascolana* that Nicholas and I prepared a couple of hours ago. There're some left if you're hungry."

"Maybe." She walked toward the kitchen. "He's back eating meat again?"

"*Sì, Padrona*. He's been studying multituberculata and other extinct animals and how paleontologists infer diet from dentition. Based on his research, and a detailed examination of his own teeth in the mirror, he concluded he is an omnivore."

Fiona opened the refrigerator and took a stuffed olive from the bowl.

"I can reheat them if you like," Hector told her.

She popped it into her mouth. "No, thanks. They're better cold."

A hand reached past her and grabbed the bowl. Nick put two of the olives in his mouth and talked around them. "That's what I told him too, but I was too hungry to wait for them to cool."

Fiona looked at her son, torn between the desire to embrace him and to punish him. Nick was barefoot, but still dressed for the day. She touched his cheek and then wrapped him in a hug.

"Careful of the bowl, Mom."

"You should be in bed."

"Too busy. You've been following the news from Mancosa? Minor damage, all things considered. Fifteen percent of the docks destroyed and less than a hundred dead. But coming right after the Governors purge? Wow. It makes it look like the Guild has declared war. With nukes."

"I seem to remember that you were in favor of the Governors issuing a statement that misguided elements within the Guild had been secretly trading with Separatist worlds and reaffirming our loyalty to the Union."

Nick laughed. "Misguided elements. You sound like a press release. All of you were in on it. Some families more than others and now they've paid the price."

"Maintaining limited trade was strategic. It demonstrated the value of being part of the Union."

"And you were *nuotare nell'oro*. Almost a quarter of revenue last year was off the books and un-taxed."

"We're conducting an audit. The Union will get their cut." She took an olive from the bowl Nick was holding. "I'm tired. We'll talk more in the morning."

"There's no time. It's only a matter of time, a really short time. The Union will question all the Governors, despite the internal purge. I reserved passage for you on an up-armored *Osro*-class packet boat bound for Malayo. It leaves at 07:00."

Fiona stopped chewing. "What do you know about Malayo?"

"Just what I can figure out from the manifests. There's a shipyard there and they're building one of your designs. You're behind schedule and over budget. I justified your trip as a critical design review when I booked it. It should get you out of the way until we know for sure how bad the repercussions will be. Official records say Malayo's just a supply depot, but a supply depot doesn't need regular deliveries of ten-thousand ton lots of ceramic composites and metal alloys."

She glanced at her watch. "07:00? I'll need to leave almost immediately."

"We."

"No. Absolutely not."

"We. You need me."

"What I need doesn't matter. You're staying here. It'll be safer for you."

Nick took a step back, holding the bowl close to his chest. "If you make me stay, I'll embarrass you. I'll find things to do after you leave, and I'll make sure the media posts it everywhere. My friend Serenella says she'll help me.

She's looking forward to it. You'll never live it down, even if you disown me. The Governors will censure you for not being able to control your family."

Fiona looked at him closely, wondering how many times Nick had rehearsed that speech. "You wouldn't dare."

"You know I will. Take me with you. You need me. You know you do."

Fiona's lips twisted into a tight, unwilling smile. "Have I told you how much like your father you are?"

"Because I'm right?"

"Not hardly. That you make me proud when I least expect it. Go pack. We need to leave in a few minutes."

Nick poured the rest of the olive *all'ascolana* into a thermal cup and screwed the lid on tight. "Already packed. My bag's sitting next to yours by the door. I just need my shoes." He turned to run.

"I suppose you're doing this to see your father."

Nick skidded to a stop. "Dad's going to be there?"

"Maybe you don't know as much as you think you do. Are you certain I need you?"

"Dad's going to be there. Wow."

Tom paced. Four steps from the bunk to the door. Still locked. Four steps back to the bunk. Gabriela still asleep. He looked at the ceiling and asked softly, "Amado? What time is it?"

"Captain Benson, really?"

"I need to talk to Captain Dias. I still can't believe she confined us to quarters."

"You tried to steal my shuttle again. She forgave you the first time, but she says she has no patience for damn fools. She is aware of your desire to speak with her."

"Please ask her again."

He waited, pacing between door and bunk.

"Dinner in one hour. The Captain has arranged an escort for you and Ms. Vendramin. Don't try anything or I'll hurt you."

"Thanks." He stood at the end of the bunk. "Gabriela?"

She answered with her eyes still closed. "I heard. What are you going to ask her to do?"

"A favor. We need to get to Mancosa. If she won't let us borrow her shuttle—"

"You mean steal."

"I'll bring it back. If we can't borrow it, she needs to drop us somewhere. She's taking us back to New Palisade after she stops at Dammeron. We'll be starting from scratch, but broke. Assuming they don't throw us in jail. We'll be back with Eric trying to find a way to rescue Kahwihta with no money. I'm not using a vibracore again."

Gabriela wiggled herself up onto her elbows. "You're making a bunch of bad assumptions. We don't know Kahwihta needs rescuing or that she's even on Mancosa. Eric probably knows where Kahwihta and her brothers really are. He'll talk. I'll make him talk. We need him and we need a reset. There're a couple of other people I need to talk to so they don't think I've gone completely rogue. We failed this time. I wish you could hear the Tarakana. Kari doesn't want to go to Mancosa anymore. She's already there, somehow. She's up to something new." Gabriela flopped back on the pillow, her arms over her eyes. "It's something to do with coffee. I smell it whenever they touch me."

"I thought it was just me."

"You smell it too?"

He smiled softly, his eyes drifting closed. "Venetian espresso. Strong and bitter, tempered by thick cream, a hint of dark creme de cocoa, and brandy."

"Um... maybe? Are you sure you don't hear the Tarakana?"

"One of them went with her. All the way back to Earth. I smelled it when we were with Gadani. It's her plan, or maybe they gave it to her. They've shared it through the whole Tarakana colony and stamped it with that scent so I'd know. Even me, who can't hear them."

"Who are we talking about?"

"Fiona. The Trade Guild. We're supposed to trust them."

"You do that." She swung her legs over the side of the bed. "I need a shower before dinner. You should shave. You look like a pirate when you don't shave. That's not good."

There was a firm knock on their door at 18:45. Tom put his hand on the keypad. Nothing happened. "Amado, tell whoever's out there to come in."

Lieutenant Keyes nodded to them when the door slid open. He was dressed in the mottled grays of the Union Marine's Universal Combat Uniform. "Captain Benson. Ma'am. Will you come to the upper lounge with me, please?"

"Why Matthew, are you to be my escort for the evening?" Gabriela smiled at him and took his arm as they passed through the door.

He smiled back at her. "Don't try anything. You played me. Both of you. But you kept me from doing something stupid and I wanted to give you my thanks. That's why I told Captain Dias that I'd walk with you on your way to dinner tonight."

Gabriela squeezed his arm and put away her legend as the ditzy Ms. Bonesso for the last time. "Thank you, Lieutenant. You have the makings of a fine officer. I'm sure you'll do well on Dammeron."

"If I ever get there. I've received new orders."

"Assigned to a combat unit?" Tom asked.

"That remains to be seen."

Tom glanced at the door leading to the bridge as they passed. They'd managed to breach it in the middle of the night with modifications Gabriela had made to the jamming cube, but Amado hadn't been as blind to them as she pretended. When Tom tried to power up the shuttle's engines, Amado had shut everything down and sealed them in until Captain Dias arrived with an armed escort. Two days passed confined to quarters with no word on their fate, two days traveling in the wrong direction, two days more without Kahwihta.

Lieutenant Keyes glanced back at Tom as though reading his mind. "Don't get any ideas. Captain Dias enhanced the bridge's security system after your last attempt. You'll never make it past the door."

"Who, me? Farthest thing from my mind."

Lieutenant Keyes placed his hand on the keypad. "Enjoy your dinner. I'll be back for you."

Captain Dias was standing by the table with her hands behind her back, bouncing on the balls of her feet. Chapman was standing next to her, head tipped slightly, watching them. Tom tried to slow his breathing. If Dias meant to execute them, it would already have happened.

The plates on the table were empty, but steam was rising from several serving dishes.

"Sit," Dias ordered. "I had Amado prepare one of my favorites. *Bolinhos de bacalhau.* There's rice and olives to go with them. Please, help yourselves."

Tom and Gabriela sat. "It smells wonderful," Tom told her. "But anything would be better than what the printer in our cabin calls food."

"Don't push me, Captain Benson."

"I'm sorry, ma'am. That was not my intention. And I apologize for trying to borrow your shuttle without permission."

"Take," Dias corrected him.

Gabriela reached across the table and spooned rice onto her plate. "No, we were trying to steal it. If we'd made it to Mancosa, you'd have never seen it or us again. Don't lie, sir. You know it's true." She passed the rice to Tom.

"I'd have found a way." He placed a couple of the *Bolinhos de bacalhau* on his plate next to the rice and olives.

"I believe you would have tried." Captain Dias stared at the fried balls of salted cod and potatoes, breathing in the warm aroma. "I was going to wait until after we'd finished dinner, but why should my appetite be the only one diminished?"

Tom lowered his fork. "What's happened?"

Chapman answered. "Your *Gattino Alato* attacked Mancosa with a nuclear weapon. In the name of the Trade Guild of the Most Serene Republic of Venice."

"Did Mancosa destroy her?"

"What? The *Gattino Alato*? I have no idea. Mancosa claims they did. She blew apart two hundred meters of the spacedock. Hundreds dead, probably. It's a miracle the whole facility wasn't lost. Do you have any idea how many people would have died had it entered the atmosphere?"

"The *Gattino.* Did they send a ship to look for survivors?"

"They say they tore it apart with directed energy weapons. I grieve with you for your crew, Captain, I really do. You're missing the point. Were you carrying nuclear weapons?"

Tom shook his head. "No, of course not. We had containers of ag products and consigned goods from Chéng Nuò. We lost all of it in the privateer attack. There was nothing like that on board. The *Gattino Alato* is a merchant ship." He turned to Gabriela and lowered his voice. "They might have disembarked and already left the spacedock before it happened. We still have to go there. There's still a chance. I have to try. I have to save her."

Gabriela frowned and pushed rice around on her plate with her fork. "No, Tom. There's nothing more you can do. You risked it all to save them, your career, your life. Sometimes that's not enough. You never get them back, no matter the price you pay. Nothing left except memories of what you had. What you almost had."

"Gabriela. Stop." He took her hand to keep her from pushing the grains of rice off her plate one by one.

A shiver ran through her at his touch and she looked up, eyes bright with tears. "Do you smell it?" She turned to Chapman. "What passed through the Mancosa DSH afterward?"

"One ship running dark thirty hours later, but too small to be a *Gattino*-class towboat. Probably a privateer. It only had seventy percent of the expected mass of a towboat."

"Where was it bound?"

"The Union resupply depot at Malayo if she holds course. Her beacons are off, but she's leaking a trail of powdered Holloman armor. If she is the *Gattino Alato*, they'll hold her at Malayo and arrest the crew when she arrives. Using a nuclear weapon is a war crime."

Tom turned to Captain Dias. "I need to go to Malayo." He glanced at Gabriela and she gave him a single nod. "Both of us do. Can we borrow your shuttle?"

Captain Dias leaned back in her chair and pushed her hands through her hair. "Well, shit. How the hell did that happen?"

Chapman chuckled. "Fate. You don't argue with it."

She pulled three sheets of flimsy paper from her jacket pocket. "New orders for me from the Mercosur Line arrived this afternoon. One." She laid it on the table in front of him. "First Lieutenant Matthew Keyes of the Union Marine Corp has been reassigned to Malayo. I'm to provide transportation if possible and expedient."

Tom gave her a tight grin. "Which means find a way to make it happen. I've had those orders."

She didn't smile back as she placed the second slip of paper in front of him. "Two. A request to provide you with transportation to, guess where? Malayo. The Trade Guild is offering the Mercosur Line a fair price for use of my shuttle so you must have friends somewhere in *La Serenissima*."

"Maybe. I'm not sure." He glanced at Gabriela and told her, "You may want to continue on to New Palisade without me."

Captain Dias laid the third sheet in front of him. "She doesn't have a choice. Neither of you do. You're under arrest. I'm to confine you until you can be securely delivered to, yes, Malayo. Union officials there want you for questioning concerning what happened at Mancosa. I've requested Lieutenant Keyes to act as your guard. You'll push away at 23:00 tonight."

"He's not qualified to fly a shuttle," Tom protested.

"The AI doesn't need help and *you* will be locked out." She shrugged. "It's a six day trip and the shuttle is small. I'm sure the three of you will be best of friends by the time you get there. And take your dogs with you. They keep getting out of their enclosure and I find them wandering all over my ship. Engineering. The bridge. There was one in my cabin when I woke up this morning. At least they don't seem to shed."

She stabbed one of the *Bolinhos de bacalhau* with her fork, closed her eyes, and breathed deeply. "No more about it while we eat. Tell me, Captain. What's it like working for the Trade Guild? I've always admired your big bulk freighters like the *Doge*-class. Have you served on one?"

CHAPTER 29

REUNION

Tom shifted uncomfortably. He'd been standing behind Lieutenant Keyes with his hands stuffed in his pockets for what felt like hours. Malayo had grown from a dot on the navigation display until details began to become visible. This was the first time Prakash had let him past the narrow door onto the bridge. The AI had been stubborn about it.

Six days in transit on board the small ship, living in one long cabin with seats they could fold down into uncomfortable bunks. No privacy. The lavatory at the aft end held a single toilet with a shower less than a meter square.

"Prakash, what is this place?" Tom asked.

"Malayo. I will transfer custody of you and Ms. Vendramin to the local military authorities at the supply depot just as Captain Dias specified. Then I can go home."

Tom pointed at the planet growing large on the display. "That can't be Malayo."

"Hands in your pockets, Mr. Benson. That was our agreement."

Tom slid his hand into his pocket. "*Captain* Benson. I keep telling you."

"Not while your Master's License is suspended, *sir*."

Gabriela glanced over her shoulder at him, eyes crinkled with amusement. She was next to Lieutenant Keyes, Prakash finding her more trustworthy for some reason, or at least more predictable. "Matthew, this can't be right."

The Lieutenant shrugged. "The coordinates are correct. No asteroid and a whole lot more than a supply depot. The planet's almost Earth sized. Looks pretty down there. Lots of ocean. The shipyard, though. It's almost as big as the one at Bodens Gate."

"That's not supposed to be here either. So where are we?" Tom asked.

"Somewhere we're not supposed to be." Gabriela answered. "Getting permission to leave is difficult once you know about a facility like this. People disappear, and we're already under arrest."

Lieutenant Keyes turned to her, trying to look serious and determined. "I won't let that happen to you. Neither of you have done anything wrong."

She laughed. "Other than trying to steal a shuttle and traveling under false papers. A butter-bar Lieutenant at a secret military base? Please promise me you won't try. There's going to be a full bird Aerospace Force colonel running the place, maybe a one-star. You follow your orders and forget about us."

He turned back to the display, his voice so low that Tom barely heard it. "I'll follow my orders, but I won't forget you."

"There, right there." Tom had his hand out of his pocket again. "My ship. God, what did they do to her?"

"No wings." Gabriela took his hand, squeezed it hard, and held it down on her shoulder so Prakash wouldn't complain. "Her belly's cracked. I can see the stains where she's been leaking."

"We'll have to replace that whole section. And the wings and the stacking frame. That's two month's work before we can get underway."

"Still under arrest," Lieutenant Keyes reminded him.

"Call Kahwihta Beauvais. I need to talk to her. Or give me my display pad back and I'll do it myself."

"No and no. Under arrest, remember? We've endured a pleasant enough voyage in tight quarters." The Lieutenant turned in his chair. "Don't end it this way. Please. If you and your crew are blameless, you've no worries. This is the Union. You'll be treated fairly."

Tom pulled his hand away from Gabriela and jammed it into his pocket. "Being blameless hasn't helped me much." He watched the shipyard growing larger as Prakash slowed and prepared to tie down into the slip the yardmaster had assigned them. "I've no complaints against you. Sorry."

"Forget it. Gabriela told me about you and your Bosun. Love can make a man do stupid things. That's kind of how I joined the Marines."

Tom tightened his fingers around Gabriela's hand and leaned forward to whisper to her. "You and I will have words later."

"Yes, sir. With Kahwihta and her brothers. We're almost there; almost a crew again."

"Right. Maybe they'll let us all share the same cell."

"Hard dock," Prakash reported. "Gather your belongings and dogs and exit the shuttle quickly. Captain Dias ordered me to rejoin her at Dammeron, and I've no time to waste. Lieutenant Keyes, you are to report to Captain Crutcher. The shipyard AI will guide you. You may address the local AI as Narva, if you like."

"What about us?" Tom asked.

There was a pause, as though Prakash didn't like the answer he was about to give. "There are no longer any charges pending against you, but you are to register with Mr. Fletcher of the DCI. I suspect he will have many questions for you regarding the crimes you committed against Captain Dias and the Mercosur Line while on board the *Ayahuasca*. Enjoy what freedom is left to you."

"Let it go, sir," Gabriela warned him. "We have a reunion waiting for us dockside."

"Right. Where's Karíhton?"

"Your menagerie is waiting for you at the airlock," Prakash answered. "They listen to me exceedingly well. Better than you. Them, I will miss."

Four dogs were lying on the deck listening to the brief whine of the shuttle equalizing air pressure. Tom gave Gabriela a questioning look and held up five fingers.

She spoke softly. "They do what they want, go where they want." She patted one on the neck, scratching behind its ear. The Tarakana leaned into it, seeming to take pleasure from her touch. "You're right. I should."

She turned to Lieutenant Keyes. "Matthew, I don't know if we'll see you again. Your duties may take you far from here, and soon."

"It's been a pleasure, ma'am." He held his hand out to her.

She ignored it, put her palm against his cheek, and kissed him on the lips for several long seconds. "You stay safe."

"Um, yeah. I'll do that. You too."

The airlock rotated open and Lieutenant Keyes walked away, following a red ball glowing in the air in front of him. Tom looked left and right down the broad passageway. "I'm not liking this."

"I'm sure it's fine. Kahwihta probably wasn't told we were coming."

"I wish I had my display pad. Narva, where is Kahwihta Beauvais?"

Narva's voice was a serious, low rumble. "Captain Benson. You and Ms. Antenori are to follow the red ball for your meeting with Mr. Fletcher. You have been extended the courtesy of not having an armed escort."

Tom gave Gabriela a crooked grin. "I'm a captain again."

"And I'm Carola Antenori. My op must be at an end. I'm not liking this."

They followed the red glow floating away to the right, three dogs trailing behind them. "Do you mind if I still call you Gabriela?"

"Would you? I'm comfortable wearing her. It's a happy legend, more than any of the others."

"You'll always be Gabriela to me."

"Hush. You'll make me cry."

Tom glanced at her. The smile in the corner of her mouth said she was kidding, but he couldn't see her eyes as she walked next to him staring at the deck.

The passageway curved and joined with a wider corridor. Workers passed them, and people wearing Union Marine and Aerospace Force uniforms.

"Children," Gabriela told him, pointing to where a man was leaving a shop with a toddler in tow. "There. See?"

"Yeah, I see them."

"The Union wouldn't allow children here if they thought it was dangerous."

"Uh huh. We still don't know what 'here' is."

They followed the red ball as it drifted into a mess hall where vendors offered a variety of food for the hundred or more people sitting and talking with friends while they ate.

The ball vanished.

Tom looked around. "Is it lunch time, or dinner? My stomach is still on Prakash time."

"Ah, there he his." Gabriela took Tom's hand and led him to a table where a man with stained coveralls was eating by himself at a table far from the crowds. He was heavily muscled, either from hard work or from living in high gravity. He seemed amused watching Gabriela's approach, his eyes crinkling into a smile.

"Mr. Fletcher?"

"Nicely done, Carola. Are you hungry?"

She shook her head.

"Captain Benson, what about you?"

Tom stood up a little straighter, struggling to maintain his patience. "No, sir. Can we be done with this? I'd like to find my crew. I'm hoping they're in better shape than my ship. The AI here hasn't been particularly helpful, and this 'supply depot' of yours is a bit large for me to search on my own."

Fletcher stood. "I'll set your mind at ease, then. Ms. Kahwihta Beauvais and her brother Tekanatoken are fine. Your engineer broke an arm yesterday, but it'll heal. For what good it will do her. Security is holding all of them for now. Walk with me."

Tom and Gabriela followed along with two of the Tarakana. "We lost Tuly on the way to New Palisade. I don't have an engineer. What about Simon?"

"I don't have any other information to share. You can visit them in the detention wedge." He placed his hand on the keypad next to an unmarked door. "Tell me, Captain. What was your motivation for trying to travel to Mancosa?"

The way he asked the question made it sound like he suspected Tom of being in league with the Separatists, maybe running supplies and weapons to them. Tom flushed, instantly defensive and angry.

"To rescue my ship and my crew. Do you know what I've gone through trying to reach them? You don't want to be standing in my way, not when I'm this close. Now, you tell me who the hell you are and why I should answer any more of your questions."

"Sir–" Gabriela stepped closer to him.

Fletcher's smile was little more than a thinning of his lips. "My name's Emil Fletcher. I'm a part-time rigger for the second shift building out the *Joseph Brant*. I also perform other miscellaneous duties as assigned."

"He's my section chief." Gabriela added softly.

One of the Tarakana pressed against Tom's leg, knocking him off balance. The distant song it was singing was urging calm, but it was hard to hear. "We weren't carrying nukes, if that's what you want to know."

"Oh, I know. That was settled two days ago when your *Gattino Alato* arrived. Her logs were explicit on that point."

"Then why are you holding my crew?"

Gabriela stepped past him into the office. Tom tried to follow, but Fletcher put one large hand on his chest. "You run along. Narva will guide you were you need to go."

"How will I–"

The door slid shut. He slammed his hand against it, but there was no answer.

"Narva, do you hear me?"

"I hear you, Captain. How may I guide you?"

"Kahwihta. Take me to the detention, um… block, or quad or whatever you call it here. Area."

"Wedge. Do you want to go there or to see Ms. Beauvais?"

"She's been released? There. Take me there. Wherever she is."

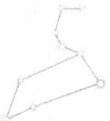

Tom placed his hand on the keypad outside cabin K/120c. His heart was beating fast and the excitement and anticipation he dimly felt from Karíhton didn't help. Her tail kept thumping his knee, urging him to go faster.

"Go away," the speaker told him. "We have nothing else to discuss unless you have Teuta with you."

"I don't have a Teuta, but I need to see you anyway."

"Oh, the hell with it. And you. I'll give you credit for at least knocking this time."

The door slid open. Kahwihta was sitting at a small desk with her back to him, engrossed in her display pad. Tek was standing next to her, arms crossed. Tom recognized the stance. Tek was eager for a fight.

Tek smiled, seeing Tom, a weary, where have you been look. He made a little 'huh' sound. "Hey, sis. I'll leave you two alone. Want anything from the mess hall?"

"No. I need to finish this report for the Guild first."

"Sure. Let Narva know when you want me back."

He embraced Tom briefly and whispered to him, "I'd go slow and gentle if I were you."

"Thanks. Good seeing you again."

Kari followed Tom the rest of the way into the cabin and the door closed behind them.

Kahwihta still hadn't turned. "I'm busy. These reports are past due. The Guild needs them and the Aerospace Force wants my estimates for repairs. I need my engineer to do it right. If you're not here to help me get Teuta back, then get the hell out."

"Ah. That's what a Teuta is. An engineer."

Her voice dropped and became soft. "Thomas. My *ákskere*. They didn't tell me. They must have known, but they didn't tell me." She turned, spinning the chair around. "These Guild reports." She glanced behind her. "Are they always such a giant pain in the ass?"

Tom moved close to her and touched her hair. He felt the softness of it between his fingers and marveled that she was real. "Yeah. Always. I'll help you. If you want me to. I came to rescue you, but you did a good job of rescuing yourself. At least let me save you from Guild bureaucracy."

She tipped her head so his hand slid down to touch her ear. "Please rescue me. I'm getting pretty good at the other captain stuff. You know, killing pirates, blowing stuff up, and bringing on crew with sketchy histories you don't want to know."

"Uh huh. The simple, easy stuff." He put both hands behind her neck, rubbing gently. Her chin came up and she looked at him with half closed eyes. There was music somewhere, distant but growing louder.

"Feels nice."

He rubbed a little harder, moving to her shoulders. "You're tense."

Kahwihta chuckled. "No shit. Turn me around so you can do a proper job. You massage, I'll tell you what's going on."

He hesitated, not wanting to talk or to listen to anything other than the song Kari was singing to him. "OK."

"I understand you. I feel what you feel. I think, even without Kari, I'd still know. You're easy to read."

He lifted her hair and kissed the back of her neck, causing a sharp little intake of breath.

"Sorry. Did I startle you?"

"No. That was just my body trying to warn my brain about what it hopes is coming next."

"Tell me about Teuta. Is she any good?" Tom pressed his fingers against the base of her neck, warming the muscles, feeling the knots.

"She's nothing but trouble, packed to overflowing in a body Tek can't keep his hands off."

Tom smiled, moving his thumbs slowly up and down. "I imagine Simon is giving him hell for it."

Kahwihta tensed and the song in Tom's head faded to silence. He wrapped his arms around her from behind and she leaned her head back against him.

"I lost him. He died right in front of me. I watched him die. I watched him die, and there was nothing I could do. I should have found a way, some way to save him."

"I'm so sorry." He held her while she rocked back and forth and sobbed.

Tom grieved with her, holding tight, crying with her, and giving her a soft kiss once in a while until she could talk again.

Kahwihta smiled up at him, her eyes still holding the sadness that had overcome her. "Kind of lost the mood, didn't we?"

"We'll find it again."

"I hadn't cried for him, not really. I needed it. I'll probably need it again. At the time, I was so angry. I killed all the privateers for him, in his name. All except one."

"I want to hear that story."

"When I'm ready. Not now." She turned her back to him and lowered her head. "I think you're supposed to be rubbing my shoulders."

"I think you're right."

"Teuta. That's her name. Kari wouldn't let me kill her. She showed me her soul instead. Wounded, lonely, beaten down over and over again. Somehow still wanting, still trying to be a good person. Stumbling over it. Making a mess. Causing chaos wherever she goes. Loving her is foolish. I'm a damn fool."

Tom pushed on her shoulder blade with the heel of one hand, slow circles, bracing it with a hand under her coveralls just below her collarbone. "Sounds like a solid recruit for my crew."

"My crew. I hired her. Officially. Filled out the Trade Guild forms."

"Captain Beauvais."

"That's official too. At least while the *Gattino* is in dry dock. Push harder."

"Where's Teuta now?"

"Detention. They don't have much use for privateers, even one that helped us take over a FAC."

Tom stopped. "You attacked a FAC?"

"Yeah. Teuta charged a Separatist Naval Infantry brigade with my knife. Saved a bunch of Union Marines, and then helped them patch up a fractured AI. Thought they'd put in a good word for her. Guess they all died before they had the chance. I've gotta find a way." She rolled her shoulder, pushing against his hand. "Gotta find a way to stop them from executing her. Attacking the judge yesterday didn't seem to do much good."

"You attacked a judge?"

"Of course not. Tek did. When they took Teuta away. Security stopped him. They were rude about it, so I stepped in to help. Lots of punching. Teuta broke her wrist hitting body armor. That pretty much ended the fight. Her howling. Tek screaming on the floor with three guys on him. We've got a few days before her trial."

Tom moved to her other shoulder, pushing hard, then soft, working the knots out.

Kahwihta arched her back and wrapped her arms around the back of his head. He kissed her upside down, feeling time stop while her mouth was on his.

She had her eyes closed when he pulled away, lips open in a soft smile. "Move your hand down a bit."

Tom moved lower on her shoulder blade.

"Other hand."

He pulled the zipper down on the front of her coveralls a few centimeters and moved his hand over the upper part of her breast, touching lightly, trailing his fingers in small circles. "Like this?"

"Like that. Yes. Down my side. Ribs. Slow. Slow circles. Across underneath, now up the middle. Again. Spiral toward the center. Then... OK, you know what you're doing."

Tom bent low and kissed the side of Kahwihta's neck and she held him there. She tugged on his hair. "This is longer than when I saw you last."

"Been too busy to cut it. Maybe tomorrow."

"No. Let it grow. I like it. It's good long."

"Giving me orders?"

"You'll like my orders. I'm a good captain. Not letting you have the *Gattino* back, by the way. She's mine now."

"We'll see about that." He kissed up along her neck, nipped the bottom of her ear, and then found her mouth again. They kissed, keeping it slow, not giving in to the desire echoing between them. Not yet.

"Chair's getting uncomfortable. Let's move. Pull my bunk down."

Tom helped her stand and she turned to face him, breathing through her teeth, her hands on his chest undoing buttons.

"Kari's in here with us, you know," he told her. "Singing to us." He pulled her zipper farther down, kissed her bare shoulder, and helped her slide her arm out of the sleeve.

She stepped close, rubbing against him. "So? I feel her in my head. Our emotions? Food to her. She's doing it right now. Eating out the power of what we feel."

He pushed the coveralls off her other shoulder and pulled them down her back. "Doesn't bother you? We watched one kill Afweyne, Gabriela and I. It ate him. Used his body to make another dog." His hands moved to Kahwihta's hips, she wiggled and the coveralls dropped around her ankles.

She stepped out of them and kissed his neck, using her teeth in gentle nibbles. "You and Gabriela. Want to hear those stories. Later. Don't care about Kari. Let her feast on what we feel. This'll be a meal she remembers forever."

CHAPTER 30

CAPTAIN MALA DUSA HOLLOMAN

Kahwihta moved up on her elbows, rocking her body as she pressed down on Tom's hips. A hot shiver passed through him that made it hard to concentrate on their conversation. She smiled at him, seeming pleased with herself.

Somewhere farther down, her toes were playing with his. They had flung the blankets from the bunk at some point, but Narva had compensated with a flow of warm air from the ventilation system.

Tom traced slow curving patterns across her lower back with his fingers while they talked. "Replacing the tank for the Holloman armor should be easy enough. They designed those hexes to be interchangeable, assuming the damage didn't warp or crack the adjacent compartments. The wings, though." He shook his head.

"The shipyard will have to fabricate them in place. The build out will take weeks, even if we can requisition the material. The construction teams here are all scheduled solid working on FACs and frigates and other military junk. They need more people that can walk the high steel. I sent a query to the Trade Guild asking for help. No answer. Not yet."

"Are they allowing comms from here? They probably blocked you."

"You're right. They'll make it look like it came from somewhere else and redact the hell out of it. If they send it at all. We're in a lot of trouble."

"I told you about Lieutenant Keyes? He said we've nothing to worry about if we're blameless. The Union will take care of us."

Kahwihta chuckled. "Blameless? I nuked a spacedock and hired a pirate. I want you to meet her. She's a good pirate."

"You got me beat. I tried to steal a shuttle a couple of times. Had forged papers. You, um. You..." Tom kissed her forehead. "Stop moving like that. We have a lot of planning to do. We need to put our ship back together. Save Teuta. I'm worried about what's happening with Gabriela. I need to find her. Talk to her."

Kahwihta rolled her hips. "You mean stop moving like this?"

"Uh."

"I like this. A lot. I move..." She moved. "And it goes from down there up to your head and then into my head."

"That's not fair."

"You really can't feel my emotions? They're loud."

"Maybe. It's hard to hear over, you know, all the other sounds you were making."

"Nasty. Let's see if you feel this."

The door to the cabin slid open and she raised her head to peer over Tom. "Tek, try knocking, all right? Go away."

"Sorry, sis. Captain. It's Teuta. They moved her. I'm trying to find out where. I need your help or I'll start punching someone again."

"OK, sure. Give us a minute. Outside with you. No punching."

Tek left and Kahwihta moved up onto her knees with her hands braced on Tom's shoulders. She looked down the length of their bodies and back to his eyes. "What did I tell you? Teuta. Even when they have her locked up she's causing me grief."

Tom touched her, running his hand slowly from under her chin, across her throat and chest, down as far as he could reach. "I feel that. Frustration. Don't worry. I plan to stay with you from here on out."

She climbed off him, stood, and started getting dressed. "I like being Captain," she reminded him. "There can only be one captain on the *Gattino*."

Tom stood next to her putting on shirt and pants. "You have a lot to learn about being a Trade Guild captain. The reports and ledgers are just the beginning. Be my first officer. The usual internship is two years, then a ship of your own. I bet I can get you ready for the exams in a year, maybe less."

"And then?"

"We'll figure it out. I've met lots of married couples serving together in the Guild. It's not perfect, but we could make it work."

She sat on the bed and pulled her boots up. "Funny. Sounded like you were proposing to me."

"I was. I am."

"Oh." She finished with her boots and adjusted the front of her coveralls, her fingers fumbling with the zipper. "Oh."

"Maybe I shouldn't have asked. You don't need to answer."

"No, you should ask. I'm glad you did. It's fine. I know how you feel. It bounces around in my head when you're this close. What happened, it wasn't a quick tumble for either of us. It's good to put it into words, better than the raw emotions, as much as I like those." She looked around the cabin. "Have you seen Kari? She must be here somewhere. I hear music." She held her hands out to Tom. "Help me up."

He took her hands and she faced him.

"I'm a difficult woman to live with."

"We've been together three years. I know what you're like."

"I'm stubborn and mean. Ask Tek, he'll tell you. And I want the *Gattino*."

"You can't have my ship. Why are you trying to talk me out of this?"

"I'm not. Just giving you fair warning. So you know what you're getting."

"Funny. It sounds like you're saying yes."

She shook her head as though not believing it. "I am. Yes. I'm saying yes."

Tom looked down at their intertwined fingers. "I love you, Kahwihta. For a long time. Ever since–"

She kissed him gently, not letting him finish.

The door slid open, the soft swish loud in Tom's ears.

"Really? Come on you two. They moved her to the Personality Alteration Lab. I don't know what that is, but it can't be good."

"Right behind you." Kahwihta told him.

Tom had to run to catch up to her. "Gabriela told me a story. About how the DCI blocked parts of her memories. It messed her up. It's still messing her up. If they're planning something like that, we need to stop them. Assuming you like her the way she is now."

The look in Tek's eyes when he glanced back at him was all the answer Tom needed.

They reached a door their palms wouldn't open. Tek pressed hard and left his hand there. "Narva, let us through."

"I'm sorry," Narva replied. "The PAL is in a restricted area. I can guide you through the process of applying for access if you believe that your current duties provide you with a Need to Know justification."

Tek punched. Narva and the metal composites of the door were unimpressed. Tom felt Kahwihta drifting into panic, the emotion sharp in his head even though Kari wasn't in sight.

"Let me try." Tom stared at the ceiling for a moment, clearing his thoughts. He'd dealt with Guild and Union officials his entire career. The key was to make the procedures work in your favor. A direct assault was usually futile.

"Narva, Captain Beauvais is Teuta's commanding officer and I am the captain of the ship she serves, the *Gattino Alato*. As such, we are responsible for both Teuta's actions and her wellbeing. We are requesting access to her so we can fulfill our obligations under the terms of her contract with the Trade Guild of Venice. Will you please inform those with her now that we would be grateful if they would allow us escorted access to her?"

"Thank you, Captain Benson. Your request is being processed and I will let you know when–" The voice in their ears stopped.

"When what?"

"Your request was accepted, although you lied to me. Please don't do that again. Captain Beauvais is master of the *Gattino Alato*. However, your new duty assignments for the Union are sufficient for provisional access. You and Captain Beauvais are to remain where you are until the door opens. Mr. Beauvais, you may use the waiting area if you desire."

Kahwihta turned to Tek. "Wait here and don't do anything stupid. Trust us, OK?"

It took a moment, but his face softened as the anger and fear diminished. "Don't let them do anything to her. I'd give my life to protect her."

"I know. So would I."

Tek nodded, believing her. "What's your new assignment, Skipper?"

Tom shrugged. "Damn, if I know. I've only been here a few hours and no one's given me time to catch my breath."

Kahwihta's eyes narrowed. "You complaining?"

"No. It's a compliment. You made me forget my worries for a while. I hope I did the same for you. We made some solid plans for our future too, for what we need to work on tonight and tomorrow." He took a step closer, reaching for her.

"And the next day." She touched his hand and wrapped her fingers around his.

He could feel her emotions crossing from skin to skin, a warm tingle. Being close wasn't enough. He had to touch her. He wanted to go on touching her. "And every day after that." He blinked a few times, trying to remember his worries. "Getting the *Gattino* ready for space, I mean. A lot of work to do."

Tek chuckled. "Uh huh, I'm sure that's what you mean. It's OK. I like seeing Kahwihta this way. Whatever the two of you are doing, keep at it. Less chance of her yelling at me."

Kahwihta's eyes narrowed. "Tek, go sit in the waiting area."

"Promise me, when you go in there... you'll get Teuta back. Find a way. Before they change her."

The door slid open. The Union Marine corporal standing with his hand still resting next to the keypad looked about seventeen, his hair buzzed to invisibility. "I'm Corporal Virtanen. Come on in." He glanced at Tek. "Sorry, not you."

Kahwihta and Tom entered the small anteroom and the door sealed behind them.

"Let's get you badged." He handed each of them a five by eight centimeter card with their picture and a large red 'E'. "I'll be your escort, so don't wander off."

Tom flipped the badge over, not sure what to do with it.

"Stick it to your shirt here." He tapped his sternum. "It will attach itself to the fabric. See the black dot in the corner? Touch it for two or three seconds to get it to let go. Don't try to yank it off; it'll take a chunk of your shirt with it." He smiled, as though speaking from experience.

Tom pressed the badge to his shirt horizontally, trying to keep his picture upright and straight. Kahwihta put hers on sideways, and then raised her chin, daring Virtanen to say something.

"That's fine, ma'am. A lot of the women here wear it that way. We weren't expecting you two to come by for your indoc briefing until tomorrow. I can show you around, introduce you to some folks, show you your quarters, but you'll still need to come back at 13:00 tomorrow."

"Our indoc? Indoc into what?"

"You'll have to wait until tomorrow. Sorry." He pressed his hand to the next keypad and led them into a passageway lined with closed doors. "There's a lot that goes on in here. Just because you make it past the front door doesn't mean they'll all open for you. There're places I can't go."

"What about where you're holding Teuta Ardian?" Kahwihta asked him. "Take us there. I need to see my engineer. You better not have done anything to her."

Corporal Virtanen's forehead wrinkled. "What do you think we're doing to her? She's with Captain Holloman in the PAL. We can go there first, if you want."

"Please," Tom told him.

"We picked up a couple of the *Onondaga's* life pods two days ago," Corporal Virtanen told them. "We've been digging into the logs, trying to find out why the AI failed."

"I was there." Kahwihta replied. Her voice broke and Tom took her hand, offering to share her pain. "Were there survivors?"

"We're still searching, but four so far. Lieutenant Bakker. She's in treatment. Unconscious, last I heard. Three from the Marine detachment. They're beat up, but they'll be fine."

"Not surprised. They were a tough group."

"Thank you, ma'am." He paused, standing outside the door to the PAL. "I know something about how AIs work, and I'm pretty good at it. I'll be Third Engineer on the *Seneca* when she goes out in a couple of months. Ms. Ardian and the Captain are working through the backups of Daga's personality silo. Listening to them talk makes me feel like I'm starting all over. I was worried about how the *Seneca's* AI would perform. Not so much now. Thanks for letting us borrow her."

Kahwihta tipped her head and Tom felt the desperate worry that had been filling her give way to a profound irritation. "So that's what the PAL does? AI personality alterations?"

"Sure. What else?"

Kahwihta gave Tom's hand a squeeze before letting go. "Why do I even worry about her? It's like she has her own damned guardian angel."

The door slid open and Corporal Virtanen touched a switch just inside. Lights embedded in the ceiling flashed a deep red. "Uncleared," he shouted. "Secure your screens."

Kahwihta pushed into the room, seeming determined to find Teuta. "Maybe you should put bells around our necks."

"Sorry, ma'am. It's the rules. If you'll follow me, please?"

Teuta was sitting in front of a large display, her back to them. A young Aerospace Force Captain with shoulder-length blonde hair was next to her, their heads nearly touching as they sifted through lines of code.

Kahwihta called to her. "Ms. Ardian, I need to talk to you."

Teuta froze. "I'll be right back. It's my Skipper. Don't start on the empathy branch without me. Promise? I want to show you something I saw when I was patching her. It's really pretty."

Captain Holloman stretched with arms up over her head. "I need another cup of coffee anyway. Up too early, long day. I'll get you one too."

"Thanks. Another one of the big cups."

Captain Holloman stopped when she reached Tom and Kahwihta. She took their hands and bit on her lower lip as she smiled at them. "You took care of my friends. Both of you. They've been telling me stories about your journey. I was right about them knowing what they were doing. They always know. Well, mostly."

She let go of them and walked to the coffee mess against the far wall.

"That was..." Tom pointed after her.

Teuta answered. "Captain Mala Dusa Holloman. Like Holloman armor, Holloman. Isn't she amazing? She rousted me out of my cell at 05:00 this morning and we've been going at it ever since. She's obsessed with what happened to Daga, since she did part of the design. She's even memorized the names of everyone that was on board. And she loves coffee almost as much as I do."

"How's your wrist?" Kahwihta asked.

She held it in front of Kahwihta's eyes. "I'll still have a cuff on it for a couple more days, but it doesn't hurt." She raised her left leg, hopping on her right to maintain balance. "And they put this tracker around my ankle. I don't know why it has to be so big. Must weigh half a kilo."

Tom's mouth came open and he licked his lips. "Um, that's not a—"

Kahwihta nudged him and he closed his mouth.

"Not a what?" Teuta looked at him, eyes bright.

"Not a bad deal. I'm Tom Benson, by the way."

"I guessed that. The Skipper talked about you most of the way here. The way she looks at you, I knew you were you. You make her emotions all gooey."

Kahwihta glanced at Corporal Virtanen who was doing his Marine best not to smile. "Teuta, not here."

"Well, it's true."

Tom smiled at her. "I see why you and Tek get along so well."

Teuta's forehead wrinkled as her eyes scrunched together. "I wish I could see him again. They won't let him into the security wedge, don't know why. Maybe I'll get to see him at my final hearing. I'd like to say goodbye to him before they... you know."

"That's not happening," Kahwihta assured her.

She shrugged. "I'm a privateer. I worked for the syndicate for five years, commerce raiding and stealing ships from Union docks. Your brother Simon died fighting my crew. He wasn't the first."

"Did you ever try to get away from them?" Tom asked.

"Huh." She shook her head. "They'd have spaced me if I'd tried. I saw it happen a couple of times. That doesn't make me innocent." She took Kahwihta's hands in hers. "It's all right, ma'am. Don't be sad. You let me do things I'm proud of. It made up for some of it. And there's Tek. He makes me forget what I am and remember what I once was. I didn't expect to have the kind of peace he gives me."

Kahwihta pulled her into a hug. "I'll never let them take you. Understand? Tell me you understand."

Teuta nodded and they held each other.

It took Tom a moment to realize they were both crying.

Captain Holloman rejoined them, a large mug of coffee in each hand. She looked at the two women with tears on their cheeks. "Interesting command structure you have in the Trade Guild. I kind of like it. There are days I could use a hug from my CO."

Tom took one of the mugs from her and tried a sip. "Captain Holloman, we need to talk."

"Talk?" Kahwihta let go of Teuta. "Talk? I am way past talking. What is your plan here? Squeeze a couple more days work out of her before her murder?"

"What?" Captain Holloman took a step back.

Kahwihta closed on her. "Her murder. Don't try calling it an execution. It's murder."

Holloman retreated, Kahwihta close behind. "I... I have no idea–"

"Don't try that. You pulled her out of her cell and let them put that *thing* around her ankle."

"The tracker?"

"You know better. Trackers are like this." She tapped the badge on her coveralls. "That anklet is there so they can blow her foot off if she does something they don't like, like maybe trying to run so they can't murder her two days from now."

Captain Holloman stopped retreating. "They told me it was a tracker. They did. Really. I need Ms. Ardian for two or three more weeks, probably longer. Why would anyone want to kill her?"

"Because I'm a pirate," Teuta answered.

"Retired," Kahwihta corrected her. "Reformed. Redeemed. Part of my crew."

Teuta sat on the floor to examine her ankle. "Will this really blow my foot off?"

Tom took one of Kahwihta's fists and held it, uncurling the fingers until it was a hand again. "Captain Holloman, did they tell you why she was being detained?"

"Questions about Mancosa. I didn't ask for details." She glanced at Corporal Virtanen. He was next to her, hand resting on his sidearm, ready to protect her. "OK," she lowered her voice, looking from Kahwihta to Tom. "I was told that I needed her. Do you understand? It kind of came to me, how important she is."

"From your friends?" Tom asked.

"We can talk later if you want, but they don't like being talked about. Forgetting you ever met them would be better. Safer for you. They, um, they sometimes kill people who talk about them."

Teuta looked up. "So, how does this work? Does it make an explosively formed penetrator or is it the force of the explosion that does the severing?" She tapped on it. "Sounds hollow. I'm betting it's an EFP."

Captain Holloman knelt next to her. "Here's your coffee." She pressed the mug into her hands. "Let's go look at that empathy branch together while Corporal Virtanen gets someone from security in here to take that thing off you, all right?"

Teuta nodded. "OK."

Virtanen seemed surprised. "Ma'am?"

"That's an order, Corporal. I'll take over escort for all of them. Go."

"Yes, ma'am."

"Need help up?" Tom asked Teuta.

"Thank you, sir, but I'm fine." She stood and smiled at Captain Holloman. "Look at you three. Are you going to cry for me? I'm not afraid. I've seen lots of people die and I deserve it more than most. Karíhton, she's one of your friends, showed me a future where I didn't, but I don't know if it's real. Do they lie some times?"

"They do, but you should believe in the futures they show you. They can all be real."

"I'd like that. I won't believe it, though. I have today. I'm doing something that's fun, and I'm with people I like. Wanting a future, any future... I won't let myself want it. Not getting it would hurt too much. Today can be enough, but I'd like to see Tek again. Can I please see him?"

CHAPTER 31

FIONA GRIMANI

Fiona touched Nicholas' shoulder. "Time to wake up. We're about a half hour out."

"W'timesit?"

"A bit after 02:00 both ship's time and station time. Do you want any breakfast?"

Nick didn't answer. Fiona watched for a moment as her son drifted back to sleep.

"Wake up, little one."

"Little? I'm as tall as you are. Give me a year and..." Nick yawned and stretched, interrupting his ability to talk.

Fiona imagined she could hear him growing a millimeter or two in the snick and pop of joints realigning. "Get dressed. I'll meet you at the airlock. I need to talk to the Captain before we disembark."

"K."

"Don't go back to sleep. Your father is meeting us."

"Right." He swung his feet out of bed. "Where's my brush?"

"Somewhere in this mess, I suppose. Good luck. I keep telling you long hair is a pain. Get it cut while we're here."

Nick's hair was wet when he skidded to a stop next to his mother thirty minutes later.

Fiona glanced at him out of the corner of her eye. The other passengers were watching, and she was maintaining her public face. She was a Governor of the Trade Guild of Venice. A haughty disinterest in those around her was expected. She was all too aware that the shipboard behavior of the Governor's son had kept them amused the past eight days. No matter. Nick would learn.

"You took a shower. I'm impressed you could do it so quickly. It's not like you."

"More a rinse, really. No brush, no time to print a new one, and my hair was all–" He put his hands on his head and wiggled his fingers.

Fiona ignored the chuckle from the man waiting next to her. "The curly hair you get from me. Your height and impudence come from your father."

Nick glanced over at her. There was a tight smile tugging at the corner of her mouth.

"Thanks, Mom. You look beautiful this morning, by the way. I like your earrings with the gold sun on blue. From the *Universitat de Barcelona*, right?"

"Are they? I don't recall."

The airlock cycled open.

Fiona stepped off the ship struggling to maintain the feeling of confidence and command others expected of her. Tom would be there, and how her heart would respond to seeing him was an open question. Nicholas was no help. She had not packed the earrings from Barcelona, yet they were the only ones she could find in her bag. Tom would notice, and she worried what he would read into her wearing them.

She glanced at her son. Was Nick really so immature as to think that reconciliation with Tom was possible? A child's fantasy. She expected better from him. Tom had a new lover, if the reports from Mr. Fletcher were accurate, and they were always accurate.

"He's not here." Nick stopped short and moved out of the flow of the other passengers. "He's not here. What does that mean?"

"It probably means he's asleep. Mr. Fletcher is here."

"Where?"

"The man in the coveralls walking this way."

"Impressive. I didn't notice him at all."

Fletcher took Fiona's hand. "Pleasant journey?"

"It got us here."

"Smart move, getting off Earth. You've been following the news."

It wasn't a question. He knew she followed Union politics. Always.

"Nicholas recommended it. He thought it would get unpleasant for a time. Better to weather unfavorable winds at a distance."

"As others fall, you will rise."

"I'm happy maintaining my current position. I've no desire to rise."

"And less to fall. It's good that you're here. The cost of the favor I did for you has increased. I think you might actually be in my debt now."

She kept her eyes straight ahead, a tightness in her chest making her aware of her heart beating a little too fast. Being in debt to the DCI was bad enough. Owing Emil Fletcher a favor could be ruinously expensive.

"Thomas?"

"Thomas is the least of your problems."

"You told me he got briefed yesterday, both him and his bosun."

"Day before yesterday. Accepted their new assignments and took to it right off. He'll get his ship repaired and then some. No more worries about the *Vendicatores*. Reinstated, just like you asked. Promise delivered."

"What's gone wrong then? It seems simple enough."

"Do they teach you that at Governor school? How to make someone feel like anything that's gone wrong must be their fault? You forget yourself. And you forget who I am."

Fiona tipped her head while they walked, waiting.

"Fine. Beauvais picked up an engineer named Teuta Ardian from Afweyne's crew and hired her into the Guild. She's a real fine catch for you. Father high up in the Separatist government. She betrayed him by shacking with a boy in the resistance all through college. We ran the kid, by the way. Smart and effective. He sucked a lot of good intel out of Ms. Ardian. It was a damn shame when Home World Security picked her up and she flipped. Led the HWS thugs straight to him and watched while they ripped him apart. Broadcast live. I've seen the pictures."

"They must have done something to her," Nick stated. "Left her no choice."

"Taking her side in this?" Fletcher glanced at Fiona. "You need to get your son out more, see what this war really looks like. It's no romantic adventure, despite what you may have read."

Nick was undeterred. "What did she do next?"

Fletcher's mouth twisted, as though tasting something unpleasant. "They dumped her with her father, but she escaped and warned every local resistance person she knew. Most of them disappeared. The HWS killed the rest. Ardian was captured a few days later."

"Knew it."

"Her father sold her to Afweyne to get her off planet and avoid the scandal her execution would have caused. She's been a good little privateer ever since, stealing ships and killing their crews."

Fiona stopped in the passageway, forcing Fletcher to come back to her. "So, of course you arrested her when she arrived."

"Of course. We gave her a fair trial. She did a few things to help the *Gattino Alato* after Beauvais killed the other privateers, and she's been helping Captain Holloman. It's enough that we allowed her to choose between life in confinement or death. She'll die this afternoon."

"And how does Thomas fit into this?" She asked it, dreading the answer. Being with Kahwihta Beauvais seemed to have done something to him. Before, he was predictable. He would have avoided becoming involved. He would have run.

"He and Beauvais showed up in the detention wedge right after the 18:30 shift change last night. They had Captain Holloman with them, and a Corporal Virtanen from the Marine detachment. They wanted to take Ms. Ardian out for one last dinner, the Corporal acting as guard. Holloman bluffed the Duty Officer. It was Holloman asking, and you don't say no to her, even if she does only wear shiny silver Captain's bars."

"They ran with her, didn't they. Did they make it? What was their plan?" Nick's eyes were bright and he seemed enthralled by the story of his father being an idiot.

"Nick, hush. Please tell me he's still alive."

"Oh..." Nick came back to reality. "They're all OK, aren't they?"

Fletcher rubbed his forehead and squinted at Fiona. "Why do you always have to show up in the small hours of the morning? Yes, of course they're all right. They made it no more than twenty meters before Narva locked down the doors. Pitiful when the AI has more sense than the human operators. We're holding them for now."

"Morons, all of you. Nicholas, you were right about me needing to be here." Fiona slid her bag off her shoulder onto the floor. Nick hesitated a moment, then did the same. "Mr. Fletcher, arrange for someone to take these to our suite. Then contact the security– what did you call it? Area? Section?"

"Wedge."

"Tell them I'm on the way there and I expect them to have processed everyone for release before I arrive. Teuta Ardian as well. Get the charges dropped. Grant her a pardon or something."

"The hell I will."

"You need to spend more time back where strategic decisions are made, not this little shipyard in the middle of nowhere. You don't win wars killing pirates one at a time, no matter how pleasurable you seem to find it. The *Rappaccini* needs to go down the ways before we start converting the

Gattino Alato into the *Asterion*. None of that can happen until Holloman finishes her work on the AI matrix. She says she needs that little pirate; I've read her reports. Have you? Every hour you hold them is an hour delay in getting my ships delivered."

His lips thinned into a smile. "And in getting you and the Trade Guild of Venice paid."

"Exactly. Do we understand each other?"

"I believe we do."

Nick walked close to her as they followed the glowing red ball toward the security wedge. "Mom, I lost track in the back and forth. Does he owe you a favor now, or the other way around?"

"If he delivers, I'll owe him."

"What do you think he'll want in return?"

"What he always wants. More spies on our ships, among other things. We transport DCI field operatives to wherever they want to go. Separatist worlds, mostly, and the DCI lets us continue trading where we shouldn't. But they report on our ships and question our crews. I'm not sure it's worth what we gain."

Nicholas nodded, seeming to be thinking about it. "Dad's going to be happy to see you."

She touched her ear. "You shouldn't have brought these. I haven't worn them in years. He'll get the wrong idea."

"You don't want him back?"

There was no easy answer to that question, so she said nothing. Her silence caused a smug smile to spread from Nick's mouth up into his eyes.

Fiona waited and watched through the one-way glass while the last release authorization flowed somewhere through the Union approval process. The shipyard security force had needed to wake the station's commanding officer to get it done. It was not how she had wanted to meet Colonel Priftakis, but dragging him out of bed at 04:00 might work to her advantage. He'd know who she was and what power she wielded.

Thomas was waiting in a chair unaware she was watching him. The woman, his bosun, was next to him. They were talking to each other, although she couldn't hear the words. He was making her laugh, a gift she remembered well. He could make her laugh even when it was inappropriate, especially when it was inappropriate. And cry too. Tears were never appropriate, not for a Governor of the Trade Guild. Not tears of frustration or anger or of loss. The last time he was home with her–

"Dad looks like a pirate."

Fiona smiled at Nick. "He could use a shave. A haircut wouldn't hurt him either."

"Is that Kahwihta? You're prettier."

"Prettier? I don't think so, not that it matters. She's like him. Do you remember *La Festa di San Marco* last year? The party we went to?"

"Stuffy. Boring. Fell asleep."

"Can you see your father there, dressed in formals, my hand on his arm as we exchange banalities with the other guests?"

"I see your point."

"I met his bosun on New Palisade. I like her." She touched her earring. "The University motto is inscribed on the back of these. *Libertas perfundet omnia luce.*"

"Freedom bathes everything with light?"

"He has his freedom, I have mine. She's making him a better person. I... I couldn't figure out how to do that."

"Who makes you a better person?"

"My son, of course."

"Complete bollocks."

Fiona smiled and looked away from Tom to study Nicholas. "Ah, so that's why you packed them. You wanted to put me in this melancholy glow, remembering simpler days."

"Not just you. Leave them in, please. I was hoping you wouldn't fight if you were both in a remember-y kind of mood."

"I'm not going to fight with your father."

Nick crossed his arms, shoulders hunched as he stared through the glass. Tom and Kahwihta had their heads leaned together and he was holding her hand. "That's what you told me last time."

Fiona kissed the back of his head. "There's his engineer coming in. The approvals must have finally come through."

"She's a pirate? She doesn't look it. She's pretty. Like, really pretty."

"She's seen things I hope you never have to see. Done things I hope you... Are you ready?"

"Sure. Dad doesn't know I came with you?"

"No. You go in first. Surprise him. I'll be a few seconds behind you."

Nicholas squared his shoulders and lifted his chin, "Narva, unseal the door to the holding area."

Fiona smiled. Perfect tone of voice, perfect posture of confident command. Now to see how long he could maintain it after Tom saw him. Would he play the proud Guild official, or... No. Nick ran into his father's arms as soon as he was over the threshold. Fiona chuckled to herself, started to take the earrings out, and then thought better of it. *Well done, Nick. You distract him for me.*

Tek had wrapped his arms around the woman Nick called pretty. Fiona tapped her shoulder. "Ms. Ardian? A word with you please. I am Governor Grimani of the Trade Guild of the Most Serene Republic of Venice."

Teuta peeled her lips away from Tek's and curtsied. "Ma'am."

Fiona held out her hand and Teuta touched it hesitantly. Teuta's fingers were cold and there was a tremor that passed through them every few seconds. Tek's eyes had narrowed to slits watching them.

"No harm will come to you. You're safe, and I'll keep you that way."

"Why?"

It was not a question Fiona expected. "Why? Because I need you and you're part of the Guild. Don't you want to be part of the Guild?"

Teuta glanced back at Tek and took his hand, looking for reassurance. "I should lie to you, but lies always get me into trouble. So does the truth, but it's easier to remember. I don't know much about the Guild. I want to be with him, my Tek, and with her, my captain. They're in the Guild, so that's where I want to be. Do you understand?"

"Loyalty and trust is important for a crew."

"And for a family."

"I need to speak to you privately."

"Sure. Tek, go talk to the boy that's keeping everyone distracted. I'll be OK."

"Ms. Ardian, I arranged your pardon because I need you to finish your work with Captain Holloman. After that, you can work on the *Asterion* and ship out on her when she's ready."

"Schiava will like that, becoming *Asterion*. They really pardoned me? No going back, no new charges?"

"You're free. The DCI and the Union have seen your past and forgiven you."

She nodded. "More than I can do."

"You elected to die instead of remaining in detention and that worries me. You can't forgive yourself for what happened to your boyfriend?"

"You know about that? Of course you do." She looked down, picking at her fingernails. "Never. Not as long as I live. But that's not why. If I stayed in detention, Tek and the Skipper wouldn't be able to move on. They'd keep doing stupid stuff like they tried last night. I can't believe they talked Captain Holloman into it. Or that nice Corporal." She looked into Fiona's eyes. "They'll get hurt, or worse. If I'm dead, they'll forget about me and go on with their lives. That's what I'd want for them. But if I'm really pardoned..."

"You are."

"Holy shit. There is so much I want to do. I want to help with the engine mods next, after the AI's upgraded. Can I do that? I nursed them the whole way here from Mancosa. I know them better than anyone."

"She's your ship. Tell them you're helping, don't ask."

"I'll tell them." She wiped her eyes with her sleeve. "Would it be all right if I gave you a hug? I need to thank you and words aren't enough. I'm still waiting for my first pay voucher or I'd buy you a gift."

Fiona hugged her and whispered in her ear. "The *Asterion* will be going in harm's way, serving the Union and the Guild. Promise me your loyalty and that will be enough."

Teuta nodded. "Yes, ma'am. I can be loyal."

CHAPTER 32

THE ASTERION

Kahwihta's hands were sweating. The tactical display showed another red flash. A third FAC had emerged from the DSH behind them and was closing fast. Three against one.

"Aster, spin us up and tell the *Lunigiana* and the *Reggio Emilia* that it's time for them to run. Start us limping. Make it look real this time, port engine at ninety percent and running hot. Drop thrust slow and jagged."

"I know what to do, *Signora*. They won't suspect a thing this time."

"Time to conjunction?"

"Six hours by plan. We'll need to watch close to see their intentions."

"Wake the Captain. He'll want to know."

"Captain Benson has only just fallen asleep. It would be better to let him rest until he's needed."

"Wake. Him." Schiava's personality had carried over from the *Gattino Alato*, but she was sharper now, less subservient, and more confident. More human.

"Have you notified him?"

"*Sì, Signora.*"

Kahwihta swiveled her chair to stare at Tom. "She's lying to protect you again."

He shrugged. "I'll talk to Captain Holloman and Teuta."

Aster's voice became petulant. "It's not fair stepping outside the simulation to talk to him like that. I was going to wake him in a few minutes. Some points in the human REM cycle are better than others."

"Continue the sim," Tom ordered. "Assume I'm awake and on the bridge now."

Aster's voice became soft, her Italian accent more pronounced. "*Si, mio Capitano*. Moving to mission time 20:14. Simulation resumed."

Kahwihta's eyes narrowed. "I'll talk to them. You're too nice to Aster. She uses that voice on you, and..."

"We'll do it together, OK?"

She looked back at him, trying to feel his emotions. It was hard without Kari close by. She nodded. "Together."

Twenty-two days, almost every hour together on the bridge rehearsing life and death through multiple sims a day in near real-time. Kahwihta spent every night studying with Tom until way too late, leaving enough time for a few hours of exhausted sleep and little else. They were learning the ship the *Gattino Alato* had become. Physically, she looked the same, or she would once her new wings were finished. She had a new name, the *Asterion*, and an updated AI that was immature and overconfident. She still sounded like Fiona Grimani to Kahwihta's ears, an irritation she did not need.

Not that there was any chance of Tom being pulled back into the real Fiona's orbit. They all met for dinner most nights and there was a flicker in his emotions when he was close to her, but stained with a painful loss and a longing for what he knew was impossible. To Kahwihta, it tasted like a memory of something he had once wanted desperately, but found the price to be more than he could afford. She had listened to their verbal dance as each tested the other and found that nothing had changed.

Kahwihta had watched Nicholas too, the hopeful look that crinkled his eyes each time his mother laughed at what Tom said. Nick's smile had faded as he listened to the gentle banter that confirmed neither of his parents was willing to compromise the lives they'd chosen. Kahwihta found it hard to feel sorry for him.

When she was finally alone with Tom, she felt the passion in him burning through the fatigue, through the distractions, powerful enough to erase all doubts and all jealousy. She was convinced she would have been able to feel his love for her even without Kari sleeping under their bunk amplifying his every emotion.

No, it was the ship that called to Tom. It was as if they had missed each other and wanted to find a quiet place to snuggle.

"Kahwihta, I think we should bugout in this scenario."

"What? Why? We have enough firepower to take on three FACs." She closed her eyes and recited from memory. "*The role of the Merchant Escort is to provide covering fire, allowing time for the convoy being escorted to move out of range or to provide tactical delay until big-deck ships can arrive.* We kill the bad guys, the convoy escapes, and the Union moves one day closer to victory." She yawned. "We've rehearsed it, what? I've lost count. Dozens of times. *Aster* is getting to be good at playing possum. We wait for all of them to be in range, then the covers slide open on the KE and HEL weapons in the fake containers strapped to our nose. End of the privateers, end of scenario."

"Not against three," Tom told her. "We're supposed to keep the M-ships a secret as long as possible. With three, they'll split up. By the time we kill one FAC, the *Lunigiana* and *Reggio Emilia* will be too far away for us to protect. We need to stay with them and try to out run the threat."

"I don't like running. We can take out three FACs if we do this right."

"Or we can lose our convoy and have them find out what we are if we don't."

"Slow everyone down with us?" Kahwihta asked.

"Union merchant ships always run. Anything else would be suspicious. Why would we slow?"

"Evacuating the crew?"

"Not allowed for a Trade Guild ship. Make it look like we're setting up for a tow?"

Kahwihta shook her head. "While one of our engines is stuttering? Risky. Not sure they'd buy it."

"We could dock wing to wing and extend the Holloman armor into a continuous shell. They'll think it's a new defensive tactic."

"And come close to inspect it before opening fire."

"Well inside our jamming range."

"Assuming they even have time to turn theirs off."

"A ship on each wing will complicate targeting. Aster, can you compensate for having sixteen containers docked on each side of you?" Tom asked.

"My spin rate will be reduced, but yes, I can compensate. It might take a little longer to have them where I want them. I can take them all for you, *Capitano.*"

Kahwihta looked at Tom, waiting.

"First Officer, I've not relieved you. The bridge is yours. Do what you need to do to set it up. I'm going to close my eyes for a bit and wait for things to get interesting."

Kahwihta settled back in her chair. "Aster, tell the other ships to come alongside. Let Teuta know we've had a change of plans and to get her ass on the bridge."

"Ms. Ardian has only just fallen asleep. It would be better to let her rest until she's needed."

"Are we really doing this again? Or do you mean she's really asleep?"

"Really asleep. Narva told me she and Mr. Beauvais were awake most of the night. He finds their relationship inspiring and their devotion to each other touching. Their story is being shared and each episode commands a high price."

"Idiots. He's out walking the high steel today, probably half asleep and daydreaming about being in her arms."

"Shall I wake her?"

"Sometime in the next few minutes will be fine."

Tom had his eyes closed, arms crossed. "You're going soft, Kahwihta Beauvais. I'm a bad influence on you."

"I know you are. I'll explain how much I hate you when we finish our after action reports tonight."

Tom opened his eyes. The words had been flirtatious, but there was a sharp edge behind them. Kahwihta had her back to him, hunched over the command console.

"What your brother and Teuta do when they're off duty isn't your responsibility, as long as it doesn't affect the *Asterion*."

"Teuta's asleep because of it."

"Ream her, but not for what she did to exhaust herself. You're not her mother. Or Tek's."

"Feels like I am. She needs one, and God knows Tek does. Back working the high steel. Dangerous work. I put a request through to the Guild asking them to raise his rating and offer him more money. I want him back with us."

"You saved him once and he learned his lesson. Let him live his life and do what he loves." Tom told her.

"Teuta will be a hopeless mess when we deploy without him."

"Malayo's our home port. She'll survive until we're back. The crew is family. Sometimes they need to go their own ways and learn through the pain."

"Hypocrite. Is that why you keep asking about Gabriela?" Kahwihta immediately regretted asking. She winced at the emotions that came back to her from him. It was as if she'd reached into his chest and squeezed his heart. "I'm sorry."

"No, you're right about me. I haven't seen or talked to her since we arrived. That Section Chief of hers, Fletcher, won't tell me anything other than she's on the surface. Training, he says. Training for what? I need to make sure they're not hurting her again."

"Aster, what follows is personal, stop recording."

"Conversation sealed as personal."

"What's the plan, Tom? Taking a shuttle down there and walking into a secret DCI training camp doesn't seem like a good idea."

"I wasn't planning on walking."

"Your prison break for Teuta didn't work out too well."

"I've learned a few things since then."

Kahwihta thought about it while she chewed on her lower lip. "OK, sure. I'm in."

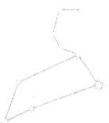

Kahwihta was mentally exhausted by the end of the exercise, and there were still reports to write. She didn't want to think about 'lessons learned' or 'opportunities for improvement'. They had survived, three simulated enemy ships were drifting debris in space, and Tom's latest message to Gabriela had bounced back as undeliverable. Kahwihta's only thoughts while they walked to the shipyard's main mess hall were how to survive dinner and how to make it back to the cabin with Tom as quickly as possible. Her neck and shoulders were desperately in need of another massage.

"How'd it go, Dad? It looked easy from the outside."

The voice had come from behind them and Tom turned to look at his son.

"How does he do that?" Kahwihta whispered to him. "The passageway was clear between here and the ship. We didn't pass anyone."

"Hey, Nick. You were watching?"

"Yeah. Mom set me up so I could watch you and your sister ships running through the sims while I did my schoolwork. The other crews were toast. You were the only ones not to lose anyone from your convoy.

Everyone ran except for you and the *Visha Kanya*. She slowed and tried to engage, but only got one FAC to stay with her. You should have heard Captain Calamai shouting *siamo fottuti* and *che cazzo* when he realized what was happening."

"Your mom lets you talk like that?" Kahwihta asked.

Nick blushed. "*I* didn't say it; Captain Calamai did. Thought it would make you laugh."

Teuta glanced over her shoulder. "It's all right, kid. We're all tired and grumpy. It is pretty funny. Did you hear what I was saying down in engineering when the number six weapons cover stuck? I almost ran out of vocabulary before–"

"Teuta. Stop." Kahwihta warned. "We're not encouraging this."

Teuta shrugged. "Can he tell us more about it over dinner? I'd like to hear what the other M-ships did. Might learn something."

"That will be in the briefing tomorrow morning," Kahwihta told her.

"Oh, shit." Tom stopped and asked Nick, "Did you hear everything we were talking about?"

"Why do you get to swear when I can't? That's not fair."

"Nick, tell me you didn't try to crack the personal conversations."

"Yeah, of course I did. Narva knows you're my dad, so he gave me access to everything. Let me help this time so you won't need Mom saving you when things go tango uniform."

"Who's teaching you how to talk?"

"I read all the time and I listen. You should hear the workers here during lunch. And I listen to Fletcher when he doesn't think I'm paying attention. I'm learning a lot. Dad, I can make your plan better because I know things you don't. I can get you down there to see Gabriela and talk to her. I know where she is and what she's doing. I know too much for you to cut me out."

Kahwihta pointed at the ceiling.

"Narva? He thinks we're talking about how well my schoolwork is going." Nick pulled a jammer cube from his pocket. "See? I borrowed this from mom. Bet you could use one."

Teuta placed a finger on the cube. "Warm. How old are you, anyway?"

"Fourteen. Almost fifteen." He stood a little straighter.

Teuta turned to Tom. "I like him. Can we bring him on as crew? There're lots of kids younger than him serving the Mancosa Federation. Ayberk Sevinç was working security on Reis's crew when we took the *Gattino Alato*. He was fourteen."

Kahwihta took a deep breath and held it, feeling as if the deck had just shifted under her feet. "I didn't need to know that."

"That's the way of it. Don't feel bad. He was cruel and a bully. Schiava shattered his bones and his guts, and Ronda helped me put his body out the airlock."

Nick took a step back. "I read and I listen. I figure stuff out and pass it to people who want to know. They do the things. I don't... I can't... I don't belong out there."

Kahwihta took a step toward him. "Except now you're out here. I think you need to see how messy it gets when people 'do the things'. You don't want to go down to the surface with us?"

"Um... Planning and research. I'll help you with those."

Tom pressed in closer, nose to nose with his son. "In or out. There's no halfway. Think about the risks carefully."

Nick wavered. "Out, maybe, I guess? At the camp, there're... guards. DCI guards. Um, I can run interference from here. Watch what's happening. I'll give you everything I know, and I won't tell anyone what you're doing."

"Good choice." Teuta told him. "It's safer up here for a kid like you. The Captain needs to make sure Gabriela's safe and is where she wants to be. We'll pull her out if she's not. It's dangerous, but she's part of our crew, our family."

Kahwihta scrunched her eyes closed. *Almost had him. So close.*

Nick's head came up, his eyes fierce as he looked at each of them. "In, Dad. In with you all the way. Make me part of your crew. I'll take you right to her and we'll make sure she's safe. We'll do the things together. Meet me at my cabin at 19:30. Mom will be out with Fletcher and we'll have a couple of hours to plan."

Kahwihta waited until Nicholas was around the corner before saying anything. "Teuta, did you do that on purpose?"

"I can't understand it. I thought we had him convinced to stay away."

"We did, Tom and I. Then you had to say family. Don't you know how much that word means to him?"

"I guess I didn't. I should have. Same as me."

She took Teuta's hand. "It's all right. Let's get dinner and figure out how to undo the damage."

"Thank you, ma'am. I really do like him. Good kid. I see the Captain in him, the way he wants to run, then doesn't. Loyal. Wouldn't mind having him on board in a few years. The Guild does that, don't they? Send kids like him out to work the ships before they stick them in an office some-where in Venice."

"Uh huh." Kahwihta walked in silence a few steps. "You made it up, about the boy on Reis' crew."

Teuta didn't answer.

"You made it up to scare Nick."

"Of course, ma'am. Reis would never have let a boy that young serve under him. I made it up."

Kahwihta nodded, studying the deck, watching her feet as they walked. "Good."

CHAPTER 33

CAROLA ANTENORI

Kahwihta put her hand on the keypad and Nicholas poked his head out into the hall and looked both ways before stepping aside to let them enter.

"I wanted to make sure you weren't followed. Narva will think you stopped by to say hi and keep me company, that's what I told him you might do. I already finished my homework for tomorrow and filed it with him so he won't be nagging me."

Teuta walked to the center of the room. "This is your cabin? How come you and your mom need this much space?"

"Oh, this is just mine. You should see Mom's cabin. It has its own sim tank. I made some snacks, if you want to eat. If you're hungry."

"You have a real kitchen? Holy–" Teuta glanced at Kahwihta. "Wow."

"There's affogato in the freezer if you want something sweet, and I programed the printer with a better coffee recipe, and, well, let me know if you want anything. I've created some charts and timelines, and a summary of what I think you'll want to know. Didn't have time to finish all of the roles and responsibilities. We can work on those together. OK?"

Nick was standing with his arms crossed tightly while he talked and it took Kahwihta a moment to see the shivers chasing through his body. They had planned to scare him again. That wasn't going to work. Nick was already terrified, but pushing through it, still committed to being part of their family.

"It's going to be OK, Nick," Kahwihta told him. "Show us what you have, then we'll sit, try some of your coffee, and talk about what we might be able to do. Your job will be done."

His forehead wrinkled. "I said I'd do the things. Don't stop me. I need to learn how to do it."

"How to do what?"

"Not hide. Not run. How not to be afraid."

Kahwihta glanced at Tom and he nodded.

"OK, show us what you have. We'll talk about how you can best help us."

Nick's shivers stopped and he seemed to relax. He waved at the couch. "I've got so much good stuff. Have a seat while I sync my pad to the display." He sat cross-legged on the floor and unrolled his pad in front of him. "This is Bituin Ulap Beach down on the surface. Really fun. Warm water and white sand. Snorkeling isn't bad. Lots of little fish things in different colors and a kind of horn coral with pink tentacles. There's a place just out of frame where the Marines built a primitive hotel sort of thing sheltered by the trees. Overnight accommodations, but it's not posh. Mom and I were there with Fletcher for a couple of nights last week."

Kahwihta felt a darkness move in Tom's thoughts and gave his hand a squeeze. Tom's dislike of Fletcher was instinctive and visceral. It went deeper than not being able to get past him to Gabriela or any lingering love he felt for Fiona. She felt it in him. He could kill a man like Fletcher and sleep well the next night believing he'd made the universe a better place. She leaned over and kissed his cheek.

He raised an eyebrow at her.

"Love you. That's all."

He looked back at her, seeming confused. "Love you too."

"Here's the kicker," Nick continued. "You'll be there on Friday and through the weekend."

"No one's told us. Are you sure?" Tom asked.

"It's kind of a surprise. All the M-Ship crews will be going. A few days of rest before they start deploying you next week."

"We've got to move fast, then. Is there transportation between the beach and the DCI camp?"

Nick looked over his shoulder at him with a smug smile. "Don't need any. The camp is less than five klicks away."

"You said it was guarded."

"It is. Sensors, virtual fence, guards, dogs. But... They're doing a land nav exercise Friday night into Saturday. The AI that sets up the individual courses talks to Narva for geospatial information. I can't get into the DCI's AI, but Narva's not as well protected, at least not his nav information. The routes are supposed to be random and they go way outside the camp borders. I can mess up Gabriela's trace instructions enough to have her show up where you can be waiting."

Teuta leaned forward, squinting at the display. "I thought we'd end up back in the detention wedge. Or dead. This could work."

"What if she wants to go with us?" Kahwihta asked Tom. "You think you can just walk back to the beach with her and board a shuttle?"

"No. Maybe. The other M-ship Captains might support us. I'll ask Fiona for another favor if I have to. If that doesn't work, then... I don't know. I'll come up with something that doesn't involve the rest of you risking your lives."

Kahwihta shook her head. "Idiot."

"All in, Dad," Nick told him. "We're family. We'll do the things."

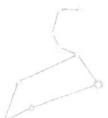

Tom waited for Gabriela in the dark. The heat of the day had lingered and it was humid. Tiny wings kept buzzing his ears, annoying, but they didn't seem to bite. The jungle was supposed to be safe, that's what the Marine sergeant doing the briefing had told them before they shuttled down. Nothing alive that was interested in eating humans. It had been more reassuring before he detailed what the Corps had gone through to make it so.

Tom resisted the urge to look at his watch. He didn't need to know. Knowing would just make the wait seem longer. A couple of kilometers to the southwest Nicholas and Teuta were supposed to be watching over him, monitoring comm traffic and orbital sensors. They'd warn him if there was any danger. Or they'd try to.

He turned away from the small clearing and watched one of Malayo's moons rising above the trees. It seemed larger than Earth's moon, or maybe it was an illusion from being so low in the sky. Several sets of eyes were watching him when he turned back around, shining green in the moonlight.

"What are you looking at?" he whispered. They winked out to the sound of rustling leaves. He stood and stretched, pacing back and forth on the trail that led downslope to the beach. He still had his hands over his head when he saw her.

Gabriela entered the clearing and circled around, staring at the stars, then at the moon. She had a small display pad glowing in her hands and it looked like she was trying to orient herself to whatever it was showing her.

Tom took a deep breath and stepped into the clearing. "Gabriela."

She turned toward him, crouching low. She was supposed to be unarmed, that's what Nick had promised him. It didn't make her any less dangerous.

"It's me. Tom."

"Tom?"

"Tom Benson. Trade Guild?"

She didn't answer, so he stepped closer, moving from shadow to moonlight. "Do you remember me?"

She straightened up. "No, I'm sorry. I was injured a couple of months back. Lost a bunch of memories. Did we serve together on the *Carlo Malatesta*?"

"No. It was after that. We were together for a few weeks on a different ship. The *Gattino Alato*."

She shook her head and shrugged, holding her hand out to him. "I'm Carola Antenori. I'm also really lost. You don't know where we are, do you?"

He pointed at the trail behind him. "Bituin Ulap Beach is a couple of clicks that way, if that helps. I was out for a walk. I wanted to see the moon come up one last time before we ship out next week. Amazing who you bump into in the jungle." He grinned and tried to ignore the sob that was stuck halfway up his throat.

Gabriela tapped on her pad. "Can't understand it. I followed all the waypoints. Should have been almost back home by now." She looked back up at him. "You knew me as Gabriela?"

"That's right."

She shook her head. "Sorry. There was an op that went sideways and they knocked me about hard. I'm lucky to be alive, so they tell me. Don't remember any of it."

Tom blinked, hoping the darkness would hide his tears. "I'm glad you're feeling better. I met a friend of yours on New Palisade a while back. Eric. I stayed with him at the Hús Trúarinnar for a few nights. He told me about how badly you'd been hurt."

"Yeah, Eric. I haven't seen him in... a while. I miss him. I'll have to look him up if I'm ever back on New Palisade." She squinted at Tom. "Wish I could remember you. You seem like a nice guy."

Tom didn't trust his voice to answer.

"Look, I've gotta go. I'm already so late there'll be hell to pay when I check in. It was good to meet you, or I guess to re-meet you. Maybe we'll bump into each other again sometime and you can tell me about who I was."

"Go carefully, Carola."

"You too. And, um, do me a favor?"

"Anything."

She smiled at him and looked up at the stars, a shy embarrassed look pulling at the corners of her eyes. "Don't tell anyone you saw me. I'd never live it down, being this lost."

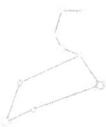

Kahwihta took a deep breath when Tom emerged from the jungle. Nick had said he was on the way back, but she wouldn't let herself believe it until she recognized him in the moonlight and could put her arms around him.

Tek was sprawled on the sand with Teuta, their legs stretched out toward the bonfire. They had been in the water a few minutes ago and the warm glow of the flames reflected off the drops of water on their skin. Nick was sitting on the sand next to them lost to whatever his display pad was showing him.

Tom sat next to Kahwihta and told them what had happened.

"And that was the end of it, Skipper?" Tek asked. "You just let her walk away?"

"I let her walk away. What was I supposed to do? She had no idea who I was or what we'd been through together. I don't even know if the memories are still in there somewhere behind a wall the DCI created. They might all be gone. They raped her brain, fucked with it while she slept, and made it all clean and shiny. She's ready to go out and die for the Union one more time."

"Tom..." Kahwihta touched his arm. She'd felt the shift in him as the pain and sorrow churned into cold anger as he told them what Gabriela had become.

"What? That's what they did." He poked the fire hard, sending sparks into the sky. "The Union. Every day it becomes less like what we're fighting to save and more like what we're supposed to be trying to kill."

"Dad, careful. I left the jammer in my room. I don't know what they can hear on the beach, but..."

"I don't care. Are my words a crime now too?" He poked the fire, softer this time.

Teuta spoke quietly. "You don't know what it was like on Mancosa. The Union wanted to kill me, but being here is still better."

"Better isn't good enough."

Teuta whispered something to Tek and they stood, brushing off sand. "Hey, sis, we're going to try and get some sleep before sunrise." Tek nodded toward Tom. "You should get some sleep too."

"Sure, OK. In a few minutes."

Nick watched them as they walked away, leaning back on his hands to see past Kahwihta as they disappeared in the darkness. He sighed, a sound full of sad longing.

"What is it, Nick?" Kahwihta asked.

"Your engineer. I like her. Did you save anyone else like her, but closer to my age?"

"Sorry. Just her."

"That's OK. I think I'll get some sleep too. See you in the morning. I'm sorry it didn't work."

Tom stood and embraced him. "We tried, Nick. You did the things. You did them well."

Kahwihta leaned against him after he sat back down, waiting until she felt his emotions settle and his anger to dull. "What are we going to do, Tom?"

"Huh. We have our orders. Dropped into my display pad while I was walking back. Shuttle at 07:00 tomorrow, and we're to make ready for a 13:30 push for Bodens Gate. Three containers of consigned goods are waiting for us there, plus our 'special' loadout. Twelve days to New Palisade alongside two bulk carriers, three day layover, and then on to Ratatoskr with a convoy of three towboats."

"They're not leaving us time to do anything. Do you think they know?"

"Yeah, I do. If it wasn't for Fiona holding Fletcher back, I think we'd all be dead now."

She chuckled. "Except little Nicholas."

"Fletcher would have killed him first. Nick's too good at what he does. And he has my eyes."

"I noticed that. Shall we turn in?"

He poked at the fire, turning the wood to make it burn brighter. "I don't think I'd be good company for you tonight."

"Let me decide. You haven't disappointed me yet."

"That's a lie, but I appreciate it."

CHAPTER 34

PUSHING CARGO

Tom made it through the brief ceremony with Colonel Priftakis wearing a tight smile on his face, eager to be underway. He didn't need reminding about the importance of their mission or the risks he had bravely accepted in service to the Union. The Trade Guild had taken his *Gattino Alato* and loaned her to the Union Aerospace Force. She still wore the Winged Lion on her bow plates, but she was the *Asterion* now, recommissioned as an armed merchantman, an M-Ship, a ship of war. She needed him to keep her safe, now more than ever. Tom shook hands with the Colonel and pretended a confidence he didn't feel.

Kahwihta was already on board helping Teuta ready the ship for flight. He was ready to join them and feel the pulse of the engines under his feet pushing them away from Malayo.

Nicholas and Fiona were waiting for him next to the airlock, Fiona with a tight grip on Nick's hand as though afraid he would try to run on board the *Asterion* if given half a chance. The look in Nick's eyes told Tom the fear was justified.

Tom stopped and Nick broke loose to give him a hug. Nick whispered to him. "I want to go with you. Mom's being unreasonable."

"She loves you and needs you. Be good to her."

"I want to go with you."

"Give it a few years. I'll be back pushing regular cargo by then."

Nick nodded, his chin digging into Tom's shoulder. "Be careful, Dad. The sims didn't include all of the dangers. I'll send you some things I just found out."

"Thanks. For everything."

Nick let go of him and wiped his eyes. "Mom?"

"Go on. Go say goodbye to the rest of them."

Nick's eyes widened. "You mean... on board?"

"Go. Don't take too long and don't try to hide."

Nick ran.

Fiona touched Tom's face, her eyes crinkled in a smile. "Thomas, you are a giant pain in the ass. Try to stay out of trouble for a few months. The cost of saving you is becoming more than I want to pay."

"Fletcher." He hadn't meant to say it, but the bitterness was too much.

"He's not the monster you imagine."

Tom didn't trust himself to answer, or to speak at all.

She stepped closer to him, pressing her hand on his chest. "I didn't know about Gabriela. Nick told me. What they did to her, it's not... unusual. Field agents need to be clear on their ops, undistracted by the past. It's reversible."

"That's supposed to make me feel better? Make it all right?"

"No. Not for you."

She put her arms around him and Tom closed his eyes. The feel of her against him, the subtle smell of citrus with clove, swept through him. Twenty years faded away and he kissed her hair. "I don't suppose saying I'm sorry begins to cover it. I owe you far more than I can ever pay."

"I like you being in my debt. It's good to have a positive balance somewhere."

He put his cheek against the top of her head. "When are you going back to Venice?"

"Soon. The situation is stable now. The senior families have sacrificed the scapegoats. The Grimani family is ascendant, along with the Loredan and Calogerà. *Capo* Angelo Calogerà has a granddaughter Nick's age. I'll introduce them when we're back home. *Capo* Calogerà is a bit of a scoundrel. He and Nick should get along well. It will be a good match."

"Keep our Nicholas safe."

"I'll try. Do you know how close you came to getting him killed?"

"Yeah. I'm not sorry about it."

"It was good for him, but it terrified me."

"How did your father ever allow you to marry me?"

"He liked you, but he knew it wouldn't work. A lesson he knew I needed to learn for myself."

"Were you ever tempted?"

"By what?"

"To stay out here with me."

"Humm. *Avrei voluto essere amato, non temuto. Ma ora non importa.* Scoundrel."

He held her close, unsure how much time was passing.

"Hey, Mom?" Nick peaked around the airlock's coaming, a big scruffy German Shepherd looking with him. "Kahwihta said I could keep him if it's all right with you. They have, like, three other ones. This one's name is Ohkwari. It means *Bear*. Can I?" He buried his face in the dog's fur. "He doesn't stink."

Tom heard the far away sound of the Tarakana singing and the smell of coffee. "Let Nick keep him. A boy like him needs as many protectors as he can get."

"All your goodbyes done with, Captain?" Kahwihta's voice was cold.

"Yes. All done. Did you manage to toss Tek out the airlock?"

"I think so. It wasn't easy."

"Where'd you find the dog?"

"Beats the hell out of me. Where do any of them come from?"

"Aster, are there any dogs on board?" Tom asked.

"Are we doing invisible dogs again? No, *Signore.* No dogs before, no dogs now."

"Engineer, are we ready to push?"

Teuta answered in his ear, her voice tight. "All green, sir. Sealed up, engines warming and ready in five. I have our new OS here with me. Ojeda, stop staring at me. Watch the strains on the containers while we push, all right?"

Kahwihta shook her head. "I think our new Ordinary Seaman must be a spy. No one can be that clueless without it being on purpose."

"You'll get him into shape, and then he can train, what's her name? Sheridan? She's supposed to be waiting for us at Bodens gate."

"Two newbs. That's the best the Guild could do for us? And no bosun until Ratatoskr. I don't like doing two jobs. I don't like the loadout, either. We have four containers strapped to our nose in slots thirteen through sixteen. Sixteen has machine tools for the Bodens Gate yards. The center two are empties that we'll drop there too. Thirteen's going with us to New Palisade. The manifest says it's empty, but it's reading a thousand kilos too heavy."

He grinned at her. "You want to crack the seals?"

"Can't. It's a dockside loader with the airlock centered on the port side. We don't have access from the frame."

"Pushing, sir," Teuta reported. "Goodbye, Tek. Stay safe."

"Who consigned it?"

"Kuća Vjere Industries. There's no record of them on the net. No one's picking it up, either. A lighter is supposed to dock with us to unload the 'empty' container and we keep it with us in to Ratatoskr."

Tom watched Malayo falling away from them on the display. "Kahwihta, do you mind if we quit this job after a few tricks? I want to go back to pushing ag products."

"Two years, I think. That's what Kari showed me. It's important. We're going to lose our engineer when we get back to Malayo in six weeks. Tek told me they're getting married. Officially. He wants me to do the toast at dinner afterward."

"Something to look forward to. You should tell how they met."

"I don't think so."

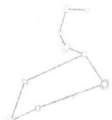

Tom made his way through the gaps in the crowd at Djemaa El-Fna square. He'd left Kahwihta and Teuta to watch over their new crewmembers and keep them away from the more sordid clubs.

This he needed to do on his own. He wasn't sure if Eric was at the Hús Trúarinnar, but it was a Saturday night and it felt right to go there.

The sanctuary was empty when he shoved the heavy wooden door open. It sealed out the last of the sounds coming from the square when he pushed it closed. Tom sat down in the back pew, resting in the dim lights and silence.

"Captain, you shouldn't be here."

"Fletcher." Tom stood, moving clear of the wooden bench. "You're the one who shouldn't be here."

Fletcher looked up at the stained glass windows and front alter. "That may be. But here I am. What brings you to the House of Faith? You should be out enjoying yourself with the rest of your crew. Your next hop to Ratatoskr is a long and dangerous one."

"I'm here looking for misplaced memories. Have you seen any lying around?"

Fletcher settled himself at the end of the pew. "Sit, Captain. Less chance that either of us will miscalculate the other's intentions."

Tom sat across the aisle, alert and ready for a fight.

"Memories are such tricky things. They can make a man retreat when he should press his advantage, or attack when the situation is quite hopeless. Most men could do with fewer memories. It would make their futures a much brighter place."

"How we live with our memories defines who we are."

"Huh. You came here looking for Eric?"

"Yes."

"And hoping to find Carola."

"Yes."

"She's here. They both are. Just down the stairs. Please don't try to see her. She's not ready for that."

"Why not?"

"Having you meet her in the jungle was the final test for the memory blocks we'd built in her head. Do you know how hard that is to get right? It's an art as much as a science. Seeing you would confirm she was ready for her next assignment."

"Well done. She had no idea who I was. Are you saying you planned for her to meet me?"

"Of course we planned it. Nicholas played his role perfectly, don't you think? Fiona wants to keep grooming him for the Trade Guild, but his talents are too great to waste them on commerce. He'll be brilliant in a few years with the right training."

"That's a lie. Nick wasn't helping you."

"Believe what you want. After you talked to Carola, she made it about ten minutes before it all came down. Not just the recent blocks. Everything. All the way back to the first time when she was sixteen. We had to go find her and pull her out. She was sitting in the middle of the trail crying, unable to walk. She thought her legs were broken. The experts don't think it's safe to try again. She's finished. The only question is if she can ever reenter society. Eric is willing to try, so I brought her to him." He shrugged. "I'm not hopeful, but it's his life to waste."

"He'll redeem her. I know he will."

"That's a lot of faith to put in a man you only knew for a few days. I guess we're in the right building for it."

"I want to talk to him."

"I knew you would. He'll be up in a moment. I asked him to give me a few minutes with you first to make you understand. Not that you ever will." He stood and walked to the door. "Good luck, Captain. Be careful out there."

"Stay away from Nicholas. And stay the hell away from Fiona."

"Fiona. Our accounts are even for now. But who knows what the future holds? I'll wager she'll need another favor or two from me before this war is over. Or I'll need one from her."

CHAPTER 35

HOME FREE

Kahwihta had one hand braced on the chair, the other playing with Tom's hair while she kissed him. She pulled away long enough to glimpse the time showing on the main bridge display. "Ten seconds." She placed her lips on his, concentrating on the kiss. "Five."

For a split second, there was nothing in the universe except the two of them. Her heart stopped beating, no sound, no air in her lungs, just Thomas and her, alone and eternal.

The first DSH was behind them. "Clean transit," Aster reported. "One-hundred fifty-two hours to the Ratatoskr DHS. All ships in the convoy are holding station."

Kahwihta collapsed against him. "Love that feeling."

"Uh huh."

"For that second, you weren't worried about anything. We were alone. We were one."

He pulled her down onto his lap. "Let's get married on Ratatoskr. We have an eight-day layover. Plenty of time for you to cure me from worrying about things I can't control."

"Tek won't be there."

"He'll forgive us. He's getting married as soon as we're back. Teuta will keep him distracted. And she'll be pregnant again."

"Can't believe she did that. One month along and she had the little guy pulled out and frozen before we left."

"She's afraid."

"I know. She seems fine on the outside, but I feel what's in her. She has trouble believing she has a future. Hurt too many times to let herself be happy. She doesn't trust it. She's expecting her life to come all apart again.

She convinced Holloman to surrogate for her if she doesn't make it back, did you know that?"

"She told me. Captain Holloman has a little girl of her own to worry about. You changed the subject."

Kahwihta wiggled back against him, enjoying the echoes of his emotions, like sharp little explosions in her mind. "What was the subject?"

"Getting married. There's a place just outside of Stordalen. Next to a waterfall. Big trees. There's a lake we can jump into afterward."

She twisted around to look at him. "What?"

"We hold hands and jump into the lake after the ceremony. Fully dressed. It's symbolic. Leaping into the unknown together. It'll be fun."

"The water's warm?"

He laughed. "No. Not at all."

"You'll take my hand before we jump?"

"I will."

"Sure, OK. Let's do it."

Aster screamed his name. "*Capitano* Benson! Unknown craft has emerged from the DSH behind us. They have not replied to my challenge and they're spinning."

"Show me."

Kahwihta slid off his lap and stood next to him. "That's more than one."

"I'm tracking two FACs with a towboat trailing behind them. Conjunction in four hours at current velocity."

Tom grinned at Kahwihta. "How do you want to play it?"

"Are you yielding the bridge to me or asking advice?"

"Let's say it's part of your training."

"We've done this scenario before. Limp back and take the first FAC by surprise, jam the second one until we can take her too. With luck we'll capture their towboat."

"Works for me."

"Aster, tell our engineer to get Ojeda and Sheridan in position."

"*Sì, Signora*. I'm feeling confident about our odds of success. We will do the things."

Kahwihta rolled her eyes. "Never should have let your son anywhere near Aster."

"Ms. Ardian has started an external inspection of the weapons pods and will be back inside in forty-five minutes. My OSs are standing by for–*Capitano*! Two additional FACs have entered range ahead of us and are at full spin. They are ignoring the rest of the convoy and are slowing to intercept us. Conjunction in thirty-two minutes. Ms. Ardian is on her way back to the airlock."

"Thomas? What are we going to do?"

"Four to one. We can't do four to one. Every sim we tried ended the same way."

She nodded, remembering Aster's voice, her cold and precise description of their simulated deaths. That's not how this was supposed to end. Kari had promised her... "The Union ordered us to abandon the convoy and run in this scenario to preserve our cover. We have the engines for it with the upgrades."

"No. We're not running. The privateers must have known we were coming. They're hunting the *Asterion*. It's what Nicholas warned us about. Our cover's already blown. Aster, tell the rest of the convoy to push hard. We'll delay the FACs long enough for them to escape."

"*Si, mio Capitano.*"

"Are you yelling for help?"

"I was able to broadcast for almost two minutes before they jammed me. The message got through."

"There's another convoy not far behind us with an *Esprit*-class escorting them. The privateers got between us, but they'll have to scatter about two hours after conjunction if they don't want to die. We can hold that long."

Kahwihta stared at the main display. "Tom, after we get married, I want to look at houses. I want a small one, but with some land around it."

"OK."

"One that backs up to the forest. Tall trees. I want to plant flowers nearby so I can smell them when the windows are open."

"There're lots of homes like that in Stordalen. Window boxes full of flowers. We'll find the right one."

"No more pushing cargo. Kari said two years. I don't want to wait that long."

"We need to do a few turns. After this, I'm sure they'll get easier."

Kahwihta closed her eyes. "You're right. I know we have to. I don't like it. I want my own ship once the Union is at peace again."

"You'll be ready. You're ready now."

"I am. I'm ready."

"We're going to make it through this."

"I know we will. Together."

"Take my hand."

Fiona tapped the keypad and waited. It was 02:38, but Captain Holloman had asked for someone to notify her in person. Fiona smiled to herself. A Governor of the Trade Guild up in the middle of the night playing messenger. Fletcher had told her not to, that the news could keep until morning. But no, a promise was a promise and it was Captain Mala Dusa Holloman asking. It was Holloman's plan and she deserved to know.

Fiona tapped the keypad again and the voice that answered sounded as tired as Fiona felt.

"Just a sec. Need to put something on."

Fiona had never seen Captain Holloman out of uniform. She hardly recognized the woman standing barefoot in front of her wrapped in a light robe, blonde hair askew. Nick said that Holloman's mother had been from Dulcinea where the people had adapted to the low gravity. Without the bulk of her Aerospace Force uniform, Holloman seemed impossibly slight. It made her easy to underestimate. But it was her armor protecting Trade Guild ships and her modifications to the AI's personality silo that put the new M-Class back on schedule. Fletcher called her a witch, and maybe she was.

"Captain Holloman, I'm sorry to wake you."

"Please, call me Mala Dusa. I'm not exactly in uniform at the moment. I wasn't sleeping. Too worried to sleep, you know?" Mala Dusa smiled and ran her fingers through her hair. It didn't help. "Just tell me."

"They're alive. Aster convinced them the shuttle was the safest place to be after the privateers stripped off *Asterion's* armor. She launched autonomously as soon as everyone was onboard. Thomas was pissed, of course. He hates to run." She shook her head, not believing she'd said it. "They're alive and bound for Ratatoskr."

"And my container?"

"Taken. The Afweyne syndicate should arrive with it at Marsa Matruh in three days. Now that the op is completed, can you tell me what makes your container worth the price of one of my ships?"

Mala Dusa stepped back from the door. "Would you like some coffee? I've been drinking it by the pot. It's standard station coffee, so it's terrible. But it's warm."

"Thanks. I could use a cup, terrible or not."

Mala Dusa walked the few steps into the small kitchen and a dog appeared next to her. That was how Fiona saw it; the big German Shepherd had appeared. It wasn't there, and then it was. He pushed up against Mala Dusa's legs and made her stumble.

"Not now, Merrimac. This afternoon, all right? Be a good boy for a change." Mala Dusa turned to Fiona. "Merrimac is as anxious to get home as I am. We'll be leaving for Kastanje this afternoon. It'll be good to be home. I have a daughter and a husband waiting for me there."

Fiona and Mala Dusa sat together at a small table and Merrimac sat on the floor between them. Fiona looked down into the dog's eyes and he looked at her with his head cocked. A thought came into Fiona's mind, almost like a voice from far away. *Every witch needs a familiar*, it whispered. There was a mocking amusement in the thought. Fiona took a sip of coffee and grimaced.

Mala Dusa smiled with her nose crinkled. "Terrible enough?"

"Perfectly," Fiona answered. "Now, about that container."

"I won't tell you. It's for your own safety. Please trust me on this. You think you want to know, but you don't. Let it be a mystery. Just know that what I did will help win the war and it will help bring the Union back together."

Fiona sat her cup down. "You said that as if those are two different things."

Mala Dusa blushed. "I suck at lying. I always have. Don't ask me any more about it. Let's talk about ships. I'm good with ships. Tell me about the fast bulk carrier you're designing."

"The *Chioggia*-class? It's still just a dream. We're a year away from bending steel."

"You should move the project to the new Chéng Nuò shipyards."

"It's too far away, the logistics alone..."

"It would be worth it. The war will end soon and the Reunification Commission will be back in the exploration business. They'll push out from Chéng Nuò to new worlds. If you have a major project in the yards, it will give the Trade Guild an advantage."

Fiona looked at Mala Dusa's hand, the way her fingers were twisting into Merrimac's fur. What was the witch up to? "Why do you care?"

"I'll help you design and build it, if you'll have me. I have an open job offer from the Trade Guild for when the Union Aerospace Force releases me, and I want to move to Chéng Nuò. I *need* to move there. It's important to me. If *Chioggia*-class construction is in the Chéng Nuò yard, I'll have an excuse."

"I'll consider it. Send me information on Chéng Nuò's capabilities and staffing. No, send it to Nick. Convince him, and then I'll see what I can do." Fiona drained her cup.

"More coffee?"

"No, thank you." Fiona stood. "I need to get back to my cabin and try to sleep an hour or two. I'm leaving for Venice at 10:00. Get the Chéng Nuò data to Nick. He needs something to keep him occupied while we're in transit."

"I'll do it this morning."

"Chéng Nuò. I hadn't considered their shipyard. I hear it's a pretty place."

"It is," Mala Dusa told her. "Lower gravity and full of excitement. They're on the edge of known space and ready to push out. Come visit. You'll be convinced."

"I might do that."

Fiona placed her hand on the keypad. "Safe travels to you back home, Captain. Fair winds."

"And following seas," Mala Dusa answered.

THE END

Thank you for reading Winged Lion!

If you enjoyed Kahwihta and Tom's journey, please check out the other books in the Reunification Series on Kindle eBook, paperback, Audible. com, and always free on Kindle Unlimited.

Wandering Star – A man on a journey, struggling to do the right thing. A woman looking for new worlds to conquer, and another trying to find her way back home. Tossed together by fate, they must learn to trust each other or die.

Wandering Soul – A young woman seeks the truth about her family on a distant world, uncovering secrets that will lead the Interstellar Union into civil war and could cost her life and the lives of all who love her.

Wandering Storm – She pledged her life and sacred honor to the Union when she joined the Reunification Commission, but the Academy changed during her time there. No longer a center of scientific learning, it became a training ground for Earth's officers corps, its graduates destined for the front lines as conflict engulfs the Interstellar Union. Now a reluctant soldier, she must fight her way through hell to save the Interstellar Union and the man she loves.

And, coming soon...

The Casino – After a life spent drifting from one failure to the next, a man is offered personal redemption when a chance meeting ushers him into a secret government facility hidden beneath a Colorado Destination Resort. The secrets revealed to him will change his life, but what difference can a short-order cook and freelance mechanic make when alien ships assume orbit around Mars with plans to colonize the Red Planet?

Follow Steven Anderson at:
https://www.amazon.com/-/e/B075KJCDGY
https://www.goodreads.com/author/show/17824113.Steven_J_Anderson
https://rucomm352.wixsite.com/theropod/
https://www.facebook.com/RuComm352
RuComm352@gmail.com

www.ingramcontent.com/pod-product-compliance
Lightning Source LLC
Chambersburg PA
CBHW060404260626
47160CB00006B/2424